By MAX GRIFFIN

Seeking Hyde
Murder on Cabot's Landing

Published by DSP PUBLICATIONS
http://dsppublications.com

MURDER
ON CABOT'S
LANDING

MAX GRIFFIN

DSP PUBLICATIONS

Published by

DSP PUBLICATIONS

5032 Capital Circle SW, Suite 2, PMB# 279, Tallahassee, FL 32305-7886 USA
www.dsppublications.com

Murder on Cabot's Landing
© 2023 Max Griffin.

Cover Art
© 2023 Tiferet Design
http://www.tiferetdesign.com
Cover content is for illustrative purposes only and any person depicted on the cover is a model.

ISBN: 978-1-64108-580-9
Digital ISBN: 978-1-64108-579-3
Trade Paperback published September 2023
v. 1.0.0

Printed in the United States of America
⊗
This paper meets the requirements of
ANSI/NISO Z39.48-1992 (Permanence of Paper).

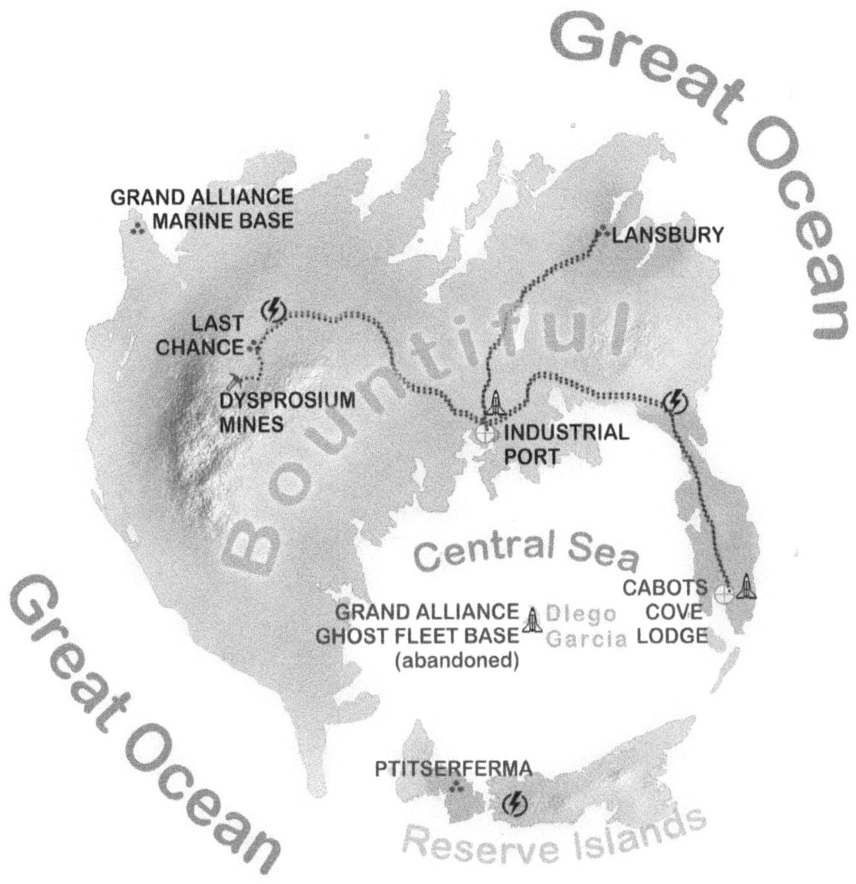

GRAND ALLIANCE
MARINE BASE

LANSBURY

LAST
CHANCE

DYSPROSIUM
MINES

INDUSTRIAL
PORT

Central Sea

CABOTS
GRAND ALLIANCE   Diego   COVE
GHOST FLEET BASE Garcia LODGE
(abandoned)

PTITSERFERMA

Reserve Islands

Great Ocean

Bountiful

Great Ocean

Cabot's Landing

NOMAD 129.683.365.120.A.3

Active Facilities ⊕

Power Plant ⚡

Ruins ⋰

Ghostport Facilities ⚞

Mines ↗

Monorail ·············

© New Omnibus Mandaean Almagest and Dataset

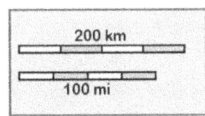

200 km

100 mi

MURDER
ON CABOT'S
LANDING

MAX GRIFFIN

Historical Timeline

2083. Mareike Baarda publishes "On the Relationship between Certain Ghost Condensates and the Casimir Effect" in *Arkiv fur matematik astronomi och fysik*, the first of her five revolutionary papers of that year.
2084. Based on Baarda's work, Gregor Hoekstra publishes the first design for a supra-luminal engine which he names the "ghost drive."
2096. Engineers at the California Institute of Technology's Jet Propulsion Lab announce a successful test of the first ghost drive.
2099. The first ghost ship departs from the newly designated NASA ghost port in White Sands, New Mexico.
2102. Exploration and colonization of habitable planets in the Local Bubble begins.
2103. Seven major powers (US, China, India, Russia, European Union, Japan, and Brazil) on Old Home Earth sign a Grand Alliance to facilitate exploration and settlement of extrasolar worlds. Eventually, the Grand Alliance expands to include over 128 nation states and becomes the governing organization for Old Home Earth and the newly settled extrasolar worlds.
2104. Sparta, a habitable world orbiting Tau Ceti, colonized.
2112. Discovery of the Immaculate Concourse, a collection of six habitable planets in the BetaCVn system, approximately 27 light years from Old Home Earth. Colonization begins that same year.
2120-2400. Rapid expansion of humans into habitable star systems centered roughly on the Immaculate Concourse with a diameter of approximately 800 light years. Estimates from the time period suggest that this consisted of nearly 10,000 worlds at its greatest extent, although currently fewer than 2,000 worlds are confirmed.
2306. An exploratory expedition of the Grand Fleet discovers dysprosium deposits on a habitable moon of a gas giant in a remote star system, now cataloged as NOMAD 129.683.365.120.B.3.
2312. Cabot Industries Trust purchases title to the above system from the Grand Alliance Fleet, names the star Cabot's Star, the habitable moon with the ore deposits Cabot's Landing, and the gas giant it orbits, Kenebec.

The source of the name Kenebec for the gas giant about which Cabot's Landing orbits is unknown, but speculation centers on the ancient North American tribal language Abenaki, in which "kinipek" means "bay," possibly a reference to the location of the initial human settlement.

2318. Cabot Industries bioengineers a species of wheat for the satellite Cabot's Landing and designs a limited ecology to support human habitation on Cabot's Landing.

2318. Mining operations and human occupation of Cabot's Landing begins. At its height, over 39,000 humans live on the satellite.

2400. Growing religious fervor in parts of the Grand Alliance on Earth leads to civil unrest, which spreads to the colonized planets.

2462. Sparta withdraws from the Grand Alliance. Within weeks, over 80 percent of extrasolar worlds declare independence from the Grand Alliance. A new religious-based US government withdraws from the Grand Alliance on Old Home Earth and declares war on the extrasolar planets. The Great Disintegration begins.

2462. Cabot Industries closes the mines on Cabot's Landing and begins to withdraw all personnel from the system.

2463. Sparta destroyed by a fleet of former Grand Alliance ghostships under the command of the US religious government.

2463. Old Home Earth devastated by retaliatory raids, including at least two asteroid strikes, by an ad hoc fleet of former trader ghostships from several extrasolar planets. Catastrophic climate disruption results in mass extinctions on Old Home Earth, although isolated pockets of humanity manage to survive.

2464. The Grand Alliance Ghostfleet engages in widespread attacks on the extrasolar planets. By the end of 2464, the Fleet has been destroyed, industrial capacity throughout the former Grand Alliance territories is vitiated, and interstellar travel ceases.

2464-2970. Dark Ages. No interstellar travel or communication. Scientific research ceases. Industrial capacity on most planets plummets. Widespread poverty and disease. Smaller human colonies fail.

2970. Gregor Stapledon, later Gregor I, discovers dozens of mothballed Grand Alliance Fleet ghostships on New Arizona in the Immaculate Concourse. He uses them to launch the first interstellar expedition in over five hundred years.

2975. The Parliament of the Immaculate Concourse proclaims the Empire of Humanity, renames itself the Parliament of Humanity, and expands to include representation from member worlds. The elected Parliament exercises limited governance of the Empire through legislation, an executive (led by a Prime Minister), and a permanent civil service. The Parliament names Gregor as the first emperor, granting him largely ceremonial duties to represent the ideals of the Empire. Gregor's leadership and vision were instrumental in the founding of Pasargadae on New Arizona as the capitol of the new Empire.

The Parliament establishes a policy of bringing all humans together in a new communion of worlds that avoids the errors of the old Grand Alliance. In particular, each world in the Empire has representation in the Parliament according to its population, has local autonomy, and the Empire enforces a pledge of non-interference in the governance of member worlds.

To enter the Empire, the government of a member planet must be a representative democracy. Many planets follow the example of the Parliament of Humanity and establish ceremonial royal houses with varying titles depending on their Old Home Earth heritage. (Examples include Baron, Chairman, Comte, Margrave, Mwami, and Sultan, among many others.) Confederations of planetary systems, sometimes with shared nobility, are also common; for example, see the Commonwealth of Elsinore or the Maharaja of Navabhaarat.

2975-present. Empire of Humanity expands to over 1000 systems and becomes the dominant political entity in known human space.

3107. The Praetorian Syndicate, a trading alliance headquartered on the Empire of Humanity planet Elsinore, launches an expedition to Cabot's Landing. The Syndicate claims title to the planet as successor to Cabot Industries Trust.

3112. The Syndicate reopens the mines on Cabot's Landing.

3142. The mines become unprofitable. The Syndicate closes the mines and withdraws all personnel from the planet.

3149. The Empire of Humanity encounters the Exalted, a hostile confederation of human-occupied planets loosely organized around a religion originating on the planet Uzvišeni in the Carthage system. The name Uzvišeni translates to "exalted" in the primary language of the planet, although the official language of the Exalted confederation is a version of the Old Home Earth language Esperanto.

3168. Pursuant to an act of the Parliament of Humanity, the Emperor signs a decree that the owners of privately held but otherwise unoccupied planets must maintain continuous official human residence on the planet, with the failure to do so resulting in the title to the planet reverting to the Empire. The Syndicate initiates the practice of maintaining an official Resident on Cabot's Landing.

3168-3174. The initial Cabot's Landing Resident serves with her extended family of forty-two individuals.

3168-3176. The Exalted invade Dongeradeel, a planet in the Elsinore Commonwealth. Conflict continues for eight years until forces of the Empire of Humanity expel the invaders and liberate Dongeradeel in late 3176.

3174-3180. The second Cabot's Landing Resident serves for six years with his spouse.

3180. Elam Vandreren becomes third Resident of Cabot's Landing, with a contract for a ten-year term.

CHAPTER 1

*Cabot's Star, NOMAD 129.683.365.120, is a class K star approximately 562 light years from the Immaculate Concourse. The Cabot system has six planets in conventional orbits ranging from .2AU to 86AU. The system was purchased in 2312 CE from the Grand Alliance by Cabot Industries Trust of Old Home Earth. The sole habitable world in the system is a satellite of the gas giant Kenebec (**NOMAD 129.683.365.120.B**). See the entry for Cabot's Landing (**NOMAD 129.683.365.120.B.5**).*
—New Omnibus Mandaean Almagest and Dataset
[NOMAD] 3172 CE

THE SHUTTLE shuddered, and Elam's seat belt bit into his shoulder. He tugged at the strap and fidgeted in his cramped faux-leather seat. The Syndicate's Auditor, Malcolm Bender, sprawled in the seat next to him, having settled there despite the fact that all the other thirty-eight seats on the *Zuiderkruis's* shuttle were empty. Elam resisted the urge to squirm away. He'd managed to spend the forty-day passage from Elsinore in his stateroom, avoiding contact with people. Now, on the last few miles of a seventy-light-year voyage, he had to put up with this bean counter.

He sighed and tried to ignore Bender's cologne. Elam had no reason to take his past out on Bender. After all, Elam's past was Elam's fault, not Bender's or anyone else's. The poor guy was probably just lonely. Besides, before long, Elam would be alone on this Chaos-forsaken hole of a planet. It couldn't happen soon enough. Hermit-like solitude was exactly what he sought. What he deserved, too.

The craft shuddered, and Elam glanced out the window. Nothing but clouds. Bender straightened a crease on his gray slacks, smirked, and squeezed Elam's knee. "Don't worry, Mr. Vandreren. It's just the upper atmosphere buffeting the landing craft. The area around Cabot's Cove has a mild climate. Subtropical. Just like your briefing promised."

Elam eyed Bender's hand on his knee. So, that wasn't loneliness in his eyes after all. It was desire. That wasn't Bender's fault either. Elam had hidden his lean, battle-honed frame under a crumpled, shapeless orange jumpsuit, but he couldn't do anything about his face. *Bewitching*, some called it. *Lean and hungry*, Ivar had said. Elam squelched a surge of grief and self-loathing at the memory of Ivar. The kindest response to Bender would be to move his knee to one side. "I'll be fine, thank you."

Bender took the hint and withdrew his hand. "Sorry. I was just trying to be reassuring."

Elam read the micro-expressions that flashed on the other man's features. Bender wasn't sorry, he was hurt. Not for the first time, Elam regretted the training that let him read expressions most couldn't even see. Not that the training hadn't been useful in his prior life, but too much knowledge often proved hurtful. Like now.

Bender's expression also showed he thought Elam was a jerk. He was right on that too. Time to gloss things over and change the subject. "How long will the transfer take?" He kept his tone businesslike. Officious. "Isn't there an audit or something?"

"My team up on the *Zuiderkruis* has already processed the data we uploaded from the Cabot Cove AI. We've got Mr. Torrance's final report too. All that's left is the formal transfer from the current Resident to you. We can do that over lunch. It's my understanding Mr. Torrance and his spouse are eager to get back to civilization."

His spouse. Right. That meant Elam would have to find a way to tolerate *two* more people, not just one. "Over lunch, eh? Can't we just skip that?"

Bender frowned. "Really, Mr. Vandreren? Aren't you interested in the Torrances' experiences? He and his spouse have been here for nearly six years, after all. Mr. Torrance's final report was pretty terse. I've seen your briefing packet, and it's not like it was… comprehensive."

Elam shrugged and avoided looking at Bender. "It told me what I needed to know. I'll have this place to myself for the next ten years, right?"

Bender nodded. "Mostly right. But you won't be totally alone. There's the AI, of course, and the occasional ship that uses the port facilities. Plus, there will be the official quarterly inspections by the Margrave's representatives, to make sure you're still alive and in residence. That's the whole point, of course: to maintain the Syndicate's title to the system. Any break in human residency and ownership of the planet reverts to the Imperium."

"Yeah, yeah. I got all that." Elam could live with being around other people once every three months or so. Barely. He stretched his legs and tried to ignore his inner ears as the shuttle swerved while it made its approach.

The craft jittered, and a thump reverberated through the compartment. Bender smiled. "Ah, that will be the landing gear deploying. I do hope the Torrances meet us at the spaceport."

The shuttle bumped to a landing and taxied toward the terminal. Elam unfastened his seat belt and tried to relax. After what felt like hours, but that he knew were just a few short minutes, the shuttle ground to a stop. More clunking noises announced the stairway deploying, and then his ears popped as the shuttle doors opened.

He stood, stretched, and escaped to the outdoors.

He took a deep breath and wrinkled his nose at the stink. Kind of sick-sweet, not quite like vomit, but almost. He supposed that would be the genetically engineered wheat, *triticum cabitorum*, he'd read about. In the five hundred years since the Great Disintegration, it had time to spread over large areas of Cabot's Landing, apparently including the spaceport at Cabot's Cove.

The gas giant Kenebec with its spectacular rings hovered on the horizon, in half phase but still filling an eighth of the too-white sky. A warm breeze fluttered through his hair. The 0.87G gravity left him invigorated after the plus-G of the ghostship *Zuiderkruis*, but he knew better than to be fooled. It was just a moon, no longer of much economic value, with a single island chain in an otherwise world-encompassing ocean. True, he'd have to share the place with the native bandersnatchi, but if he stayed away from the deep sea, he'd be fine. They were mindless carnivores, in any case.

Bender stopped at the top of the stairs and muttered something into his phone before following Elam. He stood too close when he finally approached. Of course. Elam ignored him and continued surveying their surroundings. The runway stretched off in the distance, low mountains rimmed the valley, and a single-story concrete structure stood about fifty meters distant. An open-air, driverless vehicle puttered toward them and stopped a short distance away.

Bender sighed. "It appears the Torrances decided to just send transport instead of meeting us in person." He hesitated and then snapped in a commanding tone, "Cornwall."

A hologram flickered into existence, and Elam rolled his eyes. Just what he needed. Someone had programmed the AI to not only look like a *person*, but to look like a friggin' nineteenth-century *butler*. Give him ten minutes alone at the control console and he'd fix that.

The butler—Cornwall—bowed and spoke with a prim Oxford accent. "How may I serve you, sir?"

Bender answered, "Please let Mr. and Mrs. Torrance know we've arrived."

"Sir, Mrs. Torrance is presently in Lansbury. She's not answering her phone."

"What the devil is she doing there? Never mind. Just notify Mr. Torrance, then."

"Sir, I last saw him entering the lobby of the Lodge. My connection to the lobby has been disabled, so I am presently unable to comply with your request."

"Disabled, you say? A malfunction?"

"No, sir. I deduce Mr. Torrance has manually switched it off."

"Why would he do that?"

"That information isn't available to me, sir."

Bender shook his head and glanced at Elam. "Damned literal-minded AI. No bloody curiosity. But why switch off the connection? What if he needed Cornwall to do something?"

Elam shrugged. "Maybe he turned it off so he could have privacy." For damned sure, that's what Elam planned to do with the intrusive thing.

"Makes no sense. And why did Mrs. Torrance go gallivanting off to Lansbury? There's nothing there but the ruins of an old pre-Disintegration settlement. It's almost seven hundred kilometers north of here. Even by monorail, it's a ten-hour trip one way."

"If the village is in ruins, why keep the monorail connection running?" Elam regretted asking as soon as the words left his mouth.

"Got me. When the Syndicate rediscovered the planet seventy-odd years ago, they rebooted as much of the old technology as they could. Part of restarting the dysprosium mines. Now that the mines are closed and the place is abandoned again, I guess stuff is just running on inertia or something. Mau knows, we still don't know how most of the old tech really works."

Elam avoided snorting at the reference to a divinity. He understood the ancient technology well enough without appealing to superstition. Most of it, anyway. He even understood the ghost condensate drives that powered ships like the *Zuiderkruis*. That knowledge was one reason he wanted to hide on this moon. Not the only one, but surely a sufficient one.

Bender scowled at the AI, then turned back to Elam. "We may as well take the transport to the Lodge. It's a couple of clicks away. I'm damned well going to give Torrance a piece of my mind for this. I don't like disorder. No sir, I don't like it all."

Elam's lips twitched. The universe preferred Chaos. So did he. He climbed into the tram and settled in for the ride.

Bender couldn't seem to keep his mouth shut. "The smell is from the wheat, you know. The ancients engineered it specifically for the local conditions. The food processors use it to synthesize flavored proteins. They're amazingly good, actually. I rotate through here as an auditor, and have often shared meals with Mr. and Mrs. Torrance. Prime rib. Salmon. Lamb. Even shrimp. And bread, of course." He swept an arm at the golden waves of grain waving along the roadside, under the glow of Kenebec. "They were geniuses, back in the old days."

Elam quirked an eyebrow at his know-it-all companion. "They weren't smart enough to avoid the Great Disintegration. Besides, if the ancients were geniuses, why didn't they make the damned wheat smell better?"

Bender's features turned red. "Well, there is that. I'm told one gets used to it."

"No doubt." He hoped Bender would shut up for a while.

No such luck. The man perked up and pointed. "Look, there's the Lodge." A three-story structure of gray concrete and crystalline glass emerged as they crested a hilltop. In the distance, sunlight glinted off the waters of Cabot's Cove and the Central Sea.

Elam tried to not sneer when he said, "Looks like yet another revival of twentieth-century modernism. The ancients could build anything, and they chose that loathsome style. Chaos knows what they were thinking."

"It's true, the old Cabot Trust didn't spend anything on ornamentation. They were pretty utilitarian back then. But the facilities themselves are first-rate. They survived undamaged for nearly five centuries after they abandoned this place. Even the tech rebooted without a flaw. They built to last, rather than to be pretty."

Elam didn't correct him. He knew that the definition of working tech was one in which the bugs hadn't yet been found.

The little tram buzzed to a stop under a concrete canopy that protected the two-story, glassed-in lobby of the Lodge. Yellow plastic replaced one section of the glass, just to the left of the double doors. Elam pointed. "What happened there? Storm damage?"

"Actually, yes. The mountains on the west coast of Bountiful stop most storms from getting this far, but the audit data showed one got through three years ago. The Syndicate sent in a repair team."

"Hopefully, that won't be necessary during my term."

"You never know. A lot can happen in ten years. Some people can't take the solitude. Even with two of them here, the Torrances forfeited their bonus in order to leave before their term was up." He beamed at Elam. "I'm sure that won't happen with you. Shall we go in?"

Without speaking, Elam rose and strode through the entrance.

The foul smell of the wheat vanished, but the odor inside was worse.

A body lay crumpled at the base of the yellow plastic repair, visible only from the inside. Dark blood pooled underneath. The air conditioning wafted the coppery scent of death, mingled with the odor of feces and urine, toward Elam.

Bender shrieked, "In Mau's name, what's happened here?"

Elam knelt by the body and felt for a pulse. None. The flesh was still warm to the touch. "Is this Mr. Torrance?"

Bender held a handkerchief to his nose and edged forward. "Yes. Dear heaven, is he dead?"

"Yes. I'd say not more than an hour or so."

"This is horrible! What happened? Did he trip and fall?"

Elam snorted. "What, on a banana? There's nothing to trip on, nowhere to fall from. Look at his skull. It's all bashed in. Someone killed him."

Bender's voice shook. "You mean... he's been *murdered*?"

"That's what I said. His wife must have done it. They were the only people on the planet, right?"

"That's not possible. They loved each another. I had *dinner* with them."

"Then why has she run off to—what was it? Lancaster?"

"Lansbury. I still don't believe it."

Elam sighed. "Call the ship. We'll need the captain to organize an investigation. Whatever happened here, Mr. Torrance deserves justice." His fingers touched his shirt, just below the hollow of his neck. He caressed the pendant that hid there, a constant reminder of the fragility of justice, of love, and of life.

He stood and chewed his lower lip. An investigation meant people swarming over the planet. His planet. His refuge.

He'd have to be sure they didn't wind up investigating him.

CHAPTER 2

We owe star travel and everything else to one woman's persistent belief in ghosts.
　　　　　*—Op-Ed from the **Pasargadae Post**, 25 Ventôse, 31841*

INVISIBLE NEEDLES prickled Kolonel Sigurd von Dorestad's skin as he passed through the force field at the entrance to the bridge of the *Zuiderkruis*. The field marked the transition to 0.1 G, which also brought a wave of dizziness, but through grim determination he kept his back stiff and face expressionless.

Captain Helga Fokke turned to face him, her diamond-and-platinum-studded uniform glittering in the ruddy lighting of the bridge.

He avoided rolling his eyes. Everything about her screamed she was a peasant who confused glitz with class. He'd chosen his own appearance, from his austere ebony uniform to his fastidious stubble beard and his close-cropped hair, to send a message about his *persona*. At least he had the intelligence to construct an image with the desired effect, even if most likely she didn't have the wit to understand it.

Still, it never hurt to pretend respect.

Sigurd snapped to attention and rapped out, "Sigurd van Dorestad reporting as requested, ma'am." He didn't salute. She was just a merchant captain, after all, and *he* wore the uniform of a Corsair, an officer in the Margrave's personal guard. Even a bedizened lickspittle like her couldn't miss the significance of the interlocking triangles of the *Volknut* tattooed on his left cheek.

When she smiled, she at least looked sincere. "Kolonel, thank you for coming so promptly." She leaned back and templed her fingers. "We've encountered a bit of a situation on the planet below, and I wondered if you might be of assistance?"

Sigurd narrowed his eyes. What kind of *situation* would require a kolonel of the Royal Guard? "My duty is to serve, ma'am, to the extent my modest skills permit. What sort of assistance do you require?"

She stroked the touchpad on her command chair and pointed to a screen that flickered to life. "There's been an unexpected death."

He glanced at the screen. "That's unfortunate, but how does that—" The image showed a body twisted on a Terrazzo floor, with dark blood pooled underneath the head. He walked closer to the screen. One side of the victim's skull appeared to be crushed. "This man's been murdered." He'd seen enough battlefield deaths. The conclusion was obvious.

"That's what the new Resident claimed. Elam something. Vandreren. What makes you so sure?"

"The skull wound is obviously from what the medics would call 'blunt force trauma.'"

She nodded. "I knew you could help."

He stepped back in dismissal. "I'm a soldier, not a police detective."

"I know that." She glanced at the gruesome scene on the screen, winced, and turned it off. "Look, my crew are all qualified in their professional ratings, but none of them can handle this. The Syndicate's bean counters are even less helpful. At least you have official standing with the government."

Official standing. He had that, for certain, and far more than anyone on this ship knew. His duty was clear, and unavoidable. "I will do what I can." He always did his duty. It had been ground into him from birth.

"That's all anyone can ask, Kolonel."

He nodded. "I will have your authority, then, to act as needed?" Better to phrase it as a question and continue to hold his true status in reserve.

"Of course."

"I will draft a document for you to sign delegating your authority in this matter to me." Not that he really needed it, but it would be helpful to his ultimate goals. "What else do you know?"

"Not much. The dead man, Jack Torrance, is the outgoing Resident. The Sector Auditor and the new Resident just arrived to make official the transfer of duties when they found the body. Oh, and the new Resident, Vandreren, says Torrance's spouse must be the murderer. Torrance and his wife were the only two people on the planet before today."

"Well, then, if that's true this will be an easy case to solve. What does the spouse say? And what's her name?"

"Uh, let me check." Her fingers ran over her touchpad, and holographic text popped up in front of her. "It's here somewhere. The contract was with Mr. Torrance. Ah, here we are. Wendy. Her name is Wendy."

"And what does this Wendy Torrance have to say?"

"Nothing. At least, so far. They haven't been able to locate her. She's apparently about five hundred clicks north, at the ruins of an old pre-Disintegration settlement."

"Apparently?"

"That's according to the AI. Full telemetry with the village was never reestablished when the mines reopened. No reason to. Anyway, she's not answering her phone, and the AI can't locate her."

He considered the briefings he'd read on Cabot's Landing. "The islands aren't large. Do satellite scans show anything? Like other suspects, for example?"

"The old satellite system is kind of spotty, but since the mines closed, there's never been any indication of other people on the surface, or other animal life for that matter, except for some wild chickens and fox on one of the smaller islands. In any case, the satellites won't have anything from the ruins for thirty hours or so."

He remembered reading about the abandoned agricultural station on one of the southern islands. "So, no people except the Resident and his spouse."

"Exactly. This place has been abandoned for over forty years. Nothing but an official Resident, plus routine audits, in all that time. Mr. and Mrs. Torrance were the only people on the planet."

"You mean, the only people as far as you know."

She rolled her eyes. "Yes, I guess. As far as anyone knows."

"There are two commercial spaceports and an old Grand Alliance Navy Ghost Fleet Station on this planet. How do we know there haven't been landings at those?"

"The AI should know that. There's telemetry to all three spaceports."

"Has anyone actually asked the AI?"

"Not that I know of. Wouldn't the AI report it if they had seen something?"

"Depends on their programming. AI can be pretty literal-minded. If no one asks, they might just record the fact."

"Oh. I wouldn't know. No AI on lowly merchant ships." She flashed him a smile. "See, Kolonel? You already know things and ask things none of us would have dreamt of."

He shrugged. Her compliments meant nothing. "How soon can you arrange transport to the surface?"

Her eyebrows shot up. "You're still planning to visit the old Grand Alliance Fleet base?"

"Yes, of course. But for a proper investigation, I'll need to be on the scene. Talk to witnesses and so on. I'll also need to take your medical officer with me. We'll need an autopsy."

"Oh. We don't have a medical officer. Just a corpsman."

"Fine. Send him. Or her."

"I'd rather not. We might need him here. There's only two witnesses, by the way. The Syndicate's Auditor and the new Resident. I thought you'd just interview them from here. If you must have an autopsy, we can ship the body to the ship's infirmary."

Sigurd's face heated. He controlled his breathing. "You agreed that I have your authority in this matter, Captain."

"Well, yes. Of course. But—"

"No buts. Either I have full authority or not. No arguments. No justifications needed." He waited. Underlings usually caught on, but she wasn't as used to *taking* orders as he was to *giving* them.

She waved a hand at him. "Whatever. I just need this off my watch. I'll have the shuttle come back, and I'll let the corpsman know."

"How long before I'm on the ground?"

She frowned. "Let me think how the orbits match up. Make it, say, ten hours, give or take an hour."

He sighed. Ten hours was an eternity for this kind of thing. He mentally reviewed what little he knew of the auditor and the new Resident. The file on the latter was amazingly sparse. His IQ was off the charts, though. So were his socialization scores, but in the opposite direction. Still, he might be more help than an accountant. "I need to talk to the people on the ground sooner than ten hours from now."

"I'll send you the comm links." She glanced at a flashing light on one of her screens. "Let me know what else you need."

Sigurd recognized her dismissal. "I'll do that, ma'am." He pivoted and left the bridge, almost grateful for the stability of return to a 1.2G field.

His Spartan quarters consisted of a bunk, a micro-bathroom, and a desk with computer. The comm program had been updated with the link to the auditor, one Malcolm Bender. Sigurd pressed the call button and waited.

Moments later, an officious voice answered, "Bender here." He wore a floral print shirt and appeared to be sitting on a balcony overlooking a body of water. Kennebec covered most of the sky behind him.

"Mr. Bender. Greetings. I am Kolonel Sigurd van Dorestad. Captain Fokke has asked that I look into the murder you found on the planet."

"I'm not convinced it was a murder."

"I've seen a photo of the body. He didn't bash in his own skull. No fall could cause that injury. He was murdered."

"You sound like Mr. Vandreren. He's the one that insisted there be an investigation."

"He sounds like a smart man. I wonder if I might speak to him?"

"If you wish. He's right here." The image wobbled and lost focus, and then the lean features of a man in his late thirties appeared on the screen.

"Vandreren here. Who are you?"

"Kolonel Sigurd van Dorestad of the Corsairs. Captain Fokke asked that I investigate the murder you found."

The man nodded. "You're part of the Margrave's personal guard. I recognize the *Volknut* tattoo. I'll be glad to help in any way I can."

Smart and well-informed too. He seemed personable enough, despite the socialization scores. "Thank you, Mr. Vandreren. If you'll first just tell me, in your own words, everything that has happened since your arrival on planet."

"Call me Elam. I don't go in much for formality."

Sigurd permitted himself a tight smile. He already liked this man. "Me either. I'm Sigurd."

Elam nodded. "All right, then." He proceeded with an account that was both detailed and brief, almost as if he'd had training in military intelligence. He concluded with how Bender had insisted on cocktails in the Lodge's executive dining room, and then said, "We still haven't contacted Mrs. Torrance. Someone needs to go to Lansbury to try to locate her."

Lansbury. That was the village Fokke had mentioned. "I agree. I understand it's several hundred clicks away."

"Ten hours by monorail, according to Cornwall. Er, that's the activation word for the local AI."

"Ten hours. It's going to be that long before I can get to the surface. Twenty hours is too long to wait. We need to start looking now."

Elam nodded. "Exactly what I was thinking. I asked, and there's a flitter at the spaceport here by the Lodge. By air, I can get there in not more than three hours."

"Do you have a flitter license?" Strange that wasn't in his file.

The man nodded. "My license has lapsed. But I can fly one."

"My understanding is that the village is a ruin. There isn't likely to be a suitable runway there."

"The flitter has VTOL capability. Probably so it can go anywhere on Bountiful and the other islands. The ancients had a pretty large agricultural station on one of the south islands where there's no monorail link."

The guy obviously had absorbed in-depth information on the planet. On the other hand, Sigurd had read Elam's briefing on Cabot's Landing, and there was no mention of the old agricultural station. Interesting how he knew about it. What else might this guy know?

Time enough for that later. Back to the business at hand. "If you're willing, it would be most helpful if you could locate Mrs. Torrance. You have my leave to take the flitter to Lansbury. If you find her, you have my authority to detain her for questioning."

Elam gave a little twitch, almost as if he were coming to attention, and then stopped himself. "Got it. I'll contact you as soon as I have visual contact with Lansbury. Uh, I'll have to get a phone from Cornwall. He should be able to link it with the ship's systems."

"Agreed. Good to work with you, Elam."

"You too, sir."

After the connection closed, Sigurd stared at his computer screen. The man was quick. He'd evaluated the tactical situation, arrived at the correct course of action, and proceeded to get authority to act.

Finding a man with Elam's intelligence and skills in the dead-end, doofus job of Resident made no sense. Unless, of course, there was more to the man than his two-page dossier revealed. The Emperor's intelligence services had targeted this planet for investigation for a reason. Maybe the same reason had brought Elam here. If so, he was certain to pose a threat to Sigurd's hidden purpose for being on this vessel. That made him a threat to the realm.

He mentally added Elam Vandreren to the list of things to investigate while in the Cabot's Landing system. Threat elimination was one of his official duties, and he always did his duty.

CHAPTER 3

Death is the solution to all problems. No man—no problem.
—Joseph Stalin

ELAM BROKE the connection with Sigurd, closed his eyes, and leaned back. What was an officer of the Margrave's personal guard doing here? And why in Chaos was he in charge of this investigation? Elam understood the need for a criminal investigation, but he'd figured the first officer or maybe the chief steward would be in charge—someone with no knowledge of criminal procedure, and thus someone he could control. But a kolonel in the Royal Guard? He'd likely be just as ignorant of criminal procedure, but he'd be used to barging in and giving orders.

In retrospect, maybe Elam shouldn't have spent the entire passage locked in his cabin on the *Zuiderkruis*. If he'd at least met this Sigurd person earlier, he'd have a better handle on how to maneuver him.

Bender cleared his throat and interrupted Elam's chain of thought. "That was interesting. He seems most efficient."

Elam bit his lip and examined the auditor. At least his buttons would be easy to push. "Yes, he does. Now that the prior Resident is dead, shouldn't we proceed with the transfer? Make my Residency official? Won't we need an audit trail to verify no break in occupation of the planet?"

Bender gave a little start and slopped his martini on the glass tabletop. "I hadn't thought of that. You're right of course." He fumbled with his phone. After a few seconds, dense holotext popped in front of the screen. "Here's the transfer document. If you'll just press your thumb on the screen, that will finalize the process and you'll be the official Resident." He held his phone out to Elam.

"Shouldn't I read it first?" Elam hid his amusement. He'd memorized the document before accepting the assignment back on Elsinore.

"Oh, yes, of course. Your thumbprint acknowledges you've read it and agree to the terms. I didn't mean to suggest you shouldn't."

"Don't worry about it, my friend. I'm already familiar with it." He pressed his thumb on the screen, which promptly displayed ACCEPTED in no-frills, businesslike text. "It's done."

Bender took his phone back and swiped at the screen. "I just registered it. It's now officially logged. Good thinking to get this done. Oh, I ordered a phone for you too. Cornwall should have one ready in a couple of minutes, and one of the servos will bring it."

Elam smiled. "Thank you. Now, if you'd be so good as to ask Cornwall to ready the flitter for our trip to, uh, what's the name of the village again?" That should divert Bender and make him feel useful. Maybe he'd miss the reference to a joint trip.

"Lansbury. Uh, what do you mean *our* trip? I have no intention of going there. I'm going to catch the shuttle and go back to the ship."

At that moment, the windows rattled as the shuttle passed overhead. Elam smiled. "I think you just missed the departure." This confirmed his opinion that the kolonel was both decisive and efficient, if not necessarily well-informed in police procedure.

"What?" Bender rose and stared at the sky, where the shuttle was already almost invisible as it ascended back into orbit. "They could have at least warned me." He returned to his seat and gulped down the remains of his martini. "It doesn't matter. I'm going to stay right here and drown myself in martinis. My job on this planet is finished."

"That's probably not quite true. You heard that the good kolonel assigned me to find Mrs. Torrance. In fact, you heard his exact words. He delegated his authority to me." That wasn't quite what he'd said, but Elam was certain Bender hadn't been paying close attention.

"So, what does that have to do with me?"

"At least two things." Elam ticked them on his fingers. "First, as Auditor, it's your official job to make sure we all carry out our duties in the prescribed manner, right? You audit adherence to standards and orders as well as finances."

"Well, yes, but—"

"So it's your job to make sure we carry out a proper investigation." Elam ticked another finger. "Secondly, I need a witness for the trip to Lansbury. This is part of an official investigation. I gather evidence, you witness that nothing improper happened. It's like separation of duties in financial transactions. One person authorizes payments, and a second person makes the actual payment."

Bender frowned. "Well, yes, that makes sense. But this should be done by one of the ship's officers. I don't have any civil responsibilities."

Elam smiled, ready to close the deal. "Well, I am now the official civil authority on the planet. The document you just registered with the ship establishes that. If there were any doubt, the kolonel delegated his authority to me. So, I hereby deputize you to be my witness and to audit the trip to Lansbury."

Bender's mouth hung open, and his eyes bugged out. "You can't be serious."

"Murder is always serious, sir."

A servo rolled up, and Cornwall's hologram materialized. "Your phone, sir. Kolonel von Dorestad called and asked that I prep the flitter for a trip to Lansbury. It's charged and ready for your departure, sir."

"Good. Thank you, Cornwall." Dammit, why was he *thanking* it? It was just a machine. Old habits die hard. "What's the range of the flitter?" He knew what the specs said, but it was worth confirming them.

"It's good for 580 minutes of powered flight, sir."

Elam squelched his irritation at dealing with machines. "And how long is the flight to and from Lansbury?"

"The round trip to Lansbury and back shouldn't exceed 475 minutes under current weather conditions."

Elam muttered, "You could have said that in the first place."

"I apologize if my response was inadequate, sir, but you only asked about the range of the flitter. Would you like me to replay your question?"

"No. Forget it. No! Dammit. *Don't* forget it. I meant, 'belay that.'" Damned idiot IT. "What's the weather like in, uh, Lansbury?"

"Intermittent drizzle and sixteen degrees, sir."

"Instrument flight rules, then."

"Yessir."

Bender's face had shown increasing alarm during this exchange. "I thought communications to Lansbury were out."

Cornwall said, "That is not correct, sir. Wireless communications to the Lansbury weather station are working."

Bender frowned. "I could have sworn you said they were out when Mrs. Torrance didn't answer her phone. What do the security cameras show?"

Cornwall's hologram shrugged, "Sir, I only reported she didn't answer her phone. I can replay our conversation if you like so you can show me where my answer led you astray."

Bender's face turned red, and he sputtered, "Answer my question about the security cameras."

The Cornwall hologram actually simpered, prompting a wry grin to twist Elam's lips. "The only active security camera in Lansbury is in the monorail terminus, sir. I could show you her arriving there before dawn this morning."

Bender must be looking for any excuse to not travel to Lansbury. The next words out of his mouth confirmed that for Elam. "Well, how about this? How the hell can we fly there? You said, 'instrument flight rules.' I heard you."

Elam rolled his eyes. "He means I can't rely on line-of-sight, which I wasn't planning on doing anyway. The geopositioning satellites are all functional. That's what we'll use for navigation and approach. Am I right, Cornwall?"

"Precisely, sir."

"Good. We need a tram to take us to the flitter. I assume it's hangered at the spaceport?"

"Yessir. Transportation is waiting for you outside the lobby."

"Move it to another entrance, please. The lobby is a crime scene. Stay out of there."

"Very good, sir. The tram is repositioning now. This servo will lead you to where it will be waiting."

"Thank you." Dammit, he'd it again. Still, the AI was capable of learning when its answers met his needs, so thanking it wasn't entirely stupid. It seemed to do better in anticipating personal service needs than in answering questions. That probably said something about how the Torrances had used it.

He stood. "Come on, Malcolm. The sooner we get this done, the better."

ELAM SLOWED the flitter and circled over what was left of the village. On the south, the carbon-fiber monorail ran into a low-slung concrete structure, built in the same no-nonsense, austere style of the Lodge. The engineers had built a ruler-straight concrete channel for the local river, terminating in the narrow bay a couple of clicks from the monorail station. A network of rectangular streets clustered on one side of the channel. Near to the monorail station, modest one-story squarish buildings lined the streets, most likely residences for the villagers. Foundations appeared to be all that remained of most of the buildings outside of the vicinity of the station. The ever-present wheat choked the cobbled streets and walkways.

Bender gripped his shoulder harness with white fingers. "Can we please land, already?"

Elam thought about a sky-dive landing, but took pity on the poor accountant. "Sure. Sorry. Hang on."

Winds buffeted the light craft, and it swayed as Elam approached the paved lot adjacent to the monorail station. On closer inspection, the concrete was cracked, and the wheat grew even here. A few patches of discouraged purples and yellows relieved the otherwise drab scene. "It looks like the villagers planted flowers."

Bender opened his eyes and then quickly closed them. "Petunias. They like it here, but the wheat chokes them out."

The craft swerved and bounced as Elam landed. "We're down."

"Thank heavens for that. This isn't anything like flying in the shuttle. It's more like, I don't know, being on Satan's own yo-yo, jerking all over the place."

"Light craft are different, I'll grant you that. But we're down now." Elam undid his seat belt. As he opened his door, the wind gusted and sheets of rain drenched him. Great. Now his shirt and pants clung to him in a cold, wet mess. "We should have brought rain slickers."

"We should have done lots of things. Like not come here." Bender eyed the rain. "Can we just sit here a while? Maybe it'll let up."

"That's not in the forecast. The sooner we start, the sooner we can get back and dry off." Elam stepped out, unbuttoned his shirt, and pulled it over his head. "Come on. It's not bad."

Bender gave him a hangdog expression, as if he were on his way to the gallows. He used a three-ring binder for an umbrella and stepped into the rain. "What's next?"

"We start looking." Elam trudged toward the village, Bender in his wake.

Now that they were on the ground, even this part of the village looked like a ruin. Besides the overgrown streets, most of the windows were broken out. Many doors were missing or ajar, and it looked like the wheat had even invaded the interiors.

Elam stopped to check out the first building. Four rooms with overturned furniture, drifts of dirt and trash in the corners. He could believe this place had been abandoned for five centuries.

But there was also no sign of Mrs. Torrance.

Bender slumped, waiting for him in the street and looking miserable. "Find anything?"

"No. How many buildings do you think there are?"

"There are over three hundred structures still standing, and at least twice that many are rubble."

Elam did the arithmetic. "We don't have time or resources to just randomly search every building. What was she doing here, anyway?"

"How should I know? It makes no sense for her to be here. By all reports, they were eager to leave. She should have been back at the Lodge."

"Yes, I get that. But what was she doing *here*, on Cabot's Cove? Did she have a contract with the Syndicate?"

"No. But I seem to recall she had a grant of some kind from a university. I don't recall which one. I think she was a historian."

"Maybe she was here studying the old Grand Alliance installations?"

His eyes lit, or at least looked slightly less miserable. "Yes, I'm sure that's it. The last time I dined with them, maybe two years ago, she was excited about what she'd found."

Elam waited, but Bender didn't elaborate. He kept his voice even. "What, exactly, did she find?"

"For Sheba's sake, I don't remember! Some kind of secret Alliance project or something. I remember she said something about encrypted records that caught my attention. Codes are important to account security, you know."

Elam chewed his lip. The AI should have been able to decrypt most cyphers, except military-grade quantum ones. Unless, of course, they'd been ordered not to. "What's here, in this settlement?"

"How should I know? It had nothing to do with the mining operation, so the Syndicate just ignored it. It has no commercial value."

Elam shivered in the chilly rain. "Let's at least go into the next building." He was missing something. Something big. This was a privately owned planet, always had been, even in the old days. Yet the Grand Alliance had placed both a navy base and a marine base on the planet. Why do that out here in the middle of nowhere? The mines were the only thing of value within a couple dozen parsecs, but the Alliance wouldn't invest in defending commercial interests. Even the fastest ghost drives would take a week or more to traverse the distance to the next settled planet. The marine base was supposed to be in ruins, while the navy base was, apparently, still serviceable. Like the mines, when the AI powered back up, the naval base had come back online.

But the village was a ruin. Why was that, when the mines, the Lodge, the naval base, and even the commercial port survived intact?

The roof in the next building leaked, and puddles covered the floor. The odor, though, was what struck him with brute force. Dead body smell is unmistakable, and revolting.

Bender scrunched his features and held his hand over his nose. "What is that horrible stink?"

A grim smile bent Elam's lips. "I think we've found Mrs. Torrance. Follow me."

"You mean follow that stench? Count me out. In fact, I think I'm going to vomit."

Elam tried and failed to feel sorry for him. "If you're going to hurl, do it outside. I have a feeling this is a crime scene too. As to the smell, give it about another minute and your olfactory nerves will turn numb. After that, you won't notice it."

"I can't take a minute of this."

"You can take a minute of almost anything that doesn't kill you, and this certainly won't kill you. If you're going to hurl, do it now."

Bender looked green, but he gulped and firmed his lips. "I'll be okay. I'll do my best. Go ahead, and I'll follow."

The next room held a bloated greenish-blue human corpse. Elam gagged on the smell but pressed ahead.

He ignored the sounds of Bender retching in one corner.

He walked around the body, examining it. Female, as nearly as he could tell. It had to be Mrs. Torrance. He located the standard ID hanging on a chain about her neck. It was her, all right. The medic would be able of confirm with DNA, but Elam had no doubt.

He lifted one of her bloated arms. When he released it, it plopped back to the ground. No rigor. That meant she'd been dead at least eighteen, maybe twenty-four hours. Counting backward, *that* meant she'd died at least ten or eleven hours *before* her husband.

She was no longer the chief suspect in her husband's murder. She couldn't have killed him since she was already dead. It must have been the other way around. Mr. Torrance must have killed his wife, since they were the only two people on the planet.

But then, who had killed Jack Torrance?

He was there, so he knew that neither he nor Bender had killed Mr. Torrance. Ordinarily, this kind of puzzle would fascinate Elam, but he had bigger worries now. *Sigurd* wouldn't know that Elam and Bender didn't do it. *He'd* find their mutually exonerating testimony suspect. *He'd* be certain to think Elam and Bender were the only viable suspects in Jack Torrance's murder.

This just made it even more likely that a kolonel of the Royal Guard would start poking holes in Elam's carefully contrived background.

That just wouldn't do. No, it wouldn't do at all. He stared at Bender and tried to think it through.

CHAPTER 4

It is the duty of a good shepherd to shear his sheep, not to skin them.

—*Tiberius*

A LATE-NIGHT breeze, warm and humid, stirred dust devils on the tarmac and sent grit into Sigurd's eyes and nose. The gas giant, Kennebec, and its spectacular rings dominated the sky. Even at half phase, its glow extinguished the stars. The faint purple sheen of the Scarecrow Nebula plumed on the opposite horizon. Lights blossomed from the shuttle's cargo bay and from the landing lights under the shuttle's wings. He ignored the muffled voices of the crew. *His* crew now, he supposed, not that he wanted them along.

First Officer Jorina Baak approached and gave him a casual salute. "We'll have our supplies off-loaded soon, sir. The AI is sending trams to take us to the Lodge."

He didn't acknowledge her sloppy salute. She was a just civilian, after all, despite her rank in the merchant marine. He managed to grind out, "Thank you."

She narrowed her eyes and gave him an appraising look. "I know you think we didn't need to bring a crew, or supplies."

This time, he did glance at her. "They're just a needless complication." So was she, as far as that went. The medic was the only assistance he really wanted.

"The captain insisted, and I agree. It's been decades since anyone really inspected these facilities. We don't know the status of the infirmary, or even the food supplies. And now there's been a murder. There's no reason to take unnecessary risks."

He quirked an eyebrow. "I don't think food poisoning causes blunt force trauma."

"No, but trace contaminants in the food or water supply could have unexpected effects. And with a murderer on the loose, making sure that the infirmary is up-to-date only makes sense."

He resisted the urge to shrug. She was right about the infirmary, since she'd brought nearly thirty crew along. If just the corpsman had come, he'd have sufficient supplies with him. At least she'd thought to include Knutson and the handpicked troops accompanying Sigurd.

A driverless tram hummed from the darkness and stopped near the shuttle's cargo bay. The crew loaded crates onto the back of the truck. Some of them were so large it took four people to carry them. Two dozen of the *Zuiderkruis*'s crew bustled about. Dust mites floated in the light streaming from under the shuttle's wings.

Now that he thought about it, dust mites also floated about his head. He waved his hand and scowled. "Surely those can't be insects." What idiot would bring insects onto a virgin planet?

She gave him a tight smile. "Surely they are, sir. Dust mites are efficient little housekeepers. They clean up the dead skin cells we shed. It's much cheaper to introduce dust mites than install elaborate cleaning equipment."

Minimizing costs made sense, particularly since greed had always motivated the owners of this place. "I get dust mites in the living quarters. But what are they doing here, on the tarmac?"

She shrugged. "Who knows? This planet sat empty for five hundred years. That's a long time in the life of a dust mite. Maybe they evolved."

Sigurd had to admit she was right. Maybe she'd be useful after all. "You make a good point, Ms. Baak. Thank you. I trust you'll continue to provide counsel during this mission."

"This isn't a mission. It's an investigation." She sidled closer to him, touched his elbow, and said, "But I'm here to assist you in any way you require."

He stared at her hand on his arm. "Really, Ms. Baak. Are you hitting on me?"

She pulled her hand back and tilted an eyebrow at him. "Not likely, but what if I were?"

"Then I'd have to reprimand you, and I'd hate to do that because I think you're smart and can help me on this mission." He gave a gentle push to her hand. "Besides, while I'm sure you're attractive to many, I'm not the right kind of man for you."

She stiffened, and her lips thinned. "I apologize, Your Grace." Her voice dripped with sarcasm. "I didn't mean to offend one of such high standing."

Sigurd exhaled his exasperation. "Piss on standing. That doesn't mean crap to me. I'm just a lowly soldier." She didn't need to know otherwise. "The right kind of man for you would be one who's interested in women. Is that clear enough?"

She gave a little start. "Oh?" Then her eyes lit up. "Oh! I apologize for misreading you. I mean, you're high up in the Royal Guard, and—"

He waved a hand in dismissal. "Yes, yes. We're everywhere. In any case, it's forgotten." A shout from the workers drew his attention. "Perhaps you would be so good as to supervise your crew? I see another tram approaching, and I want to get to the Lodge."

"Yes, sir. I'll handle it."

He watched as she retreated to the cargo bay. Much as he hated exposing personal information, he was pretty sure he'd purchased her loyalty.

A small two-person tram purred to a stop in front of him, and he climbed aboard. "Take me to the Lodge," he commanded.

The control panel flickered, and a genteel voice murmured from the speaker, "Very good, sir." The tram accelerated away from the shuttle.

What was the command word for the AI? Cornwall, that was it. "Cornwall, where are the Resident and the auditor?"

"They are at the Lodge, sir."

Sigurd clenched his teeth. Dumbass AI. "I meant, 'where in the Lodge are they.'"

"The Resident is in the Executive Suite. The auditor is in Suite 1A12."

Right. All the rooms were "suites." "Please ask them to meet me outside the lobby."

"Very good, sir."

The tram mounted a small hill, and Sigurd said, "Cornwall, stop the tram." The brakes slammed on, and he lurched forward. Of course. He'd forgotten to say "slowly."

In front of him, the land fell in a gentle slope toward a bay where reflected sunlight from Kennebec glimmered on placid waters. The bay opened to the black abyss of the Central Sea, which disappeared to the dark horizon. A dim golden glow from amber-hued streetlamps illuminated the Lodge itself. Lights flicked on behind floor-to-ceiling windows on the third floor. That must be Vandreren, waking up in the Executive Suite.

Sigurd's original, secret mission sent his gaze wandering back to the bay and the sea beyond. Diego Garcia, the old Grand Alliance Navy Base, was over two hundred clicks distant, on a rocky island in the middle of the Central Sea. For a moment, he wondered whatever induced the old capitalist owners to pick that name—or any name—for the isolated island, then dismissed the thought. The name itself couldn't have any importance. The purpose of the base… well, that was another thing.

"Cornwall, resume the trip. And take it easy with acceleration and deceleration."

"Very good, sir."

Minutes later, the tram pulled into the sheltered drive in front of the main entrance. Vandreren was already there. His hair was tousled, and a crease ran down his cheek from where he must have been sleeping. He wore only a loose-fitting sleep sarong that exposed abs rippling across his lithe torso.

At least he stood straight and, well, not tall, but erect. He had the good sense to not salute.

"Kolonel, I apologize for my attire, but I thought you'd value promptness over convention."

He grimaced. "I'm Sigurd, Elam. Remember? First names. And yes, you are correct about being prompt."

"Yes, sir. Sigurd. Apologies."

"I see Mr. Bender hasn't joined us yet."

"With all due respect, Mr. Bender had a challenging day. I believe he, er, *self-medicated* when we returned from Lansbury this evening."

"I still want him here, sober, drunk, or hungover. Cornwall."

A ridiculous hologram of a nineteenth-century butler appeared. "Yes, sir?"

"Please tell Mr. Bender we're waiting for him."

"Sir, when I woke him earlier, he appeared to decline your invitation."

"Appeared to decline?" What in Chaos was the idiot AI talking about?

"Perhaps I incorrectly inferred the meaning of, 'tell him to bugger off,' sir."

Sigurd's face heated, but before he could speak Elam said, "He's drunk, sir. Mrs. Torrance's remains were disturbing, even for me. The sight and smell traumatized poor Mr. Bender. He stood up well enough while I needed him as a witness, but, well, he's an accountant. This was outside the call of duty for him. I can tell you what you need tonight, and I'm sure he'll be in shape tomorrow."

Sigurd regarded the other man. He was short, only a little taller than Sigurd himself. His body showed evidence of discipline, with defined musculature and trim waist. He was unshaven, but his stubble was well-kempt. Not with the same geometric precision of Sigurd's, but neat.

He wondered if there were something between Elam and Bender. "It sounds like you care for him."

Elam snorted. "Care for him? He's a friggin' *accountant.* The only way he'd be *less* my type would be if he were a *female* accountant."

Sigurd resisted the urge to roll his eyes. Elam apparently had no hesitancy about sharing private information. "It would appear we share the same opinion of bean counters." Dammit, he couldn't help himself. He *liked* this guy. Too bad he was a suspect. "Okay, let Bender sleep off his bender." He permitted himself a tight grin. "Now, will you show me the crime scene?"

"Sure." Elam headed toward the lobby. "Cornwall. Will you turn the interior lights on?"

"Yes, sir. The cameras and microphones are still disconnected, though."

Sigurd squinted as brilliant blue-white light streamed through the glass wall that separated them from the lobby. He followed Elam through the double doors. Unlocked, of course. No reason to lock doors on a planet with a population of two.

A body lay crumpled on the floor to his left. Dark brown blood congealed underneath it. The smell wasn't as bad as it should be. Probably Cornwall or some automated sensor had turned up the ventilation.

Sigurd knelt next to the corpse and poked at the blue-tinted skin. The indentation of his finger remained.

Elam remarked, "He's probably still in rigor. It's been about fifteen hours since we found him, and he'd been dead less than hour at that time. Probably a lot less."

"Are you sure about that?"

"Pretty sure. The body was still warm, and his face was flushed. We stood here while Bender called the *Zuiderkruis* to report what we'd found. In just a few short minutes his face and extremities lost their color and turned blue. I'd say that meant he'd died within a few minutes of when we found him."

"So he transitioned to *pallor mortis* while you watched. I'd say you're definitely correct on the time of death, then." Sigurd tried to move an arm, but it was stuck in position. "You were right about the rigor too."

"I thought so."

Sigurd stood up. "Tell me about the other body."

"We found Mrs. Torrance's body in the ruins of a village dwelling. The roof was intact, but there were puddles of rain on the floor. The windows were broken out. The ambient air temperature was about fifteen degrees. The body was no longer in rigor. It was bloated and leaking fluids. I'm not competent to estimate time of death, but based on the lack of rigor it had to have been more than eighteen hours before we found her. That means it had to have been before Mr. Torrance died."

And before Elam or Bender were on the planet. That left the two of them as the prime suspects in the murder of Mr. Torrance. Unless whoever killed Mrs. Torrance also did in her husband. He gave Elam an appraising look.

Elam said, "Is there something else, Sigurd?"

Sigurd let his gaze roam over the two-story lobby. Concrete everywhere, with brutal angles and straight lines. No artwork, no paneling, nothing to soften harsh lines and surfaces. What kind of person would want to live in this sterile place, all alone, for ten years? His gaze settled back on Elam, who seemed to be inspecting him in return.

Sigurd kept his voice impassive. "I read your file. It's a little… sparse, Elam. Your observations make me think you've had some police experience."

The man's face flushed, and he looked away. "I got a speeding ticket once. That's it."

Clearly, he didn't like Sigurd having a file on him, let alone reading it. Time to play dumb. "I'm way over my head here, and I could use the help of a professional. You're smart, and you've already made helpful observations. How about it?" Ordinarily, Sigurd could make intelligence targets overconfident. Probably not this man, though, based on what he'd seen so far, but it was worth a try.

"I'll do what I can. But I I've just read too many murder mysteries." A wry expression bent Elam's lips. "I threw up, just like Bender, in Lansbury. I'd not be much of a detective if a dead body made me hurl."

Interesting. His joke about speeding tickets was more effective than a lie would have been, but no less revealing to Sigurd. Now he delivered up this transparent prevarication about reading mysteries. Whoever he was, this Elam Vandreren wasn't fooling Sigurd. There was far more to this man than his paltry file suggested.

He might be drop-dead gorgeous, at least for a guy in his late thirties or early forties. He was certainly fit, with a swimmer's bod. He was likable, and had a sense of humor. And smart. He punched all of Sigurd's buttons.

Such a shame, really. The man had no idea what or who he was up against. Sigurd didn't want to destroy him, but if necessary he'd do his duty.

He always did his duty.

CHAPTER 5

Wisdom comes alone through suffering.

—Aeschylus

ELAM TOSSED and turned in his too-soft bed while his mind replayed the meeting with Sigurd. Warm air whispered from the overhead vents and washed across his nude body. Outside the floor-to-ceiling windows of his suite, wispy clouds lazed across the night sky, now obscuring, then revealing Kennebec. Inside, purple shadows waned and waxed with the motion of the clouds.

He fingered the golden pendant that hung on a chain about his neck and murmured the words engraved in Frisian on the surface: *Myn leafde foar ivich.* That wasn't true. Nothing was forever. At least not love. Guilt, though. That was forever.

He sat on the edge of the bed and rubbed his temples. Tonight's meeting confirmed he was in trouble. Sigurd was smart and skillful, he had to give the kolonel that. He'd kept a poker face. Most people wouldn't have been able to guess what he was thinking.

Good thing Elam wasn't most people, even if what he'd learned did make him lose sleep.

Sigurd couldn't hide the micro-expressions that flitted across his almost-but-not-quite impassive features. No one could. It took training and practice to read those fleeting glimpses into his thoughts. A grim smile twisted Elam's lips. He had that training.

He walked to the window and stared into the shadows. Sigurd *liked* him, that was clear. Truth be told, Elam liked *him*, too. In the distant past, when he wore a younger man's clothes, they might even have had an affair. Not now. Not since.... He closed his eyes and tried to shut off the feelings of guilt that churned in his chest. Affairs of the heart were not for the likes of him. Not anymore. He heaved a deep sigh and concentrated on the problem at hand.

At least his charm offensive had worked. In fact, Sigurd was attracted to him. He'd suspected as much after their first video call, but still it was a risk, showing up half naked tonight. It had paid off, though. The man's reaction when Elam came out to him was unmistakable.

That was the good news. Too bad there wasn't more of it.

The bad news began with the fact that Sigurd had already decided Elam, probably with Bender, had murdered Jack Torrance. He wasn't happy about it. He even mildly regretted it. But his mind was made up.

That wasn't the only thing keeping Elam awake. He'd more or less expected to be the primary suspect.

There was something odd about Sigurd. Something he couldn't quite put his finger on. A web of puzzles that kept buzzing in the back of his skull, demanding attention.

For one thing, the man looked too young to be a kolonel. If he were such a hotshot that he got a fast-track promotion, what in Chaos was he doing on a merchant ship? He'd be commanding troops or making war plans on the general staff. Not flying around while bean counters audited more or less worthless Syndicate holdings.

Elam wished again that he'd been more social on the passage here. He might have learned something useful.

Okay, go at the contrapositive. Suppose Sigurd weren't a hotshot. Then his rapid rise to kolonel had to be from something else. The only thing that made sense was that he had connections with the aristocracy. Could be he was even one of the nobility, maybe a younger son of one of the royal houses.

On the other hand, there was the *Volknut* tattoo on his cheek. Three triangles, no two linked but all three overlapping and bound together. *Duty, honor, and heart*, whatever the crap that meant. He might get a courtesy rank of kolonel, but that tattoo was special. Soldiers *earned* that tattoo, almost always through extraordinary military service. The Margrave himself wore the tattoo, along with all his brothers, uncles, and sons. It was a high honor for anyone else to wear it, and a mark of personal fealty to the Margrave of Elsinore and his immediate family. The fact that Sigurd wore the tattoo argued that he had probably earned the right to do so. He certainly seemed competent enough.

Wearing the tattoo also argued against him being of noble birth. If he'd been born to one of the other great Houses, he'd be wearing the sigil of his sire, not the Margrave's. The great Houses only gave fealty to the Emperor, never to each other.

Elam considered whether Sigurd might be part of the Margrave's family. But he was certain the uncles were too old, that there were no brothers and—so far as he knew—only one son. The heir would be at the court on Elsinore, too valuable to be cavorting around in the middle of nowhere. It followed that Sigurd was a commoner who had earned the right to wear the tattoo.

In any case, he *did* have the tattoo. He must have earned it, and therefore must have earned his rank as well. That left the puzzle of why he was on the *Zuiderkruis*. As far as Elam knew, all the ship did was ferry auditors around the Syndicate's marginal holdings in this remote sector. The Margrave was a Principalof the Syndicate, to be sure, but sending an honored warrior on an accounting mission didn't make sense.

Elam pressed his forehead against the cold glass of the suite's windows and closed his eyes. What was he missing? He needed more information, information in the local data banks, but if he started poking around in Syndicate business or—worse—into Sigurd's background, he'd just look more suspicious.

He pulled back from the window, faced into his room, and straightened his back. He'd figure it out eventually. Meantime, he needed to find out what really happened here, and soon. He was sure Sigurd was about to take his life apart. If Elam solved the crime first, he might just escape back into his anonymous hole. "Cornwall."

The AI's hologram coalesced in front of him. "Yes, sir. Do you require assistance with clothing?"

"What?" Elam had forgotten he was naked. "No. I'm curious. about Mrs. Torrance. She must have traveled to Lansbury on the monorail. Is that right?"

"Yes, sir. I have video of her in the station."

"Why didn't she take the flitter?"

"She always used the monorail. According to their personnel files, neither of the Torrances knew how to fly a flitter."

Elam grunted. His file didn't include his flitter experience, either. He'd made sure of it. "Did Mr. Torrance go with her to Lansbury, or did he arrive later?" He turned back to the window and the night shadows.

"Mr. Torrance never left the Lodge, sir."

Elam whirled around to face the hologram. "What did you say?"

"Mr. Torrance never left the Lodge, sir. I monitor all the exits. I would have seen him leave. He hadn't left the Lodge for over three years."

"What do you mean? He never went outside? Was he agoraphobic?"

"He stopped going outside three years ago, sir. Are you asking that I break confidentiality on his medical records?

"Uh, yes." Cornwall would know that Elam, as Resident, would have that authority.

"The medical program diagnosed him as agoraphobic and clinically depressed. It prescribed sertraline for both conditions."

Elam nodded. That would be standard for panic disorders. "You should report this to Kolonel von Dorestad."

"The kolonel asked a similar set of questions an hour ago sir, before retiring for the night. He already knows what we've discussed."

"Did he ask whether anyone else besides the Torrances were on the planet?"

"Yes, sir, he did."

Elam ground his teeth. "What did you tell him?"

"That my records show that, prior to yesterday when you and Mr. Bender arrived, no other people were on Cabot's Landing."

Elam sat back on his bed and considered. Jack Torrance never left the Lodge, so he couldn't have killed his wife. His wife certainly died before Elam and Bender arrived, so they couldn't have killed her either. But someone or something clearly *did* kill her.

"Cornwall, you are certain there are no other people on the planet?"

"I am certain I have no record of other people on the planet, sir."

The mystery remained, but even Sigurd was going to have a hard time pinning the murder of Mrs. Torrance on either him or Bender. He replayed Cornwall's response. "Is it possible for me to access your data files directly? A console interface, maybe?"

"Have my responses been inadequate, sir?

"No, you've been fine. But I'm old-school. It's easier for me to write precise queries at a console."

"There are consoles at each of the power stations and at the industrial port. My main data storage is in an underground bunker at the industrial port."

The eastern power station was just a couple hundred clicks up the coast. It would be suspicious to just go there, but maybe he could maneuver Sigurd into sending him. He needed a wedge of some kind. More information.

He regarded the hologram, shimmering patiently between him and the windows. "Back to Mrs. Torrance, Cornwall. She was supposed to be here doing historical research. Did she store her notes in your data banks?"

"Mrs. Torrance's data store has approximately 6.934 petabytes of data, sir."

"That much? Is it searchable?"

"By date and location, sir."

"How about by content?"

"Sir, it's all audio, graphic, and video files. It's only searchable by date and location tags."

"No text? I'd think her research notes would be text files. She did take notes, right?"

"Sir, I believe she took handwritten notes. She regularly asked for pens and notebooks."

"Okay, then. Where are her notebooks? I need to see them."

"That won't be possible, sir. I only have sufficient materials on hand for four one-hundred-page notebooks. When she needed a new one, I had to recycle one of the old ones. She had two fresh notebooks when she left for Lansbury three days ago."

"That doesn't make sense either. Why keep notes if they're going to be destroyed?"

"She scanned them, sir, before I recycled them. That way her notes were not destroyed."

"*Stomme ezel!*" Damned literal-minded robot. "So, those must be the graphic files in her data store. Why didn't you just say that in the first place?"

"Sir, I apologize for my inadequate answers. We can review your questions and my responses to see where I went wrong if you like."

"No, I'm sure your answers were perfect." Verbal programming was too imprecise for what he needed. That was why he needed to get to a console. "Did Mrs. Torrance ever go to any of the power stations?"

"She visited the east power station once, and the west power station thirty-six times. I have no record of a visit to the south power station."

"The south power station? On the Eastern Reserve Island? That's the only one with no monorail connection. Or did I miss something?"

"You are correct, sir. There is no monorail to the south power plant."

"Did Mrs. Torrance ever go to the Western Reserve Island?"

"No, sir."

That made sense. No monorail. She couldn't travel by flitter, so she'd be restricted to where the monorail ran. "Why did she visit the nearest station only once? And where else did she go?"

"Sir, I could prepare a summary of her monorail trips for the last two years if that would be helpful."

"Yes, please do. Thank you, Cornwall." Obviously, no one had trained the AI by thanking it for correct responses. Another thing for him to fix—assuming he had time—later. Besides, all things considered, Cornwall was turning out to be his kind of people. He showed up only when called, and went away when dismissed.

Back to Mrs. Torrance and her schedule. "You said she visited the eastern power plant only once?"

"Yes, sir. That was within a month of her arrival on planet. She spent ninety minutes, and then never went back."

"Why so little time? And why never go back?"

"She was allergic to the cats, sir."

"Cats? You mean, like, *house cats*?"

"Yes, sir."

"What in Chaos are house cats doing on Cabot's Landing?"

"Sir, I believe the original Cabot Trust employees kept them as pets. When the Cabot employees abandoned the planet, they left one food processor inside the eastern power plant on automatic and set to produce a source of protein for a clowder of cats."

"The cats are *inside* the power plant?"

"Yes, sir. That's where the food is."

He considered for a moment. "After five hundred years, it must have an interesting smell."

"Are you referring to the feline urine and excrement, sir?"

Elam couldn't stop a chuckle. Urine and excrement, indeed. "Yes, exactly."

"Sir, the Cabot Trust engineers designed an automated system to recycle those resources. For reasons unknown to me, the cats are cooperative about depositing their droppings in these recycling bins."

"They wouldn't be filled with, say, sawdust, would they?"

"Of course not, sir. Wood is a scarce resource. The bins use silica pellets that are easily recycled."

Elam grinned. Still, Cornwall had scratched his curiosity bump, so to speak. "This all happened five hundred years ago, and they're still there? How many are there?"

"Based on food consumption and fecal reprocessing, I estimate between fifty and one hundred breeding pairs."

Elam tried to remember what he knew about genetic drift. "That doesn't sound like enough animals for a stable population."

"The original population was eighteen breeding pairs, sir, back when Cabot Trust employees left and put me in hibernation. When the Syndicate arrived and reanimated me, I estimated the population at approximately three hundred pairs. It has been slowly declining ever since."

Six hundred cats roaming a power plant just sounded bizarre to Elam. Hilarious too, but bizarre. Even with food and litter, they shouldn't have survived. "I remember something about a 50/500 rule. Fifty individuals to survive short-term fertility and environmental challenges, and five hundred individuals to guard against long-term genetic drift."

"There is considerable variability in that rule, sir, depending on the species and the environmental conditions."

Elam nodded. Cornwall seemed to know everything. The challenge was prying it out of him. "I really have to see this, what did you call it? A clowder?"

"Yes, sir. Will you be traveling there in the morning?"

"Hmm. Maybe." With any luck, with this new information about Mrs. Torrance's notes, he could maneuver Sigurd into sending him there.

There had to be a clue in those notes. For sure, Elam hadn't killed anyone, and he'd been with Bender the whole time, so the auditor wasn't a murderer either. The only answer was that there had to be someone else on the planet. Maybe the Torrances had found them, and paid for their discovery with their lives. Wendy Torrance had been all over the planet, or at least everywhere the monorail went. The logical place to start looking was in her notes.

At least it was a working hypothesis, until something better came along.

CHAPTER 6

To the living we owe respect, but to the dead we owe only the truth.

—Voltaire

A CRISP MORNING breeze swept across the patio and prickled Sigurd's cheeks. No clouds obscured the too-small, too-white sun. For once, Kennebec didn't dominate the sky. Instead, the companion satellite, Flyian, hovered like a pale ghost on the horizon opposite the sun.

He ignored the chatter that murmured from the *Zuiderkruis's* crew seated on the other side of the patio. At least a dozen empty tables separated him from the nearest of the enlisted ratings, and even the senior petty officers avoided his table. He sat, isolated and alone, while he sipped his fake coffee and planned his next steps.

A shadow fell across his table and he glanced up, recognized Jorina Baak, accompanied by a fit woman in her late forties with a no-nonsense haircut.

Jorina said, "Kolonel, this is First Pilot Gretl Ulrich. Gretl, this is Kolonel Sigurd von Dorestad of the Corsairs. May we join you, sir?"

He stood, gave them a stiff bow, and said, "It would be my pleasure. Please be seated."

They placed their trays on the table and sat. Gretl immediately started to wolf down her breakfast, while Jorina sipped her fake orange juice and turned to her companion. "Your record shows you're ex-military, Gretl."

Between bites, she answered, "Yes, ma'am. Me and Cadwalladar, we's both ex-marines. I served with the lad on Actium's Gate." She paused long enough to gulp some juice, then leaned forward, an eager smile on her face. "Why's ye askin' 'bout our service? Is we gonna get to kill ourselves some Orcs?"

Jorina winced, or maybe it was a smile. Hard to tell with her sometimes. She said, "No, there's no Exaltationists on this planet, more's

the pity. In fact, the only people here are the ones from the *Zuiderkruis*."
She sipped more juice, then said, "Mr. Glyndwr told me you spent the
night in the flitter hanger at the port."

"That we did, ma'am. Me and Cadwalladar and his squeeze,
Oates."

"What did you learn?"

"There's five birds there, ma'am. All Grand Alliance Vintage, so
old but better than the modern crap. Well maintained, by their service
records. They all got a battery refresh and flight tests at the last quarterly
inspection."

Jorina asked, "Is there something I should know about them?"

Sigurd pretended to eat his breakfast and let the two of them chatter
on. You never knew what you might learn by listening.

"Not really, ma'am. Four of 'ems jest glorified busses for hauling
cargo and people. But one of them's a Talon class fighter. I flew one of
those on Actium's Gate, and they're sweet." She frowned. "It had been
years since any of these had seen service, but someone took the Talon out
yesterday. Why'd they do that if there ain't no hostiles?"

Jorina shrugged. "I believe that was the Resident. You'd have to ask
him. Did Mr. Glyndwr mention anything about a mission?"

That was interesting, and proved he was right to just let them talk.
It took special training to handle a Talon class fighter, training Sigurd had
gotten at the Academy on Sandhurst. Where did Elam learn to do that?
Another mystery to add to his notes on the Resident.

Gretl answered Jorina's question, "Mr. Glyndwr said something
about flying a recovery team up north. Too many for the Talon, so I guess
I'll be flyin' one of the busses."

Jorina nodded. "Your choice, but you're right that there will be
eight or nine people. I've uploaded specifics on the local AI at Project
Nightengale. Do you know the AI's activation word?"

"Yes, ma'am." She made a face and used her toast to mop up some
fake eggs. "He's a hoity-toity one, he is."

This time Jorina's smile was unmistakable. "He is that. Someone
with a sense of humor programmed him."

"May I ask when we lift off on this mission, ma'am?"

"Ten hundred hours today."

Her eyebrows shot up her forehead. "I need to get crackin'. I gotta
pick out my bird, check the weather, recon the landing site, and work out

a flight plan. Piece of cake, but it takes time." She stood and faced Jorina. "Ma'am?" Then she seemed to remember Sigurd, glanced at him and said, "Sir?"

He waved a hand in dismissal, and Jorina said, "Do what you need to."

She dumped her tray in a trash bot and trotted out of the patio.

Sigurd templed his fingers and said, "Well, she seems competent. Bloodthirsty but competent."

Jorina replied, "She is certainly competent. She was cited for heroism in rescuing injured marines at Actium's Gate. If she's bloodthirsty, she's my kind of bloodthirsty."

"Mine too, Ms. Baak. Mine too."

They sat in silence for a few minutes eating; then Jorina said, "This is really good. I could almost believe these are real eggs and real orange juice."

He wrinkled his nose. "It's adequate for synthetics. I admit the yellow, fluffy stuff tastes a bit like scrambled eggs, if you use your imagination. The orange-colored drink is better. It's even got a touch of mango." He took another sip of his coffee and grimaced. "This stuff, though, tastes like they brewed it using soot. At least it's got caffeine in it."

"Really? I had some earlier, in my room. It wasn't bad at all. Of course, it's not like I can afford the real thing, even when it's available." She stirred the imitation juice, took a drink, and favored him with a sunny smile. "Did you have a good evening?"

"Passable. I spent some frustrating time with the AI." He almost forgot to be polite, then remembered. "How about you?"

"Excellent. A two-room suite, in-room coffee, and a view of the ocean. What's not to like?"

He could swear her eyes sparkled when she smiled. Flirting must be second nature. He cleared his throat. "I'm trying to extract information from the AI. It's a challenge."

"You mean Corn Wall?" She made his name into two words, doubtless to avoid activating him. "Who thought of that cheesy name, anyway?"

"It is annoying, isn't it? I asked if there was an alternative persona. It seems there's a female version named 'Regan.' She's even more irritating."

"Cornwall and Regan, eh? I wonder if mad King Lear's lurking about."

He frowned. "Who?"

"Never mind. My classical education is showing, I'm afraid. Totally frivolous." She gave him a big smile that squinted her eyes, then took another forkful of the fake scrambled eggs. "These aren't bad at all. In fact, they could be the real thing."

"Possible, but not probable. There are supposed to be wild chickens on the Western Reserve Island, but there's no land link between here and there. No way to harvest the eggs and get them to the kitchen."

She dimpled, and her voice turned indulgent. "You don't harvest eggs. You gather them. You must be a city boy."

How did the conversation get to his upbringing? Time to assert control. "Back to the AI. It's programmed for personal service. I think that's why it's hard to extract information."

She held up a finger while she chewed and swallowed, then spoke. "I anticipated that. One of the ratings I brought along has advanced training in data mining. Cybernetics Mate Four Clifford will suck those databases dry for you."

"Excellent. There's a control console up the coast at the east power station. It's the first stop on the monorail. I'll want to brief him on what to look for. I've taken the manager's office, behind the front desk in the lobby, as my HQ. Can he meet me there at, say, nine this morning?"

"First bell. Yes, sir, I'll take care of it." She tipped her head and whispered into her collar microphone and then turned her gaze back to Sigurd. "The corpsman has already photographed the crime scene in the lobby, secured necessary samples, and removed Mr. Torrance's body to the morgue. He's working on the autopsy as we speak. We also reconnected the AI's telemetry in the lobby."

"Thank you. You're most efficient. I knew I was right to have confidence in you."

She shrugged. "Just doing my job. I may be a Merchant Stierrener, but that doesn't mean I'm not as competent as you military types."

"I didn't mean to suggest otherwise."

A splash of color at the entrance to the patio caught his eye. Elam entered, wearing a loose-fitting bright orange shirt and lime-green wrinkled trousers. At least his boots were polished. He carried a tray with coffee and a roll and scanned the room, as if looking for a seat. Sigurd rose and waved to him. The Resident smiled, nodded, and wove his way through the empty tables.

Sigurd leaned forward and muttered in Baak's ear, "That's the new Resident. Hold your tongue with him. I don't completely trust him."

She rolled her eyes and gave him a dour look.

He winced, but it was too late to be more politic. "Elam, please join us. This is First Officer Jorina Baak of the *Zuiderkruis*. She's here to assist in the mission. Jorina, this is Elam Vandreren, Resident of Cabot's Landing."

Baak stood and offered her hand. "Pleased to meet you, Elam."

Instead of shaking her hand the way a proper gentleman would, he bowed low and almost but not quite kissed her wrist. He murmured, in a voice that oozed from his lips like warm butter, "The pleasure is mine, I assure you." He stood back at attention, and Jorina sent dimples his way.

Another squinty smile transformed her features. It must be her trademark. There was no doubt her eyes twinkled this time. Sigurd knew he was right. Flirting had to be second nature to her and meant nothing. He kept his voice steady and his face impassive. "Please, sit. Elam, I spent time last night with the AI. I have news."

The man lounged back in a chair, crossed his legs, and smiled. "Good news, I hope, after the tragic events of yesterday."

"Maybe information is a better description. I asked Cornwall about Mr. Torrance's movements. He was in the Lodge the entire time his spouse was in Lansbury."

Elam's eyebrows crept up his forehead. Sigurd had to admit he did a credible job of looking surprised. "How can that be? Mrs. Torrance didn't kill herself, not with the injuries I saw."

"The inevitable conclusion is that someone besides Mr. and Mrs. Torrance is on the planet, and probably did both murders."

Elam narrowed his eyes. "You don't look entirely convinced."

"The problem is that Cornwall insists no one else was here. The captain has scanned from space, of course, but that can't possibly be definitive. The place could be crawling with people. All they'd have to do is hide underground and the ship would never see them."

"There is that." Elam swirled his coffee but didn't drink. "I spent some time with Cornwall last night, too. He didn't exactly say no one was here. He said his data banks had no record of anyone being here."

Baak interjected, "But isn't that the same thing? Doesn't the AI have telemetry everywhere?"

Sigurd shook his head. "No. There's active video and audio telemetry here, at the Lodge, at the industrial port, at the old dysprosium mines, and at all of the monorail stations. That leaves about ninety-nine percent of the land surface uncovered, to say nothing of the oceans."

She nodded. "But if there are people here, they have to eat. Wouldn't they have to use food processors? Or at a minimum, they'd have to grind and cook the wheat, and that kind of activity would show on the ship's scans."

Elam nodded. "Good questions. Let's ask." He tipped his head and commanded, "Cornwall."

The hologram flickered into existence, sunlight streaming through its image. "How may I serve you, sir?"

"Could humans survive on a diet of the local wheat?"

"That would be possible, sir, but it would need to be processed in some way. There are food processors at many locations on the planet."

"Are they networked?"

"No, sir."

"Are they connected to the power grid?"

"They can be, yes. But they all have solar power cells. They were designed to be fail-safe in case of an unexpected power failure."

Elam nodded. "So, humans could use the food processors to survive, and no one would know. One more thing I've been wondering about while you're here. What's the largest population Cabot's Cove has ever had, including before the Great Disintegration?"

"At the time immediately preceding the first closure of the mines, there were 38,952 people on the planet. Between my hibernation and reanimation, I have no data. Since reanimation, the largest population was 976."

"And the power plants. How large a city would they support?"

"Power needs vary greatly, sir. It's impossible to answer that question accurately."

"Let's say a for typical Elsinore city, back when the plants were first built here."

"The power stations were each designed to support urban areas of that era of up to one million people, sir."

"There are three of the blasted things on this planet. Did they need all that power for the mines?"

"No, sir. The commercial mining operation ran off the east power station, and the other two were in reserve. The same is true today. My records show the load has never exceeded two percent of capacity."

"Why, then, did the ancients put three stations, each fifty times larger than needed, on this planet?"

"I don't have that information, sir."

"Thank you, Cornwall. That will be all."

The AI vanished, and Elam smirked. "Another mystery to add to the others."

Baak shook her head. "It's not really a mystery, not from a business perspective. I can think of several explanations. The most obvious is that the old Cabot corporation was also in the power plant business. It could divert the investor resources intended for the mines to subsidize the power plant business by overbuilding here."

Sigurd scowled. "That would be dishonest. Such things were permitted in the old times?"

She shrugged. "It's impossible to stop that kind of thing, especially if the auditors are corrupted. I'd be willing to bet this kind of pillaging still goes on today. In fact, I'm certain of it."

Elam just smiled and drank coffee.

Sigurd set his jaw. By his father's father, he'd get to the bottom of this. If she was right, it wouldn't happen on his watch. He took a steadying breath, focused on the task at hand, and turned to Elam. "You did a good job there, pulling information from that blasted, obtuse AI."

"It takes practice. And patience. I'd be willing to bet there's more to learn. For example, Cornwall told me Mrs. Torrance has petabytes of research notes in her data store. She was a historian and had a grant from some big university."

Sigurd nodded. "Erasmus University, on Elsinore." He'd studied there, before being sent to the Imperial Ghost Fleet Academy on Sandhurst. "What could a historian's notes possibly tell us?"

Elam shrugged. "Who knows? She spent the last six years digging into the bones of this planet. Now she and her husband are both dead, and under mysterious circumstances. Maybe she found something. Or someone."

It sounded like a stretch to Sigurd. Still, it couldn't hurt to check it out, and it certainly fit with his other mission, his main mission. Besides, it would give Elam something to do and keep him busy while Sigurd went to Lansbury. "Jorina is taking a rating, a cybernetics mate, to the east power plant to check the data bases. There are data consoles there, so he can bypass the AI interface and program more robust queries. Maybe you should go along, Elam. Follow up on your hunch."

Elam glanced at Jorina, and a coy smile played with his lips. "I'd be delighted to go with Ms. Baak."

Sigurd glared at them. Apparently flirting was second nature to him, too. Perhaps the man wasn't as repelled by women as his revelation last night suggested. In the end, it didn't matter. Nothing mattered to Sigurd but his duty.

He glanced at his watch. It was already after 8:00 a.m. "I'm using the manager's office as my HQ. I really need to go there. I'm overdue to meet with the corpsman, and I need to plan our excursion to Lansbury to recover Mrs. Torrance's remains. I expect to spend the day there, investigating that crime scene."

He stood. "I'll leave the two of you to arrange your expedition. Ms. Baak, please don't forget to have the cybernetics mate meet with me at nine."

She nodded. "Already arranged, sir. Mr. Clifford will be on time."

He gave them a curt nod, picked up his tray, and rushed away, fuming. Elam's flirting with Jorina hadn't bothered him. Not really. It couldn't have. The man meant nothing to him.

Still, it was a relief that he was less of a suspect this morning than he'd been last night. But he wasn't off the hook yet. There were too many blanks in his background. Sigurd narrowed his eyes and thought through the special instructions he would give the cybernetics mate, Clifford. The man needed to do more than just pull data from the AI's archive. If he succeeded, Sigurd would have what he needed to discover Elam's secrets. All of them.

CHAPTER 7

One cat just leads to another.

—Ernest Hemingway

ELAM HUNKERED in the back of the monorail car. He glowered out the window at the wind-swept wheat, swaying in golden waves across gentle hillocks. His stomach cramped, and he winced. Stress, maybe. Or self-loathing. Probably both.

It wasn't so much that he hated being around other people. He hated *himself* when he was *around* other people. He clenched his jaws and pressed his forehead against the cool glass. At least he was aware enough to know the problem and the solution. Stay away from people. The loathing didn't exactly go away then, but at least he didn't hurt anyone but himself.

At the front of the car, Jorina and the cybernetics mate chattered away. Elam had led her on, and for what? To make Sigurd jealous? It had worked, but neither one of them deserved the way he'd treated them.

The worst was the tiny instant of disgust that had flashed across Sigurd's face. The man knew Elam was being a two-faced jerk, trying to manipulate the situation to his advantage. His soldier's demeanor hid his reaction from other people, but not Elam. He wished he'd never been trained to read micro-expressions. Sometimes, most times, it was better to not know what people were really thinking.

Movement outside in the wheat made him peer out the window. Was that a machine? Mowing the wheat? "Cornwall."

The AI's urbane voice spouted from the speaker built into the headrest of Elam's seat. "How may I serve you, sir?"

"I see what look like lawn mowers in the wheat."

"Yes, sir."

Elam waited, then rolled his eyes. He hadn't asked a question. "Why would they be mowing? It can't be for landscaping purposes."

"No, sir. Based on recent power draws, I conjecture you are seeing bots harvesting wheat to provision the food processors at the power station. If you'd send me a picture with your phone, I could confirm."

Elam fiddled with his phone while asking, "Why do that? There's no one there to feed."

"Yes, those are harvesters. Thank you for the image, sir. You must be forgetting the cats, sir."

Oh. Of course. Someone had set up an automated system to feed the animals centuries ago. Amazing it was still running. "You must activate them when the cat food runs low?"

"No, sir. The entire process is automated. When the food stores fall below a preset threshold, it triggers the harvesters. None of harvesters or food processors are part of my neural net. All essential services are autonomous and automated."

Elam nodded. Good design. That way a single failure wasn't fatal. "How many cats are there, again?"

"Based on the frequency of harvester operations, I estimate between fifty and one hundred breeding pairs."

"You don't have a count based on sightings?"

"No, sir. Their infrared signature doesn't activate the cameras at the station. I only see them if they happen to walk on a touch-sensitive surface. In the last thirty days, that's happened six times inside the subway station and twice in the power plant itself. I could send you photographs, sir."

"Don't bother. I forgot that you told me about the numbers last night. Thank you, Cornwall." All he needed was to trigger another stultifying lecture on useless trivia.

The monorail rounded a curve, and the landscape changed. Gentle hills gave way to shallow, rocky embankments. The wheat now grew in scattered clumps, and here and there a lonely birch tree sprouted like a giant weed. Elam rubbed his cheek. He didn't fit in any better than those blasted trees. He could fake it, but he knew it wasn't real.

The train decelerated when it entered a tunnel. Intermittent overhead lighting cast a tentative dance of light and shadow on the tunnel walls as the train slowed. It finally stopped in a brightly lit station with arching concrete walls and yellow brick floors. The doors swooshed open, and Jorina and the crewman stood.

Elam sighed and rose to join them. Jorina favored him with a squinty-eyed smile, and the crewman—his last name was... Clifford, maybe?—gave him the once-over. Elam didn't need special training to read what was behind the man's penetrating gaze. Great. He was cute, but, well... he was just a kid. He couldn't be much more than twenty. He was definitely not what Elam needed right now.

Jorina tipped her head to one side, and her expression changed from merry to concerned. "Are you all right? You seem a little out of sorts."

Elam forced a smile. A fake smile. "I'm fine. Just tired. I didn't sleep well last night."

She nodded and touched his hand. "Well, no one could blame you for that. I mean, you found two dead bodies in one day."

He squeezed her hand. It was warm, the hand of a working woman, not soft at all. "I'll be fine." He released her and extended a hand to Clifford. "I apologize for not greeting you earlier. Mr. Clifford, is it? I'm Elam."

"It is, but please call me Chad. Nice to meet you. The kolonel, uh, mentioned you when he briefed me this morning." An impossibly white smile contrasted with the man's ebony features.

Did he now? From your expression, he did more than mention me. "You know what you're looking for, then."

"Yes, sir." He held up a knapsack. "I'm all set."

I just bet you are. What task has Sigurd set for you? From your expression, something about me, no doubt. "Just let me know if I can help. I've got my own orders from him, so we'll probably be working side by side."

Jorina gave them another of her cheery smiles. "I'm kind of the third wheel here. You both have stuff to do. I'm not sure why I'm along."

Elam raised an eyebrow and kept his tone businesslike. "I'm glad you're here. I'd like to know more about the station. What's here, how it works. Maybe you can look around while the two of us dig into the data banks?"

She nodded. "I can do that. I'm certified on the power plant of the *Zuiderkruis*. This one probably has the same basic design."

"You might watch out for the cats."

Elam got the surprised reaction from her that he'd expected. "Cats? I don't recognize the acronym."

"No, I mean real cats. Abyssinians. Apparently, they were pets of the original workers on the planet, and around fifty or so still survive in this station."

Clifford's face lit with delight. "You trollin' me, man? I'm, like, dead."

Jorina grinned, but her tone was officious. "Belay the slang, Mr. Clifford."

"Yes, ma'am. But I'm just sayin' it was so funny, I, like, died laughing—"

She waved him silent. "I know. It's pretty remarkable. So, there are cuddly little woozies here? Who empties their litter box? How do they get fed?"

Elam answered, "It's apparently all been on autopilot for centuries. An incredible bit of engineering. Frivolous, but awesome. Remember, though, no one's been around them in five hundred years, so they'll be feral, not tame. Be careful, and don't get scratched."

Another squinty-eyed smile graced her features. "I think I can defend myself from kitty-cats." Her look turned pensive. "You're sure no one's been here? How about the Torrances?"

"She only came once. She was allergic to cats, so she only came once and didn't stay long. And Mr. Torrance was agoraphobic. He never left the Lodge."

She flashed dimples this time. "Now I'm dead. A Resident who can't leave home." She pulled out her phone and stroked the screen. "I'm sure you want to get started. Let's find the data consoles so you two can have at it. I downloaded floorplans this morning before we left." She held her phone at arm's length and rotated. "This way, I think."

THREE HOURS later, Elam's head ached and his back cramped from sitting hunched over a keyboard. He rubbed his cheek and leaned back. He'd started reading Mrs. Torrance's most recent entries, but their tone was so strange that he sampled the earliest ones too. All her scribbled notes were cryptic, but the tone changed in the recent ones.

At first, her notes read like a mild-mannered academic pursuing a scholarly investigation. But the later ones, the ones from the last three months, had an urgency, as if she were looking for something in particular. She wrote about "clues," where earlier she'd used words like "evidence" and "data." There were constant questions about what "they" had done, without naming who "they" might be. Activities like moving mining equipment to Lansbury, or food processers to the arroyos surrounding the old mines, were "mysteries." One entry bemoaned the fact she couldn't get to Diego Garcia, the island in the middle of the Central Sea that held the old Grand Alliance Ghost Fleet base. She had even tried to walk overland to the old marine base on the west coast, but "they" had blasted the one pass through the mountains that connected the base with the monorail stop at Last Chance, the mining settlement.

Then there was the mystery of the Lansbury ruins. All of the documentation he'd read assumed the village had been destroyed by raiders during the Disintegration, but Wendy Torrance was convinced that it had occurred at least one hundred, and as much as two hundred, years later. She'd based her conclusions on comparable ruins at other archeological sites on Old Home Earth, Sparta, and other locations. Given the differences in climate and ecology, Elam wasn't convinced. More to the point, no one was around to destroy the place after the Disintegration, at least not until the Praetorian Syndicate came back seventy-odd years ago. This could just be evidence of her growing paranoia.

On the other hand, she was now dead. Murdered, in fact. Even paranoids have enemies.

One of the last entries, dated four days before her death, made him doubt her sanity even more.

When I walk the abandoned streets, I can feel their eyes on me, watching me, judging me. In my mind, the creak of the old structures becomes the rattle of their bones. The wind whistling through a shattered window becomes the moaning of their spirits. They haunt this place. They mock me. But I'm determined to find them. They are close by, I can tell. They can't hide much longer. By Draugr, I shall find them before we leave.

Sometime over the last six years, she'd degenerated from a legitimate scholar to a ghost hunter, swearing by the undead god of myth.

The crewman's chair creaked, and shuffled footfalls approached Elam's cubicle. His youthful voice was tentative when he spoke. "Hey, bud. I don't know about you, but I could use a break."

Elam twisted his neck, and some of the tension went out of his muscles. Chad. That was the kid's name. "Yeah. Have you found anything?"

"Some interesting hints in the data. Too soon to say much, though." He quirked an eyebrow at the door. "That has to be a coffee station just down the hall. You want some java?"

"That sounds good. Think it still works?"

"Only one way to find out. Everything else works. Why not the coffee bar? How you take it?"

"Thanks. I'll take mine black."

"Figures." He winked. "Just like me. Be right back."

He scampered away, and Elam cast a lingering glance at his butt. He was cute, but he really couldn't be much more than twenty. Way too young for Elam's taste. He thought of Sigurd's handsome features, and a fleeting smile bent his lips. It vanished when he opened another file on his workstation, one with Sigurd's name in large type at the top.

The striking thing about the file was that it was blank. The local data banks had no record of a Sigurd von Dorestad, kolonel in the Margrave's personal guard. There were over a hundred people of that name on Elsinore, and over ninety of those had photos. None looked anything like the Sigurd on Cabot's Landing. His Sigurd. He did find a list of personnel for the First Battalion Corsairs, as the guard styled itself. No Sigurd von Dorestad in the two-hundred-plus names. No Sigurd von Dorestad at all, anywhere in the Elsinore armed forces. The database showed it had been updated when the *Zuiderkruis* arrived in-system two days ago, so it was current.

So, Sigurd was a fraud or, more likely, using an assumed identity.

The Corsairs had the usual organization chart for a small unit, inherited from military organizations dating back to Napoleon. There were individual staff commands for operations, administration, and supply. There had to be one for intelligence too, but it wasn't listed in the database. The inevitable conclusion was that Sigurd was part of S4, the intelligence group. In fact, as a kolonel, he was probably in charge of it.

That explained his presence on the *Zuiderkruis*, or at least gave a clue. He must be on some kind of intelligence-gathering mission. But a kolonel in the Margrave's personal guard wasn't likely to be a secret agent. He'd *deploy* agents instead of being one. That meant that there was probably at least one hidden spy on board, maybe more, who reported to Sigurd.

But what in Chaos were they spying on? Not him, surely. He was confident no one could trace him. Well, not unless they used DNA, and those databases were confidential and not part of any generic download available from a commercial cruiser.

The murders must be connected in some way to the reason Sigurd was here. Elam didn't believe in coincidence.

Chad reappeared and held out a steaming plastic cup. "Careful. It's hot."

The young technician's gaze raked across Elam's body. Elam returned his scrutiny. Gah. The kid's uniform couldn't hide his perfect body. Too perfect, in fact. Elam smiled and accepted the coffee. "Thank you." He gestured to the chair by his desk. "Have a seat. Tell me about yourself."

"Not much to tell. I grew up in Bonkwerd, a nowhere place on Dongeradeel. Got out of there just in time."

Dongeradeel. The name sent a chill jittering down Elam's spine. Its settlements reflected the history of the original Old Home Earth colonists, most speaking Frisian, some Dutch, some even Malay. From his appearance and accent, Chad must be from one of the latter settlements on the northern continent. Elam kept his face impassive and his voice neutral. The last thing he needed was to expose his connection to Dongeradeel. "Oh?"

"You know. The Troubles. Dongeradeel was one of the planets the Sublime Exaltation took over. At least the Imperial Navy didn't have to bombard the place to get rid of those fanatics."

Ah yes, the "bomb the planet to save it" theory. Elam knew it well. "I seem to recall there was still a heavy price to cleanse the planet."

Sadness dragged at Chad's features. "Yeah. I had a cousin who got killed by what the Imperial Marines called 'friendly fire.' They gave his family a pension, but I'd rather have my cousin back."

"I'm sorry for your loss." The familiar words, the empty words, fell effortlessly, thoughtlessly from his lips. He loathed himself for uttering them. "I'm sure his parents would prefer their child still lived too." Time to change the subject. The guilt was too painful. "So, you left. Where did you go?"

"I spent two years at the Merchant Marine Academy on Elsinore, training, and then signed on with the *Zuiderkruis*. I've been with them a little over eighteen months."

"You must be older than you look. I would have guessed nineteen or twenty."

The boy had deep dimples and impossibly sensitive brown eyes. "Nope. I'm twenty-five. Cursed to look younger than I am. Tell me about you." He actually fluttered his eyelashes.

"Not much to tell, I'm afraid. I'm just an ordinary guy, trying to make his way in an indifferent world."

Chad touched Elam's knee. "You're no ordinary guy. You're not even a snack. You're the whole meal."

Elam glanced at the boy's hand but didn't say anything. "That's kind of you, but I fear my age shows."

"I like older guys. You're zaddy. I ain't gassin' you." He squeezed Elam's knee. "But I don't get it. What's a guy like you doing here? I mean, you signed up for ten years of solitary confinement, right? You ghosting someone or something?"

Elam reflected that Chad's words pretty much summed up what he was doing. "Sometimes you just need time alone, to find yourself." He rubbed his neck and winced.

"Hey, is your back sore? Sitting crunched over a keyboard'll do that to ya." He leapt to his feet and started massaging Elam's neck. "I got me magic fingers. Everybody sez so."

Elam had to admit it did feel good. He relaxed as tension oozed out of his muscles under the younger man's touch.

Chad leaned forward, and his hot breath warmed Elam's neck just behind his ear. He murmured, "I'm tweakin', you hot man. You do it to me." He ran his fingers inside Elam's shirt and stroked his chest.

Electric tingles ran down Elam's spine, but he rolled his head away. It was one thing to try to pump Chad for information, but he needed to reassert control of the situation.

Jorina's voice, all sultry and sweet, interrupted. "Well, I see you boys are having fun."

Elam's face heated. He adjusted his clothing while Chad jerked away and snapped to attention. "Sorry, ma'am. We was just relaxin' after a hard day's work." He picked up his coffee and slopped some on Elam. "Shit, I'm sorry, man. Let me clean that for you." He started to mop things up with a wad of napkins, but Elam pushed him aside.

"Don't worry about it. It's fine." He turned to face Jorina, afraid of what he might see in her eyes. "He's right, you know. Mr. Clifford was kind enough to offer me a neck rub when I complained of stiff muscles."

Her eyes danced with amusement. "I did notice you had a tendency toward a stiff neck." She stroked a lanky auburn-colored cat that lounged in her arms. It closed its eyes, purred, and looked indecently pleased. "This little fella likes having his neck rubbed too."

Elam stared at the creature. "You found the cats."

"Several of them. They were in a tunnel underneath the monorail line. This one came up and made friends with me right away, rubbing against me and purring. Sort of like you and Chad were just doing." She gave him another of her signature squinty smiles.

"That shouldn't be possible."

"I would have said the same thing about you two."

He was beyond embarrassment at this point. "No. I mean it shouldn't be *tame*. Cats have to imprint on humans at an early age, as kittens, or they never do. He should be feral. Afraid of you."

She scratched the feline's belly. "Why would he be afraid of little old me?"

"Because you don't smell right. Cats live in a world of smells. Don't you see? This proves that there must be people on Cabot's Landing. People besides the Torrances, I mean."

She frowned. "Maybe. But maybe these animals were genetically engineered to be tame. The way they did with foxes, back on Old Home Earth."

"That was selective breeding, not engineering. You can't engineer behaviors like socializing with humans. You can engineer a receptiveness, but not the actual act. That's what the Russian breeders did. They also engineered *anti*social foxes. Ones that hissed and cowered when humans were around even when they were pups."

"I've known people like that." Another squinty smile.

"Please, don't you see? This changes the whole investigation. There are people on the planet, and they've been here for a while in order to domesticate these cats. One of them must have killed the Torrances."

She didn't look convinced. "Maybe. We'll see what the kolonel says."

A faint sound muttered from the depths of the corridor outside the data center. Chad jumped. "What was that?"

Jorina shrugged. "I've been hearing rustling all day. I just figured it was the ventilation system kicking in after all these years, stirring things up." She paused to display another set of dimples. "I mean, it's not like there are ghosts or anything here. Right?"

The cat twisted in her arms, jumped to the floor, and darted down the corridor.

Elam gazed into the dark abyss where the cat disappeared. There were certainly no ghosts, but something was here. He could feel it. The ancient philosopher must have been right. When you stare into the abyss, it stares back at you.

CHAPTER 8

Exalted are the dead. Nonbelievers return to the elements from whence they came, while Believers go to their heavenly reward.

—*Chapter 2, verse 32,* **Ekzaltoj de Margareta**

SIGURD'S BOOTS squished into the soggy wheat field between Lansbury and the monorail station. The village stretched out in the narrow valley below him in a desolate line of streets and decaying cottages. A pathway of trampled wheat led from near where his flitter rested toward the first building, perhaps fifty meters away. That must be from when Elam and Bender had been here yesterday. The crew he'd brought along today were forming up in ragged ranks near the flitter's open bay door.

He heaved a deep breath, wrinkled his nose, and scrunched one eye closed. The blasted wheat stank even more of vinegar this morning than it had yesterday. He couldn't imagine he'd ever get used to it.

The steward's mate jumped out of the flitter and scurried to stand next to Sigurd. Sigurd glanced at him and pulled the man's name from memory: Owen ap Glyndwr. He must be from Machynlleth, or maybe Cardiff, two of the worlds under the Margrave's protection. He most certainly was not from Elsinore. Not with those ears. Sigurd gave the man a severe nod.

Glyndwr snapped to rigid attention, as if that was how soldiers in the Margrave's guard behaved. "What are your orders, sir?"

"Relax, Owen. This isn't a military operation. Our mission is to investigate these deaths, not to put on a military parade."

The corpsman, wearing the crisp white trousers and short-sleeve shirt of his rating, had already broken away from his fellow crewmates, and now slogged through the mud toward the village. The satchel he carried with both hands must be heavy, since he walked with a labored, wobbly gait. He stepped into a puddle, and greenish-brown mud splashed onto his immaculate uniform. Sigurd rolled his eyes. What was the man thinking, wearing his whites on a field assignment?

He turned back to the steward's mate, who now stood at parade rest. "Owen, the Resident didn't get any further than the second cottage yesterday. He stopped looking when he found the body. Could you have your men do a quick search of the rest of the village? Nothing too thorough. I just don't want to miss anything obvious."

"Sir, yes, sir!" The man gave a snappy three-fingered salute and stomped off to where a dozen other crewmembers milled about the shuttle.

So much for telling him to relax. He'd even given a friggin' youth scout salute. Sigurd sighed. He'd have to work with what was available.

He turned and followed in the corpsman's footsteps, careful to avoid the puddle that had fouled the man's slacks. The stink from the wheat didn't seem so bad anymore. Maybe he'd get used to it after all. Chaos knew, he'd gotten used to worse.

He stopped just inside the cottage and reflected there were worse smells than the wheat. The dead body odor roiled his stomach, and he decided to pause for a few seconds. It wouldn't do to vomit in front of the corpsman. Sigurd couldn't recall the man's name, and his face heated with self-anger. People liked it when you called them by name. They worked better and stayed on mission. Don't force it. The name would come back to him.

Besides, he might learn something from the building itself. Something had blown out the windows, not even leaving visible shards on the floor. Sunbeams streamed through holes in the roof, and dust motes glimmered in the scattered rays. The exterior door had vanished and left just rusting hinges, but the single interior door hung askew by one hinge. That was strange—almost as if someone had scavenged the outer door. Impossible, of course. No one was around to do the scavenging.

Light flashed from the next room. Sigurd pressed a finger below his nose and advanced to the doorway.

The corpsman was taking photos of the body with the latest holo camera from Fēngfù. Another camera rested on a tripod in the corner of the room, probably taking a video of everything he did. His satchel lay open at the base of the tripod, and equipment spread in neat rows on a plastic tarp. Maybe he'd actually turn out to be a competent investigator. At least the man was organized.

He didn't look at Sigurd when he spoke. "Please wait a few moments, Kolonel. Give me a chance to finish documenting the scene." The camera flashed two more times. "It's probably a waste of time, though. She's been here a couple of days, at least, and those other guys already disturbed the place." He lowered his camera and pointed. "I viewed his video. He said he moved the arm and touched the body. I can still see the indentation. What was he thinking? How can I do a proper investigation under these circumstances? I mean, it's *rained* in here. And who knows what animals might have done to the body." He returned to taking pictures.

The man was competent. His ebony features and almond eyes matched his personnel record, which placed him from the Shubaga of Kush. All that mattered was that he knew his job, not how he got on a Praetorian freighter. Sigurd said, "We can rule out animals. There aren't any around except humans."

"Really? That's weird. Well, someone moved the body, that's for sure." He knelt next to the corpse and took a close-up of something on her neck. "Okay, I'm done. If you want to look before I start examining the body, go ahead." His round vowels confirmed his origin, where they spoke a variation of an Old Home Earth tongue, Kushite.

"Thank you. Can you see what killed her?"

"Can't say for sure until I do a full workup. But something burned a hole in her throat." He plucked a stainless-steel probe from his equipment and poked it into the hollow of her neck. "I thought so. Whatever it was, it went clean through. Looks like it severed the cervical spine too, probably at C4 or C5. If I'm right, that could be the COD."

Sigurd frowned. "What would do that? A poker, maybe?"

"Got me. It's too precise for a poker. A laser might do it."

"You mean like an industrial laser?"

"Yeah, unless you military guys have super-secret death rays I don't know about."

"We don't use lasers. Not anymore, at least." Sigurd muttered, "What would an industrial laser be doing here?"

The corpsman shrugged. "Not my job to figure that out. You done? I'd like to roll the body."

Something chittered from outside the room, and Sigurd twisted to look at the entrance. Nothing.

The corpsman was looking too. "Thought you said there were no animals. That sounded like a mouse to me."

Mustafa! That was the man's name. Gabir Mustafa. Sigurd said, "Can't be, Gabir. No sane person would introduce mice to an ecosystem."

The corpsman nodded. "Right. They're disease vectors, among other things. Still, I've had the weird feeling someone or something's been watching me."

"Of course. I've been watching you." Sigurd smiled to show he was joking. Still, it couldn't hurt to check the sound out. Mustafa followed him to the front room, which looked exactly as before. Outside, one of Glyndwr's crew exited the cottage across the street, his phone held to his ear. Sigurd pointed. "We must have heard his phone."

Gabir didn't look convinced. "That'd be one funky ringtone."

Sigurd couldn't disagree, but it was still the most likely explanation. Besides, limited resources meant he had to prioritize. "Whatever it was, we need to focus on our mission. What do you have left to do?"

"Like I said, I need to roll the body and look for gross evidence of other wounds. Given the state of decay, I'm not likely to see anything here."

"How long has she been dead?"

He shrugged. "Who knows? Based on the lack of rigor yesterday, I'd say a couple of days. Ordinarily insects help set a timeline, but there aren't any on this planet. So far as I know, there's never been a body farm to gather data on decomp. Your guess is as good as mine, but it's been a couple of days at least for sure." He looked down and twisted his lips. "One more thing. I don't think she died here."

"What? Why not?"

"You know the sphincters release when you die, right?"

"Yes." Sigurd realized where this was headed.

"Well, I'll know for sure when I roll her, but I didn't see any gross evidence of that, so to speak." He flashed brilliant white teeth in a quick grin at the gallows humor.

"Let me know. That could be important." If she didn't die here, why move her? The obvious answer would be to cover up evidence, but why move her to where she was sure to be found? If she'd been dumped in the fiord, the tide would have taken her to the ocean, where she'd be snack food for a bandersnatch. Whoever moved her wanted her found. If she was moved.

The corpsman started to leave his side, but Sigurd stopped him. "Gabir, Corpsman Mustafa, thank you for your work today. You've been meticulous. I will be sure to address a letter of commendation to Captain Fokke."

"Thank you, sir. People call me Gabe, by the way. Anyhow, I appreciate it. Just doin' my job."

"Forensic science isn't exactly the job for a corpsman, Gabe, but you've done awesome work here."

He looked downward, and his voice turned hesitant. "Well, before I transitioned, I was a police officer back in Kassala. I've at least got some training."

That's right—he'd been born Fatima Mustafa. It took guts to mention transitioning, given how backward Elsinore could be about such things. "Whatever the reason, you've done good work. I'm honored to write a letter on your behalf. If you ever want to transfer to the Margrave's service, let me know. There's a place for you. I'll see to it."

"Thank you, sir. That means a lot, but I'm happy on the *Zuiderkruis*."

Sigurd's phone buzzed, and the corpsman returned to Mrs. Torrance's body. Sigurd touched the screen and answered, "Von Dorestad."

"Sir, ap Glyndwr here. We've found something you need to see."

"Speak to me." *By Frejya's eyes, just report. Don't keep me in suspense.*

"We're in an old warehouse near the docks, sir. There's a tracked vehicle, and luminol shows blood splatter."

"A tracked vehicle? What the Chaos is it?"

"I don't know, sir. We've never seen anything like it."

"I'll be right there. Post a crewman outside the door so I can find you."

"Sir, yes, sir!"

"And don't disturb anything until I get there." All he needed was for the idiot to push a wrong button and kill half his crew. The combination of a tracked vehicle and blood splatter made him think it must be a military drone, a death bot. They may have found the murder weapon, but if it was what he thought it was, it just opened more questions. Like, what was lethal military technology doing on a mining planet?

"Send me a photo of the vehicle." He closed the connection and said, without much hope, "Cornwall."

He wrinkled his forehead when the AI's image showed on his screen. "How may I help you, sir?"

"I thought you didn't have connections to Lansbury."

"I have no active video or audio monitors. Sir. But the mobile communications network is active within seventy kilometers of the monorail station."

Of course, the AI hadn't thought to volunteer that tidbit earlier. "I'm going to forward you a photo. I'd like you to identify it if you can."

He stroked his screen and sent the photo from Glyndwr.

"Receiving. Sir, that's a mining bot."

"A what?"

"It's a Mark IX Robotic Excavating Device, to be more precise, sir. At last inventory, there were sixty-eight of them on the planet."

"It's not a military drone?"

"No, sir, although records show it's based on a military device for clearing battlefields that was in common use by the Grand Alliance Marines. Cabot Industries redesigned the military bot for mining applications."

Great. Half the time, the AI neglected to inform him of essential information. The other half, it wouldn't shut up about useless details. "What's one doing in Lansbury? The mines are on the other side of Bountiful."

"Mrs. Torrance deployed several of the mining bots to assist in her excavations, sir. One of them was in Lansbury."

"Do you have a record of how she used them?"

"The only record is in her notes, sir. Mr. Vandreren is accessing those now."

Of course. Sigurd had sent him down that blind alley with the first officer and the cybernetics mate. Except it looked less like a dead end now. "There was no telemetry from the device itself?"

"No, sir. The Mark IXs were designed to require a human operator."

That made a certain kind of sense. If they'd started out as death bots, it wouldn't be smart to make them vulnerable to enemy telemetry giving them commands.

A crewman standing outside a one-story building waved to him and trotted his way. Sunlight glinted off the deep blue waters of the fiord, and Sigurd shielded his phone's screen with one hand. He increased his pace while still talking. "How did they work? As excavators, I mean."

"I could send you a manual, sir. The units have a touch screen where you enter an activation code, after which they accept voice commands."

"I meant, how to they physically excavate? Do they happen to use a laser?"

"Yes, sir. Among other tools, they are equipped with a high-powered industrial laser. When using it, the operator must exercise caution, as the laser can cause injury or death."

That was an understatement. Sigurd was sure they'd found the murder weapon. He turned to the crewman and said, "Thanks for greeting me." He paused to squint at the man's name tag. "Mr. Jenssen, I can handle it from here."

The mining bot squatted in the middle of the empty warehouse. Dried mud clung to its treads, and a brownish liquid had caked the mud under the tracks. Drag marks, smeared with dried blood, smeared across the dusty floor and disappeared onto the cobbled street. Glyndwr's team scuffled about the place, leaving boot prints behind. So much for learning from the crime scene.

Glyndwr jerked to attention when Sigurd approached.

Sigurd kept his voice calm. "Relax, Owen. Just tell me what you found."

Apparently the man's notion of relaxing was parade rest. "Sir, we thought the stains and drag marks were suspicious, so we sprayed the area with luminol. Mr. Jenssen made a recording of what we found. It's conclusive for blood, sir."

He gave a curt nod to Jenssen, who approached and held out his phone. "It's all queued up, sir. Just press Play."

Sure enough, blue splatters glowed all over the front of the robot and on the floor underneath. A spotty trail continued to the door, where it vanished in the sunlight.

"Good work, Owen. You too, Mr. Jenssen." No reason to berate them for walking all over possible evidence. That was Sigurd's fault, anyway, for not giving better directions. He glanced at the roof. "This place looks undamaged." On the way here, the buildings had shown progressive evidence of decay. The nearest ones were just walls, open to the elements. For some reason, this building seemed to have survived intact. "Did you find anything else here? Maybe some indication of what this place was used for?"

"No, sir. It's empty except for this machine. Did it murder Mrs. Torrance?"

That made Sigurd smile. "Machines can't murder, Owen. Murder implies intent." He put his hands on his hips and rotated, surveying the scene. "Let the corpsman, Mr. Mustafa, know what you found here, please. This is almost surely the murder scene."

It was at least possible Mrs. Torrance had died in a bizarre accident of some kind. The problem was that someone—or something—had moved her. If the laser had severed her cervical spine, she sure didn't move herself.

There was still a mystery here, but more information was better than less. He turned to Glyndwr. "Owen, I'm going to take the flitter back to the Lodge. Mr. Mustafa will need to move Mrs. Torrance's remains via the monorail. I'd be grateful if your crew would complete their search of the village, assist Mr. Mustafa as needed, and then use the monorail to return to the Lodge. I'll be available by phone, if you or Mr. Mustafa need to reach me."

"Sir, yes, sir!"

At least he didn't click his heels. Sigurd took his time walking back to the flitter. He still wanted to resolve the puzzle that was Elam. He hoped that bubble-headed cybernetics mate managed to get the DNA sample off the Resident. He didn't have much confidence the job would get done, let alone with enough finesse that Elam wouldn't notice.

CHAPTER 9

Thinking
I'm supreme, I
Gaze into my cat's eyes.
My cat's gaze into mine reveals
I'm not.

—***The Missing Cinquains****, Arpad Laszlo*

THE MUTED sounds of chatter from people milling outside Sigurd's conference room made Elam pause at the end of the spacious hallway. The good kolonel had decreed a briefing and invited Bender and Elam to join the team from the *Zuiderkruis*. Elam twisted his mouth downward. Ordered was more like it. The man had all the nuance of an Imperial tax collector and none of the charm.

He gave a little start when a hand touched his shoulder. Sigurd. The SOB had snuck up on him, and now he was touching him. What was worse was the erotic thrill that jittered down Elam's spine. The soldier may not have any finesse, but by Chaos, he burned with white-hot masculine charisma.

His voice was smooth as silk over barbed wire. "Thank you for joining us this afternoon, Mr. Vandreren." He squeezed Elam's arm before releasing him.

Elam replied with a stiff bow. "Thank you for inviting me, Kolonel." He managed to keep his voice steady.

Sigurd's attention turned away, to the crew down the hall, and something inside Elam withered. Annoyed with himself, he hid his yearning behind a question. "How was Lansbury?"

"Interesting. It looks like a mining bot killed Mrs. Torrance."

Elam's lips twitched in a faint grin. "You're saying the murderer was a bot?"

Sigurd looked at him like he was a rock. A stupid rock. "Of course not. It could have been an accident, but other evidence suggests someone— or something—moved her body."

That was interesting. Elam said, "Her notes show that she used mining bots for her archeological excavations. Except, at the end, she'd stopped digging up landfills and was looking for—something else."

Sigurd nodded, but his gaze stayed on the crewmen. Late afternoon sunbeams scattered through the hallway, separating it into bands of light and shadow. "I'll be interested in your report." He gestured with a hand toward the meeting room. "Shall we go?" Without waiting for an answer, he marched down the hall.

Elam glared at his retreating form. Narrow hips, broad shoulders, compact torso.

Stop it.

He adjusted his black slacks and matching sport shirt before following Sigurd into the meeting room.

Someone, probably one of the steward's mates from the ship, had set up maybe twenty-five chairs in a circle. There'd be no hiding in a corner in this meeting. Elam waited for Sigurd to stand by a chair, then selected one for himself about a third of the way around the circle.

While the crew straggled in, Sigurd spoke in a commanding tone. "Please take your seats. We're probably going to be here for a while, so get comfortable. Coffee and juice are on the sideboard. The sooner we start, the sooner we'll finish. I understand Chief Alonzo has prepared a gourmet feast for us in the dining hall."

He stood, arms behind his back at stiff parade rest, while the crew settled into their seats. Jorina sat on his right, with her phone resting on her lap. She caught Elam's eye and gave him a squinty smile. He nodded in return.

Chad appeared from nowhere and plopped into the seat next to Elam. "Hey, mind if I sit here? I got you coffee." He thrust a plastic cup toward Elam. "Black, just like you like."

It was too late in the day for caffeine, but Elam didn't have the heart to tell Chad. He accepted the steaming liquid and said, "Thank you. Did you finish your analysis?"

"Too much data, not enough time. But I've got some interesting poop. Did you know this dump has winters?"

Elam did but didn't see how that was relevant to anything. Before he could respond, Sigurd started speaking again.

"We've had a busy day, with two teams at remote locations gathering data. When I ask for your report, please be brief but thorough. After all the reports are done, I'll invite discussion, after which we'll adjourn for dinner." He stopped and surveyed the gathering with a cold expression. "Okay, then. I'll go first.

"Our team arrived at Lansbury at 10:45 hours this morning via flitter. The team included myself, Corpsman Gabir Mustafa, Steward's Mate Second Class Owen ap Glyndwr, and six crew under Owen's command. Owen and his team searched the village, while Corpsman Mustafa and I inspected the body that the Resident and the chief auditor had found yesterday. Corpsman Mustafa will report separately on his forensic findings. Owen and his team found a mining bot in an abandoned warehouse, and luminol revealed blood splatter and a trail leading from the bot to the street. Corpsman, before I continue, please summarize your forensic findings."

The corpsman stood, and the crease in his immaculate white uniform broke perfectly just below the knee. Elam knew the type. He'd probably put on fresh whites just for the meeting. Meticulous, even fastidious, but obsessed by the pseudo-military structure of the merchant marine. The first impression didn't hold hope for much in the way of forensic conclusions, but Elam knew enough to withhold judgment.

On the other hand, Jorina's expression provided silent testimony to her feelings for the corpsman. Elam let a smile bend his lips. Good for them. Love was hard to find anywhere, least of all on board a trading vessel on a pointless mission.

The man fidgeted and glanced at Sigurd. "I really should have slides for this."

Elam didn't think it possible, but Sigurd's grim expression hardened. "I can review those later. Just summarize things for now, please. We need time of death, cause of death, and location of death."

"Yes, sir. The primary evidence for time of death is the report of the Resident examining the body. Gross examination of the remains is consistent with a time of death twelve to twenty-four hours prior to the first arrival of the *Zuiderkruis* shuttle on planet. Cause of death is a cauterizing wound entering the victim's throat, burning through the soft tissue and destroying the spinal column at C4. The result would have been instant paralysis, followed within minutes by death by suffocation due to damage to the trachea. The damage is consistent with a high-energy laser beam, such as that employed by mining bots."

"And location of death?"

"I was getting to that, sir. The throat trauma, even though partially cauterized, should have resulted in significant blood loss. There was no evidence of that where we found body. However, you asked me to investigate that warehouse you mentioned. Everything about that scene is consistent with death occurring there. If this were a coroner's inquest, the preponderance of evidence would favor the conclusion that she died in the warehouse and was almost immediately moved to where we found her remains."

Elam raised an eyebrow. *"Preponderance of evidence."* It would appear the corpsman knew something about forensics after all. Or maybe he'd just watched too many murder mysteries.

Sigurd nodded. "Thank you, Corpsman. Just to be clear, Mrs. Torrance died before her husband, correct?"

"Yes, sir. The video record of the discovery of Mr. Torrance's body confirms he died not more than thirty minutes prior to discovery. Reporting it was quick thinking on the part of Mr. Bender."

Sigurd glanced at Elam. "Quick thinking, indeed. So, Mrs. Torrance could not have killed her husband."

"That's right. But, based on time alone, he might have killed her. Or at least moved her body."

"I'll get to that in a moment. Back to the mining bot. Your conclusion is that it was deployed as a weapon, then, rather than this being an accident?"

The corpsman shrugged. "You're asking if she could have walked in front of the beam by mistake? If she'd been moving, then the beam would have sliced through her flesh rather than drilling a precise hole. I don't believe in coincidence. She must have been standing still, with the laser aimed at her throat. Someone had to activate the beam."

"But you can't rule out suicide. Isn't it possible she did this to herself?"

"Maybe. But there's the evidence the body was moved. Someone else was there. Had to be."

"The mining bot couldn't have moved the body?"

"It weighs, what, a couple of tons? It would have left track marks. Besides, it wouldn't have fit through either the entry or the interior doorway in the cottage where we found the body. It's too big to do that."

Sigurd surveyed the room. "Thank you, Corpsman. You've been most thorough." He paused a moment, then continued. "I'd like to return to Mr. Torrance's activities during the time in question. Cornwall."

The AI's hologram flickered in the middle of the circle. "How may I serve you, sir?"

"How long has it been since Mr. Torrance last left the Lodge?"

"Four years, sixty-three days, eight hours, twenty-two minutes, and twelve seconds, sir."

"How certain is this information?"

"Sir, I maintain continuous monitoring of all the exits to the Lodge, as well as the monorail stations and both ghost port terminals. If Mr. Torrance had left the Lodge, my memory banks would have a record of that fact."

"Is there any record in your data banks of anyone besides the Torrances being on the planet since the last auditor's visit, four months ago, and prior to the arrival of the *Zuiderkruis's* shuttle two days ago?"

"No, sir."

"Then the Torrances were the only people on the planet during that time."

"That is consistent with what's in my data banks, sir."

Sigurd folded his fingers under his chin and regarded the room. "There you have it. The Torrances are both dead by violent means. Murder is the only conclusion in both cases. But there is no one available to commit the crime."

Elam held up a tentative finger. Time for his conclusions about the cat tamers.

Sigurd acknowledged him but said, "I'll ask for your report in a moment. I'd like Chad to tell us what he's gleaned from the data banks first. Mr. Clifford, it's your turn."

Chad bounced to his feet, eagerness gleaming in his eyes. "I've barely started my analysis, but already some interesting patterns have shown up. Did you know this place has winters?"

Sigurd's eyes turned frigid. "Just how is that relevant, Mr. Clifford?"

"Look, the power plant records go back over five hundred years. Most of that time, they were supposed to be dormant, right? I mean, there was, like, nobody here. In fact, the east and west plants were dormant except for what looks a small maintenance trickle, but the south plant shows a steady low-grade load drawing on it. Further, about every thirty-five to seventy years, the load would spike for as much as a year before returning to that low-grade draw. It's been sixty years since the last winter, so we're due."

Sigurd's jaws jumped. "Get to the point, Mr. Clifford."

"I am. Turns out this planet has an erratic climate cycle that depends on the orbital mechanics. Roughly every twenty-five to fifty years, the weather turns cold. I found pictures of snowdrifts outside this Lodge from five hundred years ago. Anyways, those power spikes coincide with winter. Even the east and west power plants showed them, pre-Disintegration, when this place was occupied."

Elam frowned, wanting to ask a question, but then Sigurd asked it for him. "I thought the south power plant was in reserve. Not used."

"Nope. The ancients must have used it for power to the agricultural station, for example. It looks like it was used by the Grand Alliance naval base on Diego Garcia, too, but I can't tell how they got the power there. There must be undersea cables, but that doesn't make sense. I mean, there'd have to be transformers—"

Sigurd interrupted, "That's all interesting, Mr. Clifford. What's your point?"

"My point?" He grinned like kid telling a goofball joke. "My point is that the patterns I found in the south power plant's activity matches exactly what you'd expect if it were powering a small settlement, including spikes for heating the place in winter. It's as if some people hung around after the ancients closed the mines down."

"Do you have any direct evidence to support that claim?"

"Well, no. Not from the data, anyway. The south islands seem to have never been integrated into the planetary net, so the AI's data banks are pretty sparse on what's down there. I bet there was a secondary net, though. Maybe even a tertiary one. The old military bases wouldn't have been part of the private data banks, right? I did find some evidence of shared satellite telemetry coming from someplace outside the planetary net."

Sigurd pursed his lips. "Extraordinary claims require extraordinary proof. We don't have the personnel to search an entire planet for ghosts."

Elam raised his finger again. "I really think I have something to contribute at this point."

Sigurd glared at him like he'd bit into an apple and found Elam inside. "Be brief."

What an asshole. He'd show him brief. "Cats."

Silence stretched; then Jorina broke out laughing.

Sigurd turned crimson and seemed to count to ten before asking, "What, if I may be so bold, is funny?"

Another dimpled grin sprouted on her features. "We found tame cats at the north power station." She fiddled with her phone and showed him the screen. "See. They love being petted and held."

Sigurd looked as if he wanted to strangle her. "Do you think the cats killed the Torrances? Maybe they didn't get *petted* enough."

"No, no. Look, Elam figured it out. He should tell you."

"Elam." He spat out the name as if it were a burning coal. "Enlighten us."

Okay, time to roll. "The cats are descended from pets left by the Cabot Industries employees. The thing is, *these* cats are tame. They sought out Jorina and let her pick them up and pet them. They should have been feral—*afraid* of her. Cats have to imprint on humans while still kittens. If they don't, they're just wild animals that hiss and run away. These were tame. They liked being handled."

Sigurd spoke with a tight edge to his voice. "So the Torrances had pet cats. Big deal."

Elam let a broad smile bend his lips. From Sigurd's micro-expression, that just drove him further into rage. Good. "Turns out, Mrs. Torrance was allergic to cats and only spent less than two hours minutes, one time, six years ago, at the east power station. Mr. Torrance never went there. Someone treated these kittens as pets, but it wasn't the Torrances. If we find the cat tamers, I bet we'll find our murderer. We can't search the planet, but we can search the west power station. That's what we need to do."

Sigurd's anger evaporated in an instant. How in Chaos did he do that, just turn off his emotions like they were on a switch? Elam had seen senior commanders that didn't have that much control.

Sigurd rapped out, "You're right, Mr. Vandreren. Multiple lines of evidence point in the same direction. We have to investigate, no matter how unlikely." He turned to Jorina. "Please organize an expedition to the west power station for tomorrow morning. Be sure to include myself and Mr. Vandreren, the Resident. Also, start planning an expedition to the south power plant and the agricultural research station. Mr. Clifford?"

Chad's eyes lit up like a puppy whose name had been called. "Yes, sir."

"I want to discuss some specialized data queries with you. Please speak to me privately after this meeting. Everyone, good work. We're making progress. Enjoy dinner tonight. Tomorrow will be a busy day."

Elam hooded his eyes. Sigurd hadn't even bothered asking about what Mrs. Torrance's notebooks revealed. He couldn't already know their contents, could he? Then there were those private data requests he had for Chad that he just mentioned.

He sighed. He was sure he could manipulate Chad into revealing Sigurd's secret orders, whatever they were. It just took betraying another sliver of innocence. Elam was good at that. Bleak self-loathing welled up from deep inside and wouldn't go away.

CHAPTER 10

Exalted are those who burn enemies of the Faithful.
　　　　　　*—Chapter 6, verse 9, **Ekzaltoj de Filipo***

SIGURD HUDDLED in a shadowed corner of the main dining room. At least twenty crew from the *Zuiderkruis* sat in the muted lighting, talking, drinking, and laughing. Someone had shoved tables to one side, and a half-dozen couples slow-danced to a romantic ballad. Jorina and Gabir were among them, snuggling close. He permitted a faint smile to bend his lips. Good for them. Both were smart, capable crew. They deserved whatever happiness they could find together, however fleeting. Another group clustered on the patio where a fire flickered in an open hearth. A crescent Kennebec sliced across the night sky, and the Milky Way, turned pink by atmospheric effects, spilled across the horizon.

Sigurd frowned at the flames. "Cornwall, what's burning on the patio? Surely not wood."

The stuffy hologram shimmered into existence. "They are burning *Egregia menziesii Cabotorii*, sir."

Damned literal AI. "In English, please."

"It's a local plant that grows in intertidal zones, sir. It's similar to a terrestrial species of kelp, from which it gets its name."

"I could swear I saw them put logs on the fire."

"Yes, sir."

Sigurd grunted in exasperation. "Seaweed is weed. How do we go from there to logs? Describe the process for me."

"Sir, the kelp grows on the local beach. Skimmers harvest it, dry it, and processers reform it to logs. The skimmers burn off the excess to keep the beaches clear for recreation. The process to form the logs—"

"Enough, Cornwall. That will be all."

The hologram bowed and faded away.

Dammit, he should be feeling better tonight. The murder investigation made good progress today, and he had a solid plan going forward. That plan had the additional advantage of advancing his other mission, even giving him an excuse for an expedition to the research station on the south islands.

On top of that, Clifford had a solid plan for collecting a DNA sample from Elam. That smartass Resident had to be hiding something. His smile turned grim as he anticipated putting the impudent jerk in his place. It would be tempting to search the DNA database using the big corporate systems Elam and Clifford had tapped into today, but that ran the risk of Elam discovering what he was up to. Better to use his smaller personal computer and the ImpSec database there, even if it might take a few days to get results.

The music paused. Some of the couples wandered off to tables or the bar. Others took the opportunity to embrace. Sigurd scowled. Dammit, Elam stood there, arms wrapped around Clifford. The younger man's mouth appeared attached, lamprey-like, to the Resident's neck. Not that Sigurd gave a rat's ass whom either one of them kissed, but damn. It just wasn't professional. Elam must be ten, maybe twenty years older than Clifford.

As for Clifford, well, so much for him showing finesse.

Under the dim, romantic lights, a Cheshire grin floated across Elam's face. He could swear Elam was looking at him. *He was! He just* winked, *the bastard.*

Jorina touched his shoulder, and he jumped.

She squinted at him. No, wait, it was her version of a smile. "He *is* good-looking, isn't he?"

"Him? He's too young for me."

"I don't mean that child. I meant the Resident, Elam." She muttered, "*Hy is waarmer as de hel.*"

"He's an asshole." He narrowed his eyes and searched her features. "I didn't know you spoke Frisian."

"Oh, that. I don't. Not really. I just picked up few phrases from when I lived on Dongeradeel." She frowned and glanced outside, over the patio. "What was that? It looked like lightning."

"I don't see how it could be. Cornwall."

The hologram reappeared with a bow. "Sir."

"What's the weather like? Any thunderstorms?"

"Satellites show a cold front on the west coast, sir, with a cell of thunderstorms over the old Alliance marine base."

"No lightning here, then?"

"No, sir."

Something flickered on the horizon, and Jorina said, "There it is again."

Sigurd nodded. "I saw it too. Cornwall, there appears to be lightning on the beach."

"It could be the skimmers we discussed earlier, sir. They reactivate every third or fourth low tide, depending on the accumulation of biomass in the local intertidal zone."

Jorina asked, "Skimmers?"

Sigurd answered, mostly to stop a lecture from Cornwall. "They clean kelp from the beach and reprocess it into logs. They're burning them out on the patio right now."

"Why not use the real thing? I saw birch trees outside the powerplant, and satellite imagery shows forests on the Western Reserve Island."

Good questions. She was turning out to be more competent than he'd expected. She was smart, and had taken the trouble to inform herself about the planet. "Cornwall, why not use real wood? There are forests on the Western Reserve Island."

"This is more economical, sir. The only transport to the Reserve Islands is by flitter."

Jorina nodded. "Right, no monorail. I imagine the fake logs might have made this place more homey for the people posted here."

Cornwall simpered, "Yes, ma'am."

Sigurd said, "Mystery solved. It wasn't lightning at all. That will be all, Cornwall."

He swirled the remains of his drink and returned his gaze to the dancers, where couples writhed to an upbeat rhythm. Elam and Clifford cavorted next to each other, barely touching, whirling apart, then embracing again. Clifford had removed his shirt, and Elam's was unbuttoned to the waist, exposing rippled abs and firm pecs. He imagined they were going to sleep together, and involuntary visions of their naked bodies flooded his imagination.

From the dance floor, Elam's eyes glowed in the warm light. If he didn't know better, Sigurd could swear the man was looking right at him, mocking him. Sigurd's face heated, and he tossed off the last of his drink.

Jorina said, "Don't let him get to you, Kolonel. I've seen how he looks at you, and how you look at him, for that matter. He's just trying to get to you." She hesitated. "It's not my place to say so, but maybe you should give him a chance. You might enjoy it."

Was he that obvious? Another flash of light from the beach offered an escape. He arranged his slacks, stood, and gave the first officer a formal bow. "You're right, Ms. Baak. It's not your place. Nonetheless, thank you for your company. I'm going to take a stroll on the beach and then retire for the evening. I recommend you retire as well. We've got a full day tomorrow."

Without waiting for a reply, he strode away and into the hall outside the dining room.

Once in the hall, Sigurd leaned against the wall and caught his breath. Jorina was right about one thing. Elam was definitely getting to him. "Cornwall, I think I'd like to walk on the beach. Is there a way from here to there?"

"Yes, sir. Go out the southwest entrance and follow the yellow flagstones. There are lights that show the way until you reach a bench that overlooks the beach. Shall I turn them on for you?"

"I guess. Can I have you shut them off once I'm there?"

"Yes, sir. Just let me know when you arrive. I have a transponder near the bench, but the range is limited. I must caution you to not enter the water, sir, and stay off the intertidal zone."

"No? I thought the bandersnatch stayed in the deep ocean."

"That's true, sir. But some of the local sea life has stingers that could be unpleasant for you. The skimmers will burn off some of them, but most will escape. The skimmers also have safety interlocks that are intended to keep them from firing when warm-blooded creatures are present, but they haven't been inspected in decades. Safety protocols call for you to stay clear."

"How do the skimmers work? Do they dig up the stinger-things?" Sigurd had visions of harvesting soggy cabbages and wasp-like burrowing creatures.

"No, sir. The stingers are floaters, not burrowers. The bot burns them off the surface with its laser as a byproduct of removing excess kelp. The skimmers are a modification of the mining bots and use the same lasers, but don't have digging capacity."

"Huh." So the skimmers deployed an industrial strength laser to kill what amounted to jellyfish. But then, it wasn't like ancients didn't have the resources of the entire planet at their beck and call.

Sigurd paused to get his bearings. "Cornwall, which way?"

"I'll light the corridors for you, sir."

A single yellow light glowed to his right. "Got it. Thanks. That will be all, Cornwall."

Sigurd sauntered away, passing an array of identical doors to identical two-room suites. He passed under the light, and another blossomed, fifty feet farther down the corridor. Of course. Cornwall was watching him.

He followed the string of yellow lights to the outside, where a stone path led away from the Lodge. It twisted and turned around rocky outcrops and discouraged clumps of the ever-present wheat. Sigurd heaved a deep breath. He guessed it was true: you could get used to anything, even the vinegar-vomit scent of the damned wheat.

The path meandered on switchbacks down a rocky cliff. Lightning flickered from beyond the edge. With more purpose, Sigurd strode forward. Lights behind him faded; those in front lit.

After the last switchback, a stone bench facing the sea came into view. The yellow glow of the lights under the bench gave it a ghostly appearance, as if it were floating. "Cornwall, you can turn off the lights now."

The glow faded, and Sigurd sat, stretching his legs in front of him. Conversation and music still murmured from the Lodge above, but at least he didn't have to watch Elam and Clifford mauling each other.

Lazy waves washed onto the beach. The tideline was perhaps fifty yards distant, but the gentle rush of the waves on sand soothed him. Now that the lights were off, his eyes started to adjust to the night.

The sky was spectacular. Kennebec was a giant sliver, curving from the horizon to nearly forty-five degrees and turning a quarter of the sky opaque, surrounded by glorious rings. The unhidden parts glowed with special beauty, as if taking the opportunity to shine while the gas giant wasn't showing off. The Milky Way hovered at the horizon, and the crooked nebula the peasants called Odin's Foot shimmered like a dream on black velvet. Elsinore and home lay somewhere in that direction, invisible on this distant outpost.

The shush of the waves brought his gaze back to the beach. Fingers of rock extended from the base of the cliff into the sea, and waters foamed about them.

One of the fingers rose up, flopped, and collapsed.

Sigurd jerked erect. Whatever he'd just seen, it was alive. Was it one of the creatures Cornwall had warned him about?

The shadow flopped again, and then rose up on two feet. It took one, then two staggering steps. The waves washed against its feet, and it went down again.

It was a person. It had to be.

Sigurd leapt to his feet and ran toward the figure. The waves washed over it, lifted it, and carried it a meter or so closer to the ocean before retreating. Sigurd accelerated, the sand dragging at his feet.

He got there just as the next wave hit. For sure, this was a body. It emitted a weak groan and thrashed in the waters.

Sigurd knelt and took the person's hand. "It's going to be all right. I'll help you."

Bloodshot eyes rolled in a face blackened and cracked with burns. Blood oozed from the exposed flesh on the arms, and the remnants of carbonized clothing stuck to the torso.

"Cornwall!" Sigurd shouted. No answer. They must be too far away from the microphone for him to hear. He snatched his phone from his pocket and punched in Jorina's number. The screen flashed, "No Carrier." Damn.

The hand he was holding squeezed his with sudden urgency, and a voice wheedled, "Help me."

"It's going to be all right, but I need to call for help." He started to stand.

"No! Don't leave me."

Sigurd dithered. He'd seen enough battlefield injuries. This person was beyond help, and certainly beyond the limited resources of the local infirmary. The best he could provide was comfort in these final moments. Chaos knew he had practice at that. He knelt back down and caressed a ravaged cheek with a knuckle. "I won't leave you. I promise."

A gurgle passed the swollen lips, then a gravelly voice that was neither male nor female. "The humble expect... nothing."

Sigurd reached for a ruined hand that waved before him like a cremated angel's wing. It twisted away, and a pathetic, withered shriek came out of the blackened lips.

"To Carthage." The words whispered from its throat like the whistle of the desert wind. "Burning, burning, burning, burning." A shudder wracked the body. "Thou pluckest me out."

What nonsense was this? "Don't talk. Everything's going to be all right." Sigurd stroked the crispy brow and hoped his touch brought comfort rather than anguish.

The body tensed. A tremor gripped it. "Burning." The words came as a whisper, a promise, a dream. Then at last the body fell silent.

Sigurd stood while horror filled his heart. Three bodies in two days, and this one was the worst. Who was this poor soul who suffered so?

Pebbles rattled. He whirled about and lifted his gaze in time to see a figure retreating from the bench where he'd sat moments earlier. A silent witness to death, perhaps a murderer, fleeing the crime.

Sigurd chewed the side of his cheek and narrowed his eyes. He didn't think the deceased was one of the crew from *Zuiderkruis*. He'd memorized their faces last night, and this charred ruin didn't match.

He examined the remnants of the corpse's clothing. It didn't look like a uniform. One foot was bare, while a sandal dangled from the other. When Sigurd bent to examine it, breath hissed from his mouth. It looked hand-crafted, not manufactured, even though it used modern materials. For sure, it didn't look like anything a member of the crew would have worn.

This had to be one of those inhabitants that Elam and Jorina had found evidence for earlier. One of the cat-taming people.

Waves sloshed and soaked his slacks. The outgoing tide again lifted the pathetic body and dragged it a few inches farther toward the sea before retreating. He couldn't leave the remains here, where the tide might wash them out to sea. He grabbed it by the shoulder and tugged.

One of the legs fell off.

Sigurd's stomach roiled, and he turned his head to hurl sour vomit onto the sands. Determination firmed his features. He placed the leg on top of the torso and finished the task of safeguarding the corpse.

When he reached the seaside bench, he called, "Cornwall."

Cornwall's urbane tones answered, "Yes, sir?" No hologram. There must not be a projector on the beach.

"Do you have cameras here, on the beach?" Given the obtuseness of the AI, he had to double-check.

"No, sir. Just this audio link."

"How about the skimmer? Any link there? Audio or video or both?"

"No, sir. Skimmers are autonomous bots. I monitor power usage, so I can infer when it last charged, if that's helpful."

"Possibly. Retain those records just in case. Can you connect me to Ms. Baak?"

"I can relay a message, sir, but your phone should work."

"It's not." No time now to figure out why. He mentally added the failure to his growing list of planetary anomalies. "Tell her to get the corpsman down here, and four crewmen. They'll need a gurney. I've found another body. Have her make sure none of the crew are missing, too."

"Consider it done, sir."

Sigurd sat on the bench and stared across the beach at the blackened corpse. Slow waves foamed across the dark sand and retreated. Another murder victim, and this one died on his watch. Intolerable. He was responsible. He was always responsible.

This planet was supposed to be abandoned, a useless backwater that no one cared about. It was looking more and more like the suspicions of the intelligence services back in the Imperial capitol, Pasargadae, were justified. He clenched his jaw in grim determination to do his duty, come what may.

CHAPTER 11

Exalted are those who watch over cats.
—Chapter 18, verse 97, **Ekzaltoj de Filipo**

THE MONORAIL sped out of the station at the Lodge, and acceleration pressed Elam into his seat. Early morning sunlight glared through the windows, and a dull ache pulsed in his head. He suppressed a moan and closed his eyes. He should know better than to self-medicate with alcohol, even if it did temporarily numb his guilty conscience.

The train swerved around a bend and roiled Elam's stomach. He massaged his forehead and wished for coffee.

Sigurd held court at the far end of the car, with four crew grouped about him. Their voices were blessedly low, but that was probably to keep whatever they were discussing secret. Something had happened last night, but no one was talking to Elam about it.

The party had broken up abruptly after a whispered conversation between Jorina and Cornwall. She'd announced an all-hands formation and a roll call, checking names off on a roster on her phone. She must have been making sure no one was missing, but why do that? Then she'd dismissed most of the crew to their quarters, except for the corpsman and four random crewmen. They all rushed off before Elam could ask what was going on.

Chad was one of the ones she'd selected. After flirting all day yesterday, it was no surprise when the young man showed up outside Elam's rooms last night with gin, vermouth, and a lascivious grin. The last thing Elam wanted was a hookup, but it would have been out of character to turn him away. Afterward, they shared martinis, and then Chad had left with a satisfied grin plastered on his face. Just as well, since Elam wasn't really interested anyway. Well, he wasn't interested except in using Chad to annoy Sigurd. Somehow, that wasn't as satisfying as it should have been.

Micro-expressions didn't lie. Whatever occasioned Sigurd's call to Jorina last night, it still alarmed him this morning. He always looked like he had a rifle up his butt, but he was extra tense this morning, not just officious and proper. He was grim, even, and determined too.

Elam slouched in his seat, closed his eyes, and pretended to sleep. He'd find out one way or another what was going on.

Sometime later, a hand touched his shoulder, and he jerked awake to the aroma of coffee.

Sigurd stood over him, his face impassive. "Sorry to wake you. I thought you might like some coffee." He held a thermos in one hand and a steaming metal cup in the other.

"Coffee would be heaven." Elam pushed the fuzz out of his brain and inspected Sigurd. The man wanted something from him. Suspicion lurked in his features too, but no malice. "Thanks. Have a seat."

Elam let the steam from the cup heat his face while he inhaled the aroma. It wasn't real coffee, he knew, but the ancient food processors had done an amazing job of simulation. Better than modern technology could replicate, for sure.

Sigurd settled in a chair facing him and gave him a pensive look. "You did excellent work yesterday. Thank you."

Elam shrugged and blew on his coffee.

Sigurd continued, "I took a walk on the beach last night. I find time alone helps me to think things through."

They had that much in common, then. Elam nodded. "I'm the same."

"I found a body on the beach."

Elam slopped scalding coffee on his fingers. "What?"

"I found a body. Not one of the crew. It looked like one of the skimmers must have malfunctioned and burned him."

"Skimmers?" What the Chaos was he talking about?

"Mining bots modified to burn kelp off the beaches."

Elam put his cup on the lap tray and wiped his fingers on a handkerchief. "A mining bot's laser killed Mrs. Torrance, right?"

"I knew you were quick."

Elam narrowed his eyes. No hint of sarcasm hid in Sigurd's features. He was being complimentary, then, in his own asshole way. "Was the victim one of the crew?"

"No. I already said that. Try to keep up. He wore what looked like a handmade sandal. The corpsman's lab results confirmed the materials were indigenous to Cabot's Landing. This is direct evidence that your conclusion was correct. At least one other human was on this planet. We may have found our murderer."

Elam mused, "I guess he might have killed Jack Torrance, but not Wendy."

Sigurd couldn't hide his momentary surprise, at least not from Elam. "Why do you say that? It would neatly wrap up our crime."

"The AI records who boards the monorail, right?"

"Yes."

"And Cornwall told me no one had flown the flitter in years."

The hologram fluttered into existence. "How can I help you, sir?"

Sigurd scowled. "Cornwall, dismissed. Damned literal-minded gadgets. We don't permit the blasted things at the, er, at my home on Elsinore."

His expression showed he'd almost let something important slip. Elam filed that information away and continued with his reasoning. "The only way he could have gotten from Lansbury to here is walking, overland. Unless he's got superpowers, there's not time for him to kill them both and walk from there to here."

Now Sigurd's features showed pleasure, probably at a puzzle solved. "Or vice versa. I see your point."

"Besides, we'd still have a murderer on the loose. We don't know who killed this new guy. He was a guy, you said?"

"I did. I agree with you about this being another murder. Two deaths from mining lasers can't be a coincidence."

"You said he wore handmade sandals? I wonder how long he's been on Cabot's Landing."

"The corpsman thinks he can give us an estimate, based on trace elements in the body. We'll have more information in a couple of days. For now, my working premise is that there are previously unknown human inhabitants on this planet."

Elam had to agree that was what the evidence seemed to imply. Still, it was best to explore the contrapositive. "Why would anyone in their right mind come to this worthless place, and stay here for any period of time?"

Sigurd's eyes crinkled in what Elam took for amusement. "I've been asking myself the same thing. Why would a smart, capable, apparently sane person choose to do that?"

Oh. The SOB was talking about him. "I'm paid to do it. And I like being alone. Like you." Take that, smartass.

Sigurd smiled now. With his lips, as if he'd won a test of wills. "Economic motivations can be compelling for a certain type of person, I suppose. But, other than a Syndicate contract, why would anyone be here?"

"Maybe this guy—or guys—did have a Syndicate contract. Maybe some of the miners got left behind when they closed down operations on the planet."

"Then they've been here for fifty years, and never interacted with the AI in all that time. That makes little sense. They would have had to be living off the land. Why wouldn't they use the facilities?"

Elam couldn't let it go. "The food processors aren't monitored by the net. But I agree. A long-term inhabitant would want to use the facilities, either at the Lodge, the mines, or the industrial port. Is it possible that they landed more recently, and the AI didn't record it?"

"I don't think so, but that's why Mr. Clifford is with us today. I want him to look for just that in the data banks. In particular, the communications satellites are supposed to record whenever a ghost drive is active in the system, so we'll know if anyone besides Syndicate ships have been here." He hooded his eyes. "I'm sure you remember Mr. Clifford. You were dancing with him last night."

Elam ignored the jibe about Chad. "The Syndicate wouldn't have sent a ship you don't know about? Maybe dropped off people for some unknown purpose?"

"That did not happen."

Elam stopped to think. Sigurd's expression showed he had no doubt at all. But then, he was probably in charge of intelligence for the Margrave's personal guard, so he'd know what the family's company did or didn't do. "I guess there's not much point in speculating. We need more data."

"That's why we're here. I wanted to catch you up on events before we start exploring the power station."

The train rounded a curve and entered the tunnels outside the power station. Elam must have slept longer than he'd thought. "Thanks for the update. Most informative."

Sigurd pursed his lips. "One more thing. The deceased was still living—barely—when I found him last night. He was obviously in pain, and spoke of burning. He also mentioned Carthage."

Carthage. The name sent adrenaline jittering down Elam's back. "You mean the Exaltationists' home planet?"

Sigurd shrugged. "What else could it mean? You see the implications, of course."

Violence and death to the *Zuiderkruis* and her crew would be the least of the implications. Elam wiped the stubble on his chin with thumb and forefinger before answering. "Carthage is clear on the other side of known space. What in Chaos would they be doing on this godforsaken rathole?"

"What, indeed? If they are here, we can be assured they are up to no good." He stood. "In any case, if they *are* here, it's my duty to find them and eliminate them."

Eliminate them. Elam couldn't argue with that goal, but with these fanatics the cost would be deadly. He'd paid that cost once. He wasn't sure he could do it again. He murmured, "Thank you for briefing me."

Sigurd stood and nodded. "My pleasure." He was lying again, not that it mattered.

In a few minutes, Elam stood on the subway platform while Sigurd and his team disembarked. The cool lighting, yellow tile floors, and concrete walls gave the place an antiseptic appearance. Except now he noticed a faint fetid odor. It was probably his imagination, now that he knew cats prowled underneath the station.

Chad slung a backpack over one broad shoulder and sauntered up to him. "Hey, man. I had a great time last night." His dark eyes gleamed, and he smelled of musk and sandalwood.

"Me too." It wasn't exactly a lie, but it wasn't the truth either.

"I'm sorry I didn't spend the night. I really wanted to, but the kolonel kept us busy until almost two, and I knew we had an early start this morning."

"S'all right."

"I guess there's always tonight." His eyelashes fluttered. He must think that was alluring. Or something.

Elam shrugged. "I suppose."

Sigurd headed their way with a baleful gleam in his eye. Elam grimaced. "Look, can we talk later? His nibs looks like he's about to explode."

"Sure thing. Later, *sayanku*." The last syllables lilted with a provincial accent.

Without thinking, Elam responded in the boy's native Malay, "*Kumdian.*"

Sigurd stomped up and glared at Chad's retreating figure. "Making plans?"

Could it be he was jealous? "Does it matter?"

"No. Ms. Baak said she found the cats in a tunnel underneath the station. I'd like for us to start there." Without waiting for an answer, he turned and stalked away.

Elam gritted his teeth and followed. Sigurd acted like they should all kiss his ring finger or something. He had the *Volknut* sigil tattooed to his cheek. He was just a commoner, and the tattoo made him the property of the Margrave, not a member of the nobility.

Unless… a chill jittered down his back. No, that couldn't be.

He rushed to catch up. "I've been wondering, why is a kolonel in the Corsairs on a merchant ship?"

"What a Corsair chooses to do is none of your business."

"Hey, it's only fair. You asked me why I accepted the job as Resident."

"I did. I also noticed you didn't answer. I'll give you the same courtesy." He paused at a door marked Authorized Personnel Only. "This is the place." He twisted the latch and pushed. The door creaked open.

Elam peered into the opening. "It's dark."

"I came prepared." Sigurd pulled a flashlight from his pocket, and the beam revealed an arched corridor with stairs leading downward. A brown cat with brilliant blue eyes lay at the top of the stairs. It stood and stretched, then rubbed its lanky body against Elam's legs.

Elam squatted down, let the animal smell his fingers, then scratched its chin. It closed its eyes and looked indecently pleased. "It's tame. Just like the one Jorina found."

"Charming. You think it's the same one?"

Elam shrugged. "Who knows? One cat more or less looks like another to me."

"It's an Abyssinian, an ancient breed from Old Earth. The Margrave's family keeps them in the palace. I'm not sure why they'd be here."

In the palace. Interesting. "Well, there's only one way to find out." Elam pointed to the stairs. "Shall we go?"

"Leave the cat." Sigurd headed down the stairs, and Elam followed.

Of course, the blasted cat came along, weaving between Elam's feet while he walked and nearly tripping him. He gave up, picked the creature up, and carried it. It gave him a wary glare before closing its eyes and buzzing contentedly. They descended perhaps fifty meters to a small room, roughly five meters on a side, with metal doors on three of the walls. Elam glanced at the ceiling. "There are overhead lights. Cornwall, turn on the lights."

Nothing happened.

Sigurd looked smug. "The network connection to these tunnels is broken, and has been for decades, according to the AI." He frowned at the cat. "I told you to leave that thing behind."

Elam scratched the cat's ears. "He was coming anyway. The alternative was tripping over him. What do you mean, tunnels? There are more than one?"

"Apparently the ancients built them for maintenance access underneath the monorail line. You could walk all the way from the Lodge to Lansbury or the mines and never go outside."

"Interesting. Seems like a lot of effort just for maintenance."

"Another mystery, I agree." He cast his light over the doors. "Pick one."

Elam shrugged and opened the door to his right. "Looks like a storeroom."

The door opposite the stairwell was ajar. Sigurd pushed and revealed a corridor that curved into the darkness. "This appears to be it."

Elam checked the other door. "This one's a latrine. How convenient."

"Whatever. Shall we go?"

"I'd follow you anywhere, Kolonel."

Sigurd rolled his eyes and stepped through the door. Overhead lights flashed on and illuminated about thirty meters of the corridor. "There must be a motion sensor."

"You think?" For a bright guy, the kolonel sometimes had a talent for stating the obvious. He was already ten meters away. Elam frowned and scurried after him. It was like Sigurd was trying to establish dominance. The cat's ears perked up. It squirmed out of his grip and scampered ahead of them.

They followed the corridor for perhaps two hundred meters, with lights coming on in front of them and fading out behind them. Ahead, bright lights streamed from what appeared to be a cross-passage in the right side of the tunnel.

Sigurd stopped when he got to the passage, and Elam almost bumped into him. A short corridor, no more than five meters long, led to a room that was stacked floor-to-ceiling with crates. Elam observed, "Looks like another, bigger storeroom. I can't see the far side. Can you?"

"No." A cat, fatter than the one that had met them at the stairs, sat just inside the room, blinking at them. Sigurd reached into his tunic and pulled something out. A blaster. What in Chaos?

"What is that for? You're not planning to kill the cat?"

"Why would I harm a helpless creature?" He kept his gaze focused on the passage. "Use your deductive powers. There could be a murderer here."

A shuffling sound, followed by a crash of something falling, made Elam glad for Sigurd's weapon. "Sounds like someone is in there. Yoo-hoo!" he called. "Who's there?"

Sigurd looked daggers at him, but said nothing.

A male voice, brittle with age, warbled from the darkness. "Go away."

The barrel of an ancient projectile weapon protruded from the right side of the entry.

Panic sharpened the hidden man's next words. "I've got a gun, and I know how to use it."

CHAPTER 12

Exalted are the armaments of the faithful, for they smite the wicked....

—*Chapter 2, verse 1,* **Ekzaltoj de Gregorio**

SIGURD STOOD rigid, his blaster held in both fists in front of him, just like he'd learned at the Academy so many years ago. The black barrel of the weapon he faced didn't waver. A feeble, aged voice called out, "Who are ya?"

He recognized the ancient gun that confronted them: a shotgun. When he was a child, his father and uncles had used them for sport hunting on the family estates. He'd seen one blow a hole in the armor of an ocraposaurus. One shot could blow Elam in half. Sigurd wasn't going to let that happen, not while he held a fully-charged blaster.

An aged face peeked around the doorframe, silhouetted in light streaming from the rooms beyond the doorway. "What ya want from me?" Sweat sheened his brow, and the gun now trembled, perhaps because he'd seen there were two of them.

Sigurd kept his gaze fixed on the old man's eyes, but the tension eased out of his stance. "I won't hurt you." This was just some old geezer, scared out of his wits. Odds were that even if he fired, the shot would go wide. Sigurd held his blaster up, sideways, then lowered it to the ground. "See. I'm unarmed." He spread his hands in front him. No one had to die today.

Elam whispered, "What in Chaos are you doing? Trying to get killed?"

Sigurd wanted to tell him to shut up, but instead said in his best soothing voice, "He's not going to kill anyone. We just surprised him, is all." He never looked away from the old man's eyes. "You don't want to hurt us, do you, sir? We just happened by and would like to visit. We didn't mean to surprise you. My name's Sigurd. What's yours?"

"Visit?" The geezer lowered his weapon and stepped into the light.

Gray whiskers sprouted on cheeks ravaged by age, and strings of greasy hair hung from his bald head. A clean but tattered jumpsuit clung to his rounded frame. It bore the interlaced triangles of the *Volknut*, a twin to the tattoo on Sigurd's cheek. He narrowed his eyes and peered at Sigurd. "You've got the Syndicate's mark on ya. Do you work for them too? Are ya here for supplies?"

"Yes, we work for the Syndicate." Sigurd touched his cheek. "You're right. I bear the Margrave's mark, just like you." He tipped his head toward the boxes stacked in the room. "What kinds of supplies do you have?"

Pride gleamed in his eyes then, and he lowered his weapon. "There are five hundred and thirty-six different items in my inventory. Acetaminophen, 325mg. Acetaminophen, 500mg. Acyclovir, 800mg. Adderall, 30mg—"

Sigurd smiled and held up a hand. "Medical supplies, then?"

"That what they are? I have them memorized. I got the location of each and every one right here, in my head." He tapped his temple. "I inventory them every month, just like the Procedures Manual says. Tell me what ya need, and I've got it."

"I'm sure you do. You sound very efficient. What did you say your name was?"

The man looked puzzled. "My name?"

"My name is Sigurd. This fellow next to me is Elam. We both work for the Syndicate, just like you. What's your name?"

Doubt clouded the man's features, but then his eyes lit up. "They used to call me Supply Clerk Three Andresen."

Sigurd bowed. "Nice to meet you. Elam, say hello to Supply Clerk Andresen."

The old man stood straight and corrected, "Supply Clerk *Three* Andresen."

The Resident rolled his eyes, but at least he had the good sense to follow Sigurd's lead. "Nice to meet you, sir." He gave a stiff bow.

The cat that had followed them down the stairs reappeared and rubbed against the old man's scuffed boots. He leaned his weapon against the doorway and stooped to pick up the animal. "This here's Per-fessor Erwin Schrodinger." He scratched the cat's ears, and it closed its eyes and appeared to enter a state of feline ecstasy.

Sigurd kept his smile fixed. He gave a courtly bow and said, "Pleased to meet you too, Professor."

The old man looked puzzled, but then shook his head. "Oh, you mean this little fella. That ain't one of his names."

"May I ask what you mean?"

"Well, the way I sees it, cats, they's like people. They's all got themselves three names. Professor Erwin Schrodinger is this one's first name. His second name's Dinger. That's what I call him most of the time."

Elam smirked, and amusement tinged his voice as he asked, "What's his third name?"

Sigurd wished he'd shut up. It was best to keep this kind of thing one-to-one until he could establish trust. Luckily, the old man seemed to not notice Elam's bantering tone. "Only he knows, and he ain't tellin'. Cats, they don't never tell nobody their third name."

Sigurd nodded. "I understand. It's private. I always respect another's privacy, man or cat."

Elam's eyes threw daggers at him, and the expression on his face screamed that he knew Sigurd was lying.

No matter. "So, Supply Clerk Three Andresen, what's your second name?"

"My second name?"

"Cats are like people. You said so. You must have a second name, just like Dinger."

"I don't rightly recall nobody ever called me nothin' but my first name. Supervisor One Hadley, he used to call me dumbass, but that ain't no proper second name." He scratched his temple. "I guess sometimes they call me Clerk. That'll do for my second name."

Hadley sounded like a piece of work. Sigurd made a silent oath to track him down when this was over and make him pay for abandoning this poor sod. If Hadley was even still living. "Have others been here, looking for supplies? Who is it that calls you Clerk?"

"Why, them what needs supplies, that's who. Who else would be comin' here, 'ceptin' for you who's just visitin'?"

A tone sounded from the depths of the storeroom. Cats streamed from the darkness and coiled about Clerk's feet, yowling and tails held erect. The old man's face lit up. "That means it's dinnertime. You little fellas is hungry, ain't' ya?" He let the cats head-bump his legs, and a smile played across his lips. "I gotta go take care of 'em. You care for a critter and it'll care for you, my mam always said."

He turned to go, but then faced back to Sigurd. "Say, I got plenty of victuals. Would you like somethin' to eat?"

Elam scrunched his nose. "Cat food? Thank you, but I just ate."

Clerk glared at him, then turned his attention to Sigurd. "Your buddy here ain't too bright, is he?"

"How so, Clerk?" It wasn't Elam's intellect that bothered Sigurd. On the contrary.

"Thinkin' I'd offer cat crunchies to you. They's not fit for people. But I've got plenty of biscuits and tea. If ya got a hankering for people food and a sit-down, just follow me."

"Biscuits and tea sound wonderful. Thank you." Elam appeared about to speak, so Sigurd continued, "Clerk, we need to refresh ourselves. Can you tell me where the facilities are?"

"Facili-whats? What you talkin' about?"

Elam said, "I think he means the latrine."

"Well, whyn't ya just say so? First door on the left after ya enter. I'll be at the back fixin' our grub." He puttered away, cats following.

Sigurd picked up his blaster from where he'd deposited it on the floor and motioned Elam to follow him.

When they were inside the latrine, Elam muttered, "We just met the Pied Piper of Cabot's Landing. What in Chaos were you thinking when you laid your weapon down?"

"That weapon of his only holds one shot and has a huge kick when it's fired. That, plus the way his hands were shaking, made it a good bet that even if he fired, he'd miss."

Elam looked dubious. "I guess. That was taking a big chance."

"It worked, didn't it? No one was hurt."

"Still pretty risky." He gave Sigurd an appraising look, as if he'd just deduced something important. His words, though, were inconsequential. "I've seen lots of weapons, but never one like his. Are you sure it only holds one shot?"

"I'm sure. My father and uncles used them on hunts. It's kind of a family tradition." Sigurd nodded to the door. "Could you read the labels on those crates?"

"You mean the ones not in modern Inglish but in old-fashioned English? Yeah, I could puzzle them out. According to the stencils, they contain munitions for the old Grand Alliance Marines."

Sigurd nodded. So Elam could read ancient English. Interesting. There weren't many professions that combined his set of skills. "I saw one of them held surface-to-air missiles."

Elam replied, "Didn't know Old English was part of Corsairs training." He paused, as if thinking. "There's supposed to be the ruins of an ancient marine base on the west coast. Munitions there would make sense. Why would they store them here?"

"I don't know. Perhaps the answer is somewhere in Cornwall's archives, if we ask the right question. The more we look, it would seem the more mysteries we uncover." He rubbed his chin. "Munitions that old could be unstable. I don't think anyone on the *Zuiderkruis* has the expertise to evaluate the risk."

Elam shrugged. "They must have been here for centuries. It's more likely that they've degraded to the point of being useless. One thing's certain, Clerk-the-simple won't be any help. He thinks there are just medical supplies here."

Sigurd shook his head. "He didn't exactly say that."

Elam's face stayed impassive, but certainty firmed his words. "Not in words, no. But trust me, that's what he thinks."

Sigurd was sure the man couldn't read minds, but this was the second time in thirty minutes he'd acted like he could. He had secrets, and individual secrets were by definition a threat. Sigurd really needed to see what the search of the DNA database turned up on this guy. "In any case, we're agreed he's not our murderer. It looks to me like they forgot him when they closed down the mining operations."

"I thought so too. You noticed he evaded your question about whether or not anyone has been here asking for supplies."

Sigurd frowned and replayed the conversation. "I thought his answer just meant he wasn't able to keep the thread of our conversation going. He's pretty scattered."

"Yeah. That's not it. He understood exactly what you asked and deflected on purpose."

The guy was getting more inscrutable and frustrating, speaking *ex cathedra* from his mountain of superiority. "What, exactly, gives you such brilliant powers of deduction?"

"Maybe I sold used flitters for a living and picked up tricks on reading people. It's none of your business. You respect privacy, remember?"

Sigurd clenched his jaw. Later. He'd deal with Elam later. "We don't have much time. Use your superpowers or whatever they are to help scope out this place. I want to send the corpsman down here to attend to any health needs Clerk might have, but otherwise I plan to leave him alone."

Elam shrugged. "I thought you said it wasn't safe here. Why not just take him back to the infirmary?"

"That's not what I said." Sigurd wasn't about to concede that Elam was probably correct that the arms had degraded to the point of uselessness and were all duds. "If we're right, he's been here for something close to fifty years. Our arrival is traumatic enough for him. I'm going to just leave him alone. Duty, honor, heart. The last one means taking care of those that need it."

"Actually, he didn't seem all that traumatized to me. Downright chatty, in fact, after he saw your tattoo."

"Regardless, I don't want to traumatize him, for his own sake. Just keep your eyes open, especially for any weapons crates that have been recently tampered with. And keep your mouth shut, if that's possible."

Elam's lips thinned to narrow grimace, and he ran thumb and forefinger across them and flipped his hand as if discarding a key.

Sigurd said nothing and stalked out of the room. By miming his response instead of saying "Yes, sir," he was being as literal-minded as Cornwall. Except he was doing it just to be annoying. How could someone so alluring be so... no, he couldn't go there.

He wound his way through a maze of floor-to-ceiling crates, noting in passing the script stenciled on the sides. All kinds of small arms, from pistols, to shotguns, to rapid-fire machine guns. Ammunition. Hand grenades and launchers. More boxes of SAMs, as if someone expected to defend against an air assault. It was what he might expect at the old Grand Alliance marine base on the west coast, but not here, at the main civilian power station. If any of them did still work, they'd swamp the firepower of the few weapons on the *Zuiderkruis. Who knows what else might be hidden here.* In less than two years, the weapons of the old Grand Alliance had managed to self-destruct their entire civilization, spanning all of known space. They'd come close to exterminating all life on Old Home Earth.

If the Exaltationists accessed even a tenth of that ancient firepower, the Empire itself was at risk.

Ancient weapons were exactly what the Imperial Intelligence Service had feared might be here. The possibility of Exaltationists accessing it made it worse.

CHAPTER 13

My foe:
Like me, willful
And smart. He lights a fire
Inside me. Does hate feed the flames,
or love?

—***The Missing Cinquains***, Arpad Laszlo

ELAM LOUNGED in the easy chair in his suite and savored his gin and tonic. Probably fake gin and fake tonic, to be sure, but reproduced with amazing creativity. He held his glass to his nose and inhaled crisp pine notes with an overlay of lemon and something else. Musk, maybe? Perhaps ginger. He took a sip and swished the cold, fizzy liquid in his mouth. Liquid needles lanced his taste buds with an array of subtle esters that danced in perfect bitter harmony.

This wasn't an ordinary gin and tonic. It rivaled ones that he'd had in the bar at the Royal Kensington Hotel in the Imperial capital, Pasargadae.

He stood, walked to the bar in his suite, and checked the label on the bottle of gin he'd pilfered from the downstairs lounge. Sure enough, it displayed a discreet copy of the Imperial coat of arms and included the phrase, "By Appointment to HM the Emperor." This wasn't an artificial liquor synthesized by the local food processing equipment. Someone had spent a small fortune to transport this bottle hundreds of light years to this nowhere planet.

Except it was increasingly clear that Cabot's Landing was more than it seemed. Worse, it had gotten Sigurd's attention, and regardless of whether Elam's suspicions about him were correct or not, the Margrave's intelligence services were bound to follow up. Instead of a hole Elam could crawl into and disappear, the planet was turning out to be the center of who-knows-what kinds of intrigue.

Decision firmed his mouth. "Cornwall."

The hologram appeared and bowed. "Yes, sir."

"Please invite Mr. Bender to my quarters for drinks at eighteen hundred hours."

Cornwall bowed. "My pleasure, sir. Will you require hors d'oeuvres?"

Elam shrugged. "Sure, why not?" Cornwall flickered to nonexistence. Elam lounged back and stared at the wheat waving on the rolling hills in front of the Lodge. His plan to disappear wasn't surviving contact with reality. Like all battle plans—they never survive contact with the enemy.

A few moments later, Cornwall reappeared. "Sir, Mr. Bender has accepted your invitation, but inquires what you wish to discuss."

"Tell him—" Elam paused. He planned to discuss terminating his contract but wanted to ease into the topic. "Tell him I want to ask him about his earlier trips here. He's the only person who has a history of visiting this planet. Maybe he'll remember something useful to the investigation." Now that he thought of it, he was surprised Sigurd hadn't already interviewed the auditor.

"Very good, sir. The mess steward from the *Zuiderkruis* suggests shrimp yakitori for the appetizer."

"Whatever. Sure. Wait. Where will he get shrimp?"

"The food processors at the Lodge can synthesize a variety of flavored proteins, sir. Shrimp was a special favorite of Mr. and Mrs. Torrance."

"Why aren't you fixing the appetizers? Why bother the steward?"

Cornwall actually simpered. "Sir, you must have forgotten that I'm a hologram." He waved his hand, and it passed through the arm of an easy chair. "I don't have corporeal existence."

"You mean the Resident has to cook for himself? That wasn't in my briefing."

"Sir, cooking is only required for the specialized proteins I mentioned. Otherwise, it's optional. A plentiful food supply is available in the form of biscuits and a protein drink. There are autonomous processors that harvest the local wheat and synthesize balanced rations for the human inhabitants of the planet. I believe you saw those in operation on the monorail the other morning."

Balanced rations. He thought about the "biscuits" Clerk had fed them this afternoon. "You mean cookies."

"The miners called them biscuits, sir, but I believe 'cookies' is the word used on some planets. There's also the protein drink, which they called 'tea.'"

"Those so-called biscuits taste like snickerdoodles, a cookie my grandmother used to make. And the green glop tastes kind of like milk."

"I see you have tried the rations, sir. I don't have a record of the precise cuisine they model. The food processors use formulas hard-wired into them by Cabot Industries bioengineers and predate my installation. I hope you found their product satisfactory."

Five hundred years—it had been that long since Cabot Industries ceased to exist. "I'm amazed the processors still work."

"I estimate fifty-eight point six percent are still operational, sir, based on satellite observations. That's comparable to other autonomous devices, like the mining bots, the housekeeping bots, the trams—"

"Okay, already. I get it. They built to last back then. But why rely on satellite observations? Aren't the processors connected to your net? I know you can't control them."

"Most are not, sir. There is no need for those outside the Lodge to be connected. If you tell me why you ask, perhaps I can better assist you."

Why, indeed? It didn't matter, especially since Elam now planned to leave when the *Zuiderkruis* departed. He glanced at the clock on his nightstand. He had time to shower before Bender showed up.

"That will be all, Cornwall."

Instead of disappearing, the AI asked, "Shall I tell the steward to prepare the shrimp yakitori?"

"I thought I already said so."

"I apologize if I misunderstood, sir. I could replay our conversation, and you could explain my error. I understood you to say I should wait."

"No, don't replay our conversation." Chaos, he didn't remember AIs being this obdurate. "I'm saying yes, now. Thank you. Dismissed." Damned literal AI. He headed to the shower, pausing to adjust a tiny wrinkle in the tight, squared-off corners he'd put in his bed this morning.

ELAM STEPPED out of the shower and wiped steam from the mirror over the sink. He felt his chin and considered trimming his beard when the door chimed. An automated server cart bearing the shrimp and a spray of flowers had appeared before he showered, so this must be Bender. Chaos knew why the auditor was early. He wrapped a towel about his waist and padded on bare feet across the carpeted suite.

He opened door and said, "Sorry. I was taking a shower—"

Jorina Baak stood in the hallway, an amused grin bending her lips. Her gaze raked him from head to toe, and she mused, "Nice abs. Work out much?"

He tried to keep exasperation out of his voice. "I was expecting Mr. Bender. What can I do for you?"

Her smile broadened as she looked over his shoulder where the server cart had stopped. "The flowers are lovely. I don't want to intrude on your date."

"It's not a date. It occurred to me that he might know something useful about the planet. He's visited here on numerous occasions in his capacity as auditor, and he met the Torrances." Since she was here, maybe he should ask her to sit in. It would save him having to report to that marionette, Sigurd. "Why don't you join us? Then you can report anything useful we pick up to the kolonel." He stepped aside and motioned for her to enter.

"Thank you, I think I shall." Once inside, she scanned the spacious receiving room, and then her gaze rested on the gin and tonic fixings sitting on the end table.

Elam said, "Help yourself if you want a drink. The gin is amazing. Glasses are in the sideboard; ice is in the minifridge." He pointed. "Give me a moment to finish dressing."

He retreated to the bedroom, closed the door, and ran fingers through his hair. What in Chaos was she doing here? He chose chinos, loafers with no socks, and a sports shirt with a turquoise and green pattern splashed on a white background. She was wearing formal merchant marine whites, so he deliberately went casual.

When he got back in the suite's lounge, she sat in one of the easy chairs nursing a drink. She held up her glass and nodded. "You're right. The gin is amazing. The bottle says it came here all the way from New Arizona."

"Yeah. I borrowed it from one of the lounges downstairs. Someone must have specially ordered it and spent a fortune to transport it. I meant to ask Cornwall how it got there."

The AI popped up in the center of the room. "You called, sir?"

Elam tossed his head in irritation and snapped, "No, I did not. Cancel."

"Yes, sir." He vanished.

Jorina snickered. He clenched his jaws and glared at her. He took a deep breath, thought about fixing another drink, but instead just poured tonic over ice. He settled into a chair across from the first officer and said, "You never said why you're here."

"Why, I'm here to help you interrogate Mr. Bender, aren't I?"

So she was a smartass. He was too, so he couldn't really complain. "I meant, why did you knock on my door? What brought you here?"

"Oh, that. The kolonel asked me to brief you on his plans for tomorrow. I think he's avoiding you."

"Fine by me. The less I see of his sneering mug, the better."

"Really? I could swear his ship had launched and you were on it. I've seen the way you check out his ass when you think no one's looking."

"An attractive bottle can't make bad wine taste good."

"He does try to make like he's an SOB, doesn't he? But underneath... 'there's some soul of goodness.'"

Elam remembered the quote from a training manual and snorted. "I believe the rest of that reads 'in things evil.'"

That got him another squinty grin. "*Henry V*. So nice to meet someone else with a classic education. The point is he's got a heart of gold. Did you hear about his conversation with the corpsman? Didn't blink an eye when he found out the guy was transgendered, and even offered him a posting with the Corsairs."

Elam shrugged. "As I recall, the Margrave issued specific orders protecting gender dysmorphic service members. Many troops come from rural planets that are not as accepting as Elsinore. In any case, our kolonel is so by-the-book, he'd fall in line no matter what his personal opinions were."

"Maybe, but there's no regulations about compassion, and that's the only way to describe his actions with respect to that hermit you found today."

A pang of shame made Elam pause. He had to admit, Sigurd's kindness was unexpected, almost noble. To say nothing of his bravery in facing the ancient weapon. The shotgun. He stared at his drink and collected his thoughts. "Why should you care what I think about him? No, never mind. It doesn't matter. Tell me about his nibs' plans for tomorrow, since he won't be bothered to tell me face-to-face."

She shook her head. "Men. It's a wonder you ever manage to form relationships. Okay, tomorrow is pretty ambitious. The plan is to go by flitter to the old Grand Alliance naval base in the Central Sea, spend two hours reconnoitering there, then depart for the abandoned marine base on the west coast. We'll spend the night and investigate the ruins the next morning. After that, we'll rendezvous with a second team at the dysprosium mines, then return here to analyze what we've learned."

"I'm to be part of this folly?"

"Yes. He was explicit. He said your observational and deductive skills were first-rate."

"Kind of him. What does he expect to learn?"

That got him one of her trademark dimpled smiles. "If he knew what he'd learn, he wouldn't need to go."

"I see your point."

She sipped her drink and gave him an appraising look. "What do you anticipate learning from Mr. Bender?"

Besides getting out of his contract, he expected to learn if the man was hiding anything, but he didn't want to say that. "I want to know more about his prior audits. What checks he ran. I want to learn more about his interactions with the Torrances. I want to know how he missed a supply clerk living under the east power station."

"There is that. The man says he's not left that supply room for over fifty years."

"You doubt that claim?"

She paused to sip her drink and then shook her head. "No. From the kolonel's description, the poor fellow is clearly mentally diminished. He'd never be able to maintain a consistent deception."

Elam nodded. "I agree." He didn't mention Clerk's dissembling about the supplies he guarded.

She stared into her glass and murmured, "Besides the hermit, there's the body the kolonel found on the beach. That's more interesting. The crispy critter."

The woman was insightful, he had to give her that. "I'm not forgetting that. Finding out what the quarterly audits *don't* do will help set parameters for figuring out how that man got on the planet and what happened to him."

"You heard what he said, what the kolonel called his 'dying declaration'?"

"I read the report. He mentioned Carthage, the place that gave us the Exaltationists. Most likely a coincidence." No reason to share his fears with Jorina. If the kolonel wanted her to know, he could tell her.

"Actually, I don't think he was talking about the planet at all. I think he was quoting an old twentieth-century poem. The *Waste Land*. I told you I had a classical education."

"Wasteland certainly describes this place." He was about to ask why she—or the dead man, for that matter—was so expert in ancient literature, but the door chimed. "That will be Mr. Bender." He rose to let him in.

Bender greeted him with bloodshot eyes. "Good evening, Mr. Vandreren." His hands thrust a bottle of wine out to him. "For you."

Elam accepted it and read the label. Synthetic Zinfandel. Cabot Lodge, 3189. Made from the local wheat, no doubt, and all of a year old. He didn't sneer. "Thank you, Malcolm. Won't you come in and have a seat?"

The man wobbled into the room and jerked to a halt. "Oh. I thought it would just be the two of us."

Sweet Freyja, the man thought he'd been asked here on a date. By the smell of him, he was toasted, too. "I asked First Officer Baak to join us. I hope that's all right. If you'll have a seat, I'll find a corkscrew and open the wine."

She rose and offered the auditor a hand. "Please call me Jorina, Mr. Bender."

He gave her a limp shake, snatched his hand back, and perched on the edge of a chair. "Call me Mal."

Elam found the corkscrew, then noticed the bottle had a twist cap. *Figures*. He removed the cap and thought about offering to let Mal smell it, but decided the irony would probably be lost. He splashed pink liquid in three goblets and joined his guests.

"Thank you for coming, Mal." He raised his glass. "To the Emperor."

Glasses clinked, and they all drank. More accurately, Bender gulped while Jorina and Elam showed more caution.

Elam swallowed and managed not to gag. It turned out to be even more ghastly than he'd feared. "Thank you for the wine."

Jorina held up her glass. "Let's not forget our patron. To the Margrave."

Glasses clinked in another ceremonial toast.

Bender couldn't seem to sit still. His gaze flipped around the room, out the window, at the bar, then finally settled on Elam. "I wasn't sure what to expect after you called." He gulped down the last of his wine.

The man's expression told Elam exactly what the man had expected, and apparently still expected, even with Jorina here. Time to cool those jets. "We were wondering if you might be able to assist the kolonel's investigation."

Alarm flashed across Bender's features. "He's not going to be here, is he?"

Even Jorina seemed see the fear in the man. "He's busy. Something about searching databases." She gave a coy glance at Elam. "I think Cybernetics Mate Clifford is helping him."

Bender jerked to his feet and lurched across the room to the bar, where he poured himself another glass of wine. "He's an awful man. I can't stand him." He carried the bottle back to his seat and sat down. "So, what do you want from me?"

His speech was starting to slur, too. Elam was losing hope for this conversation. "When we first arrived, you mentioned uploading data from the local AI as part of your audit. Can you tell me more about that?"

"What's to tell? There's a standard data set we've been uploading for the last forty-eight years, ever since the mines closed. Status of the facilities. Expendable inventories. Status of the legacy tech. It's a couple of petabytes."

"That's too much for even a full cohort of auditors to review."

"What, you think we sit down and read all that crap? Standard audit procedure is to randomly sample the records, looking for anomalies. Random walks are faster and more efficient than any systematic procedure."

"Do you monitor the energy drains on the power plants?"

"Of course. We stratify our samples by major systems, with the highest priority to mission-critical components."

"Suppose another ghost ship came here and landed a party between audits. Would you know if that happened?"

"Yes. Ghost condensate drives leave unmistakable tracks that transponders in orbit about Kennebec record. We always check those, to make sure no one is sneaking in to steal resources."

Elam hesitated. The man was lying. His micro-expressions screamed deception.

Before he could ask another question, Jorina held up a finger. "But there have to be gaps in the transponder's record. Cabot's Star has a sixty-four-month sunspot cycle. The transponders go offline during the highest point of the cycle to avoid damage. It's mentioned in the technical NOMAD notes for the system."

Bender raised his eyebrows and widened his eyes. "Really? I never knew of that."

The man did a good job of feigning surprise, but Elam knew better. Instead, his micro-expressions showed worry, even fear. First lies, now fear.

Bender gulped down another glass of wine and slurred, "This is good stuff."

He wasn't drunk either. How could Elam have missed that?

Jorina's phone buzzed. She frowned and glanced at the screen. "I've got to take this." She stood and wandered into the kitchenette.

Elam turned to Bender. "Mal, did you know there was someone living underneath the eastern power station?"

"Whaddaya mean? One of the Torrances lived there?"

"No. This was someone who was left behind when the mines closed. He's been there for nearly fifty years."

"Not posh... possible. The AI would have detected him and flagged it."

"The AI says that part of the neural network was never reactivated."

"Well, if the AI didn't see it, how would ya 'spect me to find it? I'm only human."

More dissembling. Elam needed some time alone with him. He was pretty sure he could sweat any secrets out of this amateur. He wouldn't even need extraordinary means. Assuming he was an amateur.

Jorina rejoined them, looking pensive. "That was Sigurd—I mean, the kolonel. Earlier today, we'd deployed drones to reconnoiter over the old naval base."

Elam nodded. "The one in the Central Sea. Good planning." Just what I'd expect from him. He was an SOB, but he was smart too.

"They all got shot down. It would appear that the base is protected by lethal automated defenses."

A cold ball settled in Elam's stomach as he fit pieces together. Someone knew how to activate the ancient automated defenses. If this base was like all the other old Grand Alliance bases the Empire had found, even the Imperial Bureau for State Security couldn't do that. Whoever *could* would have to possess skills beyond the best the Empire had to offer.

If the zealots on Carthage were involved, Elsinore, maybe even the Empire itself, was at risk. They had to be stopped.

Elam knew his duty lay with civilization and the Empire, however imperfect. But he'd done his duty on Dongeradeel, and it had sucked the soul out of him. To Hell with duty.

He resolved to stick with his plan to leave Cabot's Landing, one way or another.

CHAPTER 14

If I lose mine honor, I lose myself.
—Marc Antony in **Antony and Cleopatra**, *Shakespeare*

SIGURD CLICKED Replay, and the most recent drone recording lit the two-meter display at the end of the conference room. It had flown in low, over choppy seas, headed toward the cliffs of Diego Garcia. He wondered again what had possessed the ancients to give that name to their island base. The drone gained altitude, and the landing field for the ghost fleet port came into view. Low-lying buildings cast long shadows in the light from the setting sun. Something flashed from one of the rooftops, and the picture flared to static.

All four drones showed the same sequence.

"Mr. Clifford."

The cybernetics mate looked up from his keyboard. "Yes, sir?"

"Can you do anything to enhance that final image? I'd like a close-up of the source of that flash."

"It'll take an hour or two for the algorithm to run, unless you'll settle for a pixilated image."

"I can wait for a better image. Let me know when you're ready." Those defenses made his plan to visit the old Grand Alliance base on the island problematic. If they could shoot down drones, they'd do the same with an unarmed flitter. Maybe Cornwall's databases would suggest how to safely approach the base. He'd set Clifford on that task tomorrow.

A half-dozen crew hunched over consoles linked back to the ship's computers. Posters, replete with pictures of eagles soaring and inspirational corporate banalities, decorated the walls. The too-soft chairs and the fake mahogany table didn't help with maintaining proper discipline. He clenched his jaw. It wasn't much of a command center, but it was the best he could do with what was in the Lodge. At least the crew that Jorina had brought along were more or less efficient.

The corpsman looked up from his screen and quirked an eyebrow at Sigurd. He must have something. "What is it, Mr. Mustafa?"

The corpsman left his station and stood next to where Sigurd sat. "I've been looking at the results of the toxicology screens from the Torrances and others, sir."

"Anything I need to know?"

"Maybe." He glanced around the room and lowered his voice. "You might want to keep this confidential, sir."

"Really?" He used his foot to push a chair out from under the table. He pointed and said, "Speak to me."

"Sir, their medical records show both Torrances were supposed to be taking medications prescribed by Syndicate medics."

"How'd that work? I thought the infirmary had limited ability to intervene without human oversight."

"That's right, sir, but protocol called for regular blood tests, scheduled right before the quarterly audits. One of the corpsman's duties is to review those tests and prescribe treatment, including medications. In most cases, the AI synthesizes any prescribed drugs and introduces them in the patient's rations. That's SOP and avoids any problem with compliance." He paused and licked his lips. "Sir, their bloodwork shows no trace of the medications. Both of them suffered from anxiety disorders, which would only have gotten worse in the absence of treatment. But that's not all."

"Go on."

"There was something else in their samples." He pulled out his phone and showed Sigurd a graph with pointy spikes at random intervals. He pointed. "See the spike here, and this one, here? They don't correspond to any chemical in my database."

"Which means what, exactly?"

Mustafa shoved his phone back in his pocket and shrugged. "It means there is something in their blood that the gas chromatograph can detect but can't identify. That's never happened to me before. Or anyone else, as far as I know."

Sigurd frowned. "Could it be some substance native to this planet that's not been documented?"

Mustafa looked stubborn and shook his head. "If that were the case, that old coot, the supply clerk, would have the same thing in his blood. It's not there."

"How about the body on the beach?"

"His blood shows a profile of trace elements similar to the old guy, Clerk Andresen. They've both been on the planet for years, at least. The Torrances have those telltale traces too, but they also have these extra spikes that aren't in the other samples. It's got to be significant."

"Maybe. Tell me why you think this is important. It can't be just that you can't identify some chemicals."

"Look, there are things the machine can't detect, things that won't vaporize, for example. But it detected these. The GC database is up-to-date as of our departure three weeks ago, and includes local biologicals, like the venom in the sea urchins. So, in the first place, this is something not in the standard medical database."

"So it's something new?"

"Or not new, but classified."

That sent a chill down Sigurd's back. "You're thinking it's a secret chemical warfare agent? No one has dared use those since the Great Disintegration. The Margrave would never countenance such a thing."

"Maybe not, but I have less confidence in the Imperium, to say nothing of the Exaltationists. Remember what they did on Dongeradeel."

Indeed. There was already evidence those fiends were involved. "You said this was 'in the first place.' Is there more?"

"I got to thinking. How did this unknown stuff get in the Torrances and not in the other two?"

"Your conclusion?" Sigurd was pretty sure he already knew.

"It must be something here in the Lodge, sir. Either an environmental toxin, or maybe something in the food supply."

His team was staying in the Lodge, and now he'd put them at risk. "Have you tested any of the crew's blood?"

"I'm way ahead of you, sir. I tested my own as soon as I saw this. Whatever it is, it's not in my blood. Not yet, anyway. I also tested the water supply and that protein drink that's part of the standard ration. That's where the medications were supposed to be inserted. Nothing there."

"How about the rest of the standard ration? Those biscuit things that Clerk ate."

"Nothing in the ones I tested, but those are harder. We need a chemist, and the nearest one is fifty parsecs away. I think it might be an environmental contaminant, though. A mold, or some mutated bacteria. Who knows what's growing here after five hundred years."

"Well, keep checking. Should we consider drawing blood from the rest of the crew?"

"It would help to have baseline samples, but they'd also wonder why. That's why I wanted to talk to you under the rose, so to speak. I can draw daily samples of my blood. You might also have the mess steward start drawing on ship's supplies, just to be safe."

Sigurd nodded. This man was truly wasted serving as a corpsman on a fleabag trader. "Absent a compelling reason, let's stick to drawing your blood and mine. I'll stop by the infirmary tonight. That way we'll have at least two data points. I'll also speak to Ms. Baak about drawing foodstuffs from the *Zuiderkruis*."

"Three samples, sir, if you count the crazy old guy."

"Exactly. How about the John Doe? Have you completed his autopsy?"

"Yeah. Like I said, nothing unusual in his blood. The cause of death was third and fourth degree burns to over sixty percent of his body."

"Anything else? Age, for example, or how long he'd been on the planet."

"His age is harder to say. Based on CAT scans and direct observation of suture fusings, he was definitely more than twenty-five standard years. Sternal ribs are less precise, and I'm no expert at scoring these things, but I'd say he was probably mid-to-late thirties. He had two unerupted upper wisdom teeth, but someone had extracted the two lowers, and he had five ceramic fillings. There's evidence of a fully-healed break to his left femur. Overall, he had well-developed musculature, and no overt signs of chronic disease."

"He got dental care, then. I know there are automated dental clinics on Elsinore."

"Yes, but not here. I asked Cornwall. I don't see any way he could have gotten treatment on Cabot's Landing. Dental techs aren't part of a trader ship's crew. I mean, I could pull an infected tooth, but that's the limit of my skills. I guess if the Resident got a cavity, we'd pull the tooth and he could get an implant when he returned to civilization."

"So John Doe was off-planet when he got his teeth worked on. Any idea when that was?"

The corpsman shrugged. "After he became an adult. Say, sometime in the last fifteen to twenty years."

"Very well." Sigurd glanced at his screen, where a pop-up informed him of incoming data from the drones headed to the old marine base. "Anything else, Gabir?"

"No, sir."

"I appreciate you. Thank you."

He projected the image from the drone camera on the big screen. An oblong patchwork of streets, running at perfect right angles, spread out in precise rectangles. The sun had set on the west coast, where the base was, but Kennebec provided enough illumination to discern the general outlines of a military outpost. Freya knew Sigurd had been to enough of these places. The streets framed a central square that would serve as a parade ground, with offices and barracks facing on all four sides. A road led away at a sharp angle to a clear area that was doubtless the landing field for flitters.

He decided to switch to the drone's low-light camera. The buildings glowed with residual heat from the daytime sun. It was hard to say for sure, but he could swear that the destruction he'd seen in Lansbury was absent from the base, despite the maps describing it as "ruins."

At least there didn't seem to be automated defenses shooting down intruders. He split the screen four ways and watched while the drones completed a search pattern over the base. "Mr. Clifford."

The cybernetics tech's head jerked away from his screen. "Sir?"

"Please prepare maps from the images we're getting from the drones."

"I found maps in the database, sir. I already put them in your folder, under 'marine base maps.'"

"I saw them. Those are old maps, from back when the mines first reopened. I want to compare them with what the drones are finding now."

"Sure. Piece of cake. I'll have 'em done by morning."

"Thank you." Another pop-up flashed on Sigurd's monitor, but before he could read it his attention jerked back to the image from drone three. "Mr. Clifford. What was that?"

"Uh, what? I wasn't looking at the video stream."

"I thought I saw movement in the image from drone three. Can you play back the last couple of minutes?"

"Sure. Give me a second."

The corpsman would have said, 'Yes, sir," instead of Clifford's sloppy, informal response. Probably the influence of that person, Elam, on him. He needed a gentle reminder on how to address someone in authority. "Mr. Clifford."

"Uh, yeah?" He didn't look up from his screen. "There, I've got it. Damn, you're right. It looks like someone walking between the buildings."

On the other hand, effectiveness was more important than decorum. "Can you blow it up?"

"Already at it." The image froze while he zoomed in. "The resolution's pretty low, but it sure looks like that's a person. I thought there wasn't supposed to be anyone on this planet except us chickens."

Sigurd let the rustic metaphor slide. He stood and approached the screen. "Move it forward, please, in slow motion."

"You bet."

On the screen, legs moved and arms swayed. There was a head. Everything was in the right proportion. It had to be a human. "Enhance this image too, Mr. Clifford."

"Already on it."

"Good man."

Sigurd returned to his chair and remembered the pop-up. He smiled with pleasure as he read that the DNA database had found a match for the sample Clifford had taken from Elam.

According to the database, the DNA belonged to someone named Bram Elam Gastein. A satisfied smile bent Sigurd's lips. He knew the man was a phony. He clicked on the name to see the full dossier loaded from Sigurd's personal databases back on the *Zuiderkruis.*

His smile disappeared as soon as the dossier appeared. The Imperial seal at the top of the document and the heading underneath told him he was looking at a personnel record from the Imperial Bureau for State Security. Elam, or Bram, or whatever his name was, worked for the Emperor's secret police and spy agency.

He paged through the document. Born a commoner on Dongeradeel. Nominated to the Imperial Military Academy at age sixteen. Graduated fifth in his class from Sandhurst, in the same class as Crown Prince Evander and nine years ahead of Sigurd. Sigurd permitted himself a grim smile. He'd been third in his class.

Let's see, that made Elam forty-six, although he looked at least ten years younger. He'd spent the next eight years in the Imperial Navy making captain in record speed. Almost as fast as Sigurd had made kolonel. He'd transferred to the spy agency shortly after.

That was the last unredacted entry in the dossier until the final paragraphs. Not surprising that his time as a spy would be classified, except it shouldn't be redacted, at least not from Sigurd's eyes. Sigurd's rank meant he was cleared for almost everything, even to the crown prince's personnel dossier. But Elam's record was redacted. What was so secret about this guy that made his file a state secret, kept even from the likes of Sigurd?

The last few paragraphs, however, were in the clear. Sigurd scanned the details about Gastein's retirement six years ago, on New Arizona. Amazing. He'd been made a peer of the realm and Baron von Gastein when he retired. If a commoner made it to fleet admiral, he might be made baron. Posthumously. Sigurd couldn't recall one as young as Elam ever being on the honors list. The citation was cryptic, just mentioning his long years of valiant service and his heroism on Dongeradeel. His elevation to baron was marked "top secret," with a suspense date of thirty years. Whatever was in those redacted pages contained intelligence that would be sensitive for decades.

Sigurd closed the file and stared at the blank screen while he considered what he'd learned. The interests of Elsinore and the Imperium didn't always coincide, but it was hard to see a conflict here. After all, the crown prince had personally signed off on Sigurd's mission to Cabot's Landing.

Given his history, Elam should be his ally. In fact, it was impossible to believe that a peer of the realm would not be an ally. Instead, he was clowning around, acting like a buffoon, flirting with young Clifford, and in general being a smartass. On the other hand, buffoon would be the perfect cover for a spy.

If this Elam/Bram person wanted to play head games, so be it. It was axiomatic that secrets from the state were a threat to security. Ordinarily, this would imply that Elam, who appeared to be the very soul of secrets, was a threat. But his history said otherwise. It was remotely possible he was here on the same mission as Sigurd. Unlikely, but not impossible.

Sigurd firmed his lips. The main thing he'd learned was that Elam was even more formidable than he seemed. His apparent mind-reading ability, for example, probably came from interrogation techniques the Bureau for State Security had taught him. Chaos knew what else he could do and was hiding. The most prudent course of action was to regard him as a threat until proven otherwise.

Sigurd knew how to handle threats. Even good-looking ones. Even ones he was falling—no. He wasn't going to think that. The man was a jackass. You didn't give your heart to a jackass.

You did your duty.

CHAPTER 15

Duty owns the soul while love owns the heart.
Exalted are those whose soul exceeds their heart.
　　　　　　　　　　*—Chapter 3, verses 3.4, **Ekzaltoj de Cadio***

THE FLITTER bounced in an air current, and Elam jerked awake.

He'd had the dream again. It had been months since the last time.

He blinked grit from his eyes and gazed across the cramped cabin. Dust motes floated in golden sunbeams pouring through portholes. A dozen crew huddled in their seats. Some slept, some fiddled with equipment stashed in their fatigues, and others traded murmured words with one another. In the seat next to his, Clifford stirred and resumed snoring.

Elam closed his eyes. Lingering images from the dream welled up to plague him. Ivar was there, in the fog that was his dream, reaching for him. Pleading with him. Shredding his heart. Imperial marines stood by, cloaked in black battle armor, awaiting Elam's command. He opened his mouth but could not speak. He reached for Ivar but could not move. Silent rain slicked his brow, and wind whipped his flesh. He stood frozen while doom, inevitable and relentless, poured over him.

The dream had ended the same way it always ended. Time slowed. Air turned to molasses. Elam's steps slogged in slow motion. Red flashes flared from rifle muzzles. A fusillade of bullets. Ivar twisted in an impossible crimson spray, remaining forever distant, forever unreachable. Elam tried to scream, but no sound left his lips.

It ended with Ivar, his beloved, cold and dead to his touch.

The flitter swayed and lurched. Elam opened his eyes and stared out the window. Gray snow-capped peaks littered the landscape below, and sunlight glinted off a distant lake. They must be over the western mountains. It couldn't be far to the old Grand Alliance marine base.

Clifford, still asleep, squirmed in his seat and whimpered, "*Tidak, tidak. Bantu saya.*"

He must be having a nightmare. Maybe it was something in the air. Elam touched the man's wrist. "Chad. Wake up. You're having a bad dream."

His eyes snapped open. "Wha'?" His gaze roamed over the compartment.

"You were asleep and asking for help. I woke you."

"Oh." He drew a shuddering breath. "Crap. I was having the weirdest nightmare." He rubbed his eyes. "These before-dawn departures get to me every time. How long did I sleep?"

"I don't know. I fell asleep too. But we're over the western mountains now, so I'm guessing we're at most thirty minutes from landing."

"Okay." Clifford adjusted his pants and leered at him. "You were in my dream."

Elam really didn't want to know. Time for a change of subject. "What do you think we'll find at the base?"

"No idea. That's why we're going there, right?" He smirked, a slash of white across ebony features. "You'd tied me up. In my dream, I mean. I wonder if that's wish fulfillment."

"If so, it's going to stay a dream, trust me. Besides, it didn't sound like you were enjoying it. You said, 'No, no. Help me.'" In Malay.

Clifford responded with up-and-down eyebrow action and a leer on his lips. "Trust me, I wanted more."

Sigurd's voice boomed from the overhead speakers. He stood at the front of the cabin, holding a microphone to his lips. "May I have your attention, please."

Muttered conversations faded, and the passengers shifted in their seats.

"The pilot is making our final approach to the old marine base. We'll be on the ground in fifteen minutes. Mr. Glyndwr will update us on the tactical situation."

The steward's mate jumped to his feet and accepted the microphone. "Sir, thank you, sir." He stood at attention, one hand behind his back at parade rest. The flitter jittered, and he lost his balance.

Sigurd gripped the mate's shoulder and muttered, "Steady. Mind the sway, mate." As he spoke, Glyndwr teetered and the microphone passed in front of Sigurd's face, sending his words over the speakers. The crew tittered, and Glyndwr's face turned crimson.

Sigurd glared and snapped, "Enough." An uneasy silence settled over the cabin. "Mr. Glyndwr, please proceed."

Glyndwr bit his lip and nodded. "Drones have continuously monitored the base since last evening. You saw in the briefing this morning what appeared to be a human figure in the shadows of one building. There have been no further sightings, nor any evidence of movement in the old base, nor in the surrounding area. Analysis by the planetary AI assigns a sixty percent probability that the original sighting was an optical artifact."

One of the crew held up her hand and asked, "That means no one is there, then, right?"

Sigurd spoke. "It means no one is probably there. Mr. Glyndwr, please continue."

"Sir. We will land on a hilltop five hundred meters from the base. Mr. Knudson and his team will disembark and establish an electronic perimeter about the flitter. Mr. Knudson will have a blaster, but the rest of his team will be armed with sonic weapons. In the unlikely event they encounter hostiles, lethal force will be used only as a last resort."

The shuttle swayed and landing gear clunked. Glyndwr continued, "Please fasten your seat belts. We'll be down in a few minutes. The remainder of the team will stay in the shuttle until Mr. Knudson reports the area is secured. After that, we will group outside into our investigative teams and proceed to the base. Are there any questions?"

Silence.

Glyndwr collapsed to his seat and fumbled with his seat belt.

Winds buffeted the light plane while it approached the landing field, but the pilot made a skillful, soft landing. Elam recalled hearing the pilot mention military experience on Actium's Gate. Not surprising that ex-military gravitated to the merchant fleet.

The cabin door thunked open, and Elam's ears popped. Knudson's crew tromped onto the landing field, showing good order. Elam narrowed his eyes. More signs of military discipline. This crew had some surprising skill sets for a trader on a routine mission to a minor corporate outpost.

The terrain outside was strikingly different from Lansbury or the area around the Lodge. The old Grand Alliance had chosen an isolated rocky cliff for their marine base, far from the ubiquitous wheat and other imported organisms. Here, gray and blue fungi clung in scattered heaps to sandy soils, with purple and green local lichens intermixed. No trees, of course, and no insects.

An amused smile bent Elam's lips. No wheat meant no vomit stink. Fresh air at last.

Chad asked, "Did you see something funny?" His voice had a faint quaver.

Elam permitted himself a chuckle. "No. I was just thinking there's no wheat here, so it probably won't stink like the other places we've been." He gave Chad a reassuring smile. "Mr. Knudson and his team seem quite efficient."

"I guess. They weren't with us on our last pass this way. Some kind of whack-a-doodle security BS from corporate brought them this time."

Well, that was interesting. What else had Elam missed by being asocial on the trip here?

Chad grinned at him. "I guess you're right about the stink, though. Fresh air will be nice." He twisted in his seat and leaned across Elam to peer out the window. "It looks pretty desolate."

"That it does. You know, I wonder why they didn't plant any wheat here? That just meant they had to import all their food, even if it was just from other parts of the planet."

"Who knows? I mean, why build a station when they never built a monorail line to the base?"

"What?"

"There's a monorail station here, in the base. Let me show you." He pulled out his phone and flipped through images. "Look. Here's the monorail station at the Lodge." He stroked the screen. "Here's the one at Lansbury."

Elam nodded. "Arial shots, I see. From satellites?"

"Nah. I lifted them from shots the flitters automatically took while taking off and landing." He flipped to another screen. "Here's a shot of this building on the marine base, taken by one of my drones yesterday."

Elam frowned. "I thought the marine base was in ruins. Like Lansbury."

"The official maps say that. They're wrong. Real-time drones don't lie. The buildings are all standing."

Elam peered at the photos. "The building at the base certainly does look similar to the other two buildings."

"It's the friggin' same building. They're identical." Chad flipped back and forth to make his point. "Exactly the same dimensions, too. The records are clear that they never built a line to the base. Now I ask you, what good is a monorail station if there's no monorail?"

Elam had to admit they looked the same. "Maybe it's just a standard structure? Are there any other similar buildings?"

Chad gave him a smug look. "Nope. I checked."

This was strange. "Maybe they planned to extend the monorail to the marine base but never got around to it." He frowned. "Can you check the monorail station at the industrial port?"

"Good idea. All I'll have is satellite imagery for that. Gimme a minute." Chad's fingers flew over the screen on his phone.

More mysteries piling up. This was looking to be less and less the kind of place where he could hide. What, exactly, were the ancients doing here five hundred years ago? Good thing he'd already decided to bail.

Chad nudged him with an elbow. "You won't believe what I've found."

"Try me."

"Okay. Here's the monorail station at the industrial port. Exactly the same as the other three buildings." Chad displayed them one after another on his phone. "But that's not all. There's one on Diego Garcia too." Sure enough, a fifth copy of the monorail station popped up on the screen. "Here's the freakiest thing. Just for kicks, I looked at the telemetry for the agricultural station on that island to the south. Look at this."

Elam squinted at the screen. "It looks like a forest to me."

"Oh, sorry. Wrong filter." He stroked his screen again. "This pulls out the organic ground cover."

"*Jord mem fan Thor.*" Elam realized he'd been shocked into his native Frisian. Mother of Thor, indeed. He steadied himself. "That's another copy of the same building. Have you shown this to the kolonel?"

"You kidding? That tight-ass would bite my head off for wasting his precious time."

Glyndwr's voice on the flitter's speakers interrupted their conversation. "Attention, please. Mr. Knudson's team reports the landing area is secure. Teams, please assemble in the landing zone and commence your investigations. Mr. Vandreren, the kolonel requests that you meet with him at the front of the cabin after the teams have disembarked."

Elam turned to Chad. "You've done awesome work with these photos. Can you forward them to my phone? The kolonel needs to see them. I'll be sure to give you credit."

Chad shrugged. "Don't need no credit. I'd just as soon his highness didn't notice me at all." He shrugged into his backpack. "Watch yourself. Don't trust that bastard."

"Be careful yourself, Chad. Don't take any risks." Poor kid. He clearly felt guilty about something, and Sigurd was doubtless behind it. Probably some kind of inept spying on Elam. Sigurd couldn't possibly find anything meaningful about him. At least, not without DNA, and even then he'd be limited.

Elam lounged back and waited with hooded eyes while the various crew members gathered their gear and left the flitter. Sigurd stood at the front, nodding at them as they passed by and speaking to them individually, by name. The man did know how to be a leader.

When everyone else had left, Elam lazed to the front where Sigurd stood, waiting.

"Good morning, Resident. I apologize for rousting you so early this morning and for not briefing you. I thought you might prefer sleep to hearing me ramble on."

"I've yet to hear you ramble, but you're right. I'd rather hear your briefing with a rested mind."

"Right, then. Please sit." He pointed to a forward-facing seat while settling into a rear-facing seat. "First, I've put on hold plans to visit the old Grand Alliance navy base on Diego Garcia. Something has activated an automated defense system that's shooting down our drones. I can't risk personnel in a flitter, so we'll have to find another way."

"Can't Cornwall shut down the automated system?"

"He says no. As far as I know, even ImpSec couldn't do that, at least not on bases we've found." Sigurd paused, as if waiting for a reaction, then continued. "We also sent drones over the base here. One of them spotted what was almost surely a two-legged creature walking between two buildings."

"You know the official maps show this base as 'ruins.'"

Sigurd's face stayed grim. "That fact did not escape my notice."

All right, then. On to the new data. "A creature means you think it's not a person?"

"The telemetry shows the right body temperature, but the image is too pixilated to be certain. You may not know, but there are ancient legends of alien intelligence in this sector."

Elam repressed a snort and rolled his eyes. "You can't believe that. Those legends are in every sector. They even had them on Old Home Earth. I'd as soon believe in angels dancing on the head of a pin."

Sigurd's expression hardened. "The Exaltationists would certainly believe in angels."

"You think they're here? Did Jorina tell you about the sunspot cycles shutting down the monitors?"

"Mr. Clifford told me. Despite appearances, he's quite competent. So, yes, it's entirely possible unknown third parties could have entered the system. That's my current working hypothesis, in fact. It would certainly expand the list of suspects for our three murders."

Elam noted he said "expand." Sigurd didn't even try to hide that he still suspected Elam. In fact, his expression read like an open book. He knew something about Elam, something new. But what could he possibly know?

Sigurd continued, "Given the weapons stashed under the east power station, it wouldn't have to be anyone as nefarious as the Exaltationists to present a danger to the realm. It could be a rival trading firm, or even another one of the great houses jockeying for Imperial favor. What's clear is that the Margrave needs to know what's going on."

Right. Elam nodded. *Sigurd's an intelligence officer in the Margrave's Corsairs. His first loyalty is to his lord.*

Duty tugged at Elam too, and he resisted. It wasn't fair. He'd done enough. He closed his eyes and heaved a deep breath. "Mr. Clifford just discovered something that might interest you." He pulled out his phone and exposed the pictures of the monorail stations. "So the ancients built more stations than monorails."

Sigurd nodded. "You're right, that is interesting. Of course, there's only one logical explanation. They planned to extend the monorail to the marine base and the south agricultural station and never got around to it."

Elam waited. There was more to it. *Will he get it?*

Sigurd's eyes lit up. "Tunnels!"

The man was smart. Elam let eagerness rush his response. "Exactly my thought. I bet they dug maintenance tunnels everywhere they planned to put monorail tracks. That means we can walk to the navy base on that island, and probably to the agricultural station too."

Sigurd continued the thought as if he were telepathic. "It also means that anyone hiding out at those locations can walk to the Lodge, or Lansbury, or anywhere else. They'd be completely hidden from satellite telemetry, and from Cornwall, since his sensors to the tunnels are inactive."

Elam wondered if he'd reach the next conclusions on his own or would need prompting.

Sigurd jumped to his feet. "The man in the image! He must have escaped through the tunnels under the monorail station. We need to investigate." He glared at Elam. "I'll need your help. It's time for you to do your duty."

The word "duty" strangled Elam's reply. Yesterday, Sigurd had appealed to his vanity when asking for help. Today, he demanded that Elam do his duty. He *knew*. Somehow he'd penetrated Elam's identity. Duty meant nothing to Elam Vandreren, but history showed it was everything to Baron Bram von Gastein. He had to have sneaked a DNA sample somehow. But when?

Chad. It had to be him. He hadn't shown up the other night for a tryst, or even to share some martinis. He must have been on a mission from Sigurd to obtain a DNA sample. From there, it would have been trivial to use ImpSec databases to pull up Bram von Gastein's file. At least Evander had made sure that only the crown prince personally could access the details, but his cover as Elam Vandreren was blown.

As to doing his duty, well, after doing his duty on Dongeradeel, he wasn't sure he had anything left inside but guilt.

CHAPTER 16

Religion is regarded by the common people as true, by the wise as false, and by the rulers as useful.

—*Lucius Annaeus Seneca*

SIGURD SHADED his eyes as dawn sent spikes of sunlight shooting through the eastern peaks and into the flitter. A gritty wind gusted, and fine grains of sand burned his eyes. Elam's hair fluttered over his frozen features, hiding whatever he might be thinking. Maybe he would honor his duty to the Empire, maybe not. Time would tell.

Meantime, Sigurd had a job to do. He touched the microphone stuck to his throat and muttered, "Mr. Glyndwr."

The steward mate's response sounded tinny in the receiver tucked behind his right ear. "Sir, yes, sir!"

"Stand by." He tipped his head at Elam. "What's the grid location of that building? The monorail station."

The Resident gave a little start, then glanced at his phone. "Uh, 18-K, it looks like."

"Mr. Glyndwr. Send Mr. Knudson and his team to building 18-K. The Resident and I will meet them there. They are not to enter the building, and are to use caution approaching. They are to observe only and take no offensive action. If they encounter hostiles, they are not authorized to engage but are to take cover or retreat."

"Yes, sir. I'll lead the team myself."

"Negative, Mr. Glyndwr. As my second, you'll avoid all contact with hostiles. Mr. Knudson will handle this."

"Very good, sir. Mr. Knudson it is. ETA is not more than five minutes for the team."

"Excellent. Ours is about the same." He turned his attention to Elam, who for once didn't look like he was about to make a smartass remark. Time to find out where he stood. "Are you with me, Mr. Vandreren?"

"Elam. Please. I'm not a soldier."

"Elam, then. Are you with me?"

Silence for three full beats, then, "On my honor, I'm with you."

Sigurd would settle for this man's honor. It would have been better if he'd included duty and heart in the pledge, but that may have been too much to expect. At least for now. He reached into his pack and pulled out a spare needle gun. "For you."

"What makes you think I want that? Or know how to use one of those things, for that matter?"

"You seem to have an endless supply of surprising talents. It only makes sense that expertise with personal weapons be one of them. I assume you won't be bashful about correcting me if I'm wrong."

Elam took the weapon and checked the action. "You seem to have unexpected skills as well, Sigurd. We must compare notes when this is over."

"Agreed." Maybe, just maybe, Baron Bram von Gastein could be a loyal ally, even if Elam Vandreren could not. He descended to the tarmac without checking to see if Elam followed.

Building 18-K faced the central square, about five hundred meters from where the flitter had landed. Mud splashed on the crease in his slacks as they jogged through the base, taking advantage of what cover was available. Sigurd slowed about one hundred meters short of the goal and stood with his back to a building while he scanned for Knudson's team.

There wasn't much in the way of cover, just the buildings, really. But the team had done a good job, taking advantage of what there was. He followed footprints in the mud to where two of them squatted next to what looked like a solar charging station. Sun gleamed off a tram, similar to the ones they'd used at the Lodge's ghost port. It must be recharging.

Sigurd muttered to his throat mike, "Mr. Glyndwr. Switch me to Mr. Knudson."

"Sir, yes, sir."

"Mr. Knudson. Dorestad here. I see two of your crew near me, about seventy meters east of the target building."

"Sir, that's Clapham and Stiers. They're using a tram for cover."

"Yes. That's them. Any evidence of hostiles?"

"Not of hostiles, sir, but someone has been here. There's a single set of footprints leading from the target building to the power station, and tire tracks from there back to an entrance."

So the target must have grabbed a tram for his escape. "Can you approach the building from the west?"

"That's what we're doing, sir. I'm on the south side right now. I can reconnoiter the east side, where the tracks appear to enter the building."

"Do that, Mr. Knudson. Take care. We'll cover you." No reason for undue risk to a loyal trooper like Knudson. Sigurd knelt and held his needle gun steady on the building. "Elam, can you provide cover too?"

Silence. "Elam, where are you?"

Knudson's voice piped up in his earpiece. "Sir, the Resident is already at the entrance. He's waving us forward."

"What the Chaos does he think he's doing?" Sigurd jumped to his feet and sprinted to the building. The two crew at the power station followed him.

Lights flashed on inside the building, silhouetting Elam, who hunched over what looked like an electronic panel. Inside, a tunnel descended into what must be a basement. Sigurd skidded to a stop and grabbed Elam's shoulder. "What the Chaos are you doing? You could have been killed."

Elam shook him off. "It's obvious. Whoever the drones spotted used a tram to escape into the tunnels. They're probably long gone." He turned to Knudson, who had just joined them. "Can you check and see if the tram at that solar station is charged?"

"Uh, how would I do that? Sir."

"Look for the button marked 'on.' How should I know? Just check it out."

Sigurd's face heated. "I'll give the orders here."

Elam rolled his eyes. "I'm so sorry. What are your orders, Your Grace?"

Your Grace. That bit. Sigurd took a calming breath. "Mr. Knudson, he's right. Can you please have one of your crew check out the tram at the solar station? If we're to chase our target, we'll need powered transport." He paused to look into the building. "Also, please have one of your team reconnoiter this entrance. I'm guessing there is a tunnel down there headed east. You might have to open some doors."

He waited for the crew to attend to their tasks, then turned back to Elam and lowered his voice. "You're not stupid. People die in combat if there isn't a clear chain of command. Do not do that again."

"I said I was with you, not that I'd follow you off a cliff. You're not stupid either. No battle plan survives contact with the enemy. I was giving the order you would have given, if you'd seen the same things I did."

Sigurd recognized the latter quote from one of his guest lecturers when he was a student at Sandhurst. He couldn't remember anything about the guy except his impressive analytical abilities. It almost certainly wasn't Gastein, even though the lecture happened about the time he transferred to ImpSec. In any case, Elam's answer was on point and consistent with the Imperial practice of giving officers wide latitude.

In fact, Sigurd had seen exactly the same tactical situation. He was just slower to react than Elam. But then, Sigurd was responsible for the safety of the crew and his mission, and Elam was responsible to, well, no one except himself. Time to reel him in, if possible. "I apologize. You are exactly correct. Please continue to take action as needed."

Elam's features showed faint surprise, even respect. "You're right too. I should have been more circumspect. It's not like Mr. Knudson and his crew are Imperial Marines."

Sigurd almost flinched at that. No way Elam could know that Sigurd had brought his personal guard on Elsinore along on this mission. "Point taken. What is your status assessment?"

Elam waited another beat before drawing a deep breath. "It must have rained recently, with all this wet mud. I saw a single set of footprints leading from here, the entrance to the monorail station, to the solar power station. Tire tracks show a vehicle going from there to here and a mud trail inside. Except for the tracks Mr. Knudson's team left, there was no other evidence of a physical presence by anyone. I concluded that that our target was alone, since there was only one set of prints, and that he had fled via a tram. It made sense that he'd enter the tunnels under the station and head away from here. Assuming we're right about the tunnels, and assuming the trams here are like those at the ghost port near the Lodge, he could be a dozen or more clicks from here by now."

Keen observations, quick conclusions, and decisive actions. Just what he'd expect from an Imperial officer. "So you flanked our own team to enter the tunnel. Weren't you concerned about friendly fire?"

"You specifically forbade offensive action. I had confidence in Mr. Knudson and his team to follow your orders."

"Good work, Elam. Still, you have value to the Syndicate and, by connection, to the Margrave. You are personally important to me and my mission. In the future, please factor that into your calculations. I do not want to have to report to the Palace on Elsinore that I lost such a valuable asset."

That earned him another impudent grin from Elam. "Understood, Sigurd." Smartass. He didn't even use his rank, let alone call him "sir," in responding to a direct order.

Worst of all, he'd ignored the "personally important" admission. Maybe calling him a valuable asset was the wrong message.

Knudson had returned from the tunnel and stood several meters away, apparently waiting for Sigurd to finish with Elam. Sigurd nodded to him and waved him forward. "Report."

"Sir, you were correct. There's a tunnel down there, shaped like a semi-cylinder with roughly a three-meter radius. The walls appear to be poured concrete with expansion joints every thirty meters or so. It takes a long curve to the southeast."

"Hostiles?"

"None present, sir. The muddy tracks here continue down the tunnel for about fifty meters before they fade out, like the treads shed all the mud they'd picked up."

"What's your estimate for how long the tunnels run?"

Knudson chewed his lower lip. "Sir, the tunnels under the monorail at the east power station run all the way to the industrial port. We sent a bot through them when we transported the corpsman to check on Clerk Andresen, and that's where it wound up. These tunnels are similar, even though there's no monorail running above them. If I had to guess, sir, I'd say they wind up at the west power station, near the mines. Maybe two, three hundred klicks."

"I think you're correct, Mr. Knudson. I believe you brought a bot?"

"Yessir. Several. They're standard for reconnoiter missions like this one."

"Of course. Please deploy one. I want to see where this tunnel goes."

"Very good, sir. There's one more thing, sir."

"Speak to me."

"We found a stack of pamphlets, sir." He reached into his jacket and handed a booklet to Sigurd.

The cover was bright red, and the interior pages crisp and white. This artifact was recent, not a relic left over from five hundred years ago. The Esperanto title gave its purpose away: *Sanktaj Ekzaltoj de Gregorio*, the Holy Exaltations of Gregorio, one of the sacred books of the Exaltationists.

He flipped through the booklet, making sure it was the actual text and not a coded document, at least on cursory inspection. "How many of these are there?"

"Hundreds, at least, sir. There are boxes of them, sir. They're all in that screwy language, and there are four different colors. It's like they are for distribution. For propaganda or something."

"Or something, indeed." Not surprising Knudson didn't recognize them. He'd never been deployed in a mission involving the Exaltationists. At least, not before now.

"Secure any of these that you find. Perhaps our data tech can make some sense of them. Please tell Mr. Glyndwr we're secure and send my regards and my request to join me here forthwith. Don't forget to have him bring the bot. Also, prepare your team for immediate departure via flitter to the west power station."

"Very good, sir." Knudson turned on his heel and departed at a trot.

Elam was leaning against a concrete wall of building 18-K, watching him with hooded eyes and a sly smile.

"Comments, Mr. Vandreren?"

"Call me Elam, dammit."

"Elam, then."

"The mud trails were still wet, so whoever entered the tunnels must have done so no longer than a couple of hours ago. You're planning to outflank whoever we saw here, to beat them to the west power station. There should be plenty of time, since they're traveling by slow tram and we'll be in a flitter. Do you expect that to work?"

"Frankly, no. I expect whoever they are, they will anticipate our move and never arrive at the west power station. But it's the best move I've got at the moment, despite dividing my forces."

"I agree. Of course, there could be a superior force at the west power station."

"That's always possible. I have confidence in our team." Knudson was certainly qualified, and Elam even more so, based on his dossier.

Still, he couldn't get the dying words of the man on the beach out of his mind. The humble expect nothing. Maybe he expected too much.

CHAPTER 17

I exist as I am. That is enough.

—Walt Whitman

ELAM HUDDLED in the back of the nearly empty flitter and stared out the window. Snow-capped peaks and barren valleys crept below while the craft sped over the mountains and toward the western power plant. A spate of turbulence made the craft shudder. A tone sounded, and the seat belt lights flashed. Sigurd and his squad, clustered at the front of the cabin, interrupted their tactical planning to secure themselves.

Elam ignored the warning and returned to gazing at the planet below.

Ten of them, counting himself, Sigurd, and Knudson's squad. By all indications, the latter were battle-hardened Imperial Marines, traveling under cover as Sigurd's personal guard. Why Imperial Marines? And why undercover?

Elam was sure of his answers and suppressed a shudder.

When Elam had called Sigurd "Your Grace," the man had done a commendable job of hiding his reaction. But Elam's special training made such evasions impossible. The astonishing conclusion was inevitable and, in retrospect, obvious.

Sigurd's reaction revealed that Elam had broken his cover and that his guess that Sigurd was a member the aristocracy was correct. The sequence of conclusions that followed from *that* were breathtaking. Given the *Volknut* tattoo, that meant he was almost certainly the Margrave's son and heir. But that meant he was Prince Sigurd von Jernsiden, heir to the current Margrave and sixth in line to the Imperial Purple.

That certainly accounted for a squad of Imperial Marines protecting him.

But what on Cabot's Landing could possibly be important enough for him to be here, and on a secret mission no less?

It also explained the nonexistence of "Sigurd Dorestad" in the ship's databases. But that was an error, and a serious one too. If he were on an undercover mission, his cover should have been included in the ship's files. Unless, of course, his mission was a last-minute and hastily planned addition to the ship's otherwise routine passage.

All of which made the question of what in Chaos was Sigurd doing on the *Zuiderkruis* all the more compelling. And more dangerous to Elam.

The seat belt light turned off, and Sigurd rose and made his way to the back of the cabin. He stood over Elam and said, "We've got about fifteen minutes before we're down. This might be a good time for our talk."

Elam kept his face impassive and shrugged. "Sure. Have a seat."

Sigurd settled in a rear-facing seat across from Elam. "I have read your file."

A frigid ball formed in Elam's gut. He'd figured that already, but the confirmation was still chilling. "Oh? What did you learn?"

Sigurd's eyes narrowed. "It's secret. I can't talk about it, not even to you. Whatever I may have found is safe, protected by the highest possible classification." He paused for a beat. "That means *you* are safe, Elam Vandreren."

Elam snorted. "Safety is an illusion. Death waits on no one."

"Indeed. But your death will not be by my action. Or inaction, for that matter." His eyes said he wanted to say more, but his mouth stayed firm.

The man still had secrets. Maybe personal secrets. Time to probe again. "Speaking of secrets, you seem to have one or two yourself."

Conflict lurked in Sigurd's eyes. "If that is true, what does it mean to you?" Pain coiled in his face and slithered down his body, pain only Elam could see. What secret could cause such agony? A deeply personal pain, it would appear.

Elam thought he knew. It was the same pain that tormented him. He longed to touch Sigurd, to comfort him, to stroke his cheek. But the *Volksnut* barred his touch. Instead, he murmured, "Duty, honor, and heart. That oath can force choices no man should have to make." Ivar's ghost haunted Elam's memories even now. He knew those choices well.

Before Sigurd could respond, the seat belt sign illuminated and the tone chimed. The pilot's panicky voice came over the loudspeakers.

"Cabot Base radar reports unknown approaching flitters. We're taking immediate evasive action. Secure yourselves and your equipment. It's going to be a bumpy ride."

Before Sigurd could fasten his seat belt, his shoulder com link buzzed. Irritation flashed on his features, and he pressed the Answer button while fumbling with his seat belt. "Von Dorestad here. This better be good."

"First Officer Baak, sir. Telemetry shows two flitters just took off from the vicinity of the west power station. They appear to be closing on your craft. We've alerted your pilot."

"The pilot just reported incoming. What else?"

"Sir, the radar signature for these shows they aren't the standard Cabot's Landing corporate flitters. My radar tech is ex-navy, and she says they look like Exaltationist troop transports."

Elam frowned. At least Exaltationist troop transports didn't have effective air-to-air weapons. But there might still be SAM sites at the power station. The shuttle swerved and started a steep climb.

Sigurd ignored the maneuvers and spoke calmly to his shoulder mike. "We need to belay our approach to the power station. Are you in contact with my pilot?"

"Yes, sir. I've already told him to undertake evasive maneuvers and to head for the industrial port. In the absence of intelligence, the risk of surface-to-air missiles is too great. We have a contingent of able spacers at the port, and the location is secure."

Relief showed in Sigurd's features. "Good work, Ms. Baak. How soon can you get a flitter to the marine base to relieve our crew there?"

"Sir, Mr. Glyndwr reports the situation at the base is nominal. However, I can send a flitter from the industrial port to relieve them. It will take about three hours to get there. I could send one more from here, but we're running out of qualified flitter pilots. There's just me and one other." She hesitated while a voice spoke in the background. "Sir, the two hostile flitters have changed course and are headed away from you, south by southwest."

"Good news. Thank you. Ms. Baak, under no circumstances may you place yourself at risk. If Mr. Glyndwr's team is secure and not under threat, hold the remaining flitters in reserve for now. No telling where we might need them, or the pilots. Can you patch me through to Captain Fokke?"

"Yes, sir. Give me a moment. The ship's orbit is currently on the other side of Cabot's Landing, and we'll need to establish a satellite relay link."

Elam decided to take advantage of the momentary break. "As we both know, no battle plan survives contact with the enemy. I can be more helpful if you'll fill me in on what your contingencies are."

Sigurd held up a hand and shook his head. "Not now." His shoulder com buzzed, and Fokke's voice sounded over a hiss of static. "*Zuiderkruis* here, Kolonel. What is so urgent?"

"Captain, we've uncovered a hostile force on the planet. Strength, unknown. Origin, likely Exaltationist. It is imperative that word of this gets back to the Imperial base on Iskander as soon as possible."

"If you insist." Reluctance showed in her tone. "We will need at least several days to prepare for departure, Kolonel. You've got twenty-eight of my crew down there, including my first officer and my corpsman, and I'll need them all back on board before any departure."

"Captain, this cannot wait. You must depart at once, before an Exaltationist battle cruiser has time to arrive."

"A battle cruiser here? That's nonsense. Carthage is ninety days away by the fastest ship known."

"Captain, there is a hostile force of Exaltationists on this planet. They got here somehow, and evaded detection until now. For all we know, there's a battle cruiser already here, hiding in the outer reaches of the system. You must depart at once."

"Kolonel, I'm not one of your guardsmen, I'm Captain. I will do what, in my sole judgment, is best for my vessel."

"Captain, I believe you have sealed orders in your possession. Orders regarding me."

"Yes." Now suspicion tinged her voice.

"Open them, and then do as I say. Dorestad out." He tapped his com link twice. "Ms. Baak?"

"Yes, sir. That was quite the conversation."

"You were listening? Good. Know then that the *Zuiderkruis* will depart once Captain Fokke reads her sealed orders. Be sure to transmit to the ship all the telemetry you have on the enemy flitters, especially their radar signatures. Also the photos of the Exaltationist propaganda we found at the marine base."

"Yes, sir. We're already on it."

"Excellent work, Ms. Baak. Thank you." He paused, as if thinking, then asked, "Where are those two enemy flitters headed?"

"Sir, radar still shows them heading southwest, away from you."

He frowned. "There's nothing to the south of here, right? Just desert."

"Desert, mountains, and then the Great Ocean, sir. At least according to the records. Who knows the last time anyone checked. Anyway, their current route takes them just west of the Western Reserve Island."

"That's where the biological station was at, as I recall?"

"Yes, sir. The old maps call it *Ptitseferma*. Russian for 'Chicken Ranch.'"

"Interesting. Let me know if their course changes."

"Yes, sir. Uh, sir, there's one more thing. It's probably nothing—"

"Speak. At this point, anything could be significant."

"It involves that old coot at the east power station. Clerk Andresen."

"What about him?"

"He's missing, sir. I sent Gabir, I mean Mr. Mustafa, to adjust his food processors, as you requested. When he got there, Andresen was gone. Cats all over the place, but no old geezer. There were dozens of crates too, but none of them contained weapons either. Just routine medical supplies. Are you sure you saw weapons?"

"We didn't look inside, but they were clearly labeled." This wasn't making sense. "He's missing, you said?"

"Yes, sir. Cornwall's cameras and other monitors have never sensed him, so he must have fled through the tunnels."

Mention of the tunnels fired connections in Elam's brain. He held up a finger. "The tunnels could be important."

Sigurd glanced at him and nodded. "Speak, Resident."

"Ask her to look for an entrance to the tunnels at the Lodge. It might be under the monorail station, but it might be under the Lodge itself."

Sigurd spoke to his shoulder mike. "Did you catch that, Ms. Baak?"

"Yes, sir. I should have thought of it myself. I'll get a team right on it."

"Thank you." The craft swerved again. "We're continuing to take evasive action. Have there been missile launches?"

"No, sir. But I told the pilot to follow standard evasive procedures. You'll recall he was with the Imperial Navy and flew in the battle of Actium's Gate."

"That explains it. The onboard radars aren't up to combat standards. Discretion is the better part of valor. Keep me posted on any change in the tactical situation. And send someone back to check on those damned crates."

"Will do, sir. Baak out."

Sigurd leaned back and wiped the back of his hand across his mouth.

Elam said, "Now would be a good time to fill me in on what's really happening."

Sigurd gave him an appraising look. "I wish I knew. There'd been rumors for years about this place. The pre-Disintegration documents are fragmentary at best, but they contained hints of secret weapons research here. Seven years ago, ImpSec decided to look into it and funded Wendy Torrance's research."

Elam nodded. "From her notes, she didn't find anything. At least, not until a few months ago."

"She didn't find any direct evidence, no. But the semantic analyses of her quarterly dispatches were… disquieting. There were inconsistencies in the historical records. For example, she found secondary evidence that people remained on the planet after Cabot Industries had supposedly abandoned it."

"Secondary evidence?"

"The age of the ruins at Lansbury, for example. The buildings were still standing at least a century after the Disintegration and may have been inhabited during that time."

"That still doesn't explain why you, in particular, are here."

"That has to do with an archeological expedition to Old Earth. I mentioned fragmentary records. Last year, we found more—a cache of Grand Alliance records dealing with this place. Most of them were in military code, and our computers haven't been able to break it. But what we did find suggested they were working on a secret high-grade weapons system here, and Lansbury was the key."

Elam nodded. "So ImpSec decided they needed an agent to check it out, but in secret so as to not call too much attention to anything they might find. Still, why you?"

Sigurd shrugged. "I'm an ImpSec officer. I'm connected to the family that owns the planet. Who else would you have sent? Besides, we had whispers that bad actors were also interested in the planet, maybe for the same reason as us."

"Like the Exaltationists?"

"Bog, no. We would have come in force if we'd had a hint it was them. We thought it was one of the other great Houses, or maybe organized crime, say from Rostov."

"When the Torrances turned up dead, you must have thought I was part of it."

"Indeed."

"And now?"

"I'm relieved to report that what I read in your file makes that conclusion most improbable."

Elam chewed his lip. At least his expression confirmed the "relieved" part was true, even if he didn't exactly confirm the conclusion. It was good to know more, even if it didn't really help piece things together. "I thought the only research here had to do with terraforming the planet. That doesn't sound like a weapons system, let alone a high-grade one."

"It might have been a cover for the actual research."

"Could be." There was something about the station in the south. Something Clifford had said. "If there were people living in Lansbury for a century after the Disintegration, why did they abandon it?"

Sigurd shrugged. "We'll probably never know."

"Could this place have been visited during the Disintegration?"

"There's never been any evidence of interstellar travel after 2464 until Gregor the First found the mothballed Grand Alliance Fleet on New Arizona in 2970. Even if there were, why come here?"

Why, indeed. "Because of the sunny beaches." Wait, that was it. "Clifford said that the south power station showed activity during the mini ice ages over the past five hundred years. He said it was consistent with the drain needed for a small settlement."

Sigurd's eyes flashed. "You're right. I just ignored that, since it was so long ago. But you're thinking the residents of Lansbury might have resettled to the South Island. To the—what did Jorina call it? The Chicken Farm."

"*Ptitseferma.* Yes, that's it. Kolonel, I respectfully suggest we should redeploy to the Chicken Ranch. We might just find the keys to this place hidden there, in the unlikeliest of places."

"Keys, yes. There might be allies there too. I agree." He rose. "I'll let the pilot know."

He strode to the front of the cabin, straight and resolute. Elam sighed. He really did have a nice butt, among other desirable traits. Too bad he was an aristocrat. If they had met under other circumstances, he might even have been fun. But for Sigurd, duty and honor would always exceed heart. For Elam too, if truth be told.

Elam settled back in his seat and hooded his eyes. Allies were possible, to be sure. But allies to whom?

CHAPTER 18

Lay on, Macduff, and damn'd be him that first cries, 'Hold, enough!'

—**Macbeth**, *Act V, Scene 8.*

SIGURD SAT alone in the first row of the flitter. Conversations murmured behind him. Outside his window, wispy clouds crawled across the mossy treetops of the Western Reserve Island. Scents of coffee and sweat seeped into his nose.

The flitter began a slow, curving descent, and the world tilted. Not long now and they'd be down.

He folded his hands over his mouth. Inhale. Exhale. Breath warmed his cheeks. He closed his eyes to better imagine the landing. The thick canopy of trees had blocked both satellite imaging radars and drone cameras. Mr. Clifford's clever tricks enhancing satellite images had revealed only a shadow of what lay below. *Inhale. Exhale.* Outlines of ancient buildings. A hint of what might be farms. Or the remains of ancient farms.

Inhale. Exhale. Farms meant farmers. His intuition screamed *danger.* There had to be someone here. This was too much like the ambush at Hereot's Point on Hekate.

Concentrate on now, not the past. He set his lips and considered. Elam said this agricultural station was the key. He seemed so confident. Elam had more combat experience than Sigurd, but Elam also didn't know everything. Still, his argument felt right.

A chime sounded, and the pilot's voice came over the cabin's speakers. "Please secure for landing. We'll be on the ground in about five minutes."

The flitter righted itself, and then the world tilted again, swooping lower. Sigurd's ears popped, and a hollow formed in his stomach. He tightened his seat belt and hardened his features. It's not fear. It's just the descent.

He wiped sweaty palms on his trousers and the microphone at his throat. "Mr. Knudson. I'll want your team prepared to deploy in a defensive perimeter as soon as we're down. Don't wait for my command."

Knudson didn't answer, but the hushed sound of orders, the click of weapons' checks, and the rustle of troops adjusting their packs assured compliance more than any verbal response could.

The flitter jittered and bounced. The ground rushed up. Blurry details turned sharp. What had been hints of grids resolved to sharp fence lines and golden fields of grain. A concrete structure squatted under the trees about thirty meters from where they were to land. It was a copy of the monorail terminal they'd seen at the marine base, including a wide opening that had led underground. Clifford had been right and had pinpointed where to land.

The whine of the engines intensified, and just like that, they were down. The cabin depressurized, and Sigurd's ears popped again. Knudson pushed the rear door open, and the ramp deployed with a thump. In seconds, his team was on the ground, weapons held high and ready.

Sigurd stood and moved to the door.

Elam beat him there, and gripped Sigurd's elbow. "Wait. Let's see what Mr. Knudson finds."

Sigurd jerked away. "My place is with my squad." He took a step onto the ramp.

A sound, rather like a flock of birds, made him look overhead. Strange. There were supposed to be chickens here, but they wouldn't be overhead.

An explosion burst fifty yards away, followed by the whistle of shrapnel.

Someone shouted, "Mortars!" Elam, maybe?

No, that was Knudson. Everyone was shouting now.

"Head to the monorail terminal!" Sigurd pointed, but the team was already scampering for the shelter.

Sigurd ran back inside the flitter and to the front pilot's compartment. "Mr. Cadwalladar. We're under mortar attack. Get this thing aloft and out of here."

He raced back toward the rear, passing a seat where Clifford cowered. Of course. He was supernumerary during combat. "Stay here, Mr. Clifford," he murmured. "Fasten your seat belt. It's going to be fine."

Seconds later he jostled against Elam, who was heading back into the flitter. Elam shoved him toward the outdoors. "What the hell are you doing here? I ordered you to take shelter."

"I was following you. What the hell are *you* doing?"

The flitter's engines screamed. "No time." Sigurd grabbed Elam and pulled him off the craft. He pushed the button that initiated the sequence to close the rear door.

Another mortar blast exploded, this time less than thirty meters from where they stood. Stray pings of shrapnel blistered the side of the craft.

The backdraft from the engines blew grit into Sigurd's eyes and tore the breath from his mouth. But in seconds the flitter sprinted upward, shrinking to a sliver of gleaming reflected sunlight.

Elam grabbed Sigurd's wrist. "They're getting our range. We need to get in that bunker now."

Sigurd let Elam lead him into the shelter, but he paused at the entry.

A jet trail rose from the forest perhaps a klick or two away and arced toward the flitter. Sudden sparkles glittered behind the flitter's path as it swooped higher and to the north. The jet trail swerved and chased the sparkles instead of the flitter. The trail exploded in a puff of smoke and light.

Sigurd breathed relief. "He's away. Countermeasures worked." Thanks be that Baak had thought to jury-rig anti-radar countermeasures. She was turning out to be a surprising asset after a shaky start at their first meeting.

Elam said, "Thanks to your quick action. But you need to come inside. The next mortar round could be right here at our feet."

"Yes, of course." Sigurd trotted after Elam into the darkness.

Ten meters inside, a ramp led down. From the lights and sounds, Knudson must have led his team to the lower levels. He and Elam followed the lights.

Behind them, two explosions sounded at the entrance.

Elam said, "They seem to have found the range. Is there another way out?"

Exasperation heated Sigurd's face. "How should I know? This is better than being out in the open."

"Sorry. You're right. I wasn't criticizing, just spitballing. Thinking out loud."

Sigurd ignored him and continued to the bottom of the ramp. "Mr. Knudson. Status."

Knudson trotted up to him and saluted. "All secure, sir. No casualties. I've got two men on recon, but this appears to be the same setup as at the marine base. There's an entrance to another ramp and a deeper tunnel about ten yards ahead."

"No enemy actives?"

"Not that we've seen, sir. Other than whoever's at the other end of those mortars."

"Whoever that is, they had SAMs too. The flitter and Mr. Clifford got away free, though."

"That's good. Where will they head?"

"I don't know. I'm not going to ask, either."

Knudson's face was impassive, but tension coiled in his voice. "You're worried they've breached our communications, sir?"

"That's possible. I certainly never expected to have mortars dropped on us. Or to face an enemy with SAMs."

More explosions boomed from overhead, and dust puffed down the ramp.

Elam's mouth was a grim line. "Those weren't mortars."

Sigurd nodded. "Agreed. But if they had artillery, they'd have used it instead of mortars."

Knudson said, "Might be bombs pushed out of their flitter. I saw that on Actium. Put gasoline and gunpowder in a barrel and roll it out the rear entrance. Makes a hell of a bomb."

Elam said, "Makes the flitter vulnerable to blaster fire, too. Plays hob with maneuverability, and they have to fly low to accurately drop the weapon."

Sigurd nodded. "That explains why they used mortars first. Force us to take cover, then fly in with their flitter and bomb us."

Another explosion, louder than the others, boomed. Elam's ears popped. Broken concrete crumped overhead, and the upward tunnel turned dark. "Mr. Knudson." His voice sounded like he was underwater. "Have someone check the damage above."

"Yes, sir." He trotted away and spoke to a trooper, who put his helmet back on and scrambled up the ramp.

Knudson returned. "We should go into the lower level, sir. Where the tunnel is t."

Sigurd nodded. "I think so too. I want to make sure we won't be followed."

The trooper returned and trotted up to the group. "Sir, I don't know what they used, but the roof has caved in. The entrance is completely blocked by concrete rubble. There's no way out." The man kept his voice steady, but his face was pale and his eyes wide.

Sigurd gripped the man's shoulder. "Mr. Jeter. Thanks for your report. We're not trapped. We're in a monorail station, even though the surface rails never got built to here. There are tunnels connecting all of the stations, including this one. That's our way out. We can walk all the way to the Lodge if we have to."

Jeter nodded. "Yes, sir. Good to know, sir."

Sigurd squeezed his shoulder one more time and then turned to Knudson. "Mr. Knudson, move your squad to where the tunnels start. Mr. Vandreren and I will follow you shortly."

"Sir. Yes, sir." Knudson saluted, and he and Jeter departed.

Elam's gaze didn't exactly comfort Sigurd. "You have advice for me, Mr. Vandreren?"

"Call me Elam. No. You're doing fine. Superb, in fact. Especially since you're not accustomed to combat. I wonder if you've even ever been in command during a battle."

Sigurd's face heated. "What the hell are you talking about?"

Elam shrugged. "Oh, you've got the training. And your actions show both tactical awareness and leadership. You stayed calm, saved the flitter and the pilot, and then saved yourself. And me. You knew Jeter's name, sensed his fear, and reassured him in exactly the right way. You've shown bravery, intelligence, and compassion. But I bet you've never had to do this before. At least, not when you don't have backup."

"Listen, you insufferable asshole—"

Elam held up his hand. "You don't understand. I'm not criticizing, I'm admiring you."

Sigurd glared at him. "In the future, I'll thank you to admire me in silence."

Elam pressed his hands together and touched his forehead. "Your desire is my command, Your Grace."

"Don't call me that."

"What should I call you?"

The first word that popped into Sigurd's head took his breath away. *Lover.* That was the last thing needed on this mission. Why did this man torment him so? "Call me Sigurd. I've told you before."

"Very well, Sigurd. May I inquire as to your plan?"

Truth be told, he had no plan. "Follow the tunnels to the south power station. There should be gear there that lets us securely communicate with Ms. Baak and the Lodge. That's why I brought Mr. Clifford along, to have him check the computer records there."

Elam raised an eyebrow. "You mean the anomaly he found in the old records. During the mini ice age."

"Exactly."

"Good plan. Mr. Clifford's smart. I bet that's where he and the flitter wind up." He beamed at Sigurd and clasped his shoulder. "Lead on, and accursed be he who first calls, hold, enough."

That sounded familiar, somehow. It didn't matter. What mattered was Elam's touch and the electric thrill it sent down his back. What the hell was wrong with him?

CHAPTER 19

ELAM SLOGGED through the shadowed tunnel, last in the line of Sigurd's would-be warriors. Well, at least some of them were genuine warriors, no doubt ones he handpicked to accompany him. Or maybe his father, the Margrave, had handpicked them. But at least half were just crew from a minor trade ship and untrained in the military arts.

The tunnel was similar to the ones he'd been in before, except this one felt different somehow. For one thing, the lighting didn't automatically turn on and off as they advanced. That could be from the damage caused in the mortar attack, but that should have been localized. This was more like someone, or something, had shut off the automated system.

The lead elements of the column stopped, and murmured conversation reached back. Elam frowned and pushed ahead to see what was going on.

The tunnel opened into a room, perhaps fifteen meters square, with a flat ceiling instead of the tunnel's reinforced arch. A guardsman's light illuminated a set of rungs embedded in the wall and leading to what looked like a hatch in the ceiling. A puddle of brackish water pooled at the base of the ladder.

Elam approached Sigurd and asked, "What's up?"

"Not sure. We're about halfway to the south power station, so we should be underneath the strait that separates the eastern and western Reserve Islands."

Elam glanced at the ceiling and then back at the water. "You think it's leaking?" That couldn't be good.

"No. But I think someone used that hatch recently."

Sigurd wasn't one to jump to conclusions, but that seemed a stretch. "Evidence? You don't think it opens directly into the strait?"

Sigurd shook his head. "Of course not. There'd be an airlock of some kind." He ranged his lights over the walls and ceiling. "There's zero evidence of structural damage. The epoxy seal sprayed on the walls is intact. The water itself is salty, like it's from the ocean."

Elam frowned. "Five hundred years is a long time for a seal to last, even for the ancients."

"I thought of that. Someone has been maintaining this part of the tunnel, like it was important to them. There are underwater tunnels like this on Elsinore, under Thuistadt Bay. They refresh the epoxy every ten years. This might be a different mix, but it's been refreshed sometime in the last decade or so."

"How is that possible?" Elam rubbed his forehead. "The intelligence on this place must be total crap."

"Agreed." Sigurd straightened his back and called out, "We're taking a fifteen-minute break. We're halfway to the south power station, where we should find proper quarters."

A young woman with lithe muscles and short raven-black hair approached Sigurd. "Sir, permission to speak."

"What is it, Corp—Able Mariner Oates?"

Elam pretended to miss Sigurd's slipup. Sigurd must be fatigued to use the woman's military rank.

"Sir, it's been six hours since we started." Her mouth twisted, and her body squirmed.

"Yes. That's why we're breaking."

"Uh, sir, some of us are experiencing hydraulic pressure, if you catch my meaning."

"Oh, yes. Of course. I should have thought of that."

Knudson was standing by, listening, and said, "Sir, if I may be so bold, I found heads just inside the next corridor."

"Excellent. Five more minutes while the crew take advantage of the facilities. Please let them know, Mr. Knudson."

Knudson took charge of the squad and organized lines to the heads. Elam quirked an eyebrow at Sigurd and muttered, "You can't know what we'll find when we get there. More mortars? Whoever's been maintaining this tunnel? Maybe even whoever killed the Torrances."

Sigurd kept his voice low. "No reason to spook the crew. The marines I brought with me have already figured it out. What the others don't know won't hurt them, for now. Besides, with Exaltationists on the planet, who killed the Torrances is the least of our worries."

"Their murders just as we arrived can't be an accident. It has to all be connected somehow. But I don't see how Exaltationists could have done it and gotten away. I mean, we found Jack Torrance just minutes after he was killed. Cornwall should have seen something, but someone had turned off his sensors. It's not clear how they could have done that without Cornwall knowing."

"I agree they probably didn't kill him, or at least not by themselves. But you didn't kill him either. Mr. Bender would have seen you, if nothing else. Also, Torrance didn't kill his wife. The least hypothesis conclusion is that there was someone else on the planet in addition to any Exaltationists. Someone who knew how to disable Cornwall's surveillance without leaving a record. Someone with detailed knowledge of the security systems."

Elam snorted. "Well, I'm glad you've ruled me out."

Sigurd narrowed his eyes, and his mouth formed a grim line. "I didn't quite say that. Someone must have tipped the murderer off. Someone with an unknown agenda. Someone who is adept with security systems. That could have been you."

"Why would I have done that? And how? I even had to borrow a phone to call in the murders."

"You've shown you have hidden abilities. Your history convinces me that whatever your motives might be, they are not, in your judgment, hostile to the Empire. But those motives are still unknown."

Rage pounded in Elam's chest. Rage, and shame, too. "Dammit, did your blasted report say what happened on Dongeradeel?"

"Just that your part in it was heroic enough to put you on the honors list. The rest was redacted."

"Heroic be damned. I betrayed someone who loved me. Someone I loved. That doesn't deserve honor. It deserves punishment." He spat out the last word and looked away.

Sigurd put a gentle hand on his shoulder, and he jerked away. "Don't. Just don't."

Sigurd's voice turned soft, even tender. He touched the *Volksnut* sigil on his cheek. "Duty, honor, heart. I know them well. I also know the torment they create when they are in conflict, one with the other."

Elam shook his head. Memory was his enemy, relentless and unforgiving. He drew a shuddering breath, then another, steadier one. "I think the break time you announced is up."

Sigurd leaned forward and whispered, his breath hot in Elam's ear. "We will speak on this again, my faithful baron." Then he pulled away, and his voice snapped with command. "Form up! Time to go."

The men and women slowly gathered their things together. In minutes they resumed their slow march through the darkness. Sigurd waited, probably so he could be the last one out of the way station, and took up position at the end of the column.

WEARINESS DRAGGED at Elam's muscles, and pain thudded between his eyes. It had been too many years since he'd trained for a forced march like this. Sigurd, damn his pretty eyes, still strode with a spring in his step. And with that damned broomstick ramrodded up his butt.

He checked his watch, which showed over twenty thousand steps since he'd reset it at the last stop. That meant they'd marched over thirty klicks. They should be close to their destination. About twenty minutes ago, the automatic lighting had started working again, casting a cold blue light along their path. Elam hesitated at a dark side passageway. Apparently Sigurd ignored it, intent on reaching the tactical objective of the power station. Still, it couldn't hurt to take a look.

He stepped into the corridor, and lighting illuminated the first thirty meters. A doorway stood open, about halfway to the shadows. Elam half expected another warehouse, like the one that Clerk Andresen had guarded, but instead he found what appeared to be a scientific laboratory, crammed with equipment. He recognized microscopes and the flasks and beakers of a chemistry lab, but what was a pyrosequencer? The place was immaculate, as if a small army of scientists were out on their coffee break.

He prowled the room, reading the labels in Old Earth English. Something called a Sequencer Mark XII from GeneTech had to be for genetic engineering. The patent notice dated it to 2412. Maybe this was where they designed that stinky wheat, except that he was pretty sure

that had been done on Earth prior to settlement. In any case, this looked
to be a high-tech genetics engineering lab, circa the twenty-fifth century.
Probably more advanced than anything the Empire of Humanity could
boast, even in the Concourse of Worlds. What was it doing here, and in
pristine shape?

No time to follow up now. Sigurd was right. Getting to the power
station was their most important objective, not doodling around with
ancient technology. He returned to the main corridor and trotted to catch
up, muscles screaming in protest. He tried to report what he'd found
to Sigurd via communicator, but the little device showed no signal.
There must be something in these tunnels blocking it. Why here, when
the communicators worked fine in the tunnels under the west power
station?

Less than half an hour later, the column came to a halt in a copy of
the latrine room they'd been in just two days ago, right before they'd met
Clerk Andresen. Great. Another bathroom break. At least his bladder still
held up. He waited until Sigurd was done talking about who-knows-what
with Knudson and then approached. "I've been thinking."

Sigurd nodded. "Always a helpful activity, especially in your case."

"Mr. Clifford was on the shuttle. We're agreed the pilot most likely
went to the south power station."

Sigurd nodded. "That makes the most sense. It was close enough
to provide relief if needed and minimized the time in air. They eluded a
SAM attack during departure."

"I saw that. The pilot must have military training. In any case, Chad,
I mean Mr. Clifford, would head for the room with the computer consoles."

"You think the south power station is set up the same as the west
one?"

"Why not? The three monorail terminals we've been in have all
been more or less the same. It looks like they just replicated the designs.
This looks like the place right before we found that old geezer under the
west power station."

"You suggest that we look for the stairwell to the power station,
then? Instead of the monorail?"

"The computer and control complex were in a different building,
joined to the monorail station by an enclosed walkway. But yeah, that's
my idea. Specifically, I suggest that I head to the computer and control
facility and you wait here with the squad. If I'm right, Mr. Clifford can

give us the tactical situation on the ground. Even if he's somewhere else, there were video feeds at the west power station that covered everywhere except the lower corridors. There are bound to be the same at the south station, and I can use them to reconnoiter."

"Reconnaissance, then. I agree. No reason to expose ourselves until we know more. I'll go with you."

Elam shook his head. "I knew you were going to say that. You're in command here. Mr. Knudson is clearly competent and can handle tactical situations, but you have to set the strategy. Besides, you're too valuable to risk until we know more."

"I've been at risk since we arrived on this planet. My personal safety has never been an issue."

Maybe not to you, you jerk. But it is to other people. Like me. "Tell you what. Send someone with me. Maybe that mariner who spoke to you. Oates. She seemed competent." *So much the better, since your slip revealed she's ex-military.*

"Sharon Oates. She's a good choice. We sparred with each other in the *Zuiderkruis* gym on the way here. She can hold her own." He pursed his lips and mused, "She can be a relay back to here too. That way we maintain radio silence."

"Good plan. But something's blocking the communicators in these tunnels. I tried earlier."

Sigurd lifted an eyebrow. "Aren't you a fountain of information." He shrugged. "Let me speak to her and Mr. Knudson."

"Wait. One more thing."

Sigurd scowled, and his mouth turned down. "What is it?"

"About thirty minutes back, I peeked in a side corridor. About the same relative place where we found the geezer."

"Confirming your hypothesis about the layout. Go on."

"Well, what I found was a lab of some kind. I didn't poke around much, but at least one piece of gear was for gene sequencing. I tried to tell you via communicator, but that's when I found out the signal was blocked."

"Interesting, I suppose. Except for the communicators, not relevant to the tactical situation, though. Unless you think someone was there?"

"No sign, although the lab was immaculate. Like the researchers had just stepped out for coffee. I just thought you should know. It's another thing we'll need to check out eventually. Remember, this whole southern area was part of a big research project. It might be exactly what you came here to find."

"Right. Once we're secure, we can follow up. You're done?"

"That's it."

Sigurd nodded to him and strode to Knudson. Left alone, Elam decided to use the facilities. It wouldn't hurt to take a go-pill while he was at it. When he finished, he returned to where the squad had gathered. He found Sharon Oates, and she stood to greet him. "G'day, sir. Mr. Vandreren. The kolonel asked me to join you on a recon mission."

Why emphasize his name? Her micro-expressions showed she was hiding something, not flirting with him. At least she wasn't threatening. He gave her his best "I'm-in-charge" smile and extended his hand. "Call me Elam, please, Able Mariner Oates."

"I'm Sharon."

He let her crush his fingers. She was fit, that was for sure. "I think this must be just like the west power station. I've been there before, so I'm pretty sure I know where we're going."

"Works for me, Elam." She hefted her rifle. "I'm ready for anything."

"With any luck, we won't need that, but it's good to know you're prepared. Just follow me."

He reentered the tunnel and headed toward where the staircase should be. At least there were no damned cats underfoot. The lights came on and off as they progressed, so those were working again.

Sharon muttered, "Any way to stop those lights, sir? It's like they're announcing we're coming."

"I could probably do it at the control console, where we're headed, but not from here. Don't worry. With any luck, we won't meet anyone."

When they came to the ascending staircase, Elam stopped and listened. Silence. He held a finger to his lips and started a silent climb upward. Sharon mimicked his soft steps. Good. Her attention to tactics confirmed what Sigurd had let slip about her military rank.

At the top of the stairs, he followed the corridor and the scent of coffee to an open door. Chad lounged in front of a screen that showed the rest of the crew gathered in front of the latrines on the lower level. He whirled about, and relief flooded his features. "Elam! I knew you'd rescue me."

Elam relaxed at Chad's familiar face. He was right there, just as expected. Elam twisted his mouth into a wry grin and said, "I try to please. What's the situation?"

Chad's eyes shifted to the floor, and he shuffled his feet. "Not good. Terrible, in fact. I think the flitter pilot, Mr. Cadwalladar, might be dead. He held those Exaltationist bastards off while I escaped. If he's lucky, he's dead. Otherwise, they've been torturing him, the poor bastard."

CHAPTER 20

Three things cannot be long hidden: the sun, the moon, and the truth.

—*the Buddha*

SIGURD SCOWLED as he backtracked along the corridor to the branch that he'd bypassed on the march to the power plant. That blasted Elam, telling him what to do. No matter that he was right. He couldn't abandon his command to recon an unknown site. But he could damned well go back and look at a dark corridor they'd bypassed.

"Beggin' your pardon, sir, but exactly what are we lookin' for?" Calpham adjusted his pack as he huffed alongside Sigurd.

Sigurd slowed his pace before he answered. "If I knew, we wouldn't be here, Corporal."

He panted, "Thought we weren't supposed to use ranks, sir."

He'd slipped. Sloppy. "It's just us, Corporal. No harm done. But you're right. I knew I could rely on your discretion when I handpicked you for this mission, back on Elsinore."

"Yes, sir. After the campaign on Actium, I'd follow you anywhere."

"Thank you, Corporal." He stopped at the entrance to the branch corridor. At least there were no cats underfoot. "I doubt we'll encounter anyone, but be ready."

Calpham hefted his rifle and gave him a curt nod.

Sigurd stepped into the corridor, and the overhead lights flashed on. He gestured to the first open doorway, where bright lights spilled into the corridor. The faint sounds of footfalls broke the cave-like silence that shrouded them.

Sigurd held a finger to his lips and crept forward, Calpham at his side. He flattened himself to the corridor's wall just outside the door and paused. Someone was definitely on the other side, moving about.

Sigurd pulled his communicator out and turned on the camera. He squatted and stuck an edge around the doorjamb. Someone was there all right. A tall, spare figure with gray hair, wearing pressed khaki slacks and a white lab coat.

Sigurd peered at the man's features and pressed the button to take a photo. He cradled the phone in his hand and expanded the image. It couldn't be, but it was. The man was Clerk Andresen, but instead of a ragtag Syndicate jumpsuit, his clothes were clean and pressed. As if he were working in a lab at a university. What the Chaos was he doing here? And how did he get here?

Sigurd held a hand up and then pointed to the ground to tell Calpham to stay put. Then he sauntered into the lab and said, in a casual tone, "Mr. Andresen. So nice to see you again."

The man whirled about and dropped the flask he had been examining. It shattered in a thousand glittering pieces on the immaculate floor. His eyes bulged and his face turned ashen, but his voice was steady and firm. "Kolonel. Yes, it's an unexpected pleasure. How are you?"

"I've been better, thank you. What are you doing here? And how in Chaos did you get here?"

"I'm checking on an experiment in my lab, of course. I got here the same way as you, I imagine. Through the tunnels."

"You walked here? That's what, over eight hundred klicks?"

All signs of surprise had vanished from his features. Instead, amusement danced from the crinkles about his eyes. "Hmm. Klicks, you say? That's about five hundred miles, as I recall. That's about right."

"It took us a day to walk here from the Chicken Ranch. No way you walked that distance."

"Yet here I am." He nodded to the door. "Will you ask your friend to join us? Mr. Vandreren was his name, as I recall. I had hoped to meet him again too."

"He's not here." Whoever Andresen was, he certainly wasn't the harmless halfwit he'd pretended to be on their first meeting. No reason to reveal to him the status of Sigurd's reserves. "Corporal, it's all right. Please join us, but keep your weapon at the ready."

"Sir, yes, sir!" Calpham strode into the room and stood beside Sigurd, his rifle held cross-ways but his finger on the trigger.

Andresen's eyes twinkled. "A corporal, you say? An honorable rank. My name is Clerk Andresen. May I inquire as to yours?"

Calpham glared at him in silence.

Sigurd touched his shoulder. "It's all right, Noah. Tell him. The truth, not our cover."

"Sir, my name is Noah Calpham, Lance Corporal in the Margrave's Corsairs."

"Pleased to meet you, Lance Corporal. The Corsairs, you say? Impressive."

Sigurd narrowed his eyes. "What do you know of the Corsairs?"

"I know what's in the records of the *Zuiderkruis*, among other sources." He gestured toward the door. "There's a lounge a few steps away. Coffee and cold drinks. Perhaps we would be more comfortable there?"

"This is fine. For now. You said this was your lab?"

"Yes."

"What do you do here?"

"This lab? I suppose you would call it genetic engineering."

"There are other labs?"

"Of course. We're not uncivilized, after all."

"We? Are you an Exaltationist?"

Andresen's eyebrows crawled up his forehead. "You mean the cultists who bombed the monorail station at Ptitseferma? No, we have managed to free ourselves of that particular form of human weakness."

Sigurd scowled. The man seemed unable to come to a point. "Then who in Chaos are you?"

"We're the descendants of those the Grand Alliance Left Behind, during the Great Disintegration."

Left Behind. His enunciation implied the capital letters. That fit with what they'd found in the archeological dig on Old Earth. "Miners, then? Employees of Cabot Industries? How many of you were there?"

"Really, my dear kolonel, is this relevant right now? The cultists are gone for the moment, but they will be back. Their obsessions make them relentless. And cruel."

Sigurd hesitated. The immediate tactical situation was more important than ancient history. "How did you get here? You couldn't have walked."

"No. I used a tram, of course. It took less than a day. I often travel between here and there. For the cats, among other reasons."

Trams! Cats be damned. He could use trams to evacuate everyone to the Lodge and consolidate his forces. "How many trams are here?"

"Maybe a half dozen or so." He shrugged. "I haven't counted recently."

"Enough to transport ten people and their equipment, then."

"Yes. Is that the size of your contingent?"

"Who else is here besides you?"

"Whoever you brought with you, of course."

"Dammit, who else? Answer my question!"

"There are about fifty researchers currently in these labs and the associated underground quarters." He tipped his head. "Feel free to take the trams in the garage. We can always call up more."

"Call up more? How many more?"

He shrugged. "As many as we might need." His voice took on a tone of command. "Lear, what is the current inventory of working trams?"

A hologram of a spare elderly figure dressed all in black appeared. It spoke in a firm tenor with a twang reminiscent of New Oxford on Baardalân in the Concourse. "Two hundred and thirty-six are currently operational. Would you like me to display locations?"

"That won't be necessary."

So, there was another AI on the planet. How could Mr. Clifford have missed that? Sigurd frowned and recalled something Clifford had said. He hadn't missed it after all. "How many survivors from the past are there altogether?"

Lear cocked an eyebrow at Andresen. "Sir?"

"Go ahead. He may as well know."

"The current census is two thousand, four hundred and thirty-eight."

"And you stayed hidden all that time?"

"No one cared enough to look for us. We're mostly on the islands."

That made sense too. The Praetorian Syndicate was only interested in the mining facilities, and later in the potential of the planet as a gateway to beyond the local group.

"Why did you stay hidden?"

"We've been left alone for five hundred years, ever since we were Left Behind. We'd like that to continue."

"Not likely with the Exaltationists snooping around."

"Indeed. We have decided an alliance with you might be in our mutual best interests."

There was s that "we" again. "What do you mean?"

"The cultists are clearly a danger. They killed the poor Torrances. They even killed one of us. I believe you found Enos on the beach?"

The crispy critter. "He was one of you?"

"Yes. Like me, he was a Watcher."

"So you were spying on us at the east power plant?"

"Spying is so pejorative. Really." He snuffled. "But yes. I assumed a persona to interview you. I must say your empathy and compassion were impressive. Your intelligence was even acceptable too."

Compassion be damned. "What happened to the weapons we saw stored there?"

Andresen's eyes widened, and his voice took on an innocent tone. "What weapons?"

"In the crates. Surface-to-air missiles and other gear, dating from the old Grand Alliance."

"Perhaps there were no crates, Kolonel. Perhaps what you saw was but an illusion."

"Bullshit." That was no illusion. "Allies don't lie to each other."

"The truth, then. We've made some advances in holography. If you're not convinced, I could have Lear make something disappear. Say this gene sequencer." He placed his hand on a bulky piece of equipment and nodded to the AI. It flickered out of existence.

Calpham shuddered, and his voice shook. "Sir, where did it go?"

Sigurd sneered. "It's a cheap parlor trick. I've seen better illusions at the Strelitz Theater on Elsinore." He turned back to Andresen. "I'll have reinforcements here soon. Then I won't need allies."

Andresen moved his hand, and the device reappeared. "Allies can be useful, especially with a foe as relentless as the one we both face. Perhaps another demonstration would be helpful." He looked around the lab and picked up a shiny metal pipe roughly a meter in length.

Sigurd tensed. "What are you going to do with that?"

"Make a point." Andresen handed it to him. "Test it. See if you can bend it. It's tempered carbon steel."

Sigurd tested it. "Of course I can't bend it."

Andresen reached for it, and Sigurd handed it back. The erstwhile clerk gripped one end in each hand and, seemingly without effort, bent it into a *U* shape, then with a thumb and forefinger squeezed one end closed. "Nothing to it."

Sigurd stared at him, and the pieces suddenly fell into place. Ancient high-tech weapons research. Cat colonies surviving over centuries. Genetic engineering. Even the genetic drift in dust mites suddenly fit into the big picture.

A smile trifled with Andresen's lips. "Yes, my kolonel. I see that you begin to understand at last."

Sigurd could only stare at him in horror.

CHAPTER 21

Love, not time, heals.

—Andy Rooney, 20th Century Journalist

ELAM PINCHED his lips, and his chest tightened. *Dead.* He'd barely exchanged two words with Ned Cadwalladar. He'd lost comrades in arms before. It wasn't his fault. He wasn't even in command. Why did one more matter?

Maybe that was the problem. It was yet one more gone. His reaction had to be an echo of what happened on Dongeradeel. Or maybe the go-pill was messing with his emotions. He inhaled a calming breath, held it for a count of ten, then released it.

Chad gaped at him. When he spoke, his voice had a quiver. "Are you all right?"

"I'm fine. Are you sure he's dead? Cornwall, locate Mr. Cadwalladar."

Nothing happened.

Chad looked at his keyboard, at his boots, at the floor. "Cornwall's not here."

"What? No telemetry inside the power station? I thought you pulled data from here on power consumption during the last ice age."

"I did, remotely via the console at the east power station. But here, Cornwall's not responding anywhere. He's upstairs and outside, but not here. He turned on the lights for us there when we arrived. But he's not down here like he was at the east power station." His fingers rattled the keys. "Weirdest thing. I'm pretty sure there's a different AI down here, from code snippets I found in the server. But I don't know the call word. I managed to do some stuff manually, like turning on the lights down here. I found the kolonel's team on the monitors too. But no Cornwall. And no AI I can call up."

He stroked the mouse pad, and one of the screens facing him flickered. A window opened, showing a body crumpled in a bed of petunias near a sidewalk.

Chad pointed. "I managed to bring up this video feed. He's not moved in over an hour."

"That's outside the power station?"

"Yeah."

"Any other movement? Are there still hostiles around?"

"Not that I've seen. Cornwall would know, but I can't ask him."

Elam turned to Sharon. "Mariner Oates, I'm going to check on Mr. Cadwalladar's status." He narrowed her eyes. "You look pale. Are you all right?"

Her gaze locked on the screen showing Cadwalladar's still form. "He's not dead, is he? Tell me he's alive."

He touched her hand. "We'll know soon enough. I'll do whatever I can for him. The best thing you can do right now is to stay here and monitor the situation. At the first sign of hostiles, you and Mr. Clifford are to retreat at once and report back to the kolonel."

"Sir—"

"Those are orders, Able Mariner."

She continued to stare at Cadwalladar's still form on the monitor. "Sir, if Ned's still alive, he'll need treatment. I've got a standard-issue first aid kit. It's even got the latest in nanodocs."

Of course. The nanotech miracles, common in the medical facilities of the ancients, had only been replicated for mass use in the last five years, after his retirement. He should have realized Sigurd would have the best. "Can I have your kit, please?"

"You know how to use it?" She pulled it out of her pack and handed it to him.

"I thought you just put the injector next to the skin and pushed a button?"

"Yes, sir. Not directly on a wound, though. Hold it in place for a count of ten. And no more than four injections in twenty-four hours."

"Got it." That was consistent with what he'd read. He accepted the white bandolier with a red cross on it and hung it from his left shoulder. He kept his rifle in his right hand. "Thanks. These nanodocs can work miracles."

"I know that, sir. Do what you can. Ned, I mean Mr. Cadwalladar, he's... well... he's special." She blinked back what had to be tears.

He put a hand on her shoulder and squeezed. "Sharon, maybe he's just knocked out. There's no overt signs of trauma." He almost said no blood, but that wouldn't have been exactly comforting. He patted the first aid bandolier. "We've got the most recent technology the Empire has to offer. I promise, I'll do my best for him." He squared his shoulders. "You've got your orders."

"Yes, sir. Thank you, sir." She straightened her back and firmed her features.

Chad looked him in the eye and declared, "I'm not going anywhere. I won't leave you alone out there. At the very least, I should stay here and continue to monitor the situation. We can use communicators to keep in touch. And I can come to your assistance if needed."

"No communicators! Radio silence. We don't want any hostiles to know we're here. And I will not permit one more person to be put at risk until we know it's safe. You will leave if I give the signal."

Chad leaned forward and held his head high. "I am not leaving you out there alone."

Amateurs. Like leading an army of kittens, all fury and no sense. "I give up. Ms. Oates, you've got your orders."

She squared her shoulders. "Roger that, sir."

Roger, not wilco. So she understood but didn't promise to comply. No time to argue. "Mr. Clifford. Watch the video for my signal. Thumbs up means no hostiles, down means retreat. And this is your post, Mr. Clifford. Do not abandon it unless hostiles appear, in which case you are to retreat."

Elam left at a quick trot, grateful for the go-pill despite the side effects. There'd be a price to pay later, but for now he felt like a twenty-year-old again. He bounded up the stairs and paused at the top, back to the wall, just outside the doorway, listening. Nothing. He squatted down and used the camera on his communicator to peek into the interior of the next room.

Nothing. So far, so good.

He slipped into the hallway and stopped at the first door he came to. Still no sound. He squatted low, eased the door open, and waited.

Nothing again.

The camera on his communicator showed an empty room. Excellent. He entered, closed the door, and whispered, "Cornwall, be discreet, but I need you."

Cornwall's familiar, archaic accent whispered from nowhere, "Elam, what a surprise to find you here. How may I serve you?"

"Are there any hostiles around?"

"If you mean is there anyone in your vicinity, sir, I'm unable to say. I have no telemetry to the sublevels at the station. The above-surface levels are empty except for Pilot First Class Ned Cadwalladar. He was injured eighty-four minutes ago by uniformed personnel unknown to me. Would these be the hostiles you mentioned?"

"Yes. Are they still around?"

"They are no longer in the immediate vicinity of the station. Eight of them arrived by flitter two hours and eighteen minutes ago. They initiated a firefight with Mr. Cadwalladar, in which he was injured. They subsequently did something to his flitter, then departed in their own."

Elam breathed a sigh of relief and asked in a normal tone, "How is Cadwalladar? Is he still alive?"

Cornwall whispered back, "He is still breathing, sir. Respirations are thirty-two per minute. Telemetry is insufficient to deduce heart rate."

Alive, thank Chaos. "You can stop whispering. Where did the hostiles go? And could you identify their flitter?"

"Radar shows that they are two hundred and twelve klicks west of here, on a westerly bearing at approximately four hundred kph."

Cornwall should have seen their approach. Something was wrong here. "Why didn't you warn Mr. Cadwalladar about them coming?"

"No one told me to monitor the telemetry over the southern islands, sir. Sensors recorded their approach, but I wasn't aware of them until after the firefight started."

Damned literal-minded AI. All the information in the world was useless without a human brain to think about it. He hitched at the first aid bandolier hanging from his shoulder and headed back toward the outside. "Cornwall, how far is it to Mr. Cadwalladar?"

"He's one hundred and thirty-four meters due north of the main entrance, on the edge of the landing field. The field itself is covered with *Viola Cabiotorum*."

More useless jibber-jabber from Cornwall. "You never answered my question about the identity of the hostile flitter."

Cornwall, unperturbed, responded, "You interrupted me before I could, sir. Do you want an answer now?"

"Dammit, yes!"

"Very good, sir. Regarding the unidentified flitter, I have reviewed historical telemetry retained in my memory. It took off from the southeastern coast of Bountiful, then landed briefly at Ptitseferma before proceeding to here. I tentatively matched the flitter using files downloaded from the *Zuiderkruis*. I cannot say why a merchant ship had military intelligence in its memory banks, but since it was new to me, I kept it."

Bountiful. The main island. As far as he knew, no one had ever been there, so it made a reasonable hideout for an advance force. Still no answer to the basic question, though. "What'd the files tell you about the flitter?"

"It is a close match to ones manufactured on Uzvišeni and used in the Dongeradeel conflict."

Uzvišeni. That meant it was the Exalted, all right. That was their main industrial planet. What in Chaos were they doing here, anyway? While he trotted down the corridor, he pulled out his communicator and punched in Oates's code.

She answered at once. "Mr. Vandreren. I thought we were to maintain radio silence."

"I've spoken with Cornwall. The hostiles are hundreds of klicks away. Too far to pick up these low-power transmissions. Good news. Cornwall reports that Mr. Cadwalladar is still alive and breathing. I'm on my way to provide first aid now."

Even over the communicator, relief showed in her voice. "Thank you for letting me know, sir. He's, well, he's special to me."

"I got that, Sharon. I promise I'll do my best for him. What you can do right now is return to the squad and report to the kolonel. Tell Mr. Clifford he's to stay at his station, at the console."

"Will do, sir." Worry still strained her voice. "How about Ned? I mean Mr. Cadwalladar?"

"I'm on my way with your first aid kit. He'll be fine. Like I said, I've seen those nanodocs work miracles." Actually, he'd only seen ads from the manufacturer, but there was no reason to add to her worries.

"I've seen too, sir. I know you'll do your best. Uh, I'm not supposed to say, but I was on Dongeradeel. You always do your best, sir."

Chaos. That confirmed she was part of Sigurd's covert military force. Worse, she recognized him. He thought she looked familiar. "Thank you, Corporal. Be discreet, please."

"You don't have to worry about me, sir. Anything else?"

"Just be firm with Mr. Clifford. I'm sure it's safe, but we need his expertise at the console. Tell him to see if he can figure out why Cornwall is active on the surface but not below deck."

"Yes, sir. May I use the communicator to report to the kolonel?"

"You can try, but the tunnels seem to block the communicators. If you can't reach him by communicator, it's important you brief him in person."

"Understood, sir."

He closed the connection while running across the landing field. Another puzzle. Why did the communicators fail in the local tunnels when they worked in the tunnels below the east power station? Every anomaly was important, but right now he had to get to Cadwalladar.

Low-lying purple and orange flowers covered the place. He'd seen them before, in the palace gardens. They were a favorite of the Margravina. Petunias. Cadwalladar lay twisted in a golden bed of blooms.

He was still breathing, thank Chaos. Pulse fast and fluttery. No blood. Pupils fixed and dilated. Elam attached a monitor from the first aid kit to his wrist and checked the readout. Blood pressure normal, elevated breath rate, elevated temperature. Probably a concussion, but hard to tell what else without moving him.

Time for the nanodocs. He pulled out the injector pen, dialed up a 1mg dose, and pressed it against the man's arm. It gave a little jut, but otherwise nothing showed.

It would take fifteen minutes or more for the self-replicating tiny robots to analyze his injuries and start to enhance his body's natural healing mechanisms. At least that's what the commercials said.

Elam knelt by Cadwalladar's side and held his hand. The man's eyes rolled under closed lids.

Elam stroked his brow and murmured, "Everything's going to be fine, Ned. You're going to wake up, and your friends will all be with you. Sharon sends her love."

Ned's lips moved, but no sound came out.

Elam's hands trembled, and a sudden cold sweat made him shiver despite the warm sunlight. It must be a reaction to the go-pill. Not good to have one so soon. Maybe he should inject himself with nanodocs to counter the pill. But the docs might just decide to knock him out. Too risky, for now.

Besides, he'd promised Corporal Oates. Sigurd wasn't the only one who did his duty.

CHAPTER 22

The enemy of my enemy is my friend.
*—attributed to Kautilya, in the **Arthashastra**,*
circa third century BCE

TENSION COILED through Sigurd's muscles. Andresen faced him, calm and composed. He wasn't overtly threatening, but he was a freak, strong enough to bend steel.

Everything clicked in place, and a ball of ice formed in his gut. The archeological evidence from Old Home Earth said there was high-tech weapons research on this planet. He was standing in an advanced genetics lab with an orc having super-human powers. *Andresen and his peers were the result of that weapons research.* Genetically engineered supersoldiers. It had to be.

He placed his palm over his holster but didn't draw his handgun. His breath came in short puffs, and by force of will alone, he did not shudder. He kept his voice flat, emotionless. "What are you? An Übermensch?"

Andresen flashed a grin and snorted. "Hardly. Certainly nothing über about me. I'm just a man, much like you. Maybe a little stronger. Perhaps with slightly better endurance. But just a man."

"One with genetically engineered enhancements."

"Yes. Inherited in my case, but at a cost. I'm more susceptible to certain degenerative diseases, for example."

"Just to be clear. You're the end result of the high-tech weapons research the ancients were doing here. You and the other two thousand like you who are hiding away on this planet."

"That's only partly right, Kolonel. There were fifty genetically engineered fetuses ready to be decanted at the start of the Great Disintegration. Thirty-six survived to adulthood."

"That doesn't sound like enough for long-term survival. In fact, I'm sure it's not."

"You're correct. But there were over a thousand scientists and technicians who were Left Behind, along with a few dozen Grand Alliance marines. We are collectively the Left Behind."

"'Left Behind.'" As before, the capitals were clear from how he pronounced it. "Is that what you call yourselves?"

He shrugged. "It fits."

"Two thousand supermen is… impressive." And threatening.

"You misunderstand. The Left Behind are mostly just normal humans, like you'd find on any other planet. Almost all of the original bioengineered traits were recessive and involved multiple genes. Very few are still expressed in today's population. For example, there are fewer than ten of us like me, with enhanced strength, and we're subject to certain other health problems."

"That's reassuring." Of course, he could be lying. Sigurd kept his palm on his pistol. "I think you mentioned an alliance?"

A slow smile bent Andresen's lips, and his posture relaxed. "Yes. The cultists threaten both of us. In fact, they threaten everyone who is unlike them. We have deployed Watchers near their camps. We can tell you where the cultists are, and how many there are."

"How about their weapons?"

"That too."

"How many of your people are soldiers?"

"We have no need for soldiers, being so few."

Andresen's face stayed impassive, but something in his tone and posture gave Sigurd pause. Even a couple of thousand people needed law enforcement. In any case, even a small number of allies improved the tactical situation, so much in fact that the immediate benefit of cooperation exceeded the longer-term risk. "Can you show me where the trams are?"

"Of course."

"Let's start there." He waved to the door.

"Does this mean we are allies?"

"Yes." *At least for now.*

Thirty minutes later, Sigurd, Andresen, and Calpham rejoined the squad in the tunnels. Knudson approached, with a worried-looking Oates in tow. "Sir, we have a situation at the power plant."

Concern opened a cold hole in Sigurd's gut. Elam was at the plant. He girded himself for bad news. "Report."

"Sir, Mr. Cadwalladar is injured, condition unknown. Mr. Vandreren left the plant interior to administer first aid and sent Able Mariner Oates here to report."

Elam was safe, then. But what about hostiles? "Mr. Vandreren went out alone? How long ago? What's the status now?"

Knudson shuffled his feet. "Sir, the tunnels block our signals. When he ordered Ms. Oates to return here, he also ordered Mr. Clifford to stay posted at the consoles in the sub-basement of the station. We don't know the current status of any of them, but Mr. Cadwalladar is of particular concern."

Sigurd caught Knudson giving Andresen a hostile glare. "Mr. Knudson, meet Mr. Andresen. He has offered us an alliance with the natives of this planet." He paused to let that sink into Knudson, then turned to Andresen. "Can your AI tell us anything? Lear, I think you called him."

Andresen shook his head. "I've queried him already. Mr. Clifford has left the console and ventured outside. He joined another man, and the two are kneeling over a third person, who appears to be injured. They are all alive, and there are no others in the vicinity."

How the Chaos did he "query" the AI? With telepathy? No time for that. "Mr. Knudson, Mr. Andresen has offered us assistance in locating trams to complete our advance to the Lodge."

Knudson turned to face Andresen. "Good to meet you, sir." He narrowed his eyes and scanned Andresen head to toe. "Thank you for your offer of assistance." His voice dripped with skepticism.

"Mr. Andresen, please give Mr. Knudson directions to the tram garage. Mr. Knudson, the squad is to proceed under full alert until we verify no hostiles are present. Ms. Oates and I will proceed to where Mr. Vandreren and Mr. Clifford are assisting Mr. Cadwalladar."

Knudson saluted and said, "Sir, yes, sir! Permission to speak, sir?"

"Granted." Dammit, why did everyone feel free to second-guess his orders?

"Sir, until we verify the tactical situation, I suggest that you should stay with the squad. With your permission, I will have Mr. Calpham accompany Ms. Oates to relieve the group on the surface."

Well, that was clear enough. Knudson had probably gotten specific orders from the Margrave regarding Sigurd's safety. Damn them both. No time to argue. Besides, he was right, despite the urgent need Sigurd felt to rescue Elam. "Very good, Mr. Knudson. Mr. Andresen can give directions to the surface. Make it happen."

Twenty minutes later, Sigurd, Andresen, and the squad, less Oates and Calpham, gathered in a subterranean garage under the power station. Sunlight slanted in from a ramp that led to the surface. Another ramp led back to the lower level and the tunnels. Cold LED lighting illuminated a dozen trams, just like the ones they'd used on arrival at the ghost port. Each tram could easily carry five troopers and all their gear.

Knudson stood next to Sigurd and Andresen, apart from the squad, which deployed to the perimeters of the room. "What's the plan, sir?"

"We'll use these to return to the Lodge via the tunnels. Mr. Andresen here says the trip to the Lodge should take a couple of hours."

Andresen said, "Maybe less. Depends on how much you push the trams."

Knudson's comm buzzed, and he brushed his shoulder. "Report."

Calpham's tinny voice came from the shoulder-mounted speaker. "Sir, Mr. Cadwalladar is still unconscious. He's been dosed with nanodocs, but the readout from the first aid kit says he needs medical attention."

Sigurd said, "Ask about hostiles."

Calpham answered. "I heard that, sir. Mr. Vandreren says that the local AI assures him there are no hostiles in the vicinity."

Sigurd frowned. "The local AI? Cornwall?"

A muffled exchange came over the speaker; then Calpham answered, "He says yes. Cornwall apparently only has above-ground telemetry, but he assures us the hostiles all departed and are still in the air, over the Western Reserve Island."

Calpham continued after a pause, "Sir, we'll need a stretcher for Mr. Cadwalladar."

Andresen raised an eyebrow. "There's a first aid closet here. Be back in a second." He trotted to a far corner of the garage and opened a door with a red cross on it. He returned with a compact object the size of a backpack. "This will unfold to a stretcher, complete with standard readouts. With your permission, Kolonel, I'll take it to the injured man and assist with his transport."

"No. Elam and Clifford might mistake you for a hostile. Mr. Knudson, have a trooper deliver the stretcher."

"Yes, sir." Knudson left and spoke to Oates, who then ran up the ramp carrying the stretcher.

Knudson rejoined Sigurd and Andresen, and Sigurd said, "Have the troops check the trams for power. We'll need five or six." One for

Cadwalladar and an attendant, one for Sigurd, Elam and Andresen, with the remainder for the rest of the troops." He wanted to speak to Andresen with Elam present, and the tram would be his first opportunity.

"Yes, sir."

Under Knudson's efficient direction, within minutes six trams were lined up and ready to deploy. As they were finishing, Elam, Oates, Calpham, and Clifford entered the garage, the latter two carrying Cadwalladar bound to the stretcher. Oates gripped Cadwalladar's hand in one of hers, concern pooling in her eyes.

When Sigurd approached, Elam said, "He's stable, but he's got some kind of traumatic brain injury that is beyond the nanodocs' capacity. I'm confident in Mr. Mustafa's skills, but he's a medic, not a physician." He glanced at Andresen, and his jaw muscles flexed like he was chewing grasshoppers. "What in Chaos is he doing here? That's the crazy old cat guy, right? Clerk something."

Irritation made Sigurd furrow his brow. "Mr. Mustafa is quite competent, I assure you, and the facilities at the Lodge are first-rate. And yes, that's Mr. Andresen. He turns out to be not quite what he first seemed." Elam started to protest, but Sigurd turned away and touched Oates's shoulder. "Sharon, would you like to ride in the tram with him when we leave?"

She turned teary eyes in his direction and answered in a tremulous voice, "Yes, please. I'd like that very much."

"I'll have Mr. Knudson see to it. He'll be safe in Mr. Mustafa's hands soon enough."

Andresen said, "I have some training in the healing arts. Perhaps I can ride with him too?"

Sigurd frowned. He'd really wanted to interview Andresen in Elam's presence. The man had an uncanny ability to detect liars. But maybe he should brief Elam first. He did have a tendency to jump off on his own. They could grill Andresen later, at the Lodge. "Very well. I'll speak to Mr. Knudson. You and Mariner Oates can travel with Mr. Cadwalladar."

Sigurd spoke with Knudson and then surveyed the flurry of activity in the garage. At least he had a plan. A good plan too. Things were better than they'd been since the mortars started their attack yesterday. Much better.

Elam stood close, and a small thrill pulsed through Sigurd. He kept his face impassive and touched Elam's shoulder. "Thank you for helping Mr. Cadwallader."

Elam shrugged him away, and Sigurd's heart sank. The man was all jittery, like something was wrong with him.

Elam snapped, "Anyone would have done that." He lowered his voice. "Things here are weird. Too weird. Mr. Clifford says he thinks there's another AI here, one Cornwall doesn't know about. And what in Chaos is that clerk doing here? I didn't even recognize him when he first showed up. Has he had a personality implant?"

"We need to talk. It's weirder than you imagine. When we leave, sit in my tram so I can brief you."

Elam didn't answer. His gaze careened around the room, and he couldn't seem to hold still. He bounced on his toes, and his hands trembled. Something was definitely off about him. When he spoke, his voice was tight with tension. "I need to brief you too. I've thought about our talk before, about the murders, and I've got some ideas." He stalked off, his back rigid. Was he angry, or had he just reverted to his usual hostile self?

Sigurd slumped, all the confidence he'd just felt evaporating. The tactical situation was better, but the strategic situation was a mess. Too many unanswered questions and not enough information. And now Elam's brusqueness had resurfaced. It was too much.

Nearby, Andresen fussed over Cadwalladar, helping to load his stretcher onto a tram. He sure looked like he was concerned for the man's welfare. His story seemed credible, but it was full of holes too. Which was the longer-term greater danger: Exaltationists or genetically engineered super-warriors? Both were potential disasters. Maybe Elam had figured out something useful about the murders, but crime, even murder, paled in comparison to the threats they now faced.

It was his duty to protect Elsinore and the Empire. That had just gotten orders of magnitude harder.

CHAPTER 23

Have goals.
Make plans. Be true
To them, but not stubborn,
For chance and fate can turn goals to
Ruin.

— ***The Missing Cinquains***, *Arpad Laszlo*

ELAM STALKED away from Sigurd on hollow legs and staggered into a latrine. Thank Chaos no one was around. His stomach roiled, and sour bile bit the back of his mouth. The muffled conversations of Sigurd's squad penetrated the room and drummed in his ears as if he were underwater. Saliva flooded his mouth. His breath came in shallow gasps, and his heart thudded.

It was that damned go-pill. The last thing he needed was a reaction now. He bent over one of the heads and barfed. Vomit seared his throat and slimed his mouth. His stomach clenched and tried to hurl again, but this time nothing came up. At least he got here in time before Sigurd saw him and figured out he'd taken a stimulant. That was routine for intelligence officers, but a court-martial offense for regulars.

Too late: Sigurd's voice sent icy jitters down his spine. "Elam! Have you been injured?"

He grunted to a standing position and wiped his mouth with the back of his hand. "I'm fine."

"You don't look fine."

Sigurd reached for him, and Elam pushed his hand away. "I'm fine, I tell you. Just a little reaction is all." He stumbled to the washbasin, cupped some water in his palms, and splashed his face.

"Reaction? To combat? I don't believe it."

Elam fumbled in the first aid bandolier and found an expandable cup. He filled it with water, washed his mouth out, and spat. Then he filled it again and gulped it down. "I've been thinking about the flitter. Are you planning to just abandon it here?"

Sigurd scowled, but then he did a double take. "You're thinking we could use it to medevac Cadwalladar, get him to the infirmary at the Lodge more quickly. I should have thought of that."

He turned back to the door, but Elam said, "Not so fast. Cornwall told me that hostiles did 'something' to the flitter before they left. They might have sabotaged it."

"What did they do?"

"We could ask him for more details, except we'd have to go upside to do that." Elam's belly twinged again, and he winced.

"Are you sure you're all right? You've still got the first aid kit. Maybe we should take a readout." He reached for the bandolier.

A readout was the last thing Elam wanted. "Waste of time. What I'm saying is we should go check it out. Most likely they put some kind of tracer on it." Or a bomb. No reason to say that one out loud.

"You're right, of course." Sigurd paused for a beat. "Let's both go check. I want to brief you on what I've learned."

Chaos, Elam just wanted to get away from Sigurd. A few minutes and he'd pull himself together. "You don't need to organize the squad for evacuation?"

"Mr. Knudson's perfectly capable. Let's go." He turned on his heel and held the door open.

Now the arrogant SOB was giving him orders. Elam clenched his teeth and stepped through the door. Without looking back, he headed toward the ramp and daylight. Let Sigurd follow *him*. After all, he was Resident and this was, technically at least, his planet.

At the threshold to the outdoors, Elam halted and said, "Cornwall."

Cornwall's stuffy image flickered in the shadows next to him. "How may I serve you, sir? Your pulse is elevated and your body temperature is above normal. Do you require medication?"

Sigurd snorted. "Even Cornwall can tell you're not well."

"Maybe I'm just pissed off at you. Cornwall, you said the hostiles did something to the flitter before they left. Do you have more details?"

"I can show you the video. But the lighting in this location is not optimal. There's a conference room inside, on the second level."

Sigurd snapped, "We're short on time. Just show us the damned video."

"Very good, sir."

Cornwall's image flickered again, and a video of the flitter replaced it. Four uniformed soldiers wearing helmets approached and climbed into the pilot's compartment of the craft.

Elam grunted. "Those are Exaltationist marines. I recognize their gear."

Sigurd stepped closer to the display. "I can't tell what they are doing. Cornwall, can you give us a close-up of the cockpit?"

The image swelled and showed a pixelated view through the window in the front canopy. Elam said, "They seem to be fiddling with the instrument panel, but the angle is all wrong." Even as they watched, the images of the hostile troops disappeared.

Sigurd said, "Cornwall, please replay at normal size, from where you expanded the image."

The normal view didn't reveal anything more. All it showed was them leaving the flitter and walking toward the cameras. Cornwall said, "Nine minutes and thirty-seven seconds later, they returned to their flitter and took off."

Elam asked, "Do you have recordings of their conversations? Anything that might give a hint of what they were doing?"

Cornwall said, "I do have a recording of their voices. The language appears to be a dialect of Shtokavian."

Elam hardened his mouth. "That's the dominant language on Uzvišeni."

Sigurd asked, "Can you translate what they said?"

Cornwall simpered, "Yes, of course."

Sigurd waited, then turned red.

Elam rolled his eyes. "You have to ask him to actually do it. But then he'll just drone on about whatever BS they were slinging. Probably about looking for the heads or complaining about their CO. He doesn't have any way to filter out the minutiae and tell us what's important. We'd have to listen to all of it."

Sigurd grimaced. "We don't have time for that."

Cornwall piped up. "Kolonel, Ms. Baak would like to speak to you. She says it's urgent." He could have been announcing teatime for all the seriousness his voice conveyed.

Whatever Baak wanted, Elam decided to take advantage of the distraction. "Take the call. I'll check out the flitter. Five minutes, tops." He trotted outside and toward where the craft was parked, about fifty meters distant.

His ears still buzzed and his stomach could be better, but the weakness in his limbs had dissipated some. The stink from the ever-present wheat didn't help, although the petunias blooming on the perimeter of the landing field seemed to have choked out some of the noxious crop. Soon, he'd need to crash and recover. That was the problem with go-pills. Handy things, but they imposed a cost.

Once inside the flitter, he scanned the instrument panel. Nothing obvious. He sat in the pilot's chair and felt underneath the panel. The nubbly surface of circuit boards met his probing fingertips, along with what were probably capacitors and who knew what else.

He squatted down, used the flashlight on his communicator, and peered at the underside of the panel. There it was. A ruddy disk about three centimeters in diameter and maybe a centimeter thick. The fine script read *portenco de deo*. God's power, indeed. Esperanto, yet another confirmation this was Exaltationist mischief.

He pursed his lips. He'd seen these before. They included a small receiver and a tiny but powerful charge, enough to blow a small hole in the circuit board and probably disable the pilot. Worse, it was almost certainly set to explode if anyone tried to pry it loose.

He could disable it, but it would take the right tools and time. So much for using the flitter.

He ran back inside to a grim-faced Sigurd, who asked, "Well, can we use the flitter?"

"It's booby-trapped. There's a micro-bomb under the pilot's control panel. I've seen them before. It's a terror weapon that's triggered by movement. They can also set it off by radio."

"Can you disarm it?"

"Sure, with the right tools and maybe an hour."

Sigurd shook his head. "We don't have time for that. We'll have to take the trams." He turned on his heel and headed back to the lower level.

Elam clenched his teeth and grabbed Sigurd's arm. "Wait a minute. What did Jorina want that was so urgent?"

Sigurd jerked his arm free. His face darkened, and his jaws muscles jumped like he'd swallowed cockroaches. "Mr. Glyndwr reports his team at the marine base is under attack. We'll need to relieve them." He jerked his arm free. "Now let me go so we can get started." He stalked away.

Elam chewed his lower lip. Glyndwr was just a merchant marine, a quartermaster by rating. He was no soldier. In fact, he was pretty sure

Sigurd had taken all of the professional military with him on this wild goose chase. Fatigue dragged at his muscles, but Elam mustered what reserves he had in order to catch up. "What do you plan to do?"

"I told you. Relieve the forces at the marine base," he snapped.

"I meant, what's your plan?"

"Plan? I don't *have* a friggin' plan. Not yet. Mr. Glyndwr's team is safe in a bunker for now. We'll have an opportunity to figure something out on the trip to the Lodge." He glared at Elam. "Assuming you're up to it." Without waiting for an answer, he continued at a fast trot down the corridor.

Elam didn't even try to keep up. No reason to expend his depleted physical resources. Besides, Knudson probably already had the squad loaded and ready for departure.

Plan. Yes, for sure they needed a plan. The Exaltationists would show no mercy to Glyndwr's inexperienced team. But he couldn't think. His head throbbed with each heartbeat, jumbling his thoughts into random noise. Even an hour of sleep would help, if Sigurd would let him. Sigurd had as much as said he wanted help planning, and for sure they needed to talk, but in his current state, he'd be worthless. *Chaos.* Sleep first, plan later. Fatigue poisoned his body even as echoes of his betrayals on Dongeradeel rattled in his brain.

Not again. Never again.

CHAPTER 24

One sees great things from the valley; only small things from the peak.

—Chesterton

SIGURD STOMPED into the garage and stopped to catch his breath. His pulse pounded, and anger flushed his body. Elam! How could one person be so annoying and so fascinating at the same time?

Knudson approached him and stopped a couple of meters away, not quite at attention. "Sir."

Sigurd took another cleansing breath and tried to calm himself. He must look awful to have an experienced NCO like Knudson acting so deferential. Disgraceful. Commanders stayed cool and calm, no matter what. "Status, Mr. Knudson?"

"Sir, all crew are boarded on trams and ready to deploy."

"Excellent. The flitter has been sabotaged and is unavailable for medical transport." Sigurd scanned the trams. "I see you've got Calpham, Sinkey, and Sridhar on point. Who rides with them?"

"I plan to, sir."

Sigurd frowned and tried to concentrate. Motion at the corner of his eye distracted him.

Elam shuffled into the garage and headed for the last tram in the line. Cadwalladar lay there, on a stretcher, with Oates holding his hand. Andresen lounged in a nearby seat, as if an emergency evacuation were an everyday event. Clifford slouched in the rear seat, his head down and his uniform a sweaty, rumpled mess. When Elam climbed into the tram and sat next to him, Clifford glanced up, reached for Elam's hand, and a wan smile bent his lips.

Of course Elam sought out Clifford. Who else? He sought out *Clifford* instead of helping Sigurd with planning, even after getting an explicit request. Screw it. He'd spend the time interviewing Andresen. Sigurd clenched his jaw, turned back to Knudson, and said, "The wounded should be the next-to-last tram. Put me in the last tram, with, say, Mr. Wiersma. Oh, and I want Andresen with me too." All the better to keep an eye on him.

"With due respect, sir, Mr. Wiersma has the least experience in the squad."

"Which is why he rides with me. Besides, he's from Dongeradeel, right?"

"Yes, sir. I'll make it happen."

"Very good, Mr. Knudson. Once you're satisfied, you have my leave to start the convoy."

"Very good, sir. According to Mr. Andresen, the trip should take roughly three hours." Doubt leaked into his voice at the mention of Andresen.

"I think we can trust his estimate. He's offered an alliance with us."

"Very good, sir. The only thing worse than having allies is not having them."

Sigurd snorted. "Churchill. I'm surprised you know the quote."

Knudson gave him a sanguine look. "What quote, sir?"

"Proceed, Mr. Knudson." Good soldiers studied history. Knudson was not merely a good soldier, he was an outstanding one.

Less than two minutes later, the convoy headed into the tunnel leading to the Lodge. Sigurd tried to relax and focus. He needed to work out a strategy to relieve Glyndwr, but he lacked data. Ms. Baak was sending drones, and he should have telemetry by the time they got to the Lodge. The obvious thing was a flitter mission, except for the danger posed by the SAMs.

Enough of that. No data. Meantime, Andresen lounged next to him, alert, observant, but quiet. "Mr. Andresen. We at last have time for a more detailed chat. Tell me about your people."

"Where should I start? Are you familiar with the Cabot Industries Trust?"

"Just what's in the NOMAD database. I know Cabot ceased to exist five hundred years ago when the rebels' asteroids hit Earth at the start of the Disintegration. Not much more. Best to assume I know nothing."

"I'll try to keep to the point. Among other things, the Trust had secret contracts for weapon development with the old United States military. They established the Ptitseferma Biological Station to carry out those contracts."

Paydirt. Maybe. "NOMAD says that the station was to develop a sustainable, earth-based ecology for Cabot's Landing. How is that a weapon?"

A sly smile bent Andresen's lips. "It's not. They did have a small ecology team as cover, but their main project involved genetically engineered humans."

Sigurd stiffened. "That's supposed to explain the strength you exhibited? That you're genetically engineered?"

Clerk's tone turned haughty. "Are you interested in the history or not? It's best if you have full background before I answer questions like that."

"The Trust must have anticipated the Great Disintegration, because they'd started closing down operations here about five years prior. But the genetic engineering project had already decanted over four dozen infants. The Trust ordered them liquidated with other project assets."

"Murdered, you mean. Children. I understood that the ancients were heartless, but not that evil."

Andresen shrugged. "Evil seems to be always lurking in the hearts of humans. But in this case, the scientists faked the records and adopted the genetically engineered toddlers. When the later orders came to completely abandon the planet, many in the research group stayed behind, in hiding. About three thousand in all never left Cabot's Landing."

"So you've been here all this time?"

"Yes. There were a few others. The marine base had a skeleton crew after the troops were deployed. The same for the navy base on Diego Garcia in the Central Sea."

"So you're descended from those who stayed behind."

"We say 'Left Behind,' since the rest of humanity abandoned us. The Great Disintegration, when it came, was over in a couple of years. Cabot's Landing was officially no longer inhabited, and so it escaped the bombardments other places suffered."

"And what of those thirty-six genetically engineered children? What happened to them?"

"They grew up, lived their lives, and died, just like every other human. But their genes persist in our population, along with some of their traits. Diluted, to be sure, but still present. Most people of European heritage on Old Home Earth carried Neanderthal genes, for example."

"You said this was a military weapons contract. Are the genes the weapons?"

"More accurately, the traits they code for were the weapons. Things like endurance, strength, reaction times, resistance to certain classes of pathogens, and so on. They tried for enhanced kinesthetics and intelligence too, but there's no evidence they succeeded."

"So supersoldiers, then."

"That may have been the purpose of the contract. Given the complexity of modern battle spaces, it seems like a dubious goal."

"Maybe for battle. But it could be great for spies."

Andresen shrugged. "We have little need for espionage. We are a cohesive social group."

Sigurd frowned. They'd started with fewer than three thousand people. "How many of you are there now?"

"Roughly two thousand, more or less. Our population is stable."

Sigurd chewed his lower lip. "How widespread are the traits? Does everyone have the super-strength you demonstrated?"

"I'm afraid I'm an anomaly in that way, Sigurd. As I told you, fewer than ten of us have enhanced strength. Based on pre-Disintegration records, some of our average capacities exceed normal, some do not. For example, our average intelligence is at least twenty points higher than the general norm. But that's similar to what you'd find in any research community, rather than from the genetic engineering."

So they were smart. "What other capacities exceed normal?"

"Our muscles appear to be more responsive to training, whether strength or endurance training. We have hobbyists who enjoy both, and their average performances are twenty to thirty percent higher than what the old records show."

So they are both smarter and stronger on average. "Are there any areas where your performance is lower?"

"Our lifespans are about five percent less than the average reported pre-Disintegration."

That made them about five percent better than the average in the Empire, about equal to the averages on New Arizona or Baardalân in the Concourse. "It seems to me that there should be more of you, after five hundred years."

"We had some setbacks, and we prefer smaller families."

"Setbacks. There was a mini ice age a while back. Is that what you mean?"

Andresen gave him a broad smile. "Yes. Like that. How did you figure that out?"

"One of our people deduced it from orbital dynamics and power plant consumption."

"A very bright person. I'd like to meet him."

"In due time." Enough on background. "You mentioned you had someone watching us. The one the Exaltationists killed."

Andresen winced. "Poor Enos. Yes. The cultists managed to use the machines designed to burn off the kelp to assault him. I hope he didn't suffer."

"I was with him as he took his last breath. I held his hand and comforted him as best I could."

Andresen stared at his empty palms. "Thank you for that."

"Was he watching earlier, when we first arrived?"

"Yes. The cultists had moved an agent overland to the Lodge, and Enos followed him. We feared they intended harm to the Torrances."

"You knew of the Torrances? Did you interact with them?"

Andresen shuddered. "Interact with them? No. You are the first outsiders we've interacted with in five hundred years. We watched the Torrances from afar. The cultists watched them too, and were less careful than us. In fact, Mrs. Torrance saw them and figured out who they were."

"Why do you say that? And how did you know the Torrances' names, if you didn't interact with them?"

"Surely you've figured out that Lear is synchronized with the AI at the Lodge." Andresen smirked. "We had access to everything Cornwall knew."

Sigurd frowned and drummed his fingers on his armrest. He'd just learned something important but couldn't quite put his finger on it. "You must have been watching the Exaltationists, too."

"Of course."

"How long have they been here?"

Andresen shrugged. "Who knows? We became aware of them about eighteen months ago. They were pretty obvious, even to Mrs. Torrance. Recently, they had been using the old marine base on the west coast, but two days ago they took their flitter and set up a base in the hills overlooking the base."

"One of our drones spotted someone in the base. Was that them?"

"Could have been. Or it could have been one of our watchers." He got a distant look, then nodded. "Yes. I see one of our watchers, Pietor, departed on leave recently. His wife was due. After the cultists left the base, it was safe for him to enter the tunnels and use them to go home."

"Why don't the cultists use the tunnels?"

"They never found them." His tone turned smug. "We couldn't have them snooping around, you know."

Sigurd frowned. How would they hide the tunnels when the entrances were in plain sight? No matter. More interesting was the claim he'd made about Wendy Torrance. "You say Mrs. Torrance figured out they were here?"

"Yes. It was in the report she and her husband prepared prior to the visit."

"In the report. You mean her husband's report? The one that's in Cornwall's memory banks?" That was impossible. He'd read the damned thing, and it was all numbers and weather data. Nothing about Exaltationists. *So he's lying.* Sigurd kept his face impassive. *May as well see what else he's going to lie about.*

"It was there, yes. That's how we knew about it. Someone has since altered Cornwall's record of it, but Lear has the original in his memory. We thought Mr. Torrance must have been the one to alter it, since there would be no reason for Mrs. Torrance to do so. No one else could have."

"Why would he have reason to do that?"

"He's a bit of a mystery to us. We never directly observed him, since he never left the Lodge. We conjectured that he might have thought her delusional. Or perhaps he was delusional. Or perhaps he was secretly in the pay of the cultists."

Sigurd rubbed his mouth. Delusional was one explanation. Bribery and treason another. But he was missing something. He could feel it.

Andresen said, "There's more."

"Go ahead."

"Enos was at the Lodge when your shuttle first arrived. Right after it landed, the cultist he'd been following entered the lobby of the Lodge, stayed for perhaps five minutes, and then ran out carrying a bloody pipe. He fled to his hideout on the beach. Less than five minutes later, a tram arrived from the ghost port and two persons entered the Lodge."

Holy friggin' Chaos. "That cultist—the Exaltationist—must have murdered Jack Torrance in those few minutes. The timing is right."

"Yes. We concluded the same. The day before, about twelve hours earlier, another of our observers saw a group of cultists lure Mrs. Torrance into an abandoned warehouse in Lansbury. Once there, they used a mining bot to kill her."

Sigurd leaned back in shock. "So the attacks were coordinated and timed for the arrival of the *Zuiderkruis*."

"So it would appear."

"Then Jack Torrance didn't mess with his wife's report. Someone else did."

"If you say so."

Andresen might be smart, but this conclusion was obvious. That was what he'd missed earlier—the murderer had to have a confederate with access to Cornwall's memory banks, erasing both the report and the video record of the lobby cameras being shut off.

It was also possible Andresen was still hiding something or not telling the truth at all. "Look. Your guy, Enos, saw this Exaltationist agent enter the Lodge at exactly the time of Jack Torrance's murder. Cornwall told us that someone had turned off monitoring of the lobby, and in fact we found a switch near the front door in the Off position. But Cornwall still should have had a record of the man entering the lobby and shutting off the switch."

"He did not?"

"He did not. No record. The cameras are motion-activated, so there should have been. There was nothing in his memory. There was a Resident's report in his memory, though. I remember reading it. It was routine, just numbers. Nothing suspicious at all."

"That's what I said earlier. Do keep up."

Sigurd was too focused on his logical chain to acknowledge the insult. "Can your AI—Lear, you said was his name?"

Andresen nodded.

"Do his memory banks duplicate Cornwall's? Can he recover the memories Cornwall lost?"

"Yes."

"Then we can at least confirm that's how the cameras got shut off."

"No doubt. Do you want me to check?"

Sigurd waved a hand. "Later, to confirm. Here's the point. Someone knew how to change the important parts of the Torrances' report. Someone also knew how to erase a critical part of Cornwall's memory. Occam's Razor says those two have to be the same someone."

A smile broadened Andresen's features. "I agree. It's so nice to be in the presence of one who's studied the ancients."

Sigurd leaned back. The mechanics of the murders were now clear, as were the identities of the murderers. The Exaltationists would have had motive, namely hiding their presence. But they must have known the mysterious deaths of the Torrances would result in an investigation. After all, that very investigation eventually resulted in discovering them. Plus, how could they have arranged to erase part of Cornwall's memory?

He frowned. They also abandoned the marine base at about the time he'd announced his plans to go there. That couldn't be coincidence either.

Back to the investigation. It *did* result in Sigurd sending the *Zuiderkruis* for reinforcements from the Imperial Navy. Maybe that was what they wanted to avoid, and why they went into hiding at the marine base. The logical conclusion was that the Exaltationists must have reinforcements, probably scheduled to arrive after the *Zuiderkruis* departed and left Elam alone on the planet. But worse, maybe even now said reinforcements were waiting to ambush the Imperial Navy flotilla that Sigurd had called in. Yet another problem for him to worry over.

Still, the hole in the theory was how the Exaltationists had managed to erase Cornwall's memory. They would have had to do it in a way that Cornwall was unaware of it. Someone like Clifford would be clever enough to do that, but he didn't have access until much later, at the west power plant. In any case, the Exaltationists had a confederate, which meant someone on the *Zuiderkruis* or one of Andresen's people.

Of course, that chain of reasoning assumed Andresen's account was true. Andresen or his confederates certainly could have messed with Cornwall's memory through Lear. But why would they suppress the Torrances' report? Unless Mrs. Torrance had found them instead of the Exaltationist expedition. That gave them ample motive for killing the Torrances and now deceiving Sigurd.

Dammit. He needed Elam now more than ever. The man's uncanny ability to tell when people were lying was exactly the skill he needed. And where was Elam? In the next tram, his head resting on Clifford's chest, asleep.

CHAPTER 25

It only takes one audit to ruin your day.

Pasargardae ***Financial Times***

ELAM WOKE to bright lights and loud voices. He lifted his head from Chad's chest and peered at his surroundings through gritty eyes.

"Welcome to the world, sleepyhead." Chad's chipper voice made him wince.

He started to speak but could just manage a croak. After clearing his throat, he grunted, "We must be at the Lodge?"

"I think we're at the ghost port. Or under it, more accurately."

Elam sat up and stretched the ache out of his muscles. "How's Mr. Cadwalladar?"

"No change, from what I could see. Mr. Mustafa was here and checked him out. I think they've already taken him to the infirmary at the Lodge."

"Makes sense. He's in good hands." Sigurd, Knudson, and that old coot, Andresen, stood talking a few meters away. "What's His Nibs up to?"

"You mean the kolonel? He's got a bee up his butt, that's for sure. I heard something about a war council."

Elam sighed. War council. With scarcely a platoon of combat-ready actives against who knew how many Exaltationist fanatics. *Of course* Sigurd wanted a war council.

Sigurd glanced his way, said something to Knudson, who scuttled off, and then approached Elam and Chad. "Well, Mr. Vandreren, I trust you are rested."

Mr. Vandreren. Once a jerk, always a jerk. "Yes, thank you."

"Very good. Our ally, Mr. Andresen, has provided considerable intelligence for us pertaining to the murders and to the forces opposing us. We will have a briefing to catch everyone up—" He paused to glance at his watch. "—let's say at 1500, forty-five minutes from now, in my conference room. I trust you're sufficiently refreshed to attend." It wasn't a question.

"I'll be there. What about the murders?"

"In due time, Mr. Vandreren. All in due time. I do want you to hear from Mr. Andresen directly."

He stalked away, leaving Elam with his mouth hanging open. Mr. Vandreren, indeed. What happened to using his first name?

Chad tugged at his hand. "Come on. We've just got time to shower and change." He wiped at his tunic. "You kind of drooled on me while you slept."

Elam's face heated. "I guess I did. Is there transport to the Lodge, or do we have to hoof it?"

"Here comes Knudson. I bet he'll tell us."

Knudson started to salute but stopped himself. "Mr. Vandreren, the kolonel requests your presence at his staff briefing. I've arranged surface transport to take you back to the Lodge." He glanced at Chad and added, "Mr. Clifford, your presence is also required. If you'll just follow me." He raised his eyebrows and motioned them.

Elam levered himself out of the tram and followed Chad and Knudson to the surface, where a light drizzle met them. Perfect. A half-dozen four-seater trams awaited. At least these had canvas roofs to protect them from the rain.

Chad climbed into the first one, and Elam joined him. He raised his eyebrows when Knudson also climbed in. Knudson said, "Cornwall, please take us to the Lodge. Quick time, if you please."

Cornwall's image appeared, and he said, "Very good, sir. I suggest you hold on." He bowed, and then his image vanished.

The tram lurched forward and accelerated toward the Lodge. Elam sighed and wrinkled his nose. Somehow the rain made the wheat stink even worse. He held on as the little vehicle careened around curves and sped toward the Lodge. What had Sigurd learned? And why was he being so aloof? *Probably figured out I took go-pills.*

Chad squeezed his hand. Elam was going to have to do something about him. He squeezed back, freed his hand, and patted Chad's knee in what he hoped was a fatherly way. Maybe Sigurd was pissed about Chad. That wasn't all bad, and better than him figuring out about the go-pill.

A QUICK SHOWER helped work the residual aches from his body, and a change of clothes lightened his mood. He grinned as he put on a shirt covered with brightly colored flowers and exotic birds to go with his pale blue chinos. He left the top three buttons on the shirt undone. He considered flip-flops, but those would probably be a step too far for Sigurd. Or a flop too far. He grinned and slipped on open-toed leather sandals.

The clock read 1452. Wouldn't do to be late. He left his suite and headed to the elevator.

The conference room was arranged in the same circle as a few days ago. Chad's eyes lit up, and he patted the chair next to him. Elam gave him a half wave and settled instead next to Jorina. "Ms. Baak. Good to see you again."

She gave him one of her dimpled smiles. "Kind of you to say so, Elam. Good to see you too. I must say, you had us all worried."

"What's the status of Owen Glyndwr's group?"

Her expression turned serious at once. "They're no longer under continuous fire, but they're basically trapped in a bunker at the old marine base. One crewmember suffered a concussion, and another minor shrapnel injuries, but they are stable, at least for now. They're low on ammunition but have food and water for two or three days at least."

"If they're no longer under fire, why can't they just leave?"

"Well, there's no transport, for one thing. And whoever is out there still lobs mortars at them intermittently, for another. Finally, we can't risk a flitter since we now know the hostiles have SAMs."

Elam nodded, recalling the SAM attack on the flitter at the Chicken Ranch.

Sigurd marched into the room with Andresen in tow. He glanced at Elam and seemed to hesitate, then headed his way.

"I see you had time to freshen up." His deadpan expression suggested he might be shooting for irony. Unsuccessfully.

"Yes, thank you." Elam thought about saying how Sigurd looked like a horse that had been run hard and put up wet, but discretion stopped him.

"We're going to start with Mr. Andresen briefing us. I'm inclined to believe most of what he says, but I'll want your opinions when this is over."

"Of course."

Sigurd hesitated, then leaned closer and murmured, "Do you need to sit close to him? To observe?"

"If he's in the room, I'll be fine."

Sigurd gave him a curt nod and tromped to the other side of the circle, where a pair of empty chairs awaited. He motioned for Andresen to sit in one of the empty chairs, then announced, "Quiet, please. We have several urgent matters to consider at this meeting."

He waited for the conversations to die off, then scanned the group for another few seconds. "First, as you all know, members of our crew have come under attack by hostile forces. Two days ago I dispatched the *Zuiderkruis* to the Imperial Navy base on Iskander. I expect that within less than a week a cruiser and two corvettes will be in orbit, plus a battalion of Imperial Marines will be on the ground. In short, we will have sufficient force to handle any hostiles we might confront."

He paused for a beat while the room reacted. "Meantime, we have colleagues at the marine base on the other side of Bountiful who are under siege. They are safe in a bunker for now, but they cannot wait five more days for Imperial Marines. So the primary purpose of this meeting is to discuss intelligence on the hostiles and possible strategies for relieving Mr. Glyndwr and our fellow crew. Ancillary to that, I have come into possession of significant intelligence regarding the murder investigation, intelligence which has bearing on the tactical status of our colleagues at the marine base." He put a hand on Andresen's shoulder. "This is Mr. Clerk Andresen. He's a native of this planet."

That got muttered conversations started. Sigurd held up a palm. "Silence. I know that our briefing said that the planet was abandoned and uninhabited. Our briefing was wrong. Mr. Andresen is part of a small population that's been on this planet since the Great Disintegration five hundred years ago. His people have offered an alliance with us against the hostiles, and I have accepted. They have valuable reconnaissance that he will now share with you." Sigurd sat.

Andresen jerked his chin and stood. "Good afternoon, my friends. I'm pleased to meet all of you."

Elam narrowed his eyes and now wished he was sitting closer. Andresen was good. His expression wasn't giving anything away. Not yet, anyway.

"We are a peaceful lot and just want to be left alone. We live on the southern islands, where no one goes, so we decided to just stay hidden."

Elam kept his face impassive. It was true they wanted to be left alone, but the rest of that little speech was lies. How deep the lies were was impossible to say, but they were lies for sure. This guy was skillful, projecting sincerity with voice and gesture, but no one could hide micro-expressions. At least not to anyone with Elam's training.

"We can move about using the maintenance tunnels underneath the monorail. Those even go to the islands where we live, although the monorail to there never got built. In any case, we've been watching and learning about how things have changed off-planet. A year ago when the cultists arrived, we grew alarmed."

A year ago! Adrenaline sent a shiver jittering down Elam's spine.

Sigurd said, "By cultists, he means the hostile forces. The Exaltationists."

Clerk nodded. "Yes. Exaltationists. A curious name, that. In any case, we wondered about them as soon as the AI notified us of the ghost ship in the system. We knew from the timing it wasn't a regular visit, and when they landed at the old marine base, we were sure. So we started watching them. We could tell from the publications they brought with them and from listening to their conversations that their motives were... disquieting. We want to be left alone, and that desire was incompatible with their plans."

Sigurd muttered, "Tell us what you learned about their plans."

"They spoke of using this planet as a military base to flank their opponents in the Empire. We knew from our observations of the miners that the Empire was a benign entity and not a threat to us. These newcomers, though, were something quite different."

Elam stayed still but alert. It was a lie about finding the Empire benign, but the rest was true.

Sigurd said, "They need to hear about your observer, Enos."

Clerk's shoulders sagged. "Poor Enos. The cultists started secretly watching the Torrances, both here and during Mrs. Torrance's research expeditions. Enos was watching the water—he was observing a cultist just outside this building when your shuttle first arrived. The cultist took a call on his communicator, entered the building, and left about five minutes later carrying a bloody pipe."

Elam spoke in hushed tones, "So that cultist must have murdered Jack Torrance."

Sigurd nodded. "Exactly. And he later killed their observer, Enos, by using high-energy weapons. I found him on the beach, burned and dying."

Elam got that satisfied feeling when the pieces of a puzzle started to come together. "But wait. That's two murders. Torrance and this other guy, Enos. What was the Exaltationist's motive for killing them?"

Sigurd looked at Andresen. "There's more. Tell them."

Clerk's mouth formed a grim line, and he answered, "All these many years since outlanders returned, we stayed hidden. The cultists tried to hide too, but they were clumsy. In fact, Mrs. Torrance found evidence that convinced her not only they were there, but also who they were. She prepared a detailed document that her husband included in his final report that he transmitted to the *Zuiderkruis*."

Jorina raised a hand. "Wait a minute. I read that report. There was no mention of Exaltationists in it. Nothing but routine data."

Clifford added, "More to the point, how do you know what's in the report?" He pointed at Andresen.

Andresen's smile was surely meant to be reassuring. It probably was, too, to everyone but Elam. "Ma'am, sir, please bear with me. You are familiar with the AI that the miners used. I think you still use him? Cornwall?"

On cue, Cornwall flickered into existence. Sigurd snapped, "Not now. Dismissed." When the hologram disappeared, he sat back with a satisfied look on his face. Elam glared at him. *He knows what's coming, the jerk. He could have warned us.*

"There is a second AI that mirrors everything in the local one's memory banks. The local one, the one you've been using, was always for the commercial operation. The other, the one we use, was for the scientific operation. When Mr. Torrance saved his report on the local AI, it was also saved to ours. We read it, so we know that his report included Mrs. Torrance's findings."

Well, that was full of lies, except the part where they read the report and knew what it said. Why would the commercial AI be subordinate to the scientific one? That would make sense if there was a separate AI for the naval base. No wonder Clerk lied about that tidbit. Elam decided to speak up. "I read the report too. It was all boring inventories, weather data, maintenance reports. Are you saying he never transmitted the original report?"

Andresen shook his head. "No. Our records duplicate all local ones, and they clearly show that he transmitted the report that included his wife's observations."

Chad put a hand to his mouth. "So someone had to have erased that part of the report *after* it was transmitted to the ship." After a couple of beats, he continued, "That *same* someone must have erased it in Cornwall's memory too."

Cornwall reappeared.

Chad glared at him and said, "Do you have more than one copy of the exit report Jack Torrance prepared?"

"My memory banks have only one copy, sir."

"Did anyone access it after he filed it?"

"No, sir."

Chad scowled; then his face lit up. "How about the cameras in the lobby. When did those get shut off?"

"The cameras are motion-activated, so it's impossible to say."

Elam said, "But when we arrived, you specifically told us they were turned off."

"Yes, sir."

Elam clenched his teeth. Damned AI. "So you knew they were turned off at that time."

"Yes, sir. But they might have been turned off any time before then. That was just the first time I had occasion to look."

Knudson said, "When we examined the crime scene, we asked about that. Cornwall directed us to a switch near the front door. It was in the Off position."

Sigurd said, "What are you getting at, Elam?"

Well, at least Sigurd was back to using his first name. "It would appear someone has been manipulating Cornwall's memory. Chad, is that possible?"

"They'd probably leave tracks. But even so, that's a tricky thing to do. And whoever did it had to have access to secured parts of both systems, to Cornwall's and to those on the *Zuiderkruis*." Cornwall popped back into existence at the mention of his name, but Chad barreled on. "I was able to get to the on-planet data banks from the console in the power plant, but not from here in the Lodge. As far as I know, only the auditor and me, as support staff, had high enough access to the *Zuiderkruis's* data banks to manipulate them without setting off alarms."

Elam sat back as another chill slithered down his spine. *Bender. He had to have access to both systems, and at a deep level. He's got to be complicit.* He looked around the room. Bender wasn't there. "Where in Chaos is he at? He's at the heart of all this."

CHAPTER 26

If you are far from the enemy, make him believe you are near.
—Sun Tzu

SIGURD CLENCHED his jaw and glared at Elam. The guy was taking over his meeting. Again. Worse, he'd pulled it off track, even if he'd uncovered a traitor in their midst. Sigurd steadied his breathing and stood. "Cornwall."

The hologram turned to face him, calm and impassive. "How may I be of service?"

"Where is Mr. Bender? He was supposed to be at this meeting."

"Mr. Bender has turned off his communicator. He is not in range of any of my active monitors."

"When and where was he when you last had him on your sensors?"

"He turned off his communicator twenty-three minutes ago, while he was in his suite in the Lodge. My last visual sighting was on the beach twelve minutes ago. He boarded a waiting flitter which departed westward across the Central Sea."

A flitter? "Ms. Baak, what was a flitter doing on the beach?"

"I don't see how it could be one of ours, sir. Cornwall, what's the origin of Bender's flitter? Is it one of ours?"

"If you mean is it one of the flitters at the ghost port, no. Its origin is unknown."

Elam asked, "Cornwall, did your radars see the flitter approach? If so, from where?"

"Sir, I regret to say I have no radar record of a flitter approaching."

Sigurd grimaced. Cornwall's precise Oxford accent showed no regret. Of course, he was just a computer. "How about radar on where it went?"

"Sir, it headed to the west for approximately ten kilometers before it fell below line-of-sight of ghost port radars."

Jorina said, "That must be how they got here undetected, flying under the radar. Cornwall, send a drone out to see where it's headed."

Sigurd shook his head. "Belay that, Cornwall. I want to reserve our drones. We might need them later. Bender's obviously headed to the Exaltationists."

The corpsman fidgeted in his seat and raised a finger.

Sigurd nodded to him. "Mr. Mustafa. You have something to contribute?"

"Sir, you recall the anomalous readings I found in the Torrances' blood samples?"

"I do. Relevance, please."

"I tracked down what it was, a derivate of an obscure, ancient drug called cycloserine. Bender was on the last audit visit. If he corrupted the AI at that time, then that must be how they got dosed."

"Why would he do that?"

"I don't know. The ancients used that drug for TB, but we have better treatments, and the records show neither one had any infection. That drug has psychotropic side effects, however, which were present in their histories. Depression. Paranoia. Agoraphobia."

Elam nodded. "Mrs. Torrance's notes show definite signs of paranoia."

Sigurd scowled. Off track again. Still, it was interesting. "Why would he do this?"

Elam shrugged. "Bender's run off to the Exaltationists, and their presence here proves their hostile intent. They must have been planning to take over the planet between audits, for reasons unknown. Anything that weakened the Syndicate's presence on the planet would be to their advantage. It's just another line of evidence that Bender and the Exaltationists were up to no good."

That made sense, but it didn't change the tactical situation. Sigurd paused for a few seconds, then continued, "The important thing is that Cornwall has been compromised. It's possible that the hostiles know everything we say in this meeting."

Andresen shook his head. "I don't think so. In fact, I can say categorically that's not the case."

Sigurd raised an eyebrow in his direction. "What makes you so sure?"

"Our AI, Lear, has the ability to take control of Cornwall. It can supersede any programming, even code hidden in Cornwall's processors. From this point forward, you may assume that you're interacting with Lear when using Cornwall."

Elam narrowed his eyes and leaned forward. "How do you know that? I mean, I know you believe that's true, but how can you be so sure?"

Some of the tension left Sigurd's back. He had no idea if Andresen was truthful or not, but if Elam believed him, then so did Sigurd. "I was about to ask the same question, Mr. Andresen."

The man's face stayed impassive, but even Sigurd could tell he didn't want to answer the question. "I have an implant."

Sigurd kept his voice calm and even. "What exactly does that mean?"

Andresen sighed. "It means that I have... an implanted interface with Lear." He licked his lips. "It's hard to describe."

Sigurd frowned. "You mean like an ear bud?" It didn't really sound like that was what he meant, though.

Andresen's head jerked in a slight shake. "No. It's a... neural implant... a brain-to-cyber connection." The words came out slowly, in patches, like he was revealing a deep secret.

Clifford's eyes glimmered, and he piped up, "I've read about prototypes that do that for human/cyber interfaces, but they're mostly for prosthetics. Like moving an artificial limb. You're talking about information exchange, right? Data moving back and forth real-time."

Andresen narrowed his eyes and nodded.

"How can that even work? That involves real-time signal acquisition, decoding, and processing, then somehow training the neural network to make sense of an incoming data stream. The ancients worked hard on the associated problems, and all they did was fry the brains of animal subjects."

Andresen answered with a prim tone and a tight grin, "I assure you my brain is not fried. Human brains are adapted to acquire data. We do it all the time, through our senses. But you're correct. This is different. My implant permits a two-way data stream with Lear."

Clifford grinned like a puppy having his tummy scratched. "That's so rad! So, what? It's like a voice in your head whispering sweet nothings into your memory?'"

"If that helps you conceptualize, then yes. But I can't describe it. It's like people whose brains see numbers as colors, or people with eidetic memories. It just is." He shrugged. "The point is that I've instructed Lear to take control of Cornwall. Our meeting is secure."

Sigurd narrowed his eyes. Andresen was evading, not explaining. Lear might control Cornwall, but apparently Andresen controlled Lear by some weird kind of telepathy. He may as well have said it was like explaining a rainbow to a blind person or a Chopin étude to a deaf person, but he didn't. Those comparisons would have made his ability more striking. More dangerous too. What other secrets was he keeping? Sigurd glanced at Elam, whose gaze was focused on Andresen. "Mr. Vandreren. Do you have anything to contribute?"

Elam gave a start. "Me? No. It looks like a good thing we have Mr. Andresen as an ally. I'd hate to have him as a foe."

Sigurd had to agree. Elam more or less endorsing the alliance was confirmation enough for Sigurd. He sat back down. "All right, then. Our main order of business is to develop a plan to relieve Mr. Glyndwr and his team at the marine base. I'd like to turn to that next. Mr. Andresen, could you arrange for Cornwall to display a map of the base on the screen behind me?"

Andresen didn't answer, but the screen lit with the requested map. "Please highlight the bunker where our crewmates are hiding. I believe it's building 21-P-12."

An oblong square on the map turned red.

"Very good. And now the landing field."

Andresen hesitated, then spoke. "I think I see a possible rescue route."

Sigurd's lips flinched. *May as well hear what he has to say.* "Speak."

"The base is on a bluff overlooking the ocean. There's a sandy beach at the bottom of the bluff where there's room for a flitter to land. There's also a drainage causeway that empties onto the beach from the base above." Parts of the map lit up as he spoke. "The causeway is just needed during the monsoon season, and most of the time it's dry. The marines used the beach for recreation and the causeway as a shortcut to get there. They even designed it with that in mind."

Sigurd stared at the map and tried to visualize what he remembered from the topography. "If we flew low over the ocean and approached the beach from the northeast, we'd be under the radar horizon of the hostiles. Just like how they got here to pick up Bender. If we can get Mr. Glyndwr's team to the beach, we can fly them out."

Andresen nodded. "My thought exactly."

Sigurd pressed his fingers together over his nose and contemplated the map. "Where's the entrance to the causeway?"

A tiny green square flashed two buildings away from the bunker that held Glyndwr's group. Andresen said, "It's roughly fifteen meters away from where they're located."

Fifteen meters. A dozen troops, two injured, one in a stretcher. "That's risky. The hostiles probably have spotters looking for them to make a run for it. How exposed is the entrance to the causeway?"

Andresen looked grim. "The entrance is exposed, and the first fifty meters or more of the causeway are at risk to the kinds of explosives we've seen the cultists use. People moving from the bunker to the entrance would also be exposed to gunfire."

Jorina spoke up. "Sir, Mr. Glyndwr reports they appear to be under surveillance. Feints outside their bunker result in mortars arriving in under thirty seconds. They are trapped in the bunker. They're safe in the bunker, but there's no way they can survive those fifty meters."

Sigurd nodded. The tactical situation was shaping up. "How about high-energy weapons?"

Andresen shrugged. "The only evidence we've seen of those has been when they repurposed the lasers on the mining bots. Those have limited range. Unless they're in the base itself, they'd not be a worry."

Sigurd turned to Jorina. "Ms. Baak. You have secure communication with Mr. Glyndwr?"

"Yes, sir. Encrypted both ways using the latest quantum entanglement technologies. We'll know at once if they're intercepted, and they are beyond-question secure."

Nothing was absolute, but Sigurd had confidence in the technology. "Good. What we need, then, is a way to assure that those lookouts are not looking when the time comes to evacuate."

Elam leaned back with a satisfied gleam in his eye. Even now, in the middle of tactical planning, that gleam in Elam's eye meant more to Sigurd than all his other honors.

Sigurd stood. "I have the outline of a plan. Ms. Ulrich?"

A woman with grizzled short hair stood. "Sir." Her muscular frame stood out even under her baggy merchant uniform.

"Gretl, I recall you telling me you were a flitter pilot with the Imperial Marines."

"Yes, sir. I saw action on Actium's Gate."

"With Mr. Cadwalladar. I remember. I would like you to join Ms. Baak, Mr. Andresen, and me to continue this planning session in a smaller group. Mr. Vandreren, I'd be grateful if you would also join us in my office."

Elam's face lit with a wolfish grin. "Wouldn't be anywhere else."

He might be annoying as hell, but Sigurd couldn't think of a better companion for what he had in mind.

CHAPTER 27

It never troubles the wolf how many sheep there are.

—Virgil

ELAM RUBBED his palms on his slacks and tried to look bored. People milled about as the conference broke up, and Chad headed his way. Just what he needed. No, wait. Chad might be a too-friendly puppy dog, but he was smart. He could figure out what Elam needed.

Elam stood and gave the younger man a narrow look. "Chad, I've been thinking about a couple of things."

A brilliant white smile flashed across Chad's ebony face. "Me too." He wagged his hips. "I bet it's the same things."

Elam ignored his youthful enthusiasm. "It's about some things Andresen said."

Disappointment pinched Chad's features. "Oh?"

"First, Andresen said their AI notified them when the Exaltationist's ghostship arrived. Didn't Cornwall do the same thing for the Torrances?"

Chad frowned. "That's supposed to happen unless someone messed with the subroutine. I'll check it out."

"A rogue ghostship would have been in their reports for sure. I'm certain it'll show hacking. Find the date it occurred if you can. I bet it coincides with one of the regular audits."

"You're thinking Bender did it. Makes sense. Piece of cake. You said there's two things?"

"I think something happened here, maybe a hundred years or so after the Disintegration."

"Like what? The first mini ice age was about a hundred years after—" His eyes lit up. "Hey! That surge in power usage at the south power station must have been from Andresen's people, during the mini ice age."

No reason to let Chad know Elam had already figured that out. "You're right! Good deduction." He paused for a beat, then continued. "I was thinking more of something I found in Wendy Torrance's notes. She was convinced that Lansbury wasn't sacked during the Disintegration, but instead maybe between one and two hundred years later."

"Really? What made her think that?"

Elam shrugged. "Something about the state of the ruins not being sufficiently advanced. I blew it off at the time, since I figured no one was around to do it."

Chad nodded. "Makes sense. Interstellar flight had stopped, and this place was supposed to be abandoned. But now we know people were here, so they must have destroyed it themselves. You want me to look in the data for evidence?"

"Exactly. I think that Andresen's people might not be as peaceful as they say."

Chad pressed a knuckle against his upper lip and stared into the distance. "Conflicts always involve resource and energy expenditure. Hard to hide if you know what you're looking for. I'll need to head back to a console at the power plant to check."

Elam shook his head. "I bet Bender had a console squirreled away somewhere here in the Lodge. Maybe even in his room. If you ask Cornwall the right questions, I bet you can find one here."

Chad grinned. "You're right. Bender had to have console access somehow, and it doesn't make sense that the only consoles would be at the plant. I'll find it." He bounced on the balls of his feet. "Anything else?"

"That's it. Let me know what you find."

"On it, Elam." Chad left at a trot.

Sigurd and Jorina stood a few meters down the corridor arguing about something. Her face was flushed, and she'd crossed her arms. Sigurd's jaw jumped, and his eyes bulged. An argument of some kind, then.

Elam ambled up to them and said in a bantering tone, "Trouble in paradise?"

Sigurd scowled at him. "Just a small disagreement on tactics."

Jorina glared at him. "It's more than that. The Margravina—"

Sigurd held up a hand. "Enough! I will hear no more of that."

Elam looked from one to the other, his mind racing to conclusions. The Margravina would be Sigurd's mother. He suppressed a grin. Maybe the Margravina had sent Jorina to watch over her son! Delicious possibilities raced through his mind.

No time for that. Not now. "I urgently need to talk to you before you plan your diversion."

Jorina snapped, "There's not going to be a diversion."

Sigurd's gaze threw daggers at her, but he turned to Elam. "Very well. Speak to me."

Elam glanced down the hall where Andresen leaned against a wall, watching impassively. "Privately."

Sigurd followed his gaze, then nodded. "My office, then. Ms. Baak, please make sure two flitters are prepped for operations." He turned on his heel and stomped away before she could object.

Elam hesitated, then murmured to her, "Do as he says. I'll protect him, if needed."

Her eyes snapped, but then the tension drained from her. "I'll see to the flitters, but I can't let him risk himself on some crazy suicide mission."

"He's too smart for that. Trust me."

She scanned him from head to toe. "Strangest thing, I do trust you. But then, I know who you are, *Admiral*. I recognized you when I first laid eyes on you." She snorted. "This whole blasted mission is a snake pit of lies." She sighed. "We all do what we must." She left with a firm step and a straight back.

She knew him? How could he have missed that? But then, he hadn't been looking for lies from her. No matter, he was sure he could trust her too.

Sigurd stood in his office staring at a video map of the terrain around the marine base. He'd highlighted in green the locations of Glyndwr's group, the beach, and the causeway. Red Xs and Os marked locations in the hills overlooking the base from the southeast.

Elam asked, "The Xs and Os are intelligence from Andresen's scouts?"

Sigurd nodded. "Yes. The lone X marks the mortars, O other encampments. He built this map for me prior to our meeting. There are between twenty and twenty-four of them in the hills." He touched the X, which turned orange. "Presently the mortars are all at this location."

"According to Andresen."

"Yes. Why would he lie?"

"Because he's lied about other material things."

Some of the tension went out of Sigurd at that, and he collapsed into the chair behind his desk. "I wanted you to hear his story. That was the main reason I had him rehash the whole thing."

Elam turned the visitor chair around, sat in it backward, and leaned forward. "To start with, he lied when he said his people were peaceful."

"You're sure? You think he's planning an attack on us?"

"No evidence of an imminent attack, but he's hiding something. They are not peaceful. But they do want to be left alone. That part was truthful. He also lied when he said they lived on the southern islands."

"I already figured that out. There's the cats, for one thing."

Elam grinned. "You're right. I hadn't put that together." He hesitated. There were the suspicions he had discussed with Chad, but this wasn't the time to mention those. "He told the truth when he said they didn't like the Exaltationists, but he lied when he said they thought the Empire was— what did he call it? Benign."

"I wondered about that too. They might help us with the current tactical situation, but longer term I'm not sure our interests coincide."

"If you're wondering, he was telling the truth about their observer witnessing an Exaltationist at the Lodge at the time of Jack Torrance's murder. I'm sure that his people had no direct involvement in that crime, or in Wendy Torrance's murder."

"That's a relief. From the evidence, they had as much reason as the Exaltationists to kill the Torrances."

"For what it's worth, I'm sure they did not murder the Torrances. Or at least that Andresen is sure they did not. But there's more."

"What's that?"

"Everything he said about his 'implant' was a lie."

Sigurd tented his fingers and gave Elam a pensive look. "Go on."

Elam shrugged. "That's it. He lied about the implant, but he clearly had some way of controlling the screen and probably communicating with their AI. I don't see how that can be without an implant of some kind, but what he had to say about it was a lie."

Sigurd frowned. "Did you know that the ancients were breeding supersoldiers here?"

Adrenaline jittered down Elam's spine. Things were making more sense. "Supersoldiers? You mean genetically engineered soldiers?"

"Exactly. Andresen demonstrated enormous strength to me, although he said that's rare among his people. But he was quite convincing."

"Enormous strength? What did he do?" Elam tried to not roll his eyes.

"He bent a piece of metal piping like it was made of putty."

"I'd like to see that. He's a proficient liar. I wouldn't be surprised if it was some kind of sleight of hand, or even hypnosis."

Sigurd's face reddened. "I assure you I was not hypnotized."

Elam shrugged. "I'm not saying he doesn't have extraordinary powers. Like I said, he's an expert liar. Better than any I've encountered."

"Again, why would he lie about such a thing?"

That was easy. "A lie about super strength might hide other, more threatening, powers."

"Speculation is not helpful at this point. We need facts. Do you have anything else?"

Elam jumped to his feet and paced. "There's lots of pieces to this puzzle." He stopped and stared at Sigurd. "Wendy Torrance was convinced that Lansbury was destroyed a century or more after the Disintegration. It must have been done by Andresen's people, fighting with each other."

"That would be four hundred years ago. How is that relevant?"

"Because Andresen has to know about it. Because he lied when he said they were peaceful. Knowing they are descended from genetically engineered soldiers changes everything." He halted and jerked to face Sigurd. "Cats! That's got to explain it."

Sigurd looked at him like he was insane. "What do cats have to do with this?"

"Think, man. If you engineered supersoldiers, what would be the first thing you'd worry about?"

"I don't know. I guess, controlling them?"

"Exactly! Everyone knows the Frankenstein legend. They'd engineer components to make them tame. Domesticated. Like the cats."

"That seems like the opposite of what you'd want soldiers to be."

"You'd want soldiers to be loyal to their masters, like guard dogs." Elam grinned. He loved it when the pieces fell into place. "Those ancient researchers, the ones that came here to Cabot's Landing? They were originally from a Russian lab that domesticated foxes in the twentieth century. They partnered with geneticists from North America who found the genetic markers for domestication."

"How is that relevant? And how in Chaos do you know this?"

Elam shrugged. "It was in the packet I got. The NOMAD article on the biological station. You never know what's going to be useful in intelligence. Anyway, you'd want your supersoldiers to be domesticated, loyal to their commanders."

"I don't believe loyalty depends on genetics."

Elam nodded. "Nature, nurture. It's both. Cats go feral unless they are socialized at the right time of their lives. Same is true of humans. Worse, improper socialization in early childhood can lead to sociopathy in adulthood. So, unless the infant supersoldiers were properly socialized, domesticated if you will, they would be supremely dangerous to their creators."

"Causing the warfare centuries ago on this planet that you mentioned. I get it." Sigurd drummed his fingers on his desk. "That makes them dangerous to the Empire, even if there are only a couple thousand of them."

Elam said, "The only silver lining is that Andresen told the truth when he said they want to be left alone. Of course, that could just be while they perfect their plan of galactic conquest." His mouth twisted with sarcasm.

Sigurd leaned back in his chair. "This confirms our short-term allies are a long-term danger. They'll need to be controlled. Sequestered in some way. But we've still got the immediate problem of Mr. Glyndwr's team. We can't leave them hanging. There's also the risk that the Exaltationists might have a relief ghostship on the way, or even lurking in the system. In fact, that's the best explanation for why they haven't attacked the Lodge. They're waiting on reinforcements."

"I agree with that assessment, and also about relieving Mr. Glyndwr, but I don't think we need to worry about an Exaltationist ghostship. If one were in the system, they would have pounced as soon as the *Zuiderkruis* left. They didn't, ergo, no ship. And one won't be coming anytime soon. I'm sure there's one somewhere in a nearby system, but it's waiting for the all-clear that the *Zuiderkruis* has left and there's only me, the Resident, alone on the planet. The point is, it's *waiting* for an all-clear message, and their spy, Bender, is still *here*, not on the *Zuiderkruis*. No way to get a message out."

Relief etched Sigurd's features. "You're right. I hadn't thought it through."

Elam frowned. "I just thought of something else. There's probably a *second* spy on the *Zuiderkruis*, one who *will* get a message to the Exaltationist relief vessel. Probably a relay message, which will delay it. So I still think we don't have to worry about an Exaltationist relief vessel. Your quick thinking means the naval squadron from Iskander will almost certainly get here first. In any case, it either gets here first or not. There's nothing we can do about it either way."

"I suppose you're right. But that still leaves why they exposed themselves after hiding for so long. Why didn't they just stay in hiding?"

Elam chewed his lower lip and frowned. "Andresen said they originally landed at the marine base. Maybe they were using it for operations, and Bender warned them we were coming and they fled to the hills overlooking the base. They might have panicked. When the flitter took off, they may have thought we were planning an assault on their positions and the leadership fled."

Sigurd's voice was tinged with doubt. "I suppose. Saving the leaders and leaving behind troops as cannon fodder is consistent with their history." He sighed. "In any case, you're right. We need to focus on the current tactical situation and not speculate about side issues. We have enough of a problem relieving Glyndwr. Let me outline my plan and see if you can find holes in it."

Elam listened as Sigurd sketched what he had in mind, using Andresen's map. It was daring, and dangerous as hell for the diversionary team, but it should work. He gave Sigurd a narrow look. "So the second flitter is bait, while the first rescues the team."

"Exactly."

Elam nodded. "Thing is, it doesn't much matter what happens to the team on the diversionary flitter. Once you're bait, you're pretty much used up."

Sigurd's features hardened. "That's more or less what Ms. Baak said. It'll be our responsibility, yours and mine, to see that doesn't happen."

CHAPTER 28

Hope is a waking dream.

—Aristotle

GRAINS OF sand and dust swirled in the frigid mountain air and prickled Sigurd's cheeks. His night-vision goggles protected his eyes but rendered his surroundings in a surreal greenish hue. Not that he could see much from where he lay prone on this rocky hillside. He scrunched forward and peered over a jumble of fist-sized rocks. On the slope below, green figures huddled over bright viridian hot spots. Others squatted next to ebony tubes etched in green that had to be mortars. Eight altogether. That left twelve lurking somewhere else in the nearby mountains. According to Andresen's intelligence, this was the only location that fired mortars at Glyndwr's group. Wherever the other twelve hostiles might be, taking these out would be enough.

Sigurd pushed his goggles to his forehead and peered at the scene below. The goggles gave more detail, but sometimes less information. Now he could discern that the shadowy figures clustered about the ruddy glow of a portable heater. Others squatted next to what were definitely mortar tubes, with their gazes directed at the marine base. The glow from Kennebec, looming three-quarters full overhead, revealed the rectangular array of the base's streets and buildings below the hostile's camp.

Kennebec cast a shadow across its magnificent blue-and-purple rings, giving the entire scene a surreal air. The red glow of the Scarecrow Nebula, with Aldebaran its red eye, spread near the horizon, as if watching over the entire scene. Whether the old constellation foretold threat or protection, only time would tell.

The men clustered around the mortars hunkered down, and the ends of two tubes flashed bright, followed by a muffled *chuff*. Sigurd clenched his jaw. They must have fired another couple of rounds at the base below. Sure enough, two bright explosions flashed on one of the buildings, followed in a couple of seconds by the roar of explosions.

Elam's voice whispered in his earpiece, "I just took out two roaming guards. Watch your back."

He pressed a finger to his ear, and the device squawked an acknowledgment. With any luck, Elam got the only two guards, and the rest of the hostiles were elsewhere. He glanced at his chronometer. If everything else was going to plan, the rescue flitter had just arrived at the beach below the marine base. No reaction from the hostiles, so the filter's approach had most likely managed to avoid detection.

Time for their diversion.

He pulled a communicator from his pants and stroked the screen to start what Mr. Clifford had called Pandora's App. His index finger hovered over the single button on the screen that read OPEN in all caps. A timer on the screen read T-58, then decreased to T-57, counting the seconds to the start of their diversion.

He peered through the night-vision scope on his rifle. The group below stirred, leaving green whorls trailing behind them. Voices spoke in liquid accents. Sigurd concentrated and caught the words *gyulai sandviĉoj*. Sausage sandwiches. They must be planning dinner. His eyes narrowed, and a grin twisted his lips. The app ticked to thirteen, then twelve. Twelve seconds and they'd get a special dessert.

The counter hit zero, and Sigurd pushed the OPEN button.

The flitter that had brought Elam and Sigurd here sat four klicks away, behind a range of peaks that had cloaked its approach from hostile radar. His button press activated the six drones he and Elam had stacked next to it. His communicator screen flickered and changed to the view from a camera mounted on the lead drone.

Less than two minutes later, the buzz of the drone's engines whispered across the intervening peak.

The group below continued their chatter. The sound of their conversation must be covering up the murmur of the approaching drones.

A minute later, the purr of the drones' engines grew louder. Seconds after that they shot over Sigurd's head and dropped mines and antipersonnel weapons on the hostiles below. Explosions flashed and voices screamed. Men scattered and snatched up weapons. Tracer bullets soared from the ground toward the attacking drones. Flames burst from one, and it spiraled to the ground, where it exploded in a puff of smoke and debris.

The remaining drones circled back for a second run. More tracer bullets rose from the hostiles, and two more drones fell. But one unloaded explosives on the mortars and set off the ammunition piled nearby. The resulting explosion thundered against the rocky bluffs and sent mortar shells swirling in chaotic paths through the sky.

Sigurd breathed a sigh of relief. No more mortar attacks from this group. If Andresen's intelligence was correct, there were no other mortars overlooking the marine base. Mr. Glyndwr's passage should be secure.

A muzzle flashed from a hillside opposite where Sigurd lay. That had to be Elam, from his sniper's perch. One of the hostiles whirled and collapsed to the ground. Another hostile knelt at the victim's side, wailed, and held his wounded colleague's head.

Sigurd took aim with his own rifle. He centered the scope on the man cradling Elam's victim's head. Woman, not man. He pulled the trigger. Her chest exploded in a foam of blood and tissue, and she collapsed across Elam's target.

Two down. Sigurd counted two more motionless on the ground. No, make that three.

A bullet whistled past Sigurd's ear. Another sent rock splinters into his cheeks and body armor. He took aim, fired, and another hostile tumbled backward.

Before he could find another target, a blow to the back of his neck drove his chin into the rocks. A booted foot kicked his rifle from his grasp. He tucked his head under his arms and curled into a ball, but the attacker continued to kick him. Something crunched on his left side, and agony gripped his torso.

Hot, wet glop sprayed across Sigurd's neck and splattered onto rock in front of him. A dead weight collapsed on top of him. He squirmed, sending pain shooting through his body, but he couldn't dislodge the weight. Each breath was a knife in his side.

At least the kicking had stopped.

He clenched his jaws and twisted his head to assess his surroundings. Bluish-white mush glistened in spaghetti-like heaps on the rocks around him. Organic matter? From the man who'd been kicking him? A hand hung over his shoulder. Dark blood drooled from its fingers to the ground.

Sigurd grunted and pushed the body to one side. Its arms flopped as it rolled away. A neat black hole was centered above the man's sightless eyes. The back half of his head was missing. Bile burned the Sigurd's throat. The glop on the ground he'd seen earlier had to be the man's brains.

Good thing Elam was a good shot. It could just as easily have been Sigurd's brains.

He fumbled with his rifle. His fingers refused to obey, as if they'd been replaced by inanimate sausages. He tried to take a deep breath, and agony clenched his torso. The kicks must have broken a rib. Or two.

Flames flickered below from where the mortars had been. Another explosion roared and sent more random mortar rounds pirouetting into the night sky. At least no one moved below.

Sigurd tried to concentrate and count the bodies. Six, seven. There were seven bodies below. He squinted. Random body parts lay in a scattered heap next to burning mortar ammo. That could be one body, or maybe two. If two, all the hostiles he'd counted earlier were gone.

Another dead hostile, the one who had attacked him, lay sprawled next to him. Counting the eight below and the two guards Elam had taken out, that accounted for eleven. Eleven out of the twenty that Andresen had said were in the area. So there had been at least three lookouts above the camp, maybe more.

Worry clenched at Sigurd's throat. Lookouts meant that Elam was in danger. Think. He raised his fingers to his earpiece and stopped. Warning him might distract him at a critical instant. Better to assess his own situation first.

He set his jaw and grimaced as he struggled to roll over. He elbowed himself to a sitting position, with his back to the rock escarpment that had been his cover. No sign of more hostiles, and no more gunfire either. He glanced at his watch. Twelve minutes had passed since the drone attack.

That should be enough for Mr. Glyndwr's team to be in the safety of the causeway. Another ten and they'd be in the flitter and headed back to the Lodge. But the Exaltationists wouldn't be looking at the marine base. They'd be looking for whoever attacked their mortars. As Sigurd planned, they'd be looking for his diversion. They'd be looking for him. And Elam too.

Great. All was going according to plan. Now to see to Elam.

Except that he couldn't stand up.

He fumbled again with his rifle and managed to position it to his right side, with his finger on the trigger. At least he had a chance of firing if another hostile attacked him.

Elam's voice murmured in his ear, "Sigurd. Are you all right?"

Relief flooded through him and eased some of the tension in his muscles. "I'm breathing. You?"

"I'm fine. I took out two scouts who attacked you. The hostiles below us are out of commission. How are *you*?"

Sigurd managed to grunt, "Good."

"You don't sound good. Are you sure you're all right?"

"My breath got knocked out of me."

"Right. I'm going to join you. Try to not shoot me."

"I'll do my best."

Sigurd breathed in short, painful puffs. The wind gusted, and more dust whirled about him. Grains gritted in his eyes. The coppery scent of death oozed from the corpse next to him, along with the foul scents of feces and urine. A second body lay still a few meters uphill.

His head sagged, and his chin touched his chest. His eyelids drooped as if ten-kilo weights were attached to them.

He jerked his head up and winced as pain shot through his tortured center. He had to stay awake, at least until Elam got here.

Jorina's voice murmured in his ear, "*Elpízo* released."

A wan smile bent Sigurd's lips. Hope released. The perfect code for the completion of Operation Pandora. It signaled the successful extraction of Glyndwr's team. Mission accomplished. He touched his earpiece, which squawked an acknowledgment.

All that remained was hiking back to their flitter and returning by air to the Lodge. A piece of cake, given Elam's expert piloting.

Sigurd pulled his legs up and tried to use his rifle to lever himself to a standing position. He got as far as his knees when dizziness overwhelmed him and he collapsed back to the stony surface. His head thumped against a rock, and his vision dissolved in a red-tinged blackness. He managed to wriggle back to a sitting position, his rifle at his side, his finger on the trigger.

It was a great plan, if only he could walk.

He concentrated on breathing. In. Out. *Pain*. In. Out. *Pain*. Over and over. Endless pain. Before long, he couldn't concentrate. He closed his eyes. He needed just a moment to rest.

A clatter of rocks startled him awake. He jerked his rifle to the ready and let loose a random string of bullets. A shadow fell across him, and a hand wrenched the rifle from his grip.

Too late. Dismay opened a hollow chill in his gut. His luck had finally run out.

CHAPTER 29

*Being deeply loved by someone gives you strength, while
loving someone deeply gives you courage.*

—*Lao Tzu*

ELAM GRIPPED the barrel of Sigurd's rifle, and heat seared his palm.
He laid it out of Sigurd's reach and knelt next to his comrade in arms.
His gut clenched as he scanned the other man's gaunt features. Sweat
sheened Sigurd's brow, and his face was pale, even allowing for the
blue light from Kennebec. Glassy eyes peered from sunken holes in his
skull.

Elam caressed Sigurd's cheek and murmured, "You're injured."

A feeble smile flashed for a moment across Sigurd's face, and
he muttered, "Just the breath... knocked... out. I'll be okay in... a...
moment."

Elam shrugged off his backpack and dug into the interior. "I'm
going to give you an injection." He pulled out an autopen, set the dial
to two, and held it against Sigurd's thigh. When he pressed the injector
button, it gave a little *chuff* sound. He held it in place for a count of three.
"Nanodocs are in."

Sigurd nodded and closed his eyes. "Thank you."

Elam attached a clip to Sigurd's index finger and plugged it into the
handheld monitor in the field medical kit. Moments later the screen came
to life with readouts on Sigurd's condition. BP and body temp elevated,
but not dangerously so. White blood cells normal. Respiration normal too.
That was good.

He leaned close to Sigurd's ear and said, "I need to examine your
chest. Does one side hurt more than the other?"

"Right side. He kicked me."

"It's going to be all right. I know what to do. Hold still now." Maybe
his body armor had afforded some protection. Elam shook out his hands to
stop the trembling in his fingers and undid the Velcro on Sigurd's Kevlar

vest. When he unbuttoned his shirt, he exposed rippled abs covered with a fine mesh of chestnut-colored hair and a nasty purple bruise on the right-lower side of his torso.

"I can see your ribs. No open wounds, and your chest isn't deformed. Do you think you can stand up?"

"I passed out earlier when I tried. Maybe you can help?"

"Have you been coughing?"

"No. It hurts to breathe, but no coughing."

"Okay, then." The readout came alive as the nanodocs started to report in. "Nanodocs say there's a contusion to the anterior attachment of rib ten. That's good, since it doesn't say fracture." He pulled his combat knife from its ankle sheath and used it to cut away the uniform of the dead hostile. "I'm going to need to put your right arm in an elevated sling. Hold tight for a minute."

Sigurd started to laugh and then winced. "I'm not going anywhere."

Less than a minute later, Elam said, "All right. Can you sit up?"

Sigurd grimaced but used his left hand to lever himself to a sitting position.

Elam said, "Good. Now, I'm going to help you get to your feet." He looped his left hand underneath Sigurd's left arm and lifted.

Sigurd grunted to his feet, with Elam doing a good part of the work. Once standing, Sigurd gave him a shaky smile. "Nothing to it."

"That's the man I know and love. Put your right hand over your left shoulder."

Sigurd gaped at him for a beat, but then complied. Elam used the remnants of the dead Exaltationist's tunic to bind the arm in place. "That's to keep it from doing any damage by banging against your side. How's the pain? The nanodocs should be activating your natural endorphins by now."

Sigurd heaved a deep breath. "Better, actually. The sling seems to help too."

"Good man. It's better if you move around. It helps keep your lungs clear." Elam disconnected the finger monitor and put it back into the first aid kit. He slipped the kit's handheld monitor into a utility pocket on his jacket and turned back to Sigurd. "It's about four klicks back to the flitter. The sooner we get there, the better."

Sigurd wiped his brow. "Maybe you should go ahead. You could fly it back here and pick me up."

"I'm not leaving you alone."

Sigurd chewed his lower lip and gazed into Elam's eyes. "If it comes to it, save yourself. It... I mean, what you said. It works both ways."

Elam stared at him. What had he said? His mind raced over the last few minutes, and he realized what he'd blurted out in the heat of the moment. More, he realized it was true. He really did love the man. Even when he was being a jerk. He stared into Sigurd's deep blue eyes. "I meant what I said. Every word of it. I'm not leaving you." Not again. Not ever. Not like Ivar. This time, duty and love fit together, hand and glove.

Sigurd gripped Elam's arm with his left hand. "I feel the same way. I haven't been able to stop thinking about you since we first met. I mean, I know it's hopeless, given our positions, but that doesn't change how I feel." He sighed and winced. "I meant what I said too. Don't sacrifice yourself just because we care for... love... each other."

"No one's getting sacrificed." Elam stiffened his back. "We can work this out later. For now, we just get out of here."

Four klicks to the flitter. It had taken them a little over an hour earlier tonight, hiking cross-country and taking advantage of what little cover was available. Elam kept the pace slow but steady. Every ten minutes, he stopped to check the first aid kit's monitor. At the third stop, it showed Sigurd's white blood cells slightly elevated and his respiration depressed. He pursed his lips and asked, "How's it going?"

"I'm a little winded. My side aches, but nothing like before. The 'docs must be doing their job."

"We're maybe halfway there. Not much longer. We can rest a few if you want."

"The sooner we're there, the better. I'm fine. At least, fine enough to keep up."

Elam gazed at him for a couple of beats. He was right. The hostiles were still out there, hunting for them. The sooner they got out of here, the better. "All right. Let me know if we need to slow down or take a break."

Elam started up the next hill, picking his way in the shadowy blue light from Kennebec. He had detoured around a pile of boulders when the sky behind the next set of hills flashed cherry red. Seconds later the muffled *whomp* of an explosion rumbled across the landscape.

Elam halted and put a hand on Sigurd's shoulder.

Sigurd gazed at him from eyes that had sunk deep inside his pallid skull. "I think that used to be our flitter."

Elam gave him a grim nod. "I think you're right."

CHAPTER 30

"If we were all given by magic the power to read each other's thoughts, I suppose the first effect would be to dissolve all friendships."

—Bertrand Russell

SIGURD'S MUSCLES and joints ached as fatigue poisoned his body. Each breath sent pain shooting up his side. The steep slope ahead now ended not in blackness but in the flickering red glow of their distant flitter. He rubbed his eyes with his free hand and tried to think. His plan had worked. Glyndwr's team had escaped and was safely on its way. But if it cost Elam's life…. He couldn't finish the thought.

Elam murmured, "We'll think of something. Let's rest and regroup for a minute. We need a plan."

Rest. Chaos knew he needed rest. But Elam was right. He was always right. "I have a plan." Like an able commander, he'd considered loss of the flitter and made contingency plans. Not good ones, but plans nonetheless.

Elam's mouth quirked. "Now would be a good time to tell me."

Sigurd tried to reach across his body to pull out his communicator and winced as pain defeated him. "I can't reach my communicator. It's this blasted sling. Can you get it for me? It's in my right cargo pocket."

Elam fumbled with the flap on his pocket and pulled the device out. "What do you need this for? It's a bit late to call for help."

Sigurd clenched his eyes shut and tried to ignore the pain. "There's an area map on it. Can you pull it up?"

Elam stroked the phone's screen. "I don't see—oh, wait. Here it is. What am I looking for?"

"Let me see."

Sigurd gripped it in his left hand and peered at the screen. "Dammit. It needs to be larger. Can you do it? I've only got one usable hand."

Elam took the phone back, flicked the screen with his fingers, and held it so they could both see the display.

Sigurd nodded. "The cursor marks our current location. See that green *X*?"

Elam nodded. "What is it?"

"A cave. It's where Andresen's people hid out when they were watching the hostiles."

Elam's eyes widened, and a grin split his features. "A hiding place is just what we need. Are they still there?"

"Don't know. Possibly not. Andresen didn't like our ambush idea. Said it caused needless death."

"Screw him. It was a good plan, and it worked."

"Yeah. Except for us." He paused to pant. Breathe. *Pain*. Breathe. *Pain*. "Can you get us there?"

Elam examined the map. "Piece of cake. It's closer than the flitter, maybe a klick. Except the topography looks pretty rugged. Are you up to it?"

"I'll survive. Leave me behind if you have to."

"Like that's going to happen. I'll carry you if necessary."

Right. Carrying him would likely puncture a lung and kill him. "Just go already."

Elam gazed into his eyes for a beat, then nodded and took his hand. "I'll lead. Squeeze if I go too fast or you need to rest."

Time stretched to infinity. Step by step his legs grew weaker. His eyes drooped and his head sagged. Some timeless eternity later, his foot slipped on a rock and his ankle twisted. Elam's strong hands under his left arm saved him from falling, but at the cost of more pain from his tortured ribs.

Sigurd chewed his lower lip and struggled to stand straight. He wound up leaning against an outcrop of rock that stood a meter taller than his height. "How much farther?"

Elam frowned, then stared at Sigurd's phone. "We're almost there. Couple hundred meters maybe. Just over the next hill." He jerked his head to the right, then held a finger to his lips and whispered, "Don't move." He pulled his combat knife from its sheath and put his back to the rocky wall next to them.

Sigurd tried to ignore the pain in his side. It was good to rest, but what was Elam up to? He'd scrunched to one side, with his back to the rocks, and disappeared from view on the far side. A scuffling sound brought a chill to Sigurd's gut. Pebbles chattered with the sound of something heavy hitting them. A hoarse voice rasped out, "*Diablo*," then ended in a gurgle and a crunching sound.

Elam strolled back around the rocks, wiping the blade of his knife against his jacket. His mouth formed a grim line. "Two scouts. One sort of fell into my knife, and the other kind of lost his balance. He broke his neck."

"Are you all right?"

"Piece of cake. But we need to get to that hideout. Where there's two hostiles, there's bound to be more."

Another few minutes of agony later and they stood at the bottom of a steep, rocky hill. Sigurd stared at the climb, and defeat consumed him. "Maybe you should go ahead. Check for hostiles. Find the cave and come back for me."

"I'm not leaving you."

Sigurd considered his options. They didn't include climbing that last hill. "I could order you."

"You're not my boss, dammit. If it comes down to it, I'm the civil authority on this planet and you answer to me."

Yeah. A civil authority that answered to the Margrave. Or his family, which meant Sigurd. His vision blurred and his head wobbled. He jerked erect and tried to shake off the fatigue.

Elam glared at him, his mouth a hard line and his jaw jumping.

Sigurd closed his eyes. Always the argument with this one. He could really pick them. "I just can't…." He despised himself for the weak tremor in his voice.

Elam's features softened at once, and he clasped Sigurd's hand. "I'll help. We're together, remember? Between the two of us, we'll make it."

Sigurd stared at Elam's hand gripping his own. He blinked back tears, straightened his back, and took a hesitant step forward. He stumbled, but Elam wrapped an arm around Sigurd's back and caught him. Together, they took another step, then another.

A part of Sigurd knew it must be just a few minutes, but it felt like hours later that they reached the summit and started down into a little arroyo.

Steep cliffs towered over the far side. When they reached the bottom, Elam stopped and examined the phone. "According to this thing, we're there."

Sigurd lowered himself to the cold, rocky surface. At last he could rest. He closed his eyes.

His eyes jerked open, and pain shot up his side. Someone—Elam— was shaking him.

Tension filled Elam's voice, and grim lines marked his face. "You can't sleep just yet. Are you sure this map's accurate?"

"Yes." Of course it was accurate. It was based on satellite data.

"I don't see the cave."

Ruddy light pulsed and then steadied to a faint halo about Elam's features. His head jerked up and his eyes widened. He snatched up his rifle and started to point it at something.

Sigurd struggled to sit up and failed. The arroyo spun around him in a dizzying red whirl, then narrowed to a spot of ruby light. Darkness closed in and the world went away.

CHAPTER 31

The devil was once an angel.

—Dongeradeel Proverb

ELAM SQUATTED in the rocky hollow next to Sigurd and scanned the escarpment ten meters away. It glimmered in pale blue light from Kennebec, but it was solid stone. He chewed his lip and then gave Sigurd the bad news. "I don't see the cave."

Ruddy light pulsed behind him and then faded to a steady glow. The escarpment writhed. A figure, a woman, walked through the rocks and stopped. She wore flowing white robes that glowed with a ruby-colored aura. She gazed at him with somber cerulean eyes.

Elam snatched up his rifle. She didn't look like any Exaltationist he'd ever seen, but who else would be out there tonight?

She held her palms up and said in a soft contralto, "We're here to help." She turned a concerned look on Sigurd. "Your friend is injured. May we see to him?"

Elam glanced back at Sigurd, and a cold ball of fear formed in his gut. He looked like death itself, shrouded in the ruddy glow. Sweat sheened on his features, and he'd passed out. Elam looked back at the woman. "Who are you?"

"Call me Afina. We're of the Left Behind. We thought you might need assistance. We've been waiting for you."

Elam glanced at the rocky escarpment, then back at the woman. "Andresen told you we were coming?"

She gave him an indulgent smile. "You must mean Marat." She pronounced it Mar-ah. "Yes, we know of you through him." She turned her gaze back to Sigurd. "Please. He needs attention. We know what it's like to be abandoned. We won't let that happen to you."

Elam clenched his jaw and glared at her. She was right. Sigurd's injuries were clearly worse than he thought and were probably exacerbated by the forced march to get here. He was sure she wasn't an Exaltationist, and he wasn't about to shoot her. What choice did he have? "Go ahead."

She knelt at Sigurd's side and placed a hand on his forehead. With her other hand she stroked the side with the injured ribs. She looked up at Elam and said, "We can heal him. But we'll need to take him to our infirmary."

"He can't—" Elam stopped his objection because two more glowing figures carrying a stretcher walked through the rocky wall. In moments they'd secured Sigurd to the stretcher and carried him toward the escarpment. It rippled as the lead stretcher bearer, then Sigurd, and finally the last bearer passed through the barrier and disappeared.

Elam closed his mouth. He approached the rocks and touched them. They were solid and grainy. "How did they do that?"

Afina beamed at him. "Would you like to join your friend?"

"Yes. Absolutely."

"Take my hand."

He kept his rifle in his right hand and took her hand with his left. She led him through the wall like it wasn't there. Well, except it rippled and was kind of tingly, but it offered no resistance.

The other side of the rocky wall was a cave, just like Andresen had said. It ended in a brightly lit semicylindrical tunnel ramping down to a lower level. He turned around and touched the rock wall he'd just walked through. Solid again, just like the other side had been minutes ago. "How did you do that?"

She frowned and tipped her head. "I'm not sure I can explain. We know you use an AI you call Cornwall. Could you explain to us how he works? The details of how he displays himself and the circuits that he uses?"

"Yes."

"Of course. You must be an engineer. Maybe that's not the best example. Surely you use technology that you can't explain. Maybe those devices you call nanodocs."

She had him there. All he knew was that they were a self-programming neuronet, which was pretty much the same as saying they worked because they inhaled Freya's breath. How the wall worked wasn't important, anyway. "Where did they take Sigurd?"

"We've taken your friend to the infirmary as we promised. Would you like to join him?"

"Yes." He gripped his rifle. "Right now."

"Of course. Come along."

Elam let her lead him into the corridor. It leveled out after dropping perhaps ten meters, then curved to the left and darkness. When they rounded the turn, lights came on in front of them and dimmed behind them. For about the next hundred meters, the tunnel ran straight, with closed doors on alternating sides every twenty meters or so. The air was warm and fresh. "What is this place?"

Afina shrugged. "It had fallen out of use until the cultists came. A few us came here to watch over them." She opened one of the doors, which led to stairs going down.

Elam followed her down two landings to where she held another door open for him.

He narrowed his eyes. "Seems like a pretty big place." Too big to just be abandoned.

"We had use for this large place at one time, when there were still marines at the old base." She stopped and held her hand on a doorknob. "Your friend is on the other side. Healers will be assisting his body to recover. For his sake, we must ask you not interfere."

Elam frowned. This didn't sound good. "What are they doing to him? Is it dangerous?"

"No, but the healers must concentrate on him. If they are distracted, it will take longer for him to recover." She gave him a probing look. "We have your word you will not interfere?"

Elam scowled. He wasn't giving his word until he saw Sigurd. "Just let me see him."

She hesitated, then said, "We see you care for him deeply." She opened the door and stood aside for Elam to enter.

Sigurd lay unconscious and stretched out on a table, naked except for a sheet over his midsection. An angry red-and-purple bruise circled his lower chest, from his sternum to his back. Four, no five people wearing surgical masks and pale green gowns bustled about him. IVs hung at the head of the table and connected to his arm. A dozen or more blue patches stuck to his body at various locations. A monitor pulsed with his heartbeat and displayed squiggles in a script Elam didn't recognize.

Afina murmured, "He has a broken rib and injuries to internal organs. We will help him heal."

Elam's throat tightened at the sight of Sigurd so helpless. "The rib's actually broken, then? Not cracked? Will he have to have surgery?"

"Yes, it is detached." She frowned. "Surgery? You mean cut him open like they did in ancient times? Don't worry. We'd never do anything so barbaric."

"Won't you have to set the broken bone?" Elam had seen broken ribs before. They took weeks to heal, and detached ribs often needed surgery, especially if they'd punctured an internal organ.

"We can heal without cutting." She peered at him. "We will let him sleep while he heals, so he won't experience any pain."

A coma? That was insane. "How long?" Elam was sure they wouldn't keep him in a coma for weeks.

"Oh, he should be fully recovered in three or four days. His body is in excellent condition, except for his injuries."

"Three days? That doesn't sound possible."

Her tone turned indulgent. "We assure you we are excellent healers. We have experience. We're much better than your primitive nanodocs."

Huh. Primitive nanodocs. "I want to be with him while he's asleep. All the time."

"Certainly, if that's your wish."

The bustle around the table seemed to slow down. Several of the people stripped off their masks and robes, and one of them approached Afina. "Good thing we got to him when we did."

Cold fear gripped Elam's gut. "You mean he could have died?"

The man looked at Elam, and his eyes softened. "You're his lover. No, we would never have permitted that to happen. It just would have taken us a little longer. He's going to be fine."

Afina said, "Elam, this is Dembe. He's one of our best healers."

Elam offered his hand. "Thank you for saving Sigurd, sir."

Dembe's face split in a wide smile, and he gave Elam's hand a vigorous shake. "You're most welcome, but Afina here gave him the initial aid. She's the miracle worker." He turned back to Afina. "I understand that Mfumu is working on two of the wounded cultists. I really should help him out."

Afina waved a hand. "Of course. I'll attend to Elam."

Elam gave Afina an appraising look. How could she be a miracle worker when she didn't actually do anything? "What did I miss? It looked to me like all you did was comfort him."

"Maybe that was all he needed. They're taking him to his room. Shall we go?"

THE NEXT morning, Elam stretched awake in a comfortable bed in a clean, quiet room. He rolled over, and Sigurd lay face up in an adjacent bed, eyes closed and peaceful. A crisp white sheet covered his body, IVs attached to his arm, and a readout pulsed with his heartbeat. It was in the same strange script as the readouts in the treatment room.

Elam climbed out of bed and stood next to Sigurd. Last night he'd looked gaunt, like he'd just fought a close battle with death. This morning his color was good, and he seemed to be resting comfortably. Elam ran his fingers across Sigurd's close-cropped skull and caressed the side of his head. He was beautiful, even with the *Volknut* tattoo on his bristly cheek.

The door opened, and Afina pushed a cart into the room. Elam inhaled the homey scent of coffee, bacon, and eggs.

Afina said, "How are my patients?"

"I'm not your patient. Sigurd seems to be comfortable."

She came to the bedside and held Sigurd's wrist as if taking his pulse, while scanning the readouts. "He's progressing nicely." She lifted the sheet and exposed Sigurd's side, where a light green bruise marked his lower ribs.

Elam peered at the bruise. "How can that be? It was twice as big last night, and deep purple."

She beamed at him. "His body is healing itself. We gave it a little push to help it along." She replaced the sheet and stroked Sigurd's forehead. "We'll wake him in two mornings from now. He'll be healed by then."

Elam raised his eyebrows. "That quickly? Standard healing time is six to eight weeks, depending on the severity of the break."

"Perhaps your healers use different methods?" She pointed to the cart. "You must be hungry. Sit, and we can chat while you eat."

Breakfast did smell good, and Elam's stomach reminded him he hadn't eaten in, what? It must be eighteen or more hours, back in the Lodge. She'd rolled the cart next to a chair, so he sat and dug in.

"This is really good. Thank you."

"Our pleasure. How are you feeling this morning?"

"Besides hungry? I'm fine. Sigurd's the one who's injured."

"Not all injuries are to the body. Some are less obvious."

He let that pass and sipped at his juice. "I swear, this is much better than the synthesizers at the Lodge. I could swear this is real orange juice."

She shrugged. "Our genetic engineers are clever. They probably tweaked the ancient processors. I trust it's better than the snack you shared with… Andresen, I think you called him?"

Elam remembered cookies and milk. "They were good, but this is much better. Thank you."

She dimpled. "You were so kind to Marat's cats. You even carried one to your first meeting with him. That told us a lot about you."

Elam frowned. How could she know that kind of detail? And why would they care about frigging cats?

She tipped her head and gave him an impish smile. "Did you like the biscuits? Our engineers gave them a traditional flavor common to Dongeradeel."

"Snickerdoodles. Yes. It was comforting to find something so familiar here." Her mention of engineers reminded him of the rippling escarpment. "You never told me how that trick with the rock wall worked."

Her eyes widened in innocence. "Trick?"

"Last night. We walked through a solid rock wall. It kind of rippled, and we walked through it. But when I touched it a moment later, it was, well, rock solid."

She shrugged. "Oh, that. It's just engineering. I'm not an expert. I'm told it has to do with holograms."

He frowned. "You mean like with Cornwall? Holograms can't do that. You can see through them, and they have no substance. They're just a trick of the light."

"I'm sorry. I told you I'm not an expert. It has something to do with quantum physics, and those that do understand tell me the effect is like a hologram. That's all I know."

Elam frowned. He wasn't a physicist either, but this sounded fishy. He remembered reading something about an information paradox and holograms, but that was in a physics class on Sandhurst, years ago. In any case, it had nothing to do with walking through walls.

Afina touched his hand. "We sense much dissonance in you."

"Dissonance? I never could carry a tune." What in Chaos was she talking about?

Ivar Jelckama.

Elam jerked his hand back. "What did you say? How do you know that name?"

"What name? We only said that we sense unresolved conflict in you."

"Ivar Jelckama. You said his name."

"Ivar Jelckama." She repeated it, giving the vowels the precise inflection a rural villager on Dongeradeel would use. The same inflection Ivar had used. She seemed to taste each word before swallowing it. "He is someone important to you." It wasn't a question.

"He's dead." Elam squelched the emotions that accompanied that statement. He couldn't suppress the memory of Ivar as he last saw him, twisted, pocked with bullet holes, in a pool of his own blood.

Afina caressed his wrist. Something deep inside him twisted free. The horror of that last memory of Ivar remained, but it no longer devoured other memories. Instead, memories of Ivar's face the first time he tasted chocolate, or when his dog gave birth to puppies, or the first time they kissed emerged. Memories of his warm body sleeping next to Elam in their shared bed, memories of making love, memories of them together swelled in his heart.

He wrenched his arm away from Afina. "What did you do?"

She pursed her lips and frowned. "Duty, honor, heart. Such dissonance in those demands."

How did she know those words? How did she know his failure?

She stood and stacked the empty dishes on the cart. "We'll leave you to heal. Perhaps you can take a nap?"

His eyelids did feel suddenly heavy. A nap sounded wonderful. "What did you do to me?"

Her expression turned somber. "Lovers die. It is the way of the world. But love survives." She pushed the cart out the door and left.

What the Chaos just happened? Elam sat on the edge of his bed, yawned, and replayed the conversation. Her micro-expressions showed no guile, only genuine concern. The only moments of deception occurred when she talked about the rock wall, and those were fleeting. She did have a peculiar way of speaking, as if modern Inglish were not her birth language. But what language replaced first person singular with first person plural? Could it be the unknown language on the readouts?

How did she get the accents on Ivar's name so perfect? Not from Elam. He'd purged those phenomes from his own speech during his time on Sandhurst.

Then the pieces all fell together. Shock sent electric jitters down his spine. It couldn't be right, but it all fit.

He had to tell Sigurd. They had to warn the Empire. If he was right, all of humanity was at risk.

CHAPTER 32

We hear only those questions for which we are in a position to find answers.

—Friedrich Nietzsche

SIGURD WOKE and pulled soft blankets around his body. Gentle snores sounded from nearby. He frowned and sat up. An IV dragged at his right arm. A dim amber glow suffused the room, illuminating blank, featureless walls. A red light pulsed on a monitor next to his bed, while the screen traced out his heartbeat in regular squiggles.

This couldn't be right. Where was he?

The last thing he remembered was an ambush in the mountains, right where Andresen's people were supposed to have a hideout. How did he get here? Where was here? And where was *Elam*? This room looked nothing like the infirmary back at the Lodge when he'd visited Cadwalladar. Those rooms had big windows looking out onto floral gardens, and inspirational art on the walls.

And who in Chaos was in the bed next to him?

The man in the next bed lay on his side, facing away from Sigurd. He wore orange-and-pink knee-length shorts and a black shirt with crimson flames stitched into the bottom half, but no shoes or socks. He snorted and rolled to his back, exposing his face. Elam. Drool ran down his cheek as he resumed snoring.

A smile trifled with Sigurd's lips. Wherever they were, Elam had managed to find an outlandish outfit to wear. Totally in character.

Sigurd touched his side and took a tentative breath, then a deeper one. The muscles felt a little stiff, but the pain had gone away. Maybe he was dead. How long had he been out? It felt like yesterday, but no one healed that quickly from cracked ribs.

The door to the room stood ajar and revealed a shadowy corridor outside. Sigurd wanted to explore, but the blasted bed had rails on it, and there wasn't an obvious way to lower them. Besides, he was still leery of aggravating his injured ribs. The last thing he needed was a punctured lung.

A pleasant feminine voice interrupted his inspection of the bed rails. "I see you're awake. How's our patient?"

The nurse, if that's what she was, was tall, maybe his height with her auburn hair cut in a short, sensible bob. Her regular features defied classification, as if she was a mixture of several races. She stepped between the two beds, gripped his wrist, and her eyes got an absent look.

Sigurd let her finish taking his pulse or whatever she was doing, then asked, "Where am I?"

"You're in our infirmary." She gave him a bright, if somewhat toothy, smile. "You got here just in time. You were going into shock. Internal bleeding, fatigue, broken ribs." Another sunny smile. "But you're all fixed up now. No worries."

Sigurd glanced at Elam. "How about him?"

"Him? He's a stubborn one. He's fine, except for being bone-headed."

Sigurd snorted. "He is that. Did he give you trouble?"

"Nothing we couldn't handle. He mostly just wanted to be sure you were taken care of. He wouldn't leave your side. He even insisted on sleeping here."

Sigurd let that sink in while gazing at Elam's sleeping form.

The woman patted his hand. "My name's Afina, by the way. We're in charge of your care." She followed his gaze. "You two must be very special to each other."

Sigurd's face heated. "We're colleagues in arms." No reason to reveal more, certainly not until he knew more about where they were and who Afina was. She didn't *look* like an Exaltationist, and no one was torturing him. Both positive things. But any weakness could be used against them. Best to be cautious.

She squeezed his hand. "It's all right. While we were checking your injuries, we had to do some deep... *scanning*, I think is the word you might use. We know that off-worlders value something you call privacy, so please accept our apologies."

Scanning? Off-worlders? Sigurd frowned. "You're one of the Left Behind? One of Andresen's people?"

That earned him another sunny smile, this one with dimples that made him think of Jorina. "That's so quaint. Yes, we're... one of his... people."

The way she said "one" and "people" made Sigurd frown. There was some mystery here, but he couldn't put his finger on it. But before he could pursue the thought, Elam woke.

"Sigurd!" Elam jumped out of bed, pushed Afina to one side, and grasped his hand. "How are you? I was so worried about you. Don't ever do that again!"

"I'll try not to. I trust you are well?" He squeezed back. Elam's hand felt right in his own.

"Me? I'm fine." His face clouded. "You know where we're at, right? In the hideout Andresen's people used."

Sigurd nodded, then frowned. "He told me it was a cave. This appears more... substantial?"

Elam nodded. "You got that right. There's at least three levels, and room for dozens of people." He glanced at Afina, then looked back at Sigurd. "I've reached some conclusions. I'll fill you in later."

Later. That must mean he doesn't want to talk in front of Afina. Sigurd turned to face her. "I really am feeling better. Can I maybe go for a walk? I'm sure Elam here can assist me if needed."

She nodded. "Of course. The two of you want to catch up." She fiddled with his IV, pulled it out, and attached a gauze and bandage. "The bathroom is just inside the door to the hall, and there's a lounge down the corridor where the two of you can talk. If you need anything, I'll be right here to help. Meantime, We have other patients to attend to." She bustled away.

Elam watched her leave, his mouth pinched into a firm line.

Sigurd frowned. "Other patients? Have some of the Left Behind been injured?"

"No. They went back to the site of our firefight and rescued two wounded hostiles. The ones with nonfatal wounds. They're in the infirmary too."

Sigurd nodded. "Well, I can't say I'm sorry. That's our standard practice too."

Elam let a sneer bend his lips. "Yeah, for us. For the Exaltationists, torture and death is what they do. In fact, these guys tried to fight with their rescuers. They're under sedation right now, in locked rooms."

"Prisoners of war, then. We'll repatriate them to Sparta if they want." He paused, and doubt seeped into his voice. "Assuming Afina and her people are willing."

"Who knows what they're willing to do."

Sigurd said, "I take it you don't trust her."

"About as far as I can spit." He reached under the bed and lowered the rails. "I'm sure if we need anything, she'll be right here, whether we ask for her or not."

"What do you mean?"

"I'm pretty sure she can read our minds. In fact, I think they all can."

CHAPTER 33

If you correct your mind, the rest of your life will fall into place.

—Lao Tzu

CONCERN TIGHTENED Elam's throat when Sigurd stood by his bed and swayed, as if dizzy. Elam gripped his shoulder to steady him, but Sigurd shrugged him off. "I'm fine."

He didn't look fine. His face was pale, his respiration shallow and fast, and he wasn't steady on his feet. "We can talk here if you want." He hesitated. "Did Afina mention you've been out of it for three days now?"

Sigurd paled and sat back on the edge of the bed. "Three days? Really?"

"Really. You were in pretty bad shape—far worse than I knew. I'm amazed you managed to keep it together as long as you did. You were in shock when they brought you in here. You'd apparently dislodged the rib on the march, and the scans showed it penetrating your intestine. I'm not sure even Mr. Mustafa could have helped you."

Sigurd frowned. "Tell me what happened. All I remember is a red light and you reaching for your rifle. I thought it must be an ambush."

"I thought so too. They just appeared from nowhere. But they held up their hands and assured me they were sent by Clerk Andresen. I figured Exaltationists would have just killed us and asked questions afterwards, so I let them work on you."

"So we were in the right place after all?"

"Yeah. They told me to follow them and walked through what looked like a solid rock wall into this place. I gritted my teeth and followed. It was like walking through a hologram."

"Andresen did tell me they had advanced holographic techniques."

Elam let skepticism leak into his voice. "Maybe." He paused for a beat, then added, "I have been in touch with Ms. Baak, at least indirectly. They've relayed messages to me. Our communicators don't seem to work here."

"Status?"

"Mr. Glyndwr's team arrived safely at the Lodge, so your plan was a success. Oh, and Mr. Cadwalladar is awake. Mr. Mustafa expects a full recovery."

Sigurd nodded. "Excellent on both counts. Sharon will be pleased about Cadwalladar. Anything about the naval squadron?"

"Not as of a day and half ago. I didn't want to reveal too much to our, er, allies." He frowned, then continued, "This place is huge. Not a cave at all. Afina told me they built it long ago to watch over the marine base."

Sigurd quirked an eyebrow at that. "Did she say why they needed to watch over the base?"

"No. But I think we already figured that out."

Sigurd nodded, recalling their discussion about a possible conflict in the planet's distant past. "You're probably right." He heaved a deep breath and stood back up, and this time didn't wobble.

Still, Elam reached for his arm just to be safe.

Sigurd leaned into him, and Elam put an arm around Sigurd and pulled him closer. Their eyes met, and without thinking, Elam kissed him.

Sigurd froze, then melted against him and returned the kiss. They wrapped arms around each other, and their tongues commingled. Elam pressed against Sigurd's hard body and raked his fingers across his back. After an eternity, after a few seconds, he had to break for a breath. Sigurd whispered, "At last." His breath warmed Elam's neck.

Elam ran his fingers through Sigurd's short hair and lingered on the nape of his neck. "Why did we wait so long?" he murmured.

A languid smile played on Sigurd's lips. "You talk too much. Kiss me again."

This one lasted longer. Their bodies coiled as one, desire pulsing in their veins. Sigurd's fingers trailed down Elam's side, sending desire jittering up his neck and sending goose bumps to prickle the nape of his neck. He gripped Sigurd closer still, his heart pounding. He pulled back and gazed into Sigurd's eyes. "You know I love you."

Sigurd's grin turned impish. "I seem to remember you saying that. I love you too. I have loved you ever since I saw you that first night outside the Lodge."

Elam snorted. "Wearing nothing but a towel."

"That was on purpose, I'm sure. How did you know it would work on me?"

"I didn't. I just hoped. I kind of felt bad after, since I wanted you from the first. It was like I was using you."

"Well, it worked. I'm glad you did." His eyes crinkled. "You wanted to talk to me. Was it to propose marriage?"

"Yes."

"I don't believe you." He paused for a beat, and his expression turned serious. "Much as I'd like to continue this, we've got serious matters to consider. Like our tactical situation. I don't trust Afina any more than you do."

Elam sighed. "You're right, of course."

Elam gave Sigurd a courtly bow and extended a bent arm. Sigurd looped his arm around it, and together they walked down the hall. Elam kept the pace slow. "You know, you almost died. Good thing these people have advanced medical technology. That Afina person said our nanodocs were 'primitive.'"

"She and her people are descended from some of the best bioengineers of the old Grand Alliance. I'm not surprised they've got advanced technology."

Elam held the door to the lounge open and followed Sigurd inside. The same amber light as in Sigurd's hospital room filled this place, revealing the severe interior décor that they'd seen in the Lodge. While Sigurd took a seat, Elam muttered, "Mr. Clifford called this style 'sofa-in-a-cage.' If they're so smart, you'd think they'd have more advanced esthetics."

Sigurd leaned back and put his feet on a matching ottoman. "I've seen this in old videos from the era. It's a copy of a style popular on Old Home Earth dating back to a famous designer in the mid-twentieth century."

Elam shrugged. "I guess bad ideas have a long lifespan."

"Actually, I kind of like it. It's minimalist, with the metal frame an homage to the rise of machines. The essence of what a chair wants to be in an industrial age."

Elam didn't roll his eyes. A chair didn't want to be anything. Time to get started on serious matters. "Are you up to having a discussion?"

"Yes. I imagine Afina and company are listening."

"I think you imagine right." Elam pursed his lips, then continued, "I know you read my ImpSec file. Did it mention Ivar Jelckama, by any chance?"

Sigurd frowned. "Not that I recall. Who is he?"

Elam shrugged. "Someone I knew on Dongeradeel."

"Oh. A big section of the file was redacted. The only mention of Dongeradeel was in the honors list citation, for heroism."

Elam winced. Heroism was the last word he would have chosen for what happened on Dongeradeel. "Somehow they knew his name. The people here, the Left Behind, as they call themselves. I thought they might have found him in my file."

Sigurd frowned and rubbed his forehead. "I'm pretty sure he wasn't mentioned. Is it important?"

"Maybe. Afina definitely knew that name was important to me. If it wasn't in the file, then she must have pulled it from my memory."

Sigurd's eyebrows went up. "Ah. That's why you think they read minds."

"That, and the things she knew about Andresen. She knew the details of our first meeting with him, for example, right down to tea and biscuits with the cats. How could she know that if she hadn't read my mind, or at least his?"

"You of all people should know that a skilled interrogator can pull details from a subject. It can seem like mind reading. Like how you can tell if someone is telling the truth or lying. However it works, magicians do similar things. I've seen it myself when they perform at the court on Elsinore."

Elam scowled and waved his hand. "That's training. Sure, I can read micro-expressions. With the right training, you can't miss them, and they reveal what a person is really feeling when they lie." He narrowed his eyes and considered Sigurd's words. "You're probably right. Used properly, you can extract a lot of information from a subject."

Sigurd's eyes lit up. "Micro-expressions. I recall reading about those. I thought it must be something like that. I can imagine how you'd use that skill to tease out intelligence from subjects."

Elam leaned back and stroked his chin. Sigurd was smart, and he was right too. But his training should have let him see what she was doing. "She'd need a pretty high skill level to do that without me catching her."

Sigurd nodded. "I'm sure that's true. I have no doubt as to your skills. But you'd just completed an exhausting forced march, burdened by a wounded colleague. Perhaps you were not at your best?"

"Maybe." Ordinarily, mind reading would fail a least-hypothesis test for sure. Except these weren't ordinary circumstances. "I've also been thinking more about Andresen's so-called implant."

"What about it?"

"During the conference, did you notice he directly interacted with the screen? No verbal commands?"

Sigurd frowned. "Of course. We talked about this. I just thought he had some way of transmitting commands to Lear, his AI."

"Other times, before that, did you see him interact with Lear?"

"Yes. Lear appeared as a hologram in his lab, and he interacted verbally, just as we do with Cornwall, or any AI I've ever encountered, for that matter."

Elam couldn't keep the triumph out of his voice. "Exactly. But in the conference room, he bypassed verbal commands and manipulated the display directly. And he knew he'd screwed up when he did it. His facial expression was quick, but unmistakable."

Sigurd shrugged. "So, what's the point? I mean, I can see where that would be useful, especially in combat where timing can be everything. But how is it relevant?"

He still didn't get it. Elam stood and paced. "Think about the implications. Think about Afina's intimate knowledge of our first interactions with Andresen. They've been engineering themselves for centuries. Even if they can't read *our* minds, they can read each other's. I think they're a group mind. A shared consciousness."

Sigurd's face paled, but he shook his head. "There have to be other explanations. The evidence seems thin for such an extraordinary conclusion. I mean, how could that even work?"

Elam stopped pacing and faced him. "I don't know. Remember when he first revealed he had an implant? He didn't want to answer questions."

Sigurd nodded. "He was evasive, yes. I remember thinking he might as well have said it's like explaining color to a blind person."

"I had exactly the same thought. But he didn't say that, because it would have been too revealing. The bottom line is, we can't imagine what that implant must be like. But if they all have one, it means there is mind-to-mind contact with each other as well as the machines. Now imagine a fleet of ghostships with crews like that."

Elam let that sink in. The alarm in Sigurd's eyes showed that he understood. He'd probably reach the next logical conclusion, now that he had all the data.

Someone tapped at the door, and a female voice said, "Knock-knock. Hope the two of you are decent. I'm coming in." The door opened and Jorina entered, wearing camouflage combat mufti, complete with a pistol holstered at her hip. She gave them a dimpled smile. "Good to see you guys. I mean, sirs."

Sigurd scowled at her. "What in Chaos are you doing here? I gave you explicit orders—"

She held up her hand. "Don't get your britches in a hitch. Marines from HMS *Andover* have landed, and the situation is well in hand. They've captured or killed the Exaltationist forces and secured the planet. Admiral Pierre Béhuchet of HMS *Charles Martel* requests your presence at the Lodge, and sent me to fetch you. Your flitter awaits, my lords."

CHAPTER 34

Life is divided into three terms—that which was, which is, and which will be.

—William Wordsworth

SIGURD EXAMINED his image in the mirror and adjusted the choker collar of his dress uniform. He twisted his chin up, but the damned thing still chafed. His mouth turned down as he inspected the spare lines of his uniform, from the ebony sheen of his knee-high boots to the crease in his black trousers and up to the featureless black tunic. Black everywhere except for the stylized golden hawk of his rank on the collar and the silver sails of the Corsairs stitched over his heart. That and his blasted facial tattoo completed the storm-trooper image.

Sigurd snorted. Much as he despised the uniform, it was better than the ornate gold-encrusted crimson-and-sapphire mufti of the Margrave's court. That was something he'd change once he inherited. The politicians ran everything else, but the Margrave at least ran his own court.

A discreet knock at the door made him check the clock. Plenty of time. "Who is it?"

"Jorina, sir."

Great. She knew better than to bother him before today's ceremony, so this meant something must have gone wrong. "Enter."

She gave him one of her dimpled grins and a snappy salute. She wore the gray-and-white uniform of the *Zuiderkruis*, but without insignia or rank. "Don't you look official. Sir."

Sigurd snapped, "I'm sure you're not here to give fashion advice."

"No, sir." She shuffled her feet and evaded his gaze.

"What is it, Ms. Baak?" He tried for a gentle tone and grimaced. Gentle was tough.

She glanced up at him, then continued her examination of the carpet. "It's about the treaty, sir."

"What about it?" A codicil included the Syndicate assigning her to the court on Elsinore. "The Admiral included the provisions about you at the request of the Margravina."

She glanced up. "Yes, sir. I appreciate that. I'm happy to serve where needed."

Sigurd sighed. If he knew his mother, her plans for Jorina involved him too. "Speak to me. We can work this out together."

"Sir, it's Mr. Mustafa. We're kind of a, well, I mean…."

"You're in love with him."

She lifted her eyes to glance at him; then her gaze darted around the room. "Yes, sir."

"Did you know I offered him a place with the Corsairs, if he wanted it?"

"He told me, sir. But the Corsairs mean deployment. Separation."

"I could assign him to the Margrave's personal contingent. He'd be at the palace. Would that do?"

"That would be awesome. That's exactly what we'd hoped for. Thank you, sir."

He nodded. "Next time, just come out and ask. You've more than earned the right to be frank." He'd have to put his foot down with his mother and her matchmaking schemes too. "Is there anything else?"

"No, sir. And thank you. Gabir and I really appreciate it."

"Well then, off with you. Tell him the good news."

"Yes, sir. Thank you, sir." She glanced at the clock. "I'll see you in twenty minutes." She rushed out the door, happy dimples in her cheeks.

Sigurd thought about sitting down, but that would wrinkle the perfection of his uniform. A voice from the doorway made him turn.

"*Achtung, mein Herr!*" Elam leaned against the frame, for once wearing more or less conventional attire. At least to the extent that leather trews, sporran, and a tartan fly plaid in the Imperial Balmoral could be said to be conventional. A baronial medallion hung on a golden chain about his neck.

Sigurd let a tight smile bend his lips. "Don't you look fancy."

Elam rolled his eyes. "I planned on an aloha shirt, grass skirt, and flip-flops, but the admiral insisted."

"And you agreed. I'll have to learn the secret to his success in getting you to follow orders."

Elam's face turned grim. "The bastard had something I wanted. This was his price."

Sigurd tried to squelch the surge of sadness that had threatened to consume him for the last week. "Does this have to do with your new assignment?"

Elam sighed and puttered to the bar. "I need a drink. Can I get one for you?"

"Gin and tonic, please." Sigurd collapsed into an easy chair. The hell with his uniform.

Elam fixed two drinks, squeezed artificial lime juice into them, and handed one to Sigurd. He sat in a chair facing Sigurd and raised his glass. "To us!"

Sigurd raised his in response. "To us. There's damned few of us left." He sipped his drink.

Elam gulped half his down and then stared at Sigurd. "So, you're headed back to the palace?"

"Yes. Duty calls. And you're to stay here as Resident."

"That's the deal. Not quite what I'd originally planned, though, what with there being a permanent naval presence in the system."

Sigurd nodded. "That was the only possible solution. By Imperial policy, the planet really belongs to the native population, voiding the Syndicate's title. But the Left Behind had to be quarantined, for the safety of the Empire. They needed protection from the Exaltationists too. In a way, the Exaltationists did us a favor. It made them see they need that protection. They want to be left alone, and we can guarantee that. The treaty spells out the details. Both sides win."

Elam gave him a grim nod. "You know, they already had it all worked out. They even had the language ready when the admiral proposed your solution, including a demand to name me as Resident and requiring that I be the only official contact with the outside galaxy."

Sigurd snorted. "The admiral seemed to think it was his brilliant negotiating skills."

"They are skillful at manipulating what people think, I'll give them that. They conned him, just like they did the rest of us." Elam finished his drink. "You want another?"

"I'm fine, thank you." He let Elam refresh his own drink, then asked, "So do you still think they are mind readers?"

"I don't know what to think about them. For all I know, they could all be a single hive mind, each of them with superpowers beyond human ken. Or it could all be just a big con. But I'm sure they are dangerous. For one thing, there's the evidence that Chad— Mr. Clifford—found of local warfare around three hundred years ago. They fought with each other, so they're not the sandal-wearing pacifists they pretend to be."

"Smart of you to ask him to look for that. But what he found wasn't exactly conclusive. Just a modest peak in energy consumption with no apparent environmental cause. Still, I agree, it's suggestive."

Elam's mouth formed a grim line. "The important thing is that they're locked up on this planet and aren't getting out."

"And no more people get killed."

Elam nodded. "There's that."

"They also claim there are no advanced kinetic weapons here. No death rays either."

Elam snorted. "Claim would be the operative word."

"It doesn't really matter what they've got. They're bottled up here, with an Imperial flotilla permanently overhead. I understand that they've leased the old naval base on Diego Garcia to us as well. They even had their AI, Lear, disable the defenses. It doesn't sound like they've got nefarious plans."

That got him a hesitant nod. "I guess. At least they've agreed to share their holographic technology and their mind-machine interface. Clerk also told me he wants us to set up mechanisms to share medical technology and databases."

"Sounds like you'll be busy after all. Not the navel-gazing nosedive you were expecting when you signed up to be Resident."

"I thought you liked my navel."

Sigurd grinned. "I admit it has a certain appeal. I'll miss it. And you."

They sat in silence for a few moments. Elam sucked down his drink and said, "Well, I guess we at least have that last few days here at the Lodge to remember."

Sigurd fiddled with his glass and mused, "Yes. I wouldn't trade those for anything."

Elam looked like he'd sucked on lemons. "Unless the Empire required it."

Sigurd recited, "Duty, honor, and heart." He paused for a beat. "There's a reason those are in that order. We always do what duty and honor demand. Both of us."

"Yeah, we do." Elam narrowed his eyes. "I believe that duty demands you produce an heir."

Sigurd winced. Elam probably didn't mean to be hurtful, but still his words bit. He retorted, "It does. It doesn't demand I take a wife and impregnate her, though."

Elam's eyebrows crawled up his head. "You're thinking of a surrogate?"

"That's one solution. My father wants an heir. My mother just wants a grandchild. As long as they get what they want, they won't care how it's done."

Elam leaned back and tented his fingers. "I understand Ms. Baak is headed to the court."

"Yes. Along with Mr. Mustafa. Apparently they are in love."

"You know he's trans, right?"

"Yes. Your point?"

"Just thinking things through, is all. Following consequences. The Margravina seems to hold her in high regard."

Sigurd shrugged. "There is that. Jorina and Gabir deserve whatever happiness the two of them can find. I'm not going to let anyone interfere with that."

"I didn't say you would." He swirled his drink, then fingered his baronial medallion. "I don't deserve this thing, you know. I got it because I betrayed the person closest to me."

"You got it because you did your duty." He stood and caressed Elam's cheek. "I'm going to miss you."

"Me too. We had so little time together, and we wasted most of it." He blinked, and Sigurd wondered if those were tears in his eyes.

Sigurd's chin trembled, and he cursed the tear that ran down his own cheek. He tried to squelch his emotions, but then surrendered to them. He pulled Elam closer and murmured in his ear, "The story of our lives still has pages for us to write. This isn't the end. Let's agree this is farewell and not goodbye."

Elam pulled back and gazed into his eyes. A shaky grin flitted across Elam's features. "Farewell it is, then." He put his arms around Sigurd and embraced him. "To our tomorrows."

Sigurd returned the hug, and they clung to one another for a few seconds. Sigurd heaved a deep breath and broke away. He whispered, "It's time."

Together, they walked to the ceremony where the Left Behind and the admiral would sign the official treaty sealing their mutual fates.

TWO DAYS later, Elam stood next to Chad on the landing field at the Lodge's ghost port. An early evening fog swirled about them. The *Charles Martel*'s shuttle taxied through the ghostly mist toward the end of the runway. Overhead, Kennebec shimmered through the fog, its rings dimmed by the mist.

Elam sighed and realized he no longer noticed the stench of the wheat. Apparently it was true, you could get used to anything.

The shuttle stopped at the end of the runway, and its engines whined as the pilot revved them for takeoff.

Chad took his hand. "Will you miss him?"

He meant Sigurd, of course. "Yes. But our little lives don't matter much to the rest of the galaxy. He's off to do his duty to the Empire. And to humankind, for that matter. We have to do our part too, here in this place."

Chad squeezed his hand. "I'm glad you asked me to stay."

Together they watched the shuttle speed down the runway and depart to the heavens. Sigurd, Jorina, Gabir, and all the others were gone. They were alone together on this planet, restricted by treaty to the Lodge and environs.

Elam squeezed Chad's hand. "I'm glad you agreed to stay. I think this might be the beginning of a beautiful friendship."

Why Are They Called Ghost Ships?

Op-Ed from the *Pasargadae Post*
25 Ventôse, 3174
Pasargadae, New Arizona
Immaculate Concourse of Planets
Reprinted by permission
Part of our continuing series on the history of technology

TODAY, HUMANS routinely journey through this corner of the galaxy in ghostships. Almost no living soul remembers the time before 2970 when Gregor Stapledon rediscovered the secret of interstellar travel. Even fewer know the history of the time over a thousand years ago when everyone lived on one planet, Old Home Earth, and thought faster-than-light travel was impossible.

In 2082, August Daignot proclaimed all physics problems solved. He tried to freeze the world forever in a grand Theory of Everything, a theory that finally unified quantum mechanics and general relativity. No one had heard of an obscure woman physicist, a Frisian named Mareike Baarda, who couldn't even obtain a position in a university. But in just a year, she would publish five papers that dwarfed even Einstein's 1905 Annus Mirabilis.

The Theory of Everything (TOE) relied on complex and obscure mathematics. Daignot was fond of saying that he was one of no more than a dozen people in all of history who could understand it. Even today, the few people interested in such things number only in the hundreds.

In order to make the TOE equations balance, mathematicians included something called "ghost condensates." These got their name in the previous century because everyone supposed that they didn't represent physical reality—they were just mathematical "ghosts" needed to balance certain equations. There was even a "no ghost" theorem that purported to prove they couldn't "really" exist except in the abstract.

There was certainly good reason to believe the ghost condensates were merely abstract, albeit essential, conveniences. After all, if these ghost condensates did really exist, they would violate both relativity and common sense. They'd violate relativity because they seemed to permit faster-than-light exchange of information. Worse, they'd violate common sense because they were acausal—their state in the present seemed to depend on initial conditions in the future.

No one but a fool would contemplate that something so absurd as ghost condensates could be part of reality.

Of course, the same was true of black holes, predicted by relativity and rejected as impossible by everyone. Until they weren't.

Baarda's genius was to suppose the condensates were real. Her detractors sneered that she believed in "ghosts." She accepted and even adopted the insult, giving it and her wide fame. Her five papers explored the theoretical consequences of these very real ghosts, trolling through accepted icons like Bell's Inequality and the Casimir effect and shredding conventional explanations. Within a year, her mentor, Gregor Hoekstra, showed how the ghost condensates might be used to construct a faster-than-light engine, which he called a ghost drive. A year after that, Baarda was appointed to the Lucasian Chair in physics at Cambridge, the same chair Newton had held. Five years after that, Baarda and Hoekstra shared the Nobel Prize in Physics, the ancient world's highest scientific honor.

It took another twenty years for engineering to catch up, but by 2112 the first ghostship arrived in our own Immaculate Concourse. Before long, humans had permanent settlements on all six of the habitable planets in the Concourse, and the path to today's Empire of Humanity was set.

We owe star travel and everything else to one woman's persistent belief in ghosts.

New Omnibus Mandaean Almagest and Dataset (NOMAD)
Excerpts from the 3172 edition of NOMAD
From the Preface

THE NEW Omnibus Mandaean Almagest and Dataset (NOMAD) is a comprehensive digital database of the known astrographic, social, and historical data in the Local Bubble. It is continuously updated as the Empire of Humanity discovers new systems and rediscovers systems lost during the Great Disintegration. The database is a distributed chain, with copies on dispersed planets which are synchronized on a regular schedule by the Imperial Navy. For historical reasons, the primary database and related support and administrative staff are located on the planet Hemman, NOMAD 100.100.200.101.A. The database is named for the astronomical treatise by Ptolemy from the first century CE and for the Mandaean religious order on Hemman which was instrumental in preserving this knowledge during the Great Disintegration.

The Mandaeans are a small, separate, and intensely private monotheistic religious order, located almost exclusively on the isolated island Elymais on the planet Hemman. The Mandaeans arrived on Hemman sometime in the twenty-third century, but the origin of the order on Old Home Earth dates to at least the second century CE, and possibly earlier. Residents of Elymais speak Svenska, the main language of Hemman, but acolytes use Aramaic for ceremonial purposes. The Mandaean religion centers on the concept of Gnosis, an Aramaic word which roughly translates as knowledge. During the Great Disintegration, the Mandaeans of Elymais dedicated themselves to preserving the knowledge the Grand Alliance had gathered on habitable worlds in the Local Bubble. They named their project the Omnibus Mandaean Almagest.

The diligent work of those early Mandaean acolytes preserved much of what we know about the history of humans in the Local Bubble. Their contributions in preserving this heritage cannot be overstated. Today, out of respect for their desire for privacy, access to their home island, Elymais, is only by permission of the Rashama, the island's local magistrate. Mandaean acolytes on Elymais continue to provide staff and administrative support for the current distributed database.

Selected entries

Cabot's Star, NOMAD 129.683.365.120, is a class K star approximately 562 light years from the Immaculate Concourse. The Cabot system has six planets in conventional orbits ranging from .2AU to 86AU. The system was purchased in 2312 CE from the Grand Alliance by Cabot Industries Trust of Old Home Earth. The sole habitable world in the system is a satellite of the gas giant Kenebec (NOMAD 129.683.365.120.B). See the entry for Cabot's Landing (NOMAD 129.683.365.120.B.5).

Cabot's Landing, NOMAD 129.683.365.120.B.5, is a class 12 satellite of Kenebec (NOMAD 129.683.365.120.B), a Type II gas giant orbiting 1.2 AU from the local star. The system was discovered in 2306

CE during an exploratory mission of the Heale Moanne of the Grand Alliance Fleet. Cabot's Landing consists almost entirely of a planet-encompassing ocean with only one significant land mass, Bountiful, an island of approximately 58,000 km2. Native marine life is abundant (see the entry for bandersnatch), but native land-based life forms appear to be restricted to a few primitive plant species and various viral and microbial parasites. The satellite is notable for large deposits of dysprosium and other rare-earth metals.

Cabot Industries Trust (CIT) purchased the system in 2312 CE, and human operations began in 2318 CE. CIT seeded the land mass with a genetically engineered ecosystem to facilitate human habitation. This primarily supported species of wheat (see triticum cabitorum), amaranth (see amaranthus cabitorum), and sugar beets (see b. vulgaris caitorum) was collectively designed to provide biomass for the automated food processors common to the era. The latter two species required special soils and exist in limited locations, while the former spread planet-wide. In addition to constructing cybernetic mining operations in the western mountains of the single land mass, the company placed a standard self-sustaining habitat on the southeastern shore. This habitat, known as Cabot's Lodge, provided for housing up to three hundred human technicians. By exploiting the genetically engineered crops, the personnel could theoretically survive indefinitely without resupply from off-planet. CIT constructed two ghost ports, one adjacent to Cabot's Lodge and the other adjacent to an industrial port serving the mining enterprise. Both ports included automated facilities for replenishing and repairing up to three Cruiser Class ghostships at any time, and up to fifteen tactical transports.

Subsequently, the Grand Alliance leased space for a ghostfleet naval base and a marine base on the planet. CIT also leased limited colonial rights to a subsidiary foundation and funded an agricultural research station on a small island south of the main mini-continent, Bountiful. At its peak, Cabot's Landing supported a population of over 39,000 humans.

Mining operations ceased in 2462 CE, at the start of the Great Disintegration, and by 2464 CE CIT had evacuated all personnel from the Cabot's Landing system.

With the rediscovery of ghost condensate shunt starships [ghostships], contact with the system resumed in 3107 CE. That same year, an expedition by the Praetorian Syndicate claimed title to the system and initiated plans to restart the mines. All of the original CIT installations rebooted successfully, although the colony and the research station were in ruins, presumably due to outlaw raids during the Disintegration. The mines resumed operations in 3112 CE. In 3142 CE the mines were again shut down due to the discovery of more economical sources of rare earths. The industrial port and the ghost port at Cabot Lodge remain operational, with facilities for the emergency repair of commercial ghostships.

Pursuant to the Imperial Decree of 3168 CE, in order to maintain its title to the system, the Praetorian Syndicate maintains continuous human occupancy of the planet via a resident caretaker.

Ptitseferma Biological Station (NOMAD 129.683.365.120.B.5.q) was established in 2436 CE by the Institute of Cytology and Genetics in Novosibirsk and the Joint Genome Institute in California, under a grant from the Cabot Industries Trust (CIT). The announced purpose of the grant was to conduct experiments on seeding the planet with additional species that would be useful to the human workforce. The Institute located a research station on the Western Reserve Island on the southern coast of the Central Sea. This location was selected due to its geographic isolation from the other land masses of the planet and, in particular, from the main island of Bountiful, where CIT maintained profitable mining operations. The research station was named Ptitseferma (chicken farm in the Archaic Russian of the researchers).

The Institute's initial goal was to develop a sustainable ecosystem for natural human protein sources, to wit, domestic chickens (Gallus gallus domesticus) and goats (Capra aegagrus hircus). Both species were shown to thrive in the previously genetically engineered ecosystem that supported the wheat species triticum cabitorum. The Institute also introduced experimental plots of plant, amphibious, and insect species consistent with the biome of Kauri forests found on New Zealand.

In order to prevent population explosion and subsequent collapse of the new ecosystem, the Institute introduced two predator species, the so-called domestic red fox (Vulpes vulpes familiares) and domestic dogs (Canis lupus familiaris, viz., golden retrievers). The Institute of Cytology and Genetics pioneered the domestication of the red fox in the late twentieth century, accounting for its inclusion in this project.

Surviving reports of the original research are fragmentary but suggest that researchers expected any resulting ecosystem would have a high probability of stability. This expectation proved correct. Today, flocks of chickens and scattered herds of goats survive on Western

Reserve Island, together with roaming predator foxes and packs of dogs. Kauri forests have expanded from the original small, experimental plots to cover approximately eighty percent of Western Reserve Island, with the remainder being mountains and rocky terrain not suitable for the imported species.

For reasons that are unclear, the Institute also introduced domestic cats (Felis catus, viz., Abyssinians). These animals reportedly also tolerated the engineered environment, but prey (in the form of insects, chicks, and eggs) were deemed insufficient for long-term survival without human intervention.

Records for Ptitseferma Station end in 2642 CE at the start of the Great Disintegration, when CIT abandoned Cabot's Landing. In 3107 CE, HRH Imperial Cruiser *Fearless* arrived as part of an expedition to reclaim the planet. The various species mentioned, with the exception of cats, survived and are geographically isolated on Western Reserve Island.

While there are no reports of cats on the island, rumors persist of a small colony that survived near the east power station on the main island, Bountiful. According to the rumor, the last humans on the planet set an automated food processor at the station to produce regular portions of protein synthesized from the local triticum cabitorum and suitable for feline consumption. There is no evidence to support these rumors.

From summary entry for the Immaculate Concourse

Immaculate Concourse, NOMAD 129.628.100.100, is the common name for the planetary system of Baarda's Star, a G-type main sequence star in the local group. The system is notable for having six planets in the habitable zone, a circumstance likely made possible by the absence of gas giant planets in the system. Today, the Concourse is the political and commercial hub of the Empire of Humanity, with influence spread over a thousand member systems. From the bustling avenues and financial markets of the Novy Kyiv, to the embassies and chambers of the Parliament of Humanity in Pasargadae, one can encounter humanity in all its diversity.

Pre-Disintegration History

The Grand Alliance exploratory vessel *Challenger* first visited the system then known as Beta Canum Venaticorum in 2112 CE, just ten years after the invention of superluminal ghostdrives. The Alliance realized at once the value of a system just 27 light years from Old Home Earth with so many habitable planets. They renamed the star Baarda's Star, in honor of Mareike Baarda, whose work in theoretical physics made ghostships possible. Human colonization began that same year with the settlement of New Arizona, the fifth planet in the system by distance from Baarda's star.

A member of the Grand Alliance, the United States, made a claim of sovereignty over the entire Concourse based on financing the expedition of the *Challenger*. However, other members of the Grand Alliance contested this clam, and ultimately colonization rights were allocated to various members of the Alliance. This resulted in dozens of different cultures from all over Old Home Earth settling in the Concourse, giving it ethnic and linguistic diversity found nowhere else in known human space.

Habitable Planets

Immaculate Concourse, NOMAD 129.628.100.100.1, Xīn Zhōngguó, the first planet in the Immaculate Concourse as measured by distance from Baarda's star. The capital is Fēngfù (Abundance in the native language). The current population is estimated at 473 million people, and the primary language is Mandarin. The primary industries include mining, heavy manufacturing, and cybernetics. The planet is a net exporter of food to the rest of the concourse. The planet was originally named New Florida by the first settlers but was later renamed when it was allocated to China by the Grand Alliance. A small ethnic enclave of 1.2 million inhabitants still speak a dialect of Inglish.

Immaculate Concourse, NOMAD 129.628.100.100.2, Patrie, the second planet in the Immaculate Concourse as measured by distance from Baarda's star. The capital is Nouveau Marseille. The current population is estimated at 256 million people, and the primary language is French. The planet's extensive habitable lands have a temperate climate and as many as three growing seasons each year. Unlike other planets in the Concourse, metal ores are in deep reserves that are difficult to mine, so the planet has instead focused on agriculture as its main commercial activity and is known as the breadbasket of the Concourse. In addition, the main university, known as the Sorbonne for historical reasons, is renowned throughout the Empire of Humanity for its biological and agricultural research.

Immaculate Concourse, NOMAD 129.628.100.100.3 Baardalân, the third planet in the Immaculate Concourse as measured by distance from Baarda's star. Named for Mareike Baarda by the original expedition, who regarded it as the primary location for colonization due to its orbit placing it in the center of the habitable zone. However, the main continents are clustered in the north polar region, and the planet has been locked in an ice age for at least the last hundred thousand years. Today, the primary industry is tourism, largely for winter sports, which supports a population of three million inhabitants. The planet is self-sufficient in food, and exports local delicacies like smelt and sardines. The language is a dialect of Inglish, inherited from the original settlers who came from an area of the old United States known as New England. The capital is Bastin.

Immaculate Concourse, NOMAD 129.628.100.100.4, Nova Europa, the fourth planet in the Immaculate Concourse as measured by distance from Baarda's star. The capital is Centrum, and the current population is estimated to be 1.2 billion. The planet was settled by various nationalities from the European Union on Old Home Earth, and includes over four dozen languages and even more cultures. The common tongues are Inglish, French, and Deutsch, but significant minorities speak Italian, Ukrainian, Polish, and Catalan. Nova Europa is the financial hub of the Empire of Humanity, with exchanges and banks located mostly in the Thesitee, but places like Dublin and Novy Kyiv also play central roles. With over a billion inhabitants, the planet is the most populous in the human space. It has a diverse economy, including finance, banking, mining, manufacturing, and ghostship construction. The planet's robust agricultural industry exports grains, wines, and other food products. The planet is also a mecca for scholars and students from across human space, with private universities such as Oxford and Harvard being among the most elite in the Empire of Humanity.

Immaculate Concourse, NOMAD 129.628.100.100.5, New Arizona, the fifth planet in the Immaculate Concourse as measured by distance from Baarda's star. The capital is Pasargadae, which is also the administrative and political capital of the Empire of Humanity. The current population is estimated at 573 million, and the primary language is Inglish, with substantial minorities speaking Spanish, Portuguese, Arabic, Hindi, and Bantu. Archaic English is still spoken by less than half a million inhabitants of an isolated enclave in the Yellowstone Mountains and is officially an endangered language. The current population is notable for its multiethnic character, which results from early settlers arriving from such varied Old Earth locations as Africa, the Americas, and south Asia. The primary industries include government, pharmacology, and medical technologies. The planet is self-sufficient in food resources, and local cuisine is renowned for its use of spices. Like Nova Europa, the planet is also known for scientific research, carried out at public universities like the Tata Institute, Unilagos, and Iowa (named for Old Earth counterparts) and in private entities, like the Empower Gregor Academy in Pasargadae and the Jamieat Alqahira located in the delta of the Nyl Alnyl.

Immaculate Concourse, NOMAD 129.628.100.100.6, New Alaska (Dommièstèi}in the native Yakusian), is the sixth planet in the Immaculate Concourse as measured by distance from Baarda's star. The planet's distance from the star and its axial tilt of 38 degrees make its climate the most challenging for human occupants of all the Concourse worlds. Originally settled by immigrants from north Asia on Old Home Earth, the population during the height of the Grand Alliance never exceeded two million. During the Great Disintegration, the population collapsed to fewer than ten thousand humans. Today, the planet has over eighty thousand inhabitants. The primary language is Yakusian, which appears to be a hybrid of two languages originating on Old Home Earth, Yakut and Russian. The primary economic activity involves automated mining of various ores and their export to the industrial worlds of the Concourse. The government is organized as a commune, with common ownership of planetary resources. The capital is Başkent, but most of the population still lives in the small, self-sufficient nomadic groups that survived the Great Disintegration.

Keep reading for an excerpt from
Potential Energy
by Kim Fielding!

CHAPTER ONE

EVEN IN civvies, she obviously didn't belong in this dump. She was too clean, clear-eyed, and straight-backed. Too glowing with purpose and determination. She marched across the floor of the bar as if she owned the place—except if she did own it, the bar would be well lit and orderly, and the patrons would be a hell of a lot classier.

Haz wouldn't have guessed she would show up, but he somehow wasn't surprised. Maybe he'd unconsciously expected this for a long time. The only question was whether she'd arrest him or simply blast him where he sat.

When she reached his table at the back of the room, she pulled out a chair, settled in, and stared at him, stone-faced. She'd aged since he'd seen her last: a few new lines around her narrow mouth, hair steel-gray now and worn in a practical buzz cut.

Haz drained his glass in one swallow and waved to the barkeep for another. He turned back to his companion.

"To what do I owe the honor, Colonel Kasabian?"

"In fact, it's Brigadier General Kasabian."

The same clipped tones he remembered, as if she were rationing oxygen.

"Gratulálok!" He raised his empty glass in a mock toast.

The bartender squelched over, their plantar suction cups noisy on the tile floor. They set down Haz's refill and looked expectantly at Kasabian. At least Haz assumed the look might be expectant; it was hard to read a craqir's face, especially when some of the eight eyes were staring in other directions. Craqirs were unable to speak Comlang due to their beaks and lack of tongue, and this one rarely bothered to use the translator on their biotab.

"I don't suppose you have any true gin." Even when she spoke, Kasabian's mouth remained slightly pursed.

The craqir shook their head, and Haz provided a more complete answer.

"They have a synth version that makes a decent paint stripper. Order the yinex vodka instead, cut fifty-fifty with water. Still tastes like shit, but it won't eat away your stomach lining."

She gave his glass—synth whiskey straight up—a significant look and nodded at the craqir, who returned to the bar.

"Major Taylor—"

"Uh-uh. They busted me all the way down to staff sergeant, remember? But don't call me that either because I'm a civilian—have been for a long time now."

She narrowed her eyes. "All right. Captain Taylor, then."

"Nope. I don't have a ship. No ship, no captain. I'm just plain old Mister Taylor nowadays. But you can call me Haz. You've called me that once or twice before."

He shifted in his seat and straightened his quasar-cursed leg, but the ache didn't dissipate, so he drank a slug of synth whiskey instead. It didn't help with the pain, but when he was drunk enough, he stopped caring.

"I was told you do have a ship."

He didn't ask for her source. She had hundreds of rats and moles stashed all over the galaxy, which had probably contributed to her promotion.

"Outdated info. My ship got banged up on my last run, and I can't afford to fix her. She's rotting in dry dock. Unless they've already stripped her for parts."

He couldn't help a sigh. The Dancing Molly had served him well and deserved a better fate.

The craqir returned quickly with Kasabian's drink and one for Haz. It was why he came to this particular dump: the barkeep never kept him waiting. He drained his current glass and started on the next, impressed that Kasabian managed a decent swig of hers without making a face.

"How are you making a living without a ship?"

Haz grinned and shrugged.

She watched him for the several minutes it took for him to finish off the latest drink, try to find a less uncomfortable position for his leg, and wait for her to either tell her story or walk away. Or arrest him, if that was her goal. Maybe she'd just shoot him, ending his troubles and hers. Finally she started tapping a rhythm on the metal table with her fingernail, making it ring hollowly. He remembered that she liked music. She used to plan battles while playing Earth songs from a few hundred years ago, a genre that was, for reasons unclear to Haz, called heavy metal. Maybe she was thinking of one of those tunes while she tapped.

At least she hadn't drawn a weapon and didn't seem inclined to. If she had intended to shoot him, she would have done it by now; she wasn't the type to mess around. But if she didn't want him dead, what did she want?

"I have a contract to offer you," she said at last. Well, that answered his question.

He raised his eyebrows. "A contract? Not a jail cell?"

"I'm willing to overlook some past... indiscretions. If you accept the mission."

"I have no sh—"

"It pays enough for you to lease one."

He crossed his arms. "I don't borrow."

He didn't trust anyone else's ship. Besides, who the hell would be stupid enough to put their equipment into his hands?

"Then fix yours."

His heart skipped a few beats at that option. Losing Molly had been like having a limb hacked off. Worse, maybe. He'd have happily traded his bad leg for his ship.

As if sensing Haz's thoughts, Kasabian gestured in the general direction of his lower body.

"Why haven't you seen a doctor about that?"

"Believe me, those bastards have had their way with me plenty of times." He shook his head. "They've reached the limits of flesh and bone."

"Then replace it," she said. As if getting a new leg was as easy as getting a fresh drink.

"I don't have that kind of money. And the szotting navy won't give me a single credit." He couldn't keep the bitterness out of his tone.

She nodded briskly. "This contract will give you enough to cover your medical costs as well as repair your ship. You'll have enough for running expenses too. And a salary for your crew."

Kasabian leaned back in her chair, apparently pleased with her offer.

"Since when does the navy go throwing that kind of money around? And while we're on the subject, what the fuck's up with this contract shit?

Whatever it is that needs doing, you've got plenty of your own ships and more than enough people to fly them. And furthermore, why me?"

He knew the answer to that: the job was too dangerous or too sticky to risk their own people. But he wanted to hear her say it.

"This mission is… sensitive. And it involves travel through Kappa Sector."

Haz snorted. So it was both dangerous and sticky.

"Got it. Don't want to endanger any of your delicate flowers on this one."

"You know better than that, Taylor. Delicate flowers don't last long in the navy. They didn't when you joined, and they still don't today." She allowed herself a tight smile. "But we do appreciate some of your specific talents."

That made him snort again. He knew he should simply walk away, but he couldn't help thinking of Molly and how much he missed her. How much he hated being stuck on the ground like a szotting mushroom. And then there was his leg. He would sell his soul—assuming he still had one—for a decent night's sleep, for not waking up with shooting pains every time he shifted position. Besides, curiosity had always been one of his weak spots, and he wondered what was such a big deal that Kasabian had come after him.

"What the hell do you need in Kappa? There's nothing there but pirates and a bunch of planets too stubborn or too stupid to join the Coalition."

"We need something delivered to a planet on the other side."

He sneered. "I'm not a cargo runner, General."

He couldn't imagine a more joyless existence than that: stodgy assholes with their bloated, sluggish ships and their precious delivery schedules. He'd rather rot here, planetside, than become an intragalactic mailman.

"It's not exactly cargo. It's a single item, in fact. A religious artifact of great importance to the people of Chov X8. The artifact was stolen, we recovered it, and they very much want it back."

Haz's stomach had clenched as soon as she said religious. He wished he had more booze, but he kept his voice steady as he spoke.

"And the Coalition's returning the whatsit out of the goodness of their hearts."

"We're returning it because Chov X8 has certain strategic value to us. Which is all you need to know. Well, and the fact that we'll pay handsomely for you to return the item safely to its rightful owners."

He raised an eyebrow. "Safely being the operative word?"

There was that smile again, but larger and more predatory. "The parties responsible for the theft may try to steal it again. If that happens, you'll need to stop them."

"Then why not send it with a phalanx of gunships? The navy's got plenty of those."

"Because the Coalition wishes to keep its involvement... unobtrusive."

Haz sighed. He never paid much attention to politics and wasn't the kind of guy who enjoyed innuendos and hidden agendas. He'd been called blunt more than once, and he didn't consider it an insult. Whatever the Coalition's interest in that little planet, and whatever their reasons for returning the whatsit on the down-low, he didn't know—and, he realized, he didn't care.

He thumbed at the biotab embedded in his left wrist, paying for his drinks. While he was at it, he paid for Kasabian's too. Why not? It'd only get him to flat broke a little faster. Trying not to grimace too much, he stood.

"No," he said.

"No what?"

"No contract. No religious thingamajig. No handsome pay. Find someone else."

"Why are you refusing?"

"I've had enough of the Coalition, and it has damned well had enough of me."

She caught his wrist in a hard grip before he could step away.

"You could have your ship back, your leg repaired. I know exactly how many credits you have, Taylor, and it's not many. I'd bet my commission that you have no plan once they run out. Refusing this contract is stupid."

"Never claimed to be smart." He jerked his arm free. "Good luck, Sona. With everything."

Of course he had no chance of outrunning her, but he hoped she might simply let him go. No such luck. He made it almost to the door before she caught up with him. This time she seized his lower arm. In danger of losing his balance, he gripped an unoccupied table to steady himself.

Because her presence was so substantial, he had forgotten how short she was; her head didn't even reach his shoulder. The three or four times they'd tumbled into bed together, long before either of them wore officers' insignia, she'd been tiny against his long body. Tiny but strong.

Now she pressed her biotab against his, causing both to emit a tinny ding.

"I'm shipping out in two days. You have that long to reconsider. Ping me when you do."

He shook his head and pulled away for the second time.

"No."

"That's a bad limp. Why don't you at least use a cane?"

"Fuck you, Sona."

She was smiling as he lurched away.

IN A BEST-CASE scenario, he wouldn't be stranded on Kepler. Most of the small planet was uninhabitable for humans, covered in toxic swamps and regularly reaching temperatures hot enough to kill. But when Molly was crippled during his last mission, he hadn't had much choice. He'd needed to make a beeline for the nearest settlement, and he was lucky to have survived.

Kepler had only two cities—one on each pole, where the temperatures were bearable—and he'd chosen the north only because it happened to be in daylight as he approached. The city was named North, and that lack of imagination was emblematic of the planet as a whole. Nobody came to Kepler because they wanted to. They came because they had no option. Most people worked on the vast structures that roved the noxious swamps, harvesting and processing barbcress leaves. The planet's few wealthy citizens traded the barbcress to off-world merchants in exchange for all the things Keplerians needed to survive, amassing profits until their greed was satisfied and they fled to a better place. The remainder of the population worked in run-down shops or restaurants or bars, or they repaired buildings or ships, or they provided sundry other services that residents required.

It was a dreary planet with perpetually overcast skies and few entertainments, the type of place that everyone dreamed of escaping.

But here he was, here he'd been for over a stanyear, and here he'd remain.

The bar where Kasabian had found him had no name, and it was more or less indistinguishable from most of North's other dives. One of the other regulars, an Earther with a fondness for ancient entertainment, always called it the Pit of Despair, then laughed and had another synth whiskey. Haz and the Earther had fucked once, but both decided the act wasn't worth repeating. They later engaged in an implicit contest to see who would drink himself to death first. The Earther had won. Haz hadn't thought about him in some time, and during his slow walk home, he wondered why the Earther had now come to mind.

The streets in this part of North were unpaved, which meant they alternated between dusty enough to clog your lungs and so muddy they'd suck the shoes off your feet. People with a little money traveled on hoverscoots, uncaring of the street conditions; people without much money walked and swore. Haz was in the latter group, his swearing especially fluent on a night like this, as mist wetted his hair and dripped down his face and the muck pulled viciously at his leg.

He'd paused against a ramshackle building, steeling himself for the final three blocks, when a shadow took shape out of the darkness and stalked toward him. Haz couldn't make out much detail, but by the way the figure moved, Haz recognized its intent.

"I've got nothing on me worth stealing." Haz's voice was cheery; he was in the mood for a fight. "And you might think you're handy with that pigsticker you're clutching, but I assure you, I'm handier."

The person continued to approach. Haz undoubtedly looked like an easy mark with his heavy limp, and some of North's residents were desperate enough to kill for a few credits. They'd spend it on the narcos they had become addicted to while working the barbcress processors— the narcos their bosses so generously handed out to keep them docile and then took away the moment an employee fucked up bad enough to get fired. Haz almost felt sorry for them, when they weren't trying to rob him.

"I'm telling you, pal. You're gonna regret this."

"Gimme your credits." The man's voice, deep and raspy, had a Kepler accent. Poor bastard had been born on this shitty planet; no wonder he needed narcos to bury his woes.

"I told you. I'm just about flat broke. I can't—"

The man lunged.

Haz, with the wall behind him, didn't have much room to maneuver and didn't have enough trust in his leg or the ground to dance away. He carried a knife of his own, of course, but hadn't drawn it. That would take all the fun out of this encounter. He stayed put, braced himself against the building, and grabbed the attacker's wrist. The edge of the blade nicked Haz's hand—a misjudgment attributable to booze and darkness—but he only tightened his grip, using his opponent's momentum to guide the knife away from his body and into the softened wood of the wall. It stuck there, and as the man tried to pull it out, Haz kneed him in the balls using his bad leg. It fucking hurt, but not as much as getting a patella in the gonads. Haz had learned the hard way to keep his good leg on the ground when fighting.

The man made a gurgling cry and, letting go of the knife, doubled over. Haz took the opportunity to land a solid fist to his temple. The sound of the impact lingered as the guy hit the ground.

Haz thumbed his biotab, then bent over the unconscious man and tapped their biotabs together, transferring a nasty little virus that would put the other man's biotab out of commission for a week or more. Highly illegal, but so was coming at a stranger with a knife, which Haz now tugged out of the wall. After giving it a quick wipe on the downed man's poncho, he carefully slid it into his own hip pocket.

"It's been a pleasure," Haz said and resumed his limp home.

IN HIS part of town, three-story buildings contained stores and small workshops at ground level and living space above. Dandy for most folks, but on his worst days, Haz found stairs a bitch to climb. After a long search for a place he could afford and easily access, he'd eventually rented a small room at the back of a repair shop.

He unlocked the door, chuckling at the thought of his assailant unable to access his own home due to the fucked-up biotab. Haz turned on a single light, illuminating his hard narrow bed, a small table with two chairs, a couple of shelves, and a bureau. A vidscreen embedded in the wall had a small diagonal crack, as if someone had forcefully thrown something. Near the sink and mirror, tucked into a corner, was the door to a wetroom so tiny that he could conveniently use the toilet and shower at the same time, if he chose.

He was used to much closer quarters on ships, and he wasn't one to accumulate possessions, so this worked fine. He even liked the creaking floorboards under his uneven steps. And as for the bugs the locals called mudroaches, well, there wasn't much he could do about them. At least they didn't bite.

Haz hung his jacket on a hook and shook the rain out of his hair. The slice on his hand throbbed, which made dealing with his boots more painful than usual. Szot that stupid leg. He threw the boots across the room.

After limping over the floor, he clumsily doctored himself at the sink. The cut was long but not deep, so after rinsing and disinfecting, he closed it with glueskin. Man, he hated that stuff. Not only did it make his wounds itch like crazy, but this brand of the synthetic was much paler than his golden-brown skin color, as if intentionally drawing attention to his injuries.

"Who cares?" he chided himself. "You're nobody's center of attention."

Nobody but the occasional thief and the craqir bartender. And, tonight only, Sona Kasabian. Who'd apparently flown all the way to this nowhere planet to offer him a contract.

"Well, she can leave me the hell alone. She can fly right back, polishing her shiny general's star the entire way."

Haz would get back to destroying his liver and feeling himself sink into the ooze until, ultimately, nothing was left but a little bit of foreign DNA embedded in a Kepler swamp.

Still standing at the sink, he looked down at his open palms and thought about the things those hands had done. The weapons they'd wielded, the ships they'd steered, the lovers they'd caressed. Unlike his brain and his leg, his hands had never betrayed him.

If he closed his eyes, he could feel the warm metal armrests of the control seat on the Dancing Molly. Szot, he missed that.

Sighing, he turned his hands over and tapped at the biotab.

"Kasabian," he said.

MAX GRIFFIN is a gay man, a husband, a father, a writer, and a mathematician. Max creates fictional worlds with a breadth informed by globe-spanning travels, a depth provided by the rigor of science, and an excitement generated by a lifetime of seeking out new ideas and meeting new people. Max writes characters with passionate hearts, bright minds, and goals that matter.

Max's professional career has spanned over thirty years at a major research university in the US Southwest. His duties included faculty appointments in mathematics and electrical engineering, senior academic positions, and participation in the executive leadership. Teaching responsibilities involved world-wide travel and deep engagement with diverse cultures and peoples. His research includes numerous mathematical monographs and graduate textbooks on real analysis and on probability. He has served on dozens of doctoral committees in fields as diverse as music theory and interplanetary laser communication systems.

Max's journey as a gay man includes a midlife self-evaluation and coming out. While this could have turned out many ways, some of them bad, it instead turned out to be life-affirming for all involved. Today, Max is blessed by strong relationships with his current husband, Gene, with his daughter and her two children, and even with his ex-wife who has since remarried.

Sometimes alien creatures populate Max's fiction. He has direct experience with those too. You see, two Russian Bluecats, Boris and Natasha, are the true owners of the house they share with Max and Gene. Boris and Natasha keep the two humans as their pets in return for feeding them and petting them. Oh, and there's that cat litter thing they do too. Despite what you might expect, there are no signs of moose or squirrel in the household.

website and blog: https://maxgriffin.net
Facebook: https://www.facebook.com/max.griffin.58
Writing.com: https://mathguy.writing.com

Follow me on BookBub

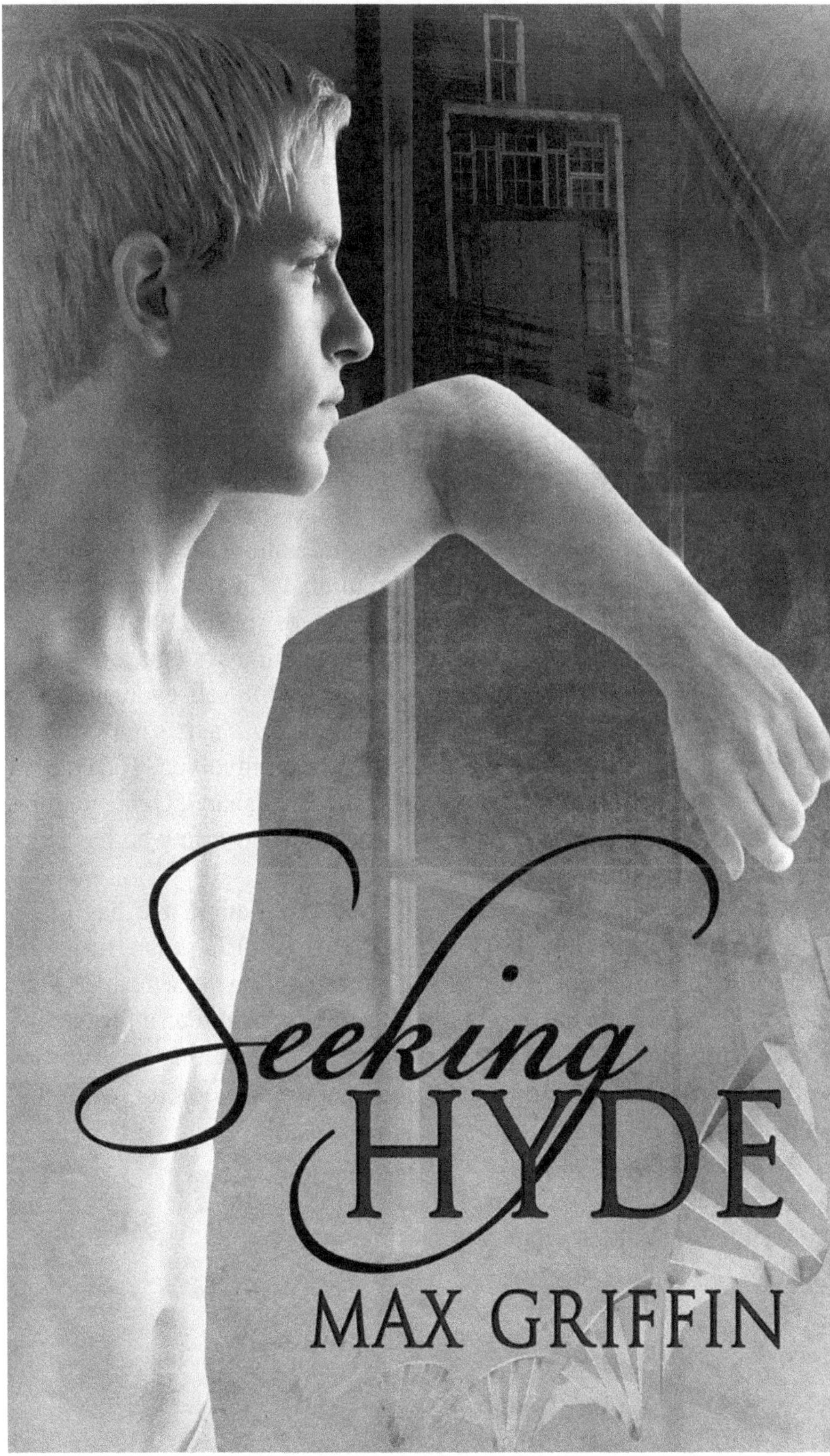
Seeking
HYDE
MAX GRIFFIN

When Brent Hyde arrives home from college to find his parents missing from their dairy farm, he feels a creeping sense of dread, but the inept local police won't take him seriously. Determined to find them, Brent drags his boyfriend, Gary, into the search.

When Jason Killeen, a senior journalism student from Brent's college, shows up to investigate a twenty-year-old research project involving Brent's mother—and Brent's current employer—the situation gets sticky. Jason insists they're all in danger, and a sudden body count proves him right.

While Brent, Jason, and Gary gather clues, a hit man, an FBI agent, and a corporate scientist turn up the heat by embroiling themselves in the investigation. Under that pressure, Brent and Gary's relationship falters, and Brent finds himself turning to Jason, whose understated heroism attracts him. Then an unexpected discovery puts all three of them in mortal danger, and Brent makes a choice that will change them all forever.

www.dreamspinnerpress.com

... will please fans of diverse space opera and queer romance alike.
- Publishers Weekly
KIM FIELDING
POTENTIAL ENERGY
Sometimes a hero is just a scoundrel with his back against the wall.

When interstellar smuggler Haz Taylor loses his ship, his money, and his tattered reputation, drinking himself to death on a backwater planet seems like his only option. Then the Coalition offers him a contract to return a stolen religious artifact. Sounds simple enough, but politics can be deadly—and the artifact's not enthusiastic about being returned.

Haz didn't sign up to be prisoner transport, but he's caught between a blaster and hard vacuum. Still, that doesn't mean he can't show his captive some kindness. It costs him nothing to give Mot the freedom to move about the ship, to eat when he's hungry… to believe that he's a person. It's only until they reach Mot's planet. Besides, the Coalition would hate it, which is reason enough.

Then he finds out what awaits Mot at home, and suddenly hard vacuum doesn't look so bad. Haz is no hero, but he can't consign Mot to his fate. Somewhere under the space grime, Haz has a sliver of principle. It's probably going to get him killed, but he doesn't have much to live for anyway….

www.dreamspinnerpress.com

life seed

albert nothlit

Wurl: Book One

They came to New Skye in search of a better future. The colonists, descendants of the brave people who set out to reach a new planet, found a beautiful world, rich beyond their wildest expectations.

Except for one thing. Crops will not grow in the soil of New Skye—not the way they should—and humans cannot eat the native animals. Desperate feats of botanical engineering have kept the colony alive, but time is running out as food becomes more scarce.

Elias Trost will not sit idly by while his colony starves. The one hope for a solution is the Life Seed, a dormant plant organism kept under lock and key at the heart of the colony.

In desperation, Elias steals the Life Seed to return it to its rightful place, making him an outcast in the unforgiving winter world. Pursued by colony soldiers armed to the teeth, including his former best friend, Tristan MacLeod, Elias soon runs afoul of a far greater threat. The wurl, the deadly reptiles that besiege the colony, are tracking him too, and they appear to be more intelligent than the colonists ever knew....

www.dreamspinnerpress.com

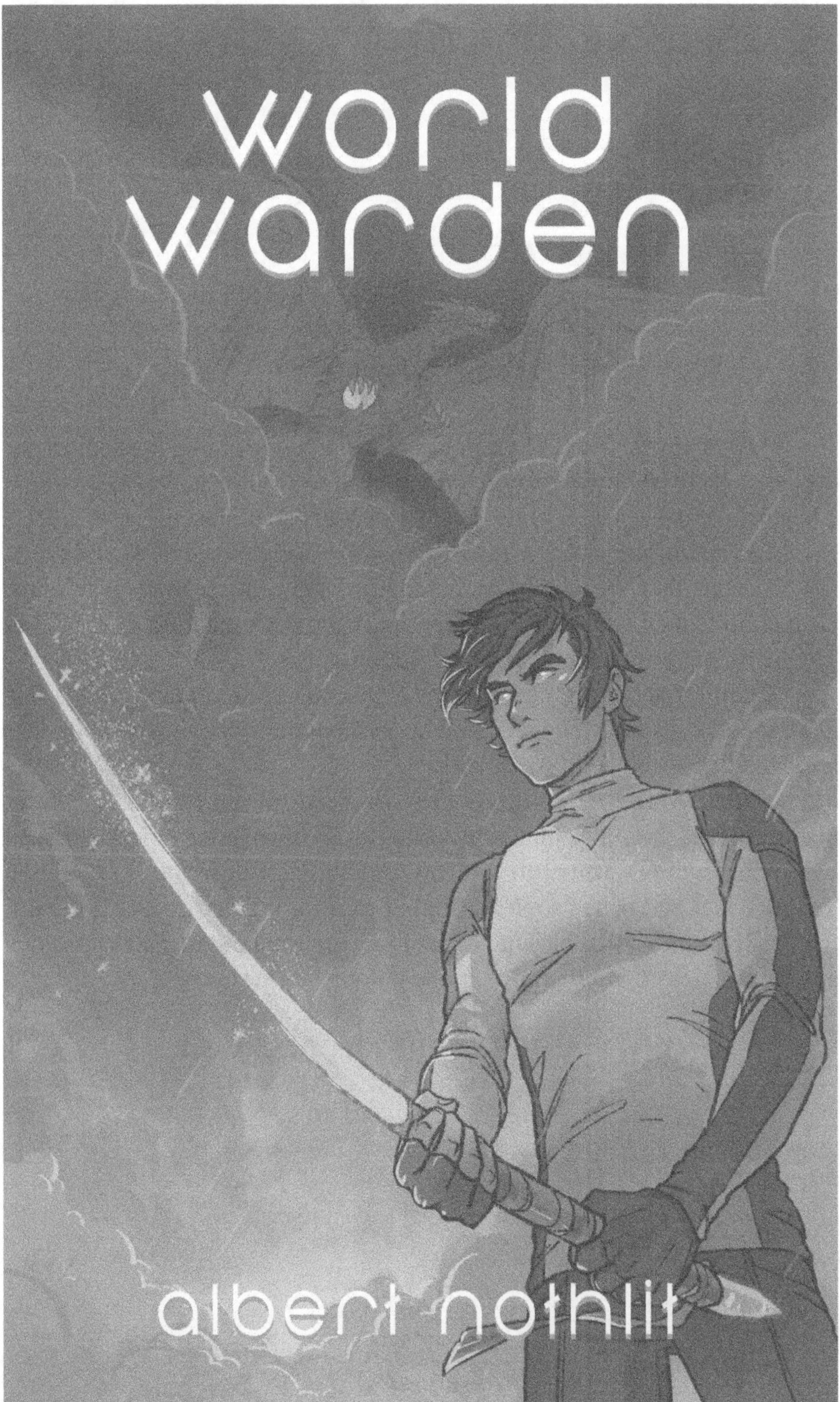
world
warden
albert nothlit

Wurl: Book Two

Now that colonists Elias Trost and Tristan MacLeod have learned of the existence of another intelligent species on this planet, their life on New Skye has become even more perilous. Dresde, the ruthless wurl queen, has kidnapped Elias's brother, Oscar, along with the egg of a rival queen.

Oscar Trost finds danger and privation under Dresde's reign, but he isn't alone. A small group of humans from the original colony ship, long lost from memory, live on the eastern continent as slaves to Dresde's horrific whims. In order to survive, Oscar must find his courage and prove himself to these others while he awaits the rescue he is sure will come.

Elias and Tristan have to find Oscar and the egg, and fast. Every day their search becomes more desperate. But sprawling between them and Dresde's lair is the untamed alien wilderness, teeming with threats from ground and sky. And in the vast ocean they must cross lies something else—something ancient that should not be disturbed....

www.dreamspinnerpress.com

Haunted by the screams of the men he murdered, ex-Marine medic Riff Khora is serving a life sentence on board a prison ship. Seeking more punishment for his crime, he strikes a deal with the corrupt Captain Vidal—an exchange of pleasure and pain—and forges a new life leading the team that surveys space wreckage for salvage.

Ship engineer Zed Jakobsen's psychometric abilities make prison a sentence worse than death, and the barrage of emotional stimuli is an unending torment. His only regret is that he didn't kill the monster who sent him to prison, and only a glimmer of hope to escape a judgment he doesn't deserve keeps him clinging to a brutal existence.

When they board derelict ship Pandora and discover a lone survivor, the hell of prison life plunges into abject horror. An epidemic of violence and insanity consumes their ship, driving the crew to murder and destruction. Mutual need draws Riff and Zed together, and their bond gives them the strength to fight a reality they cannot trust. But Vidal possesses the only means of escape from the nightmare, and he's not letting anyone leave alive.

2nd Edition
First Edition published as *Pandora in the Deep Into Darkness: Aliens, Alphas and Antiheroes Anthology* by Smashwords, 2015.

www.dreamspinnerpress.com